MCSWEENEY'S 32

2024 AD

Last year we asked a dozen or so writers to travel somewhere in the world—Budapest, Cape Town, Houston, any sleepy or sleepless outpost they could find—and send back a story set in that spot fifteen years from now, in the year 2024. Only ten returned alive (and Doerr with a broken leg), but their stories are what you'll find here. The predictions, at least on the municipal level, are pretty grim—not enough good water, too much bad water, several distressing developments in personal electronics. But civilization persists nevertheless, and it offers some small consolation that each of these stories provides a picture of the little guy or gal persistently carving out a life. One reason we asked our writers to look ahead only fifteen years, instead of fifty or five hundred, is because we wanted to hear about where *we'd* be—to see what the world could look like when things had shifted just a bit, as it seems like they're starting to, heading into the second decade of the third millennium, with the long presence of our forty-third president come to an end and a semitangible *future* at last seeming imminent. For better or for worse, this feels like a dynamic moment, in the world and in the work we do with ink and paper and in the changing physiques of our editorial board, who are all twelve years old, if you didn't know that. The best fiction set in years ahead can deepen that feeling of impending possibility; these stories, we think, are grounded in that spirit, and now is a good time to read them.

INTERNS & VOLUNTEERS: Alex Ludlum, Adrienne Mahar, Tess Thackara, Onnesha Roychoudhuri, Renae Hurlbutt, Henry Jones, Michelle Lo, Nicholas Thomson, Alexandra Brown, Emily Stackhouse, Jacqueline Berkman, Ashley Rube, Anna Brenner, Julia Kinsman, Cassandra Neyenesch, Christina Rush, Ben Jahn, Rob Sandall, Drew Dickerson, Dwight Pavlovic, Alexandra Vara, Claire Stanford, Deanna Benjamin. ALSO HELPING: Chris Ying, Michelle Quint, Brian McMullen, Laura Howard, Sean Wilsey, Eliana Stein, Greg Larson, Jesse Nathan, Christopher Benz. COPY EDITORS: Oriana Leckert, Caitlin Van Dusen. WEBSITE: Chris Monks. SUPPORT: Juliet Litman. OUTREACH: Angela Petrella. CIRCULATION: Heidi Meredith. MANAGING EDITOR: Jordan Bass. PUBLISHER: Eli Horowitz. EDITOR: Dave Eggers. COVER AND ENDPAPER ILLUSTRATION: Robyn O'Neil. INTERIOR ILLUSTRATIONS: Michael Schall.

♣ RT/features *This project was created with the help of RT/features. Thanks to Rodrigo Teixeira, Fernando Loureiro, Daniel Galera, and Daniel Pellizzari.*

MEMORY WALL

by ANTHONY DOERR

Tall Man in the Yard

SEVENTY-FOUR-YEAR-OLD Alma Konachek lives in Vredehoek, a suburb above Cape Town: a place of warm rains, big-windowed lofts, and silent, predatory automobiles. Behind her garden, Table Mountain rises huge, green, and corrugated; beyond her kitchen balcony, a thousand city lights wink and gutter behind sheets of fog like candleflames.

At three in the morning, one night in November, Alma wakes to hear the rape gate across her front door rattle open and someone enter her house. Her arms jerk; she spills a glass of water across the nightstand. A floorboard in the living room shrieks. She hears what might be breathing. Water drips onto the floor.

Alma manages a whisper. "Hello?"

A shadow flows across the hall. She hears the scrape of a shoe on the staircase, then nothing. Night air blows into the room—it smells of frangipani and charcoal. Alma presses a fist over her heart.

Beyond the balcony windows, moonlit pieces of clouds drift over the city. Spilled water creeps slowly toward her bedroom door.

"Who's there? Is someone there?"

The grandfather clock in the living room pounds through the seconds. Alma's pulse booms in her ears. Her bedroom seems to be rotating very slowly.

"Harold?" Alma remembers that Harold is dead but she cannot help herself. "Harold?"

Another footstep from the second floor, another protest from a floorboard. What might be a minute passes. Maybe she hears someone descend the staircase. It takes her another full minute to summon the courage to shuffle into the living room.

Her front door is wide open. The traffic light at the top of the street flashes yellow, yellow, yellow. The leaves are hushed, the houses dark. She heaves the rape gate shut, slams the door, sets the bolt, and peers out the window lattice. Within twenty seconds she is at the hall table, fumbling with a pen.

A man, she writes. *Tall man in the yard.*

Memory Wall

Alma stands barefoot and wigless in the upstairs bedroom with a flashlight. The grandfather clock down in the living room ticks and ticks, winding up the night. A moment ago Alma was, she is certain, doing something very important. Something life-and-death. But now she cannot remember what it was.

The one window is ajar. The guest bed is neatly made, its coverlet smooth. On the nightstand sits a machine the size of a microwave oven, marked PROPERTY OF CAPE TOWN MEMORY RESEARCH CENTER. Three cables spiraling off it connect to something that looks vaguely like a bicycle helmet.

The wall in front of Alma is smothered with scraps of paper. Diagrams, maps, ragged sheets aswarm with scribbles. Shining among the papers are hundreds of plastic cartridges, each the size of a matchbook, engraved with a four-digit number and perforated by a single hole.

The beam of Alma's flashlight settles on a color photograph of a man walking out of the sea. She fingers its edges. The man's pants are rolled to the knees; his expression is part grimace, part grin. Cold water. Across the photo, in handwriting she knows to be hers, is the word *Harold*. She knows this man. She can close her eyes and recall the pink flesh of his gums, the folds in his throat, his big-knuckled hands. He was her husband.

Around the photo, the scraps of paper and plastic cartridges build outward in crowded, overlapping layers, anchored with pushpins and chewing gum and penny nails. She sees to-do lists, jottings, drawings of what might be prehistoric beasts or monsters. She reads: *You can trust Pheko.* And *Taking Polly's Coca-Cola.* A flyer says *Porter Properties.* There are stranger phrases: *dinocephalians, late Permian, massive vertebrate graveyard.* Some sheets of paper are blank; others reveal a flurry of cross-outs and erasures. On a half-page ripped from a brochure, one phrase is shakily underlined: *memories are located not inside the cells but in the extracellular space.*

Some of the cartridges have her handwriting on them, too, printed below the numbers. *Museum. Funeral. Party at Hattie's.*

Alma blinks. She has no memory of writing on little cartridges or tearing out pages of books and tacking things to the wall.

She sits on the floor in her nightgown, legs straight out. A gust rushes through the window and the scraps of paper come alive, dancing, tugging at their pins. Loose pages eddy across the carpet. The plastic cartridges rattle lightly.

Near the center of the wall, her flashlight beam again finds the photograph of a man walking out of the sea. Part-grimace, part-grin. That's Harold, she thinks. He was my husband. He died. Years ago. Of course.

Out the window, beyond the crowns of the palms, beyond the city lights, the ocean is washed in moonlight, then shadow. Moonlight, then shadow. A helicopter ticks past. The palms flutter.

Alma looks down. There is slip of paper in her hand. *A man,* it says. *Tall man in the yard.*

Dr. Amnesty

Pheko is driving the Mercedes. Apartment towers reflect the morning sun. Sedans purr at stoplights. Six different times Alma squints out at the signs whisking past and asks him where they are going.

"We're driving to see the doctor, Mrs. Alma."

The doctor? Alma rubs her eyes, unsure. She tries to fill her lungs. She fidgets with her wig. The tires squeal as the Mercedes climbs the ramps of a parking garage.

Dr. Amnesty's staircase is stainless steel and bordered with ferns. Here's the bulletproof door, the street address stenciled in the corner. It's familiar to Alma in the way a house from childhood would be familiar. As if she has doubled in size in the meantime.

They are buzzed into a waiting room. Pheko drums his fingertips on his knee. Four chairs down, two well-dressed women, one a few decades younger than the other, sit beside a fish tank. Both have fat pearls studded through each earlobe. Alma thinks: Pheko is the only black person in the building. For a moment she cannot remember what she is doing here. But this leather on the chair, the blue gravel in the saltwater aquarium—it is the memory clinic. Of course. Dr. Amnesty. In Green Point.

After a few minutes Alma is escorted to a padded chair overlaid with crinkly paper. It's all familiar now: the cardboard pouch of rubber gloves, the plastic plate for her earrings, two electrodes beneath her blouse. They lift off her wig, rub a cold gel onto her scalp. The television panel shows sand dunes, then dandelions, then bamboo.

Amnesty. A ridiculous surname. What does it mean? A pardon? A reprieve? But more permanent than a reprieve, isn't it? Amnesty is for wrongdoings. For someone who has done something wrong. She will ask Pheko to look it up when they get home. Or maybe she will remember to look it up herself.

The nurse is talking.

"And the remote stimulator is working well? Do you feel any improvements?"

"Improvements?" She thinks so. Things do seem to be improving. "Things are sharper," Alma says. She believes this is the sort of thing she is supposed to say. New pathways are being forged. She is remembering how to remember. This is what they want to hear.

The nurse murmurs. Feet whisper across the floor. Invisible machinery hums. Alma can feel, numbly, the rubber caps being twisted out of the ports in her skull and four screws being threaded simultaneously into place. There is a note in her hand: *Pheko is in the waiting room. Pheko will drive Mrs. Alma home after her session.* Of course.

A door with a small, circular window in it opens. A pale man in green scrubs sweeps past, smelling of chewing gum. Alma thinks: There are other padded chairs in this place, other rooms like this one, with other machines prying the lids off other addled brains. Ferreting inside them for memories, engraving those memories into little square cartridges. Trying to fight off oblivion.

Her head is locked into place. Aluminum blinds clack against the window. In the lulls between breaths, she can hear traffic sighing past.

The helmet comes down.

Three Years Before, Briefly

"Memories aren't stored as changes to molecules inside brain cells," Dr. Amnesty told Alma during her first appointment, three years ago. She had been on his waiting list for ten months. Dr. Amnesty had straw-colored hair, nearly translucent skin, and invisible eyebrows. He spoke English as if each word were a tiny egg he had to deliver carefully through his teeth.

"This is what they thought forever but they were wrong. The truth is that the substrate of old memories is located not inside the cells but in the extracellular space. Here at the clinic we target those spaces, stain them, and inscribe them into electronic models. In the hopes of teaching damaged neurons to make proper replacements. Forging new pathways. Re-remembering.

"Do you understand?"

Alma didn't. Not really. For months, ever since Harold's death, she had been forgetting things: forgetting to pay Pheko, forgetting to eat breakfast, forgetting what the numbers in her checkbook meant. She'd go to the garden with the pruners and arrive there a minute later without them. She'd find her hairdryer in a kitchen cupboard, car keys in the tea tin. She'd rummage through her mind for a noun and come up empty-handed: *casserole? carpet? cashmere?*

Two doctors had already diagnosed the dementia. Alma would have preferred amnesia: a quicker, less-cruel erasure. This was a corrosion, a slow leak. Seven decades of stories, five decades of marriage, four decades of working for Porter Properties, too many houses and buyers and sellers to count—spatulas and salad forks, novels and recipes, nightmares and daydreams, hellos and goodbyes. Could it really all be wiped away?

"We don't offer a cure," Dr. Amnesty was saying, "but we might be able to slow it down. We might be able to give you some memories back."

He set the tips of his index fingers against his nose and formed a steeple. Alma sensed a pronouncement coming.

"It tends to unravel very quickly, without these treatments," he said. "Every day it will become harder for you to be in the world."

Water in a vase, chewing away at the stems of roses. Rust colonizing the tumblers in a lock. Sugar eating at the dentin of teeth, rubble sealing off a highway, a river eroding its banks. Alma could think of a thousand metaphors, and all of them were inadequate.

She was a widow. No children, no pets. She had her Mercedes, a million and a half rand in savings, Harold's pension, and the house in Vredehoek. Dr. Amnesty's procedure offered a measure of hope. She signed up.

The operation was a fog. When she woke, she had a headache and her hair was gone. With her fingers she probed the four rubber caps secured into her skull.

A week later Pheko drove her back to the clinic. One of Dr. Amnesty's nurses escorted her to a leather chair that looked something like the ones in dental offices. The helmet was merely a vibration at the top of her scalp. They would be reclaiming memories, they said; they could not predict if the memories would be good ones or bad ones. It was painless. Alma felt as though spiders were stringing webs through her head.

Two hours later Dr. Amnesty sent her home from that first session with a remote memory stimulator and nine little cartridges in a paperboard box. Each cartridge was stamped from the same beige polymer, with a four-digit number engraved into the top. She eyed the remote player for two days before taking it up to the upstairs bedroom one windy noon when Pheko was out buying groceries.

She plugged it in and inserted a cartridge at random. A low shudder rose through the vertebrae of her neck, and then the room unraveled and fell away in layers. The walls dissolved. Through rifts in the ceiling, the sky rippled like a flag. Alma's vision snuffed out, as if the fabric of her house had been yanked downward through a drain, and a prior world rematerialized.

She was in a gallery: high ceiling, poor lighting, a smell like old magazines. The South African Museum. Harold was beside her, leaning over a glass-fronted display, excited, his eyes shining—look at him! So young! His khakis were too short. Black socks showed above his shoes. How long had she known him? Maybe a year?

She had worn the wrong shoes: tight, too rigid. The weather had been perfect that day and Alma would have preferred to sit in the Company Gardens under the trees with this tall new boyfriend. But the museum was what Harold wanted, and she wanted to be with him. Soon they were in a fossil room, a couple dozen skeletons on podiums, some big as rhinos, some with yard-long fangs, all with massive, eyeless skulls.

"One hundred and eighty million years older than the dinosaurs, hey?" Harold whispered.

Nearby, schoolgirls chewed gum. Alma watched the tallest of them spit slowly into a porcelain drinking fountain, then suck the spit back into her mouth. A sign labeled the fountain *For Use by White Persons* in careful calligraphy. Alma felt as if her feet were being crushed in vices.

"Just another minute," Harold said.

Seventy-one-year-old Alma watched everything through twenty-four-year-old Alma. She *was* twenty-four-year-old Alma! Her palms were damp and her feet were aching and she was on a date with a living Harold! A young, skinny Harold! He enthused about the skeletons; they looked like animals mixed with animals, he said. Reptile heads on dog bodies. Eagle heads on hippo bodies. "I never get tired of seeing them," young Harold was telling young Alma, a boyish luster in his face. Two hundred and fifty million years ago, he said, these creatures died in the mud, their bones compressed slowly into stone. Now someone had hacked them out; now they were reassembled in the light.

"These were our ancestors, too," Harold said. Alma could hardly bear to look at them: they were eyeless, fleshless, murderous; they seemed engineered only to tear one another apart. She wanted to take this tall boy out to the gardens and sit hip-to-hip with him on a bench and take off her shoes. But Harold pulled her along. "Here's the gorgonopsian. A gorgon. Big as a tiger. Two, three hundred kilograms. From the Permian. That's only the second complete skeleton ever found. Not so far from where I grew up, you know." He squeezed Alma's hand.

Alma felt dizzy. The monster had short, powerful legs, fist-size eye holes, and a mouth full of fangs. "Says they hunted in packs," whispered Harold. "Imagine running into six of those in the bush?" In the memory twenty-four-year-old Alma shuddered.

"We think we're supposed to be here," he continued, "but it's all just dumb luck, isn't it?" He turned to her, about to explain, and as he did shadows rushed in from the edges like ink, flowering over the entire scene, blotting the vaulted ceiling and the schoolgirl who'd been spitting into the fountain and finally young Harold himself in his too-small khakis. The remote device whined; the cartridge ejected; the memory crumpled in on itself.

Alma blinked and found herself clutching the footboard of her guest bed, out of breath, three miles and five decades away. She unscrewed the headgear. Out the window a thrush sang *chee-chweeeoo*. Pain swung through the roots of Alma's teeth. "My god," she said.

The Accountant

That was three years ago. Now a half dozen doctors in Cape Town are harvesting memories from wealthy people and printing them on cartridges, and occasionally the cartridges are traded on the streets. Old-timers in nursing homes, it's been reported, are using memory machines like drugs, feeding the same ratty, over-fingered cartridges into their remote machines: wedding night, spring afternoon, bike ride along the cape. The little plastic squares smooth and shiny from the insistence of old fingers.

Pheko drives Alma home from the clinic with fifteen new cartridges in a paperboard box. She does not want to nap. She does not want the triangles of toast Pheko sets on a tray beside her chair. She wants only to sit in the upstairs bedroom, hunched mute and sagging in her armchair, with the headgear of the remote device screwed into the ports in her head and occasional strands of drool leaking out of her mouth. Living less in this world than in some synthesized Technicolor past where forgotten moments come trundling up through cables.

Every half hour or so, Pheko wipes her chin and slips one of the new cartridges into the machine. He enters the code and watches her eyes roll back. There are almost a thousand cartridges pinned to the wall in front of her; hundreds more lie in piles across the carpet.

Around four the accountant's BMW pulls up to the house. He enters without knocking, calls "Pheko" up the stairs. When Pheko comes down the accountant already has his briefcase open on the kitchen table and is writing something in a file folder. He's wearing loafers without socks and a peacock-blue sweater that looks abundantly soft. His pen is silver. He says hello without looking up.

Pheko greets him and puts on the coffee pot and stands away from the counter-top, hands behind his back. Trying not to bend his neck in a show of sycophancy. The accountant's pen whispers across the paper. Out the window mauve-colored clouds reef over the Atlantic.

When the coffee is ready Pheko fills a mug and sets it beside the man's brief-case. He continues to stand. The accountant writes for another minute. His breath whistles through his nose. Finally he looks up and says, "Is she upstairs?"

Pheko nods.

"Right. Look. Pheko. I got a call from that… physician today." He gives Pheko a pained look and taps his pen against the table. *Tap. Tap. Tap.* "Three years. And not a lot of progress. Doc says we merely caught it too late. He says maybe we fore-stalled some of the decay, but now it's over. The boulder's too big to put brakes on it now, he said."

Upstairs Alma is quiet. Pheko looks at his shoetops. In his mind he sees a boulder crashing through trees. He sees his five-year-old son, Temba, at Miss Amanda's school, ten miles away. What is Temba doing at this instant? Eating, perhaps. Playing soccer. Wearing his eyeglasses.

"Mrs. Konachek requires twenty-four-hour care," the accountant says. "It's long overdue. You had to see this coming, Pheko."

Pheko clears his throat. "I take care of her. I come here seven days a week. Sunup to sundown. Lots of times I stay later. I cook, clean, do the shopping. She's no trouble."

The accountant raises his eyebrows. "She's plenty of trouble, Pheko, you know that. And you do a fine job. Fine job. But our time's up. You saw her at the *boma* last month. Doc says she'll forget how to eat. She'll forget how to smile, how to speak, how to go to the toilet. Eventually she'll probably forget how to swallow. Fucking terrible fate if you ask me. Who deserves that?"

The wind in the palms in the garden makes a sound like rain. There is a creak from upstairs. Pheko fights to keep his hands still behind his back. He thinks: If only Mr. Konachek were here. He'd walk in from his study in a dusty canvas shirt, safety goggles pushed up over his forehead, his face looking like it had been boiled. He'd drink straight from the coffee pot and hang his big arm around Pheko's shoulders and say, "You can't fire Pheko! Pheko's been with us for fifteen years! He has a little boy now! Come on now, hey?" Winks all around. Maybe a clap on the accountant's back.

But the study is dark. Harold Konachek has been dead for more than four years. Mrs. Alma is upstairs, hooked into her machine. The accountant slips his pen into a pocket and buckles the latches on his briefcase.

"I could stay in the house, with my son," tries Pheko. "We could sleep here." Even to his own ears, the plea sounds small and hopeless.

The accountant stands and flicks something invisible off the sleeve of his sweater. "The house goes on the market tomorrow," he says. "I'll deliver Mrs. Konachek to Suffolk Home next week. No need to pack things up while she's still here; it'll only frighten her. You can stay on till next Monday."

Then he takes his briefcase and leaves. Pheko listens to his car glide away. Alma starts calling from upstairs. The accountant's coffee mug steams, untouched.

Treasure Island

At sunset Pheko poaches a chicken breast and lays a stack of green beans beside it. Outside the window flotillas of rainclouds gather over the Atlantic. Alma stares into her plate as if at some incomprehensible puzzle. Pheko says, "Doctor find some good ones this morning, Mrs. Alma?"

"Good ones?" She blinks. The grandfather clock in the living room ticks. The room flickers with a rich, silvery light. Pheko is a pair of eyeballs, a smell like soap.

"Old ones," Alma says.

He helps her into her nightgown and squirts a cylinder of toothpaste onto her toothbrush. Then her pills. Two white. Two gold. Alma clambers into bed muttering questions.

Wind-borne rain starts a gentle patter on the windows. "Okay, Mrs. Alma," Pheko says. He pulls the quilt up to her throat. "I got to go home." His hand is on the lamp. His telephone is vibrating in his pocket.

"Harold," Alma says. "Read to me."

"I'm Pheko, Mrs. Alma."

Alma shakes her head. "Goddammit."

"You've torn your book all apart, Mrs. Alma."

"I have? I have not. Someone else did that."

A breath. A sigh. On the dresser, three lustrous wigs sit atop featureless porcelain heads. "Ten minutes," Pheko says. Alma lays back, bald, glazed, a withered child. Pheko sits in the bedside chair and takes *Treasure Island* off the nightstand. Pages fall out when he opens it.

He reads the first paragraphs from memory. *I remember him as if it were yesterday, as he came plodding to the inn door, his sea chest following behind him in a hand-barrow; a tall, strong, heavy, nut-brown man...*

One more page and Alma is asleep.

B478A

Pheko catches the 9:20 Golden Arrow to Khayelitsha. He is a little man in black trousers and a red cable-knit sweater. In the train seat, his shoes barely touch the floor. Gated compounds and walls of bougainvillea and little bistros lit with colored bulbs slide past. At Hanny Street the train pauses outside Virgin Active Fitness, where three indoor pools smolder with aquamarine light, a last few swimmers toiling through the lanes, an elephantine waterslide disgorging water in the corner.

The car fills with township girls: office cleaners, waitresses, laundresses, women who go by one name in Cape Town and another in the townships, housekeepers called Sylvia or Alice about to become mothers called Malili or Momtolo.

Drizzle streaks the windows. Voices murmur in Xhosa, Sotho, Tswana. The gaps between streetlights lengthen; soon Pheko can see only the upflung penumbras of billboard spotlights here and there in the dark. DRINK OPA. REPORT CABLE THIEVES. WEAR A CONDOM.

Khayelitsha is thirty square miles of shanties made of aluminum and breeze blocks and sackcloth and car doors. A thousand haphazard light towers stand over the shacks like limbless trees. Women carry babies or plastic bags or vegetables or ten-gallon water jugs along the roadsides. Men wobble past on bicycles. Dogs wander.

Pheko gets off at Site C and hurries along a line of shanties in the rain. Someone a few alleys over lights a firework and it blooms and fades over the rooftops.

B478A is a pale-green shed with a sandy floor and a light-blue door. Three treadless tires hold the roof in place. Bars seal off the two windows. Temba is inside, still awake, animated, whispering, nearly jumping up and down in place. He wears a T-shirt several sizes too large; his little eyeglasses bounce on his nose.

"Paps," he says, "Paps, you're twenty-one minutes late! Paps, Boginkosi caught three cats today, can you believe it? Paps, can you make paraffin from plastic bags?"

Pheko sits on the bed and waits for his vision to adjust to the dimness. The walls are papered with faded supermarket circulars. Dish soap for 1.99. Juice two-for-one. Yesterday's laundry hangs from the ceiling. A rust-red stove stands propped on bricks in the corner. Two metal-and-plastic folding chairs complete the furniture.

Outside the rain sifts down through the vapor lights and makes a slow, lulling clatter on the roof. Insects creep in, seeking refuge: gnats and millipedes and big, glistening flies. Twin veins of ants flow across the floor and braid into channels under the stove. Moths flutter at the window screens. Pheko hears the accountant's voice in his ear: *You had to see this coming.* He sees the silver pen flashing in the light of Alma's kitchen.

"Did you eat, Temba?"

"I don't remember."

"You don't remember?"

"No, I ate! I ate! Miss Amanda had samp and beans."

"And did you wear your glasses today?"

"I wore them."

"Temba."

"I *wore* them, Paps. See?" He points with two fingers to his face.

Pheko slips off his shoes. "Okay, little lamb. I believe you. Now choose a hand." He holds out two fists. Temba stands barefoot in his overlarge jersey, blinking his brown eyes behind his glasses.

Eventually he chooses left. Pheko shakes his head and smiles and reveals an empty palm.

"Nothing."

"Next time," says Pheko. Temba coughs, wipes his nose. He seems to swallow back a familiar disappointment.

"Now take off your glasses and give me one of your barnacle attacks," says Pheko, and Temba stows his glasses atop the stove and leaps onto his father, wrapping his legs around Pheko's ribs. They roll across the bed. Temba squeezes his father around the neck and back.

Pheko rears up, makes exaggerated strides around the little shed while the boy clings to him. "Paps," Temba says, talking into his father's chest. "What was in the other hand? What did you have this time?"

"Can't tell you," says Pheko. He pretends to try to shake off the boy's grip. "You got to guess right next time."

Pheko stomps around the house. The boy hangs on. His forehead is a stone against Pheko's sternum. His hair smells like dust, pencil shavings, and smoke. Rain murmurs against the roof.

Tall Man in the Yard

Monday night Roger Tshoni brings the quiet little memory-tapper named Luvo with him up into the posh suburb of Vredehoek and breaks, for the twelfth time, into Alma Konachek's house. Roger has white hair and a white beard and a nose like a large brown gourd. His teeth are orange. He gives off a reek of cheap tobacco. The band of his straw hat has MA HORSE printed three times around the circumference.

Each time Roger has picked the lock on the rape gate, Alma has woken up. He thinks it might have to do with an alarm but he has not seen any alarms inside the house. Roger has given up on trying to hide anyway. Tonight he hardly bothers to keep quiet. He waits in the doorway, counting to fifteen, then leads the boy inside.

Sometimes she threatens to call the police. Sometimes she calls him Harold. Sometimes something worse: Boy. Or kaffir. Or darkie. As in, Get to work, boy. Or: Goddammit, boy. Sometimes she stares right through him with her empty eyes as if he were made of smoke. If he frightens her he simply walks away and smokes a cigarette in the garden and breaks back in through the kitchen door.

Tonight Roger and Luvo stand in the living room a moment, both of them wet with rain, looking out at the city through the glass balcony doors, a few red lights blinking among ten thousand amber ones. They wipe their shoes; they listen as Alma mutters to herself in the bedroom down the hall. The ocean beyond the waterfront is an invisible blackness in the rain.

"Like an owl, this lady," whispers Roger.

The boy named Luvo takes off his wool cap and scratches between the four ports installed in his head and climbs the stairs. Roger crosses into the kitchen, takes three eggs from the refrigerator, and sets them in a pot to boil. Before long Alma comes shambling out from the bedroom, barefoot, bald, no bigger than a girl.

Roger's hands whisper across his shirtfront, find an unlit cigarette tucked into his hatband, and return to his pockets. It's his hands, he has learned, more than anything else, that terrify her. Long hands. Brown hands.

"You're—" hisses Alma.

"Roger. You call me Harold sometimes."

She drags a wrist across her nose. "I have a gun."

"You don't. You couldn't shoot me anyway. Come, sit." Alma looks at him, confounded. But after a moment she sits. The blue ring of flame on her cooktop casts the only light. Down in the city the pinpoints of automobile lights dilate and dissolve as they travel between raindrops on the windowglass.

The house feels close around Roger tonight, its ratcheting grandfather clock and spotless sofas and the big display cabinet in the study. He wants desperately to light his cigarette.

"You got some new cartridges today from your doctor, didn't you, Alma? I saw that little houseboy of yours drive you down to Green Point."

Alma keeps silent. The eggs rattle in their pot. She looks as if time has stopped inside her: rope-veined, birdlike, expressionless. A single blue artery pulses crosswise above her right ear. The four rubber caps are seated tightly against her scalp.

She frowns slightly. "Who are you?"

Roger doesn't answer. He shuts off the burner and lifts out the three steaming eggs with a slotted spoon.

"I am Alma," Alma says.

"I know it," Roger says.

"I know what you're doing."

"Do you?" He places the eggs on a dishtowel in front of Alma. A dozen times now over the past month they've done this, sat at her kitchen table in the middle of the night, Roger and Alma, tall black man, elderly white woman, the lights of Trafalgar Park and the railway yards and the waterfront strewn below. A tableau not quite of this world. What does it mean, Roger wonders distantly, that the countless failures of his life have funneled him into this exact circumstance?

"Eat up now," he says.

Alma gives him a dubious look. But moments later she takes an egg and cracks it on the surface of the table and begins to peel it.

The Order of Things

Things don't run in order. There is no A to B to C to D. All of the cartridges are the same size, the same redundant beige. Yet some take place decades ago and others take place last year. They vary in intensity, too: some pull Luvo into them and hold him for fifteen or twenty seconds; others wrench him into Alma's past and keep him there for half an hour. Moments stretch; months vanish during a breath. He comes up gasping, as if he had been submerged underwater. He feels catapulted back into his own mind.

Sometimes, when he comes back into himself, Roger is standing beside him, an unlit cigarette fixed in the vertex of his lips, staring into Alma's wall of papers and postcards and cartridges as if waiting for some essential explanation to rise up out of it.

Other times the house is noiseless, and there's only the wind sighing through the open window, and the papers fluttering on the wall, and a hundred questions winding through Luvo's head.

Luvo believes he is somewhere around fifteen years old. He has very few memories of his own: none of his parents, no sense of who might have installed four ports in his skull and set him adrift among the ten thousand orphans of Cape Town. No memories of how or why. He knows how to read; he can speak English and Xhosa; he knows Cape Town summers are hot and windy and winters are cool and blue. But he cannot say how he might have learned such things.

His recent history is one of pain: headaches, backaches, boneaches. Twinges fire deep inside his neck; migraines blow in like storms. The holes in his scalp itch and leak a clear fluid; they are not nearly as symmetrical as the ports he has seen on Alma Konachek's head.

Roger found him in the Company Gardens, where he usually sleeps. A dozen times now, the older man has loomed up out of the night smelling of garlic and tobacco; he hustles Luvo into a taxi and they climb from the waterfront into Vredehoek and Roger picks two locks and lets them into the elegant white house on the hill.

Luvo is working from left to right across the upstairs bedroom, from the stairwell toward the window. By now, over a dozen nights, he has eavesdropped on perhaps five hundred of Alma's memories. There are hundreds more cartridges to go, some standing in towers on the carpet, far more pinned to the wall. The numbers engraved into their ends correspond with no chronology Luvo can discover.

But he feels as if he is working gradually, clumsily, toward the center of something. Or, if not toward, then away, as if he is stepping inch by inch away from a painting made of thousands of tiny dots. Any day now the picture will resolve itself; any day now some fundamental truth of Alma's life will come into focus.

Already he knows plenty. He knows that Alma as a girl was obsessed with islands: mutineers, shipwrecks, the last members of tribes, castaways fixing their eyes on empty horizons. He knows that she and Harold worked in the same property office for decades, and that she has owned three silver Mercedes sedans, each one for twelve years. He knows Alma designed this house with an architect from Johannesburg, chose paint colors and doorknobs and faucets from catalogs, hung prints with a level and a tape measure. He knows she and Harold went to concerts, bought clothes at Gardens Shopping Centre, traveled to a city called Venice. He knows that the day after Harold retired he bought a used Land Cruiser and a nine-millimeter Crusader handgun and started driving out on fossil-hunting trips into a huge, arid region east of Cape Town called the Great Karoo.

He also knows Alma is not especially kind to her houseman, Pheko. He knows that Pheko has a little son named Temba, and that Alma's husband paid for an eye operation the boy needed when he was born, and that Alma got very angry about this when she found out.

On cartridge 5015 a seven-year-old Alma demands her nanny hand over a newly opened bottle of Coca-Cola. When the nanny hesitates, grimacing, Alma threatens to have her fired. The nanny hands over the bottle. A moment later Alma's mother appears, furious, dragging Alma into the corner of a bedroom. "Never, ever drink from anything one of the servants has put her lips on first!" Alma's mother shouts. Her face contorts; her little teeth flash. Luvo can feel his stomach twist.

On cartridge 9136 seventy-year-old Alma attends her husband's funeral service. A few dozen white-skinned people stand beneath chandeliers, engulfing roasted apricot halves. Alma's meticulous little houseman Pheko picks his way through them wearing a white shirt and black tie. He has a toddler in eyeglasses with him; the child winds himself around the man's left leg like a vine. Pheko presents Alma with a jar of honey, a single blue bow tied around the lid.

"I'm sorry," he says, and he looks it. Alma holds up the honey. The lights of a chandelier are momentarily trapped inside. "You didn't need to come," she says, and sets the jar down on a table.

Luvo can smell the nauseating thickness of perfume in the funeral home, can see the anxiety in Pheko's eyes, can feel Alma's unsteadiness in his own legs. Then he is snatched out of the scene, as if by invisible cords, and he becomes himself again, shivering lightly, a low ache draining through his jaw, sitting on the edge of the bed in Alma's guest room.

Soon it's the hour before dawn. The rain has let up. Roger is standing beside him, exhaling cigarette smoke out the open bedroom window, gazing down into the backyard garden.

"Anything?"

Luvo shakes his head. His brain feels heavy, explosive. The life span for a memory-tapper, Luvo has heard, is one or two years. Infections, convulsions, seizures. Some days he can feel blood vessels warping around the columns installed in his brain, can feel the neurons tearing and biting as they try to weave through the obstructions.

Roger looks gray, almost sick. He runs a shaky hand across the front pockets of his shirt.

"Nothing in the desert? Nothing in a Land Cruiser with her husband? You're sure?"

Again Luvo shakes his head. He asks, "Is she sleeping?"

"Finally."

They file downstairs. Memories twist slowly through Luvo's thoughts: Alma as a six-year-old, a dining room, linen tablecloths, the laughter of grown-ups, the soft hush of servants in white shirts bringing in food. Alma sheathing the body of an earthworm over the point of a fishhook. A faintly glowing churchyard, and Alma's mother's bony fingers wrapped around a steering wheel. Bulldozers and rattling buses and gaps in the security fences around the suburbs where she grew up. Buying a backlot brandy called white lightning from Xhosa kids half her age.

Roger pays the boy 400 rand: four wrinkled hundreds. Luvo would like to argue for more but his headache is advancing, irrepressible; it is a deep orange flame licking at the edges of everything. Each step downstairs sends his brain reverberating off the walls of his skull. Any moment his field of vision will ignite.

He pulls his wool cap over his head and zips up his jacket and Roger locks the house behind them as the first strands of daylight break over Table Mountain.

Tuesday Morning

Pheko arrives just after dawn to the faint odor of tobacco in the house. Three fewer eggs in the refrigerator. He stands a minute, puzzling over it. Nothing else seems disturbed. Alma sleeps a deep sleep.

The estate agent is coming this morning. Pheko vacuums, washes the balcony windows, polishes the countertops until they shine a foot deep. Pure white light, rinsed by last night's rain, pours through the windows. The ocean is a gleaming plate of pewter.

At ten Pheko drinks a cup of coffee in the kitchen. Two tea towels, crisp and white, are folded over the oven handle. The floors are scrubbed, the dishwasher empty, the grandfather clock wound. Everything in its place.

He could steal things. He could take the kitchen television and some of Harold's books and Alma's music player. Jewelry. Coats. The matching pea-green bicycles in the garage—how many times has Alma ridden hers? Once? Who even knows those bicycles are here? Pheko could call a taxi right now and load it with suitcases and take them into Khayelitsha and before nightfall half of Alma's things could be turned into cash.

Who would know? Not the accountant. Not Alma. Only Pheko. Only God.

Alma wakes at ten-thirty, groggy, muddled. He dresses her, escorts her to the breakfast table. She sits in her chair, tea untouched, hands quivering, strands of her wig stuck in her eyelashes. "I used to come here," Alma mutters. "Before."

"You don't want your tea, Mrs. Alma?"

Alma gives him a bewildered look.

Upstairs the memory wall ruffles in the wind. The estate agent's sedan arrives at eleven, precisely on time.

The South African Museum

Tuesday afternoon Luvo scrubs his face and hands in a Company Gardens public lavatory and runs a wet paper towel over the toe of each sneaker. His black canvas backpack contains a bar of soap, a change of clothes, and three adventure novels—everything he owns in the world. He fixes his watchcap over the ports in his head and walks to the South African Museum.

Inside he steps past the distrustful looks of two warders and into the paleontology gallery. Hundreds of fossils are locked in glass cases, specimens from all over southern Africa: shells and worms and nautiluses and seed ferns and trilobites, and minerals, too, yellow-green crystals and gleaming clusters of quartz, mosquitoes in drops of amber, scheelite, wulfenite.

In Alma's memories Luvo has watched Harold return from the Karoo boiling with ardor, enthusing about dolerite and siltstone, bonebeds and trackways. The big man would chisel away at rocks in the garage, show Alma whole amphibians, a foot-long dragonfly embedded in limestone, little worm tracks in hardened mud. He'd come into the kitchen flushed, animated, smelling of dust and heat and rocks, safety goggles pushed up over his forehead, waving a walking stick he'd picked up somewhere, nearly as tall as he was, made of ebony, wrapped with red beads on the handle and with an elephant carved on the top.

The whole thing infuriated Alma: the walking stick, the goggles, Harold's boyish avidity. Forty-five years of marriage, Alma would announce, and now he had decided to become a lunatic rockhound? What about their friends, what about going for walks together, what about joining the Mediterranean Cruise Club? Retirees, Alma would yell, were supposed to move *toward* comforts, not away from them.

Here is what Luvo knows: inside Roger's frayed, beaten wallet is a four-year-old newspaper obituary. The headline reads REAL-ESTATE ACE TURNED DINOSAUR PROSPECTOR. Below it is a grainy black-and-white photo of Harold Konachek.

Luvo has asked to see the obituary enough times that he has memorized it. A sixty-eight-year-old Cape Town retiree, driving with his wife on backveld roads in the Karoo, had stopped to look for fossils at a roadcut when he had a fatal heart attack. According to the man's wife, just before he died he had made a significant find, a rare Permian fossil. Extensive searches in the area turned up nothing.

Roger, with his straw hat and white beard and tombstone teeth, has told Luvo he went out to the desert with dozens of other fossil hunters, even with a group from the university. He says a paleontologist even went to Alma's house and asked her what she'd seen. "She said she couldn't remember. Said the Karoo was huge and all the hills looked the same."

Interest slackened. People assumed the fossil was unrecoverable. Then, several years later, Roger saw Alma Konachek leaving a memory clinic in Green Point with her houseboy. And he started following them around town.

"*Gorgonopsia longifrons*," Roger told Luvo a month ago, when he first started bringing the boy to Alma's house. Luvo has engraved the name into his memory.

"A big, nasty predator from the Permian. If it's a complete skeleton, it's worth forty or fifty million rand. World's gone crazy for this stuff. Movie stars, financiers. Last year a triceratops skull sold to some Chinaman at an auction for thirty-four million American dollars."

Luvo looks up from the display case. Footfalls echo through the gallery. Tourists mill here and there. The gorgon skeleton the museum has on a granite pedestal is the same one Harold showed Alma fifty years before. Its head is flat-sided; its jaw brims with teeth. Its claws look capable of great violence.

The plaque below the gorgon reads GREAT KAROO, UPPER PERMIAN, 260 MILLION YEARS AGO.

Wednesday Night, Thursday Night

When Luvo wakes Roger is standing over him. It's after midnight. The shock of coming into his own tampered head is searing. Roger squats on his haunches, inhales from a cigarette, and glances at his watch with a displeased expression.

"Someone put a realty sign in front of that house today."

Luvo presses his fingertips into his temples.

"They're selling the old lady's house."

"Why?"

"Why? 'Cause she's lost her mind."

Leaves blot and unblot the cadmium-colored park lights. Dim figures move now and then through the trees. The gardens seethe. The tip of Roger's cigarette flares and fades.

"So we're done? We're done going over there?"

Roger looks at him. "Done? No. Not yet. We've got to hurry up." Again he glances at his wristwatch. "We're losing time."

Little by little, order rises out of the confusion. Luvo sits on the bed in Alma's upstairs bedroom and studies the wall in front of him and concentrates: in the center, a young man walks out of the sea, trousers rolled to his knees. Around the man orbit lines from books, postcards, photos, misspelled names, grocery lists underlined with a dozen hesitant pencil strokes. Trips. Company parties. *Treasure Island.*

Each cartridge on Alma's wall becomes a little brazier, burning in the darkness. Luvo wanders between them, gradually exploring the labyrinth of her history. Maybe, he thinks, at the beginning, before the disease had done its worst, the wall offered Alma a measure of control over what was happening to her. Maybe she could hang a cartridge on a nail and find it a day or two later and feel her brain successfully recall the same memory again—a new pathway forged through the dusklight.

When it worked, it must have been like descending into a pitch-black cellar for a jar of preserves, and finding the jar waiting there, cool and heavy, so she could bring it up the bowed and dusty stairs into the light of the kitchen to cut it open. For a while it must have worked for Alma, anyway; it must have helped her believe she could fend off her inevitable erasure.

It has not worked as well for Roger and Luvo. Luvo does not know how to turn the wall to his ends; it will only show him Alma's life as it wishes. The cartridges veer toward and away from his goal without ever quite reaching it; he founders inside a past and a mind over which he has no control.

On cartridge 6786 Harold tells Alma he is reclaiming something vital, finally trying to learn about the places he'd grown up, grappling with his own infinitesimal place in time. He was learning to see, he said, what once was: storms, monsters, fifty million years of Permian protomammals. Here he was, sixty-some years old, still limber enough to wander around in the richest fossil beds outside of Antarctica. To bend down, to use his eyes and fingers, to find the impressions of animals that had lived such an incomprehensibly long time ago! It was enough, he told Alma, to make him want to kneel down.

"Kneel down?" Alma rages. "Kneel *down*? To whom? To what?"

"Please," Harold asks Alma on cartridge 1204. "I'm still the same man I've always been. Let me have this."

"You're losing your mind," Alma tells him.

On cartridge after cartridge Luvo feels himself drawn to Harold: the man's wide, red face, a soft curiosity glowing in his eyes. Even his silly ebony walking stick and big pieces of rocks in the garage are endearing. On the cartridges in which Harold appears, Luvo can feel himself beneath Alma, around her, and he wants to linger where she wants to leave; he wants to learn from Harold, see what the man is dragging out of the back of his Land Cruiser and scraping at with dental tools in the study. He wants to go out to the Karoo with him to prowl riverbeds and mountain passes and roadcuts—and is disappointed when he cannot.

And all those books in that white man's study! As many books as Luvo can remember seeing in his life. Luvo is even beginning to learn the names of the fossils in Harold's display cabinet downstairs: sea snail, tusk shell, ammonite. He wants to spread them across the desk when he and Roger arrive; he wants to run his fingers over them.

On cartridge 6567, Alma weeps. Harold is off somewhere, hunting fossils probably, and it is a long, gray evening in the house with no concerts, no invitations, nobody ringing on the telephone. Alma eats roasted potatoes alone at the table with a detective show mumbling on the kitchen television. The faces on the screen blur and stray, and the city lights out the balcony windows look to Luvo like the portholes of a distant cruiseliner, golden and warm and far away. Alma thinks of her girlhood, how she used to stare at photographs of islands. She thinks of Billy Bones, Long John Silver, a castaway on a desert beach.

The device whines; the cartridge ejects. Luvo closes his eyes. The plates of his skull throb; he can feel the threads of the helmet shifting against the tissues of his brain.

From downstairs comes Roger's low voice, talking to Alma.

Friday Morning

An infection creeps through Site C, waylaying children shanty by shanty. One hour radio commentators say it's passed through saliva; the next they say it's commuted through the air. No, township dogs carry it; no, it's the drinking water; no, it's a conspiracy of Western pharmaceutical companies. It could be meningitis, another flu pandemic, some new child-plague. No one seems to know anything. There is talk of public antibiotic dispensaries. There is talk of quarantine.

Friday morning Pheko wakes at four-thirty as always and takes the enameled washbasin to the spigot six sheds away. He lays out his razor and soap and washcloth on a towel and squats on his heels, shaving alone and without a mirror in the cool darkness. The sodium lights are off, and a few stars show here and there between clouds. Two house crows watch him in silence from a neighbor's eave.

When he's done he scrubs his arms and face and empties the washbasin into the street. At five Pheko carries Temba down the lane to Miss Amanda's and knocks lightly before entering. Amanda pushes herself up on her elbows from the bed and gives him a groggy smile. He sets still-sleeping Temba on her couch and the boy's eyeglasses on the table beside him.

On the walk to the Site C station Pheko sees a line of schoolgirls in navy and white uniforms, queuing to climb onto a white bus. Each wears a paper mask over her nose and mouth. He climbs the ramp and waits. Down in the grassy field below them forgotten concrete culverts lay here and there like fallen pillars from some foregone civilization, spray-painted with signs: EXACTA and FUCK and BLIND 43. RICH GET RICHER. JAMAKOTA DIES PLEASE HELP.

Trains shuttle to and fro like rattling beasts. Pheko thinks, Three more days.

Cartridge 4510

Alma seems more tired than ever. Pheko helps her climb out of bed at 11:30. A clear liquid seeps from her left eye. She stares into nothingness.

Today she lets Pheko dress her but will not eat. Twice an agent comes to show the house and Pheko has to shuttle Alma out to the yard and sit with her in the chaise longues, holding her hand, while a young couple tools through the rooms and admires the views and leaves tracks across the carpets.

Around two Pheko sighs, gives up. He sits Alma on the upstairs bed and screws her into the remote device and lets her watch cartridge 4510, the one he keeps in the drawer beside the dishwasher so he can find it when he needs it. When she needs it.

Alma's neck sags; her knees drift apart. Pheko goes downstairs to eat a slice of bread. Wind begins thrashing through the palms in the garden. "Southeaster coming," says the kitchen television. Then ads flicker past. A tall white woman runs through an airport. A yard-long sandwich scrolls across the screen. Pheko closes his eyes and imagines the wind reaching Khayelitsha, boxes cartwheeling past spaza shops, plastic bags slithering across roads, slapping into fences. People at the station will be pulling their collars over their mouths against the dust.

After a few more minutes, he can hear Alma calling. He walks upstairs, sits her back down, and pushes in the same cartridge again.

Upstairs

There are blanks on Alma's wall, Luvo is learning, omissions and gaps. Even if he reorganized her whole project, arranged her life in a chronological line, first memory to last, Alma's history running in a little beige file down the stairs and around the living room, what would he learn? There'd still be breaks in time, failures in his understanding, months beyond his reach. Who is to say a cartridge even exists that contains the moments before Harold's death?

Friday night he decides to abandon his left-to-right method. Whatever order once existed in the arrangement of these cartridges has long since been shuffled out of it. It's a museum arranged by a madwoman. He starts watching any cartridge that for some unnameable reason stands out to him from the disarray pinned to the wall. On one cartridge nine- or ten-year-old Alma lays back in a bed full of pillows while her father reads her a chapter from *Treasure Island*; on another a doctor tells a much older Alma that she will probably not be able to have children. On a third Alma has written *Harold and Pheko*. Luvo runs it through the remote device twice. In the memory Alma asks Pheko to move several crates of books into Harold's study and arrange them alphabetically on his shelves. "By author," she says.

Pheko is very young; he must be newly hired. He looks as if he is barely older than Luvo is now. He wears an ironed white shirt and his eyes seem to fill with dread as he concentrates on her instructions.

"Yes, Madam," he says several times. Alma disappears. When she returns, what might be an hour later, Harold in tow, Pheko has put every book on the shelves in Harold's office upside down. Alma walks very close to the shelves. She tilts a couple of titles toward her, then sets them back down. "Well these aren't in any kind of order at all," she says.

Confusion ripples through Pheko's face. Harold laughs.

Alma looks back to the bookshelves. "The boy can't read," she says.

Luvo cannot turn Alma's head to look at Pheko; Pheko is a ghost, a smudge outside her field of vision. But he can hear Harold behind her, his voice still smiling. He says, "Not to worry, Pheko. Everything can be learned. You'll do fine here."

The memory dims; Luvo unscrews the headgear and hangs the little beige cartridge back on the nail from which he plucked it. Out in the garden the palms clatter in the wind. Alma is Madam. Pheko is Boy. Through the cartridges Luvo can watch Pheko as a young man learning to build the mask Luvo has seen on so many black South African faces, on the faces of his elders in the Company Gardens, on the face of Roger. Bafflement turns to sufferance, sufferance to endurance.

Soon the house will be sold, Luvo thinks, and the cartridges will be returned to the doctor's office, or sent along with Alma to whatever place they're consigning her to, and this strange assortment of papers will be folded into a trash bag. The books and appliances and furniture will be sold off. Pheko will be sent home to his son.

Luvo shivers. He thinks of Harold's fossils downstairs, waiting in their cabinet. He hears Harold whispering as if from the grave: *We all swirl slowly down into the muck. We all go back to the mud. Until we rise again in threads of light.*

Downstairs

In a nightmare Alma finds herself at the fossil exhibit she went to with Harold fifty years before. All its overhead lights have been switched off. The only illumination comes from sweeping, powder-blue beams that slice through the gallery, catching each skeleton in turn and leaving it again in darkness, as if strange beacons are revolving in the lawns outside the high windows.

The gorgon Harold was so excited about is no longer there. The iron brace that supported the skeleton remains; a silhouette of dust marks where it stood. But the gorgon is gone.

Alma's heart stops; her breath catches. Her hands are at her sides, but in the dream she can feel herself clawing at her own throat. Shadows rear up and are sucked back into darkness. The purpose of her errand veers past her, there, then gone.

Saturday

The southeaster throws a thick sheet of fog over Table Mountain. In Vredehoek everything looks hazy and tenuous. Cars loom up out of the white and disappear again. Alma sleeps till noon. When she wakes she comes tottering out with her wig in proper alignment, her eyes bright. "Good morning," she says.

Pheko is startled. "Good morning, Mrs. Alma."

He serves her oatmeal, raisins, and tea. "Pheko," she says, enunciating his name as if tasting it. "You're Pheko." She says his name several more times.

"Would you like to sit inside today, Mrs. Alma? It's awfully damp out there."

"Yes, I'll stay inside. Thank you."

They sit in the kitchen. Alma shovels big spoonfuls of oatmeal into her mouth. The television burbles out news about rising tensions, farm attacks, violence outside a health clinic.

"Now my husband," Alma says suddenly, not quite speaking to Pheko but to the kitchen at large, "his passion was always rocks. Rocks and the dead things in them. Always off to do, as he put it, some grave-robbing. Mine was less obvious. I did care about houses. I was an estate agent before many women were estate agents."

Pheko sets a hand atop his head. Except for a mild unsteadiness in her voice, Alma sounds much as she did a decade ago. The television drones. Fog presses against the balcony windows.

"There were times when I was happy and times when I was not," continues Alma. "Like anyone. To say a person is a happy person or an unhappy person is sort of ridiculous. We are a thousand different kinds of people every hour." She looks at Pheko then, though not quite directly at him. As if a guest floats behind him and to his left. Fog seeps through the garden. The trees disappear. The chaise longues disappear. "Don't you think?"

Pheko closes his eyes, opens them.

"Are you happy?"

"Me, Mrs. Alma?"

"You should have a family."

"I do have a family. Remember? I have a son. He is five years old now."

"Five years old," says Alma.

"His name is Temba."

"I see." She drives her spoon into what's left of the oatmeal and lets go and watches its handle slowly fall down to touch the rim of the bowl. "Come with me."

Pheko follows her up the stairs into the bedroom. For a full minute she stands beside him, both of them facing her wall of papers and cartridges. She crouches, moving here and there along the wall. Her lips move silently. On the wall in front of Pheko is a postcard of a little island ringed by a turquoise sea. Two years ago she worked every day on this wall, posting things, concentrating. How many meals did Pheko bring Alma up in this room?

She reaches for the photo of Harold and fingers its corner a moment. "Sometimes," she says, "I have trouble remembering things."

Behind her, outside the window, the fog cycles and cycles. The sky is invisible. The neighbor's rooftops are gone. The garden is gone. Everything is white. "I know, Mrs. Alma," Pheko says.

Vapor Lights

It's nine-thirty p.m. and the wind is shrieking against the ten thousand haphazard houses in Site C. As soon as he walks in the door, Pheko can tell by the way Miss Amanda has her lips pinched under her teeth that Temba has become ill. A foot away, he can feel the heat radiating off the boy's body. "Little lamb," whispers Pheko. "Little lamb."

The queue at the twenty-four-hour clinic is already long, longer than Pheko has ever seen it. Mothers and children sit on upturned onion crates or sleep on blankets. Behind them a bus-length mural of Jesus stretches supernaturally long arms across a wall. Dried leaves and plastic bags scuttle down the road.

Two separate times over the next few hours Pheko has to get out of line because Temba has soiled his clothes. He cleans his son, wraps him in a towel, and returns to wait outside the clinic. The vapor lights on their towers above Site C rock back and forth like some aggregation of distant moons. Scraps of paper and skeins of dust fly through the air beneath them.

By two a.m. Pheko and Temba are still nowhere near the front of the line. Every hour or so a bleary nurse walks up and down the queue and says, in Xhosa, how grateful she is for everybody's patience. The clinic, she says, is waiting for antibiotics.

Pheko can feel Temba's sweat soaking through the towel around him. The boy's cheeks are the color of dishwater. "Temba," Pheko whispers. Once the boy raises his face weakly and Pheko can see the wobbling pinpoints of the light towers reflected in the sheen of his eyes.

That Same Hour

Roger and Luvo enter Alma Konachek's house in the earliest hours of Sunday morning. Alma doesn't wake. Her breathing sounds steadily from the bedroom. Roger wonders if perhaps the houseboy has given her a sedative.

Luvo tromps upstairs. Roger opens the refrigerator and closes it; he contemplates stepping out into the garden to smoke a cigarette. He feels, very keenly tonight, that he is running out of time. Down below the balcony, somewhere past the fog, Cape Town sleeps.

Absently, for no reason, Roger opens the drawer beside the dishwasher. He has stood in this kitchen on seventeen different nights but has never before opened this drawer. Inside Roger can see butane lighters, coins, a box of staples. And a single beige polymer cartridge, identical to the hundreds upstairs.

Roger picks up the cartridge and holds it to the window. Number 4510.

"Kid," Roger calls, raising his voice to the ceiling. "Kid." Luvo does not reply. Roger walks upstairs and waits. The boy is hooked into the machine. His torso seems to vibrate lightly. After another minute the machine sighs, and Luvo's eyes flit open. The boy sits back and grinds his palms into his eye sockets. Roger holds up the new cartridge.

"Look at this." There is a shakiness in Roger's voice that surprises them both.

Luvo reaches and takes it. "Have I seen this before?"

Cartridge 4510

Alma is in a movie theater with Harold. They are perhaps thirty years old. The movie is about scuba divers. On-screen, white birds with forked tails soar above a beach.

Light touches the tops of breaking waves. Alma and Harold sit side by side, Alma in a bright green dress, green shoes, green plastic earrings, Harold in an expensive brown shirt. The side of Harold's knee presses against the side of Alma's. Luvo can feel a dim electricity traveling between them.

Now the camera slips underwater. Rainbows of fish flit across the screen. Reefs scroll past. Alma's heart does its steady work.

The memory jerks forward; Alma and Harold are in a cab, Alma's camera bag over her shoulder. They travel through a place that looks to Luvo like Camps Bay. Everything out the windows is vague; it is as if, for Alma, there is nothing to look at at all. There is only feeling, only anticipation, only her young husband beside her.

In another breath they are climbing the steps of a regal, cream-colored hotel, backed by moonlit cliffs. Gulls soar everywhere. A little gold-lettered sign reads TWELVE APOSTLES HOTEL. Inside the lobby a willowy woman in a white shirt and white pants with a gold belt buckle gives them a key on a brass chain; they pad down a series of hallways.

In the hotel room Alma lets out a succession of bright, genuine laughs. She gulps wine. Everything is pristine; two spotless windows, a wide white bed, richly ruffled lampshades. Harold switches on a music player and takes off his shoes and dances clumsily in his socks. Outside the windows, range after range of spotlit waves fold over onto a beach.

After what might be a few minutes Harold leaps the balcony railing and takes off his shirt and socks. "Come with me," he calls, and Alma takes her camera bag and follows him down onto the beach. Alma laughs as Harold charges into the wavebreak. He splashes around a bit, grinning hugely. "Freezing!" he shouts. As he walks out of the water, Alma raises her camera and takes a photograph.

If they say anything more to one another, it is not remembered, not recorded on the cartridge. In the memory Harold makes love to Alma twice. Luvo feels he should leave, should yank out the cartridge, send himself back into Alma's house in Vredehoek, but the room is so clean, the sheets are so cool beneath Alma's back. Everything is soft; everything seems to vibrate with possibility. Alma tastes the sea on Harold's skin. She feels his big-knuckled hands hold onto her ribs, his fingertips touch the knobs of her spine.

Near the end of the memory Alma closes her eyes and seems to slip underwater, as if back into the film at the moviehouse, watching a huge black urchin wave its spines, noticing how the water is not silent but full of soft clicks, and soon the pastels of coral are scrolling past her vision, and little slashes of needlefish are dodging her fingers like a rain of light, and Harold's body seems not to be on top of hers at all, but drifting instead beside hers; they are swimming together, floating slowly away from the reef toward a place where the sea floor falls away and the bottom is too far away to see, and there is only light filtering into deep water, bottomless water, and Alma's blood seems to swell out to the very edges of her skin.

Sunday, Four a.m.

Alma sits up in bed. From the ceiling come the unmistakable sounds of footfalls. On her nightstand there is a glass of water, its bottom daubed with miniature bubbles. Beside it is a hardcover book. Though its jacket is missing and half the binding is torn away, the title appears sparkling and whole in her mind. *Treasure Island.* Of course.

From the ceiling comes another creak. Someone is in my house, Alma thinks, and then some still-functional junction of her brain coughs up an image of a man. His eyes are brown. His nose looks like a small brown gourd. His trousers are khaki and stained and a tear in the left shoulder of his shirt shows his darker skin beneath. A faded jaguar winds up the underside of his wrist.

Alma jerks herself onto her feet. A demon, she thinks, a burglar, a tall man in the yard.

She hurries across the kitchen into the study and opens the heavy, two-handled drawer at the bottom of Harold's fossil cabinet. A drawer she has not opened in years. Toward the bottom, beneath a stack of paleontology magazines, is a cigar box upholstered with pale orange linen. Even before she finds it, she is certain it is there. Indeed, her mind feels particularly clear. Oiled. Operable. You are Alma, she thinks. I am Alma.

She retrieves the box, sets it on the desk that once was Harold's, and opens it. Inside is a nine-millimeter handgun.

She stares at it a moment before picking it up. Blunt and colorless and new-looking. Harold used to carry it in his glove compartment. She does not know how to tell if it is loaded.

Alma carries the gun in her left hand through the kitchen to the living room and sits in the silver armchair that offers her a view up the stairwell. She does not turn on any lights. Her heart flutters in her chest like a moth.

From upstairs winds a thin strand of cigarette smoke. The pendulum in the grandfather clock swings back and forth. Outside the windows there is only a dim whiteness: fog. Everything seems irradiated with a meaning she is only now recognizing. My house, she thinks. I love my house.

If Alma keeps her eyes straight ahead and does not look to her right or left, it is possible to believe Harold is about to settle into the matching chair beside her, the lamp and table between them. She can just sense the weight of his body shifting over there, can smell something like rock powder in his clothes, can perceive the scarcely perceptible gravitational tug one body exerts upon another. She has so much to say to him.

She sits. She waits. She tries to remember.

Leaving the Queue

At four-thirty a.m. Pheko and Temba are still twenty or so people from the clinic entrance. Temba is sleeping steadily now, his arms and legs limp, his big eyelids sealing him off from the world. The wind has settled down. Pheko squats against the wall with his son in his lap. The boy looks emptied out, his cheeks depressed, the tendons in his throat showing.

Above them the painted Jesus stretches his implausibly long arms. The light towers have been switched off and a dull orange glow reflects off the undersides of the clouds.

My last day of work, Pheko thinks. Today the accountant will pay me. A second thought succeeds that one: Mrs. Alma has antibiotics. He is surprised he did not think of this sooner. She has piles of them. How many times has Pheko refreshed the little army of orange pill bottles standing in her bathroom cupboard?

Bats cut silent loops above the shanty rooftops. A little girl beside them unleashes a chain of coughs. Pheko can feel the dust on his face, can taste the earth in his molars. After another minute he lifts his sleeping son and abandons their place in the queue and carries the boy down through the noiseless streets to the train station.

Harold

"Maybe it's something the houseboy didn't want her to see?" murmurs Roger. "Something that made her upset?"

Luvo waits for the memory to fade. Pain drags through the roots of his teeth. He studies Alma's wall in the dimness. *Treasure Island. Gorgonopsia longifrons. Porter Properties.* "That's not it," he says. On the wall in front of them float countless iterations of Alma Konachek: a seven-year-old sitting cross-legged on the floor; a brisk, thirty-year-old estate agent; a bald old lady. A racist, a lover, a wife.

And in the center Harold walks perpetually out of the sea. His name printed below it in shaky handwriting. A photograph taken on the very night when Harold and Alma seemed to reach the peak of everything they could be. Alma had placed that picture in the center on purpose, Luvo is sure of it, before her endless rearranging had defaced the original logic of her project. The one thing she wouldn't move.

The photograph is faded, slightly curled at the edges. It must be forty years old, thinks Luvo. He reaches out and takes it from the wall.

Before he feels it, he knows it will be there. The photograph is slightly heavier than it should be. Two strips of tape cross over its back; something has been fixed underneath.

"What's that?" asks Roger.

Luvo carefully peels away the tape so as not to tear the photograph. It takes him almost a minute. Beneath the tape is a cartridge. It looks like the others, except that it has a black *X* drawn across it.

He and Roger stare at it a moment. Then Luvo slides it into the machine. The house peels away in slow, deciduous waves.

Alma is riding beside Harold in a dusty truck: Harold's Land Cruiser. Harold holds the steering wheel with his left hand, his face sunburned red, his right hand trailing out the open window. The road is untarred and rough. On both sides grassy fields flow into steep, crumbled mountainsides.

Harold is talking, his words washing in and out of Alma's attention. "What's the one permanent thing in the world?" he's saying now. "Change! Incessant and relentless change. All these slopes, all this scree—see that huge slide there?—they're all records of calamities. Our lives are like a fingersnap in all this." Harold shakes his head in genuine wonderment. He swoops his hand back and forth in the air out the window.

Inside Alma's memory a thought rises so clearly it's as if Luvo can see the sentence printed in the air in front of the windshield. She thinks: Our marriage is ending and all you can talk about are rocks.

Occasional farm cottages whisk past, white walls with red roofs; derelict wind pumps; sun-ravaged sheep pens; everything tiny against the backdrop of the peaks growing ever larger beyond the hood ornament. The sky is a swirl of cloud and light.

Time compresses; Luvo feels jolted forward. One moment a wall of cliffs ahead glows chalk white, flickering lightly as if composed of flames. A moment later it has turned coal black. Another moment passes and Alma and Harold are in among the rocks, the Land Cruiser ascending long switchbacks. The road is composed of rust-colored gravel, bordered now and then by uneven walls of rock. A sign reads SWARTBERGPAS.

Inside Alma, Luvo can feel something large coming to a head. It's rising, frothing inside her. Heat prickles her under her blouse; Harold downshifts as the truck climbs through a nearly impossible series of hairpin turns. The valley floor with its little quilt of farms looks a thousand miles below.

At some point Harold stops at a pullout surrounded by rockfall. He produces sandwiches from an aluminum cooler. He eats ravenously; Alma's sandwich sits untouched on the dash. "Just going to have a poke around," Harold says, and does not wait for a reply. From the back of the Land Cruiser he takes a jug of water and his ebony walking stick with the elephant on the handle and climbs over the dry-stone retaining wall and disappears.

Alma sits, bites back anger. Wind plays in the grasses on both sides of the road. Clouds drag across the ridgetops. No cars pass.

She'd tried. Hadn't she? She'd tried to get excited about fossils. She'd just spent three days with Harold in a game lodge outside of Beaufort West: a tiny, cramped place encircled by rocks and wind, ticks on her pant legs, a lone ant paddling slow circles atop her tea. Lightning storms scoured the horizon. Scorpions patrolled the kitchenette. Harold would leave at dawn and Alma would sit in a fold-up chair outside their room with a mystery novel in her lap and the desolation of the Karoo shimmering in all directions.

A glitter, a madness. The Big Empty, people in Cape Town called the Karoo, and now she saw why.

She and Harold had not been talking, not sleeping in the same bed. Now they were driving over this pass toward the coast to spend a night in a real hotel, a place with air conditioning and white wine in silver buckets. She would tell him how she felt. She would tell him she had reached a certain threshold. The prospect of it made her feel simultaneously lethargic and exhilarated.

Alma blinks; the sun lapses across the ridgelines. Shadows swing across the road. Time skids and ripples. Luvo begins to feel nauseous, as if he and Alma and the Land Cruiser were teetering on the edge of a cliff, as if the whole road is about to slough off the mountain and plunge into oblivion. Alma whispers to herself about snakes, about lions. She whispers, "Hurry up, goddamn it, Harold."

But he does not come back. Another hour passes. Not a single car comes over the pass in either direction. Alma's sandwich disappears. She urinates beside the Land Cruiser. It's nearly dusk before Harold clambers back over the wall. Something is wrong with his face. His forehead is crimson. His words come fast, quick convoluted strings of them, as if he is hacking them out.

"Alma, Alma, Alma," he's saying. Spittle flies from his lips. He has found, he said, the remains of a *Gorgonopsia longifrons* on a ledge halfway down the escarpment. It is toothy, bent, big as a lion. Its long, curved claws are still in place; its entire skull is present, its skeleton fully articulated. It is, he believes, the biggest fossilized gorgon ever found. The holotype.

His breathing seems only to pick up pace. "Are you all right?" asks Alma, and Harold says "No," and a second later, "I just need to sit for a moment."

Then he wraps his arms across his chest, leans against the side of the Land Cruiser, and slides down it into the dust.

"Harold?" shrieks Alma. A slick of foamy, blood-flecked saliva spills down her husband's throat. Already dust begins to cling to the wet surfaces of his eyeballs.

The light is low, golden, and merciless. On the veld far below, the zinc rooftops of distant farmhouses reflect back the dying sun. Every shadow of every pebble seems impossibly stark. A tiny rockslide starts beneath Alma's ribs. She turns Harold over; she opens the rear door. She shrieks her husband's name over and over.

When the memory stimulator finally spits out the cartridge, Luvo feels as if he has been gone for days. Patches of rust-colored light float through his vision. He can still feel the monotonous, back-and-forth motion of the Land Cruiser in his body. He can still hear the wind, see the silhouettes of ridgelines in his peripheral vision, feel the gravity of the heights. Roger looks at him; he flicks a cigarette out the open window into the garden. Strands of fog pull through the backyard trees.

"Well?" he says.

Luvo tries to raise his head but it feels as if it will shatter.

"That was it," he says. "The one you've been looking for."

Tall Man in the Yard

Alma is thirsty. She would like someone to bring her some orange juice. She runs her tongue across the backs of her teeth. Harold is here. Isn't Harold in the chair beside her? Can't she hear his breathing on the other side of the lamp?

There are footfalls on the stairs. Alma raises her eyes. She is almost giddy with fear. The gun in her left hand smells faintly of oil.

Birds are passing over the house now, a great flock, harrying across the sky like souls. She can hear the beating of their wings.

The pendulum in the grandfather clocks swings left, swings right. The traffic light at the top of the street sends its serial glow through the windows.

The fog splits. City lights wink between the garden palms. The ocean beyond is a vast, curved shield. It seems to boom outward toward her like a loudspeaker, a great loudspeaker of reflected starlight.

First there is the man's right shoe: laceless, a narrow maw between the toe and sole. Then the left shoe. Dark socks. Unhemmed trouser legs.

Alma tries to scream but only a faint animal sound comes out of her mouth. A man who is not Harold is coming down the stairs and his shoes are dirty and his hands are out and he is opening his mouth to speak.

He is a demon. His hands are huge and terrible. His beard is white. His teeth are the color of old leaves.

His hat says Ma Horse, Ma Horse, Ma Horse.

Virgin Active Fitness

The train grinds to a halt in Claremont and Temba sits up and looks out bleary-eyed and silent at Virgin Active Fitness where it glows beyond the window, quiet, not yet open for the day. His gaze tracks the lit, unpopulated swimming pools through his eyeglasses. Submerged lights radiating out through green water.

The train lurches forward again. Looking up through the window, the boy watches the darkness drain out of the sky. The first rays of sun break the horizon and flow across the east-facing valleys of Table Mountain. Fat tufts of fog slide down from the summit.

A woman in the aisle stands with her back very straight and peers down into a paperback book.

"Paps?" Temba says. "My body feels loose."

His father's arm closes around his shoulders. "Loose?"

The boy's eyes shut. "Loose," he murmurs.

"We're going to get you some medicine," Pheko says. "You just rest. You just hang on, little lamb."

Dawn

Luvo is detaching himself from the remote device when he hears Roger say, from the stairwell, "Now, wait one minute." Then something explodes downstairs. Every molecule in the upstairs bedroom feels as if it has been jolted awake. The windows rattle. The cartridges on the wall quiver. In the shuddering concussion afterward Luvo hears Roger fall down the stairs and exhale a single sob, as if expelling all of his remaining breath at once.

Luvo sits paralyzed on the edge of the bed. The grandfather clock resumes its metronomic advance. Someone downstairs says something so quietly that Luvo cannot hear it. His gaze catches on a small, inexplicable watercolor of a sailboat among the hundreds of papers on the wall in front of him, a sailboat gliding through clouds. He has seen it a hundred times before but has never actually looked at it. Sails straining, clouds floating happily past.

Gradually the molecules in the air around Luvo seem to return to their former states. He hears no more from downstairs except the grandfather clock, banging away in the living room. Roger has been shot, he thinks. Someone has shot Roger. And Roger has the cartridge with the X on it in his shirt pocket.

A low breeze drifts through the open window. The pages on Alma's wall fan out in front of him like a flower, like a mind turned inside out.

Luvo listens to the clock, counts to a hundred. He can still see Harold in the gravel beside the Land Cruiser, his face a mask, dust stuck to his eyes, saliva gleaming on his chin and throat.

Eventually Luvo crawls across the floor and peers down the stairwell. Roger's tall body is at the bottom, slumped over onto itself, folded almost in half. His hat is still on. His arms are crimped underneath him. A portion of his face is gone. A halo of blood has pooled around his head on the tile.

Luvo lays back on the carpet, sees Alma's immaculate room at the Twelve Apostles Hotel, sees a mountain range rush past the dusty windscreen of a truck. Sees Harold's legs twitching beneath him in the gravel.

What is there in Luvo's life that makes sense? Dusk in the Karoo becomes dawn in Cape Town. What happened four years ago is relived twenty minutes ago. An old woman's life becomes a young man's. Memory-watcher meets memory-keeper.

Luvo stands. A wedge of sunlight creeps up the stairwell. He plucks cartridges off the wall and sticks them into his pockets. Forty, fifty of them. Once his pockets are full he moves toward the stairwell, but pauses and looks back. The little room, the spotless carpet, the washed window. On the bedspread a thousand identical roses intertwine. He walks back to the remote device and takes the photograph of Harold walking out of the sea and slips it inside his shirt. He sets cartridge 4510 in the center of the coverlet where someone might find it.

Then he stands at the top of the stairwell, collecting himself. From the living room—from Roger—rises a smell of blood and gunpowder. An odor more grim and nauseating than Luvo expected.

Luvo is about to walk down the stairs when the rape gate rattles and he hears a key slip into the deadbolt of the front door.

Clock

Perhaps the last thing in the world Pheko is prepared to see is a man facedown at the bottom of Alma's stainless-steel staircase lying in a puddle of blood.

Temba is asleep again, a hot weight across his father's back. Pheko is out of breath and sweating from carrying the boy up the hill. He sees the dead man first and then the blood but still it takes him several more seconds to absorb it all. Parallelograms of morning light fall through the balcony doors.

Down the hallway, in the kitchen, Alma is sitting at the kitchen table, her head resting on her arms. She is barefoot.

The questions come too quickly to sort out. How did this man get in? Was he killed with a gun? Did Mrs. Alma do the killing? Where is the gun? Pheko feels the heat radiating off his son into his back. He wants suddenly for everything to go away. The whole world to go away.

I should run, he thinks. I should not be here. Instead he carries his son over the body, stepping over the blood, past Alma in the kitchen. He continues out the back door and into the garden and sets the boy in a chaise longue and returns back inside to retrieve the white chenille blanket off the foot of Alma's bed and wraps the boy in it. Then inside again for Alma's pill bottles. His hands shake as he tries to read the labels. He ends up choosing two types of antibiotic of which there are full bottles and crushing them together into a spoonful of honey. Alma looks up at him once while he works, her stare lost and unknowable and reptilian.

"Thirsty," she says.

"Just a moment, Mrs. Alma," says Pheko. In the garden he sticks the spoon into Temba's mouth and makes sure the boy swallows it down and then he goes back into the kitchen and pockets the antibiotics and listens to Alma breathe awhile and puts on the coffee pot and when he is sure he will be able to speak clearly he pulls his telephone from his pocket and calls the police.

Boy Falling from the Sky

Temba is looking into the shifting, inarticulate shapes of Alma's backyard leaves when a boy falls from the sky. He crashes into some hedges and clambers out onto the grass and places his head in the center of the morning sun and peers down at Temba with a corona of light spilling out around his face.

"Temba?" the silhouette says. His voice is hoarse and unsteady. His ears glow pink where the sunlight passes through them. He speaks in English. "Are you Temba?"

"My glasses," says Temba. The garden is a sea of black and white. The face in front of him shifts and a sudden avalanche of light pierces Temba's eyes. Something bubbles inside his gut. His tongue tastes of the sweet, sticky medicine his father spooned into his mouth.

Now hands are putting on Temba's glasses for him. Temba squints up, blinking. "My paps works here."

"I know." The boy is whispering. Fear travels through his voice.

Temba tries whispering, too. "I'm not supposed to be here."

"Me either."

Temba's eyesight comes back to him. Big palms and rosebushes and a cabbage tree loom against the garden wall. He tries to make out the boy standing over him against the backdrop of the sun. He has smooth brown skin and a wool cap over his lightly felted head. He reaches down and tugs the blanket up around Temba's shoulders.

"My body is sick," says Temba.

"Shhh," whispers the boy. He takes off his hat and presses three fingers against his temple as if reining in a headache. Temba glimpses strange outlines on the boy's scalp, but then the boy puts his cap back on and sniffs and glances nervously toward the house.

"I'm Temba. I live at B478A, Site C, Khayelitsha."

"Okay, Temba. You should rest now."

Temba looks toward the house. Its sleek profile looms up above the hedges, cut with silver window frames and chrome balcony railings.

"I'll rest now," he says.

"Good," whispers the boy with the smooth skin and the glowing ears. Then he takes five quick steps across the backyard and leaps up between the trunks of two palms and scales the garden wall and is gone.

The Days Following

Harold's dying face, Roger's crumpled frame, and the filmy eyes of Temba all rotate behind Luvo's eyes like some appalling picture show. Death succeeding death in relentless concatenation.

He spends the rest of Sunday hiding inside the labyrinthine paths of the Company Gardens, crouched among the leaves. Squirrels run here and there; city workers string Christmas lights through a lane of oaks. Are people looking for him? Are the police?

On Monday Luvo crouches in the alley outside a chophouse watching the news on a bar television through an open window. It takes several hours before he sees it: an elderly woman has shot an intruder in Vredehoek. A reporter stands on Alma's street, a few houses away, and talks into a microphone. In the background a stripe of red-and-yellow police tape stretches across the road. The reporter says nothing about

Alma's dementia, nothing about Pheko or Temba, nothing about accomplices. The whole report lasts perhaps twenty-five seconds.

No one comes for him. No Roger shaking him awake in the night, hustling him into a taxi. No Pheko come to demand answers. No ghosts of Harold or Alma. Tuesday morning he rides a bus up to Derry Street and walks up onto the slopes of Table Mountain, through the sleek, hushed houses of Vredehoek. There is a blue van in front of Alma's house and the garage door is open. The garage is absolutely empty. No Mercedes, no realty sign. No lights. The police tape is still there. As he stands beside the gutter a moment a dark-skinned woman passes behind a window pushing a vacuum cleaner.

That afternoon he sells Alma's memory cartridges to a trader named Cabbage. Cabbage calls a red-eyed teenager out from the trees to run them through a ramshackle memory machine. The transaction takes over two hours. "They real," affirms the teenager finally, and Cabbage looks Luvo up and down before offering him 3,300 rand for the whole batch.

Luvo studies the cartridges in the bottom of his backpack. Sixty-one of them. Pinpoints of a life. He asks the trader if he can buy the remote device with its dirty-looking, warped headgear, but Cabbage only grins and shakes his head. "Costs more than you'll ever have in the whole world," he says, and snaps his bag shut.

Afterward Luvo walks back up through the Company Gardens to the South African Museum and stands in the fossil room with his backpack on and his money in his pocket. He looks into the display cases for a long time. Brachiopod, paper mussel, marsh clam. Horsetail, liverwort, seed fern.

Outside a light rain starts to fall. A warder ambles through, announces to no one in particular that it's closing time. Two tourists come through the door, glance about, and leave. Soon the room is empty. Luvo stands in front of the gorgon. He sees a slender-headed skeleton, stalking something on its long legs, its huge canine incisors showing.

Before long an Indian man in an apron comes out from a door painted the same color as the wall and stands beside Luvo, looking at the case.

"Is the gallery closed?" the man asks.

Luvo glances over at him. His thoughts feel frail, dangerous. "Soon," he says.

The Indian man blinks once, slowly. "You looking at the Permian predators?"

Luvo nods.

"Fierce, eh? And underappreciated, too. I'll take them over dinosaurs any day." He smiles down at Luvo, as if expecting the boy to smile back.

Instead Luvo says, "What could you pay if I were to bring you a complete skeleton of a gorgonopsia?"

"Ha," the man says. His smile fades, then widens. "Why don't you bring us a pterosaur while you're at it? A tyrannosaurus, too?"

"How much could you sell it for?"

"How much? A lot of money. A lot. Are you saying you know where a skeleton of a gorgon is?"

"No," Luvo says. "I don't know what I'm saying."

The man gives Luvo a sympathetic look. Again the warder shuffles through, calling out closing time.

"Well," says the Indian man.

"I should go," says Luvo.

At the street market in Greenmarket Square Luvo buys the following things: a kelly-green duffel bag, nine loaves of white bread, a paint scraper, a hammer, a sack of oranges, four two-liter bottles of water, a polyester sleeping bag, and a puffy red parka that says KANSAS CITY CHIEFS across the back. When he's done, he has 900 rand in his pocket, all the money left him in the world.

Swartberg Pass

On the morning bus heading east from Cape Town there's the impossible straightness of the N1 cutting across the desert all the way to the horizon. The road is swallowed by the bus's big tinted windscreen like an infinite black ribbon. On either side of the N1, dry grasslands run backward into sheaves of brown mountains. Everywhere there is light and stone and unimaginable distance.

Luvo feels simultaneously frightened and awed. As far as he can remember, he has never been outside of Cape Town, though he has Alma's memories riding along inside him, the bright blue coves of Mozambique, Venice in the rain, a line of travelers in suits standing in a first-class queue in the Johannesburg train station.

He pulls the photograph of Harold from his backpack. Harold, half-grinning, half-grimacing, walking out of the sea.

It's afternoon when Luvo clambers off at the intersection for Prince Albert Road.

A gas station and a few aluminum trailers huddle under a brass-colored sun. Black eagles trace slow ovals a half mile above the road. Three friendly-looking women sit behind a vinyl-covered picnic table and sell cheese and marmalade and sticky rolls. "It's warm," they tease. "Take off your hat." Luvo shakes his head. He chews a roll and waits with his duffel bag. It's nearly dusk before a Bantu salesman in a rented Honda slows for him.

"Where you going?"

"The Swartberg."

"You mean over the Swartberg?"

"Yes sir."

The driver reaches across and pushes the door open. Luvo climbs in. They turn southeast. The sun goes down in a wash of orange; moonlight spills onto the Karoo.

The pavement ends. The man drives the last hour through the badlands in silence, with the startled eyes of bat-eared foxes reflecting now and then in the high beams and a vast spread of stars keeping pace above and curtains of dust floating up behind the rear tires.

The car vibrates beneath them. Soon there is no traffic in either direction. Great walls of stone rear up, darker than the sky. They come around a turn and a rectangular brown sign, its top half pocked from a shotgun blast, reads SWARTBERGPAS. Luvo thinks: Harold and Alma saw this same sign. Before Harold died they drove right past this spot.

Twenty minutes later the Honda is climbing past one of the road's countless switchbacks when Luvo says, "Please stop the car here."

The man slows. "Stop?"

"Yes sir."

"You sick?"

"No sir."

The little car shudders as it idles. Luvo unclips his seat belt. The man blinks at him in the darkness. "You're getting out here?"

"Yes sir. Just below the top."

"You're joking."

"No sir."

"Ag, it gets cold up here. It *snows* up here. You ever seen snow?"

"No sir."

"Snow is terrible cold." The man tugs at his collar. He seems about to asphyxiate with the strangeness of Luvo's request.

"Yes sir."

"I can't let you out here."

Luvo stays silent.

"Any chance I can talk you out of this?"

"No sir."

Luvo takes his big duffel and four bottles of water from the backseat and steps out into the darkness. The man looks at him a full half minute before pulling off. It's warm in the moonlight but Luvo stands shivering for a moment, holding his things, and then walks to the edge of the road and peers over the retaining wall into the shadows. He finds a thin path, cut into the slope, and hikes maybe two hundred meters north of the road, pausing every now and then to watch the twin red taillights of the salesman's Honda as it eases up the switchbacks toward the top of the pass.

Below there he finds a lumpy, level area of dry grass and rocks roughly the size of Alma Konachek's upstairs bedroom. He unrolls his sleeping bag and urinates and looks out over the starlit talus below, running mile after mile down onto the plains of the Karoo far beneath him.

He takes a drink of water and climbs into his sleeping bag and tries to swallow back his fear. The rocks on the ground are still warm from the sun. The stars are bright and impossibly numerous. The longer he looks into a patch of sky, the more stars emerge within it. Range upon range of suns burning out beyond the power of his vision.

No cars show themselves on the road. No airplanes cross the sky. The wind makes the only sound. What's out here? Millipedes. Buzzards. Snakes. Warthogs, ostriches, bushbuck. Farther off, on the northern tablelands: jackals, wild dogs, leopards. A last few rhinos.

First Day

Dawn finds Luvo warm and bareheaded inside his sleeping bag with a breeze washing over the ports in his scalp. A truck grinds up the switchbacks of the road in the distance, HAPPY CHIPS painted across its side.

He sits up. Around his sleeping bag are rocks, and beyond his little level spot of grasses are more rocks. Indeed, there seem to be sandstone and limestone blocks everywhere, an infinity of rocks. The slopes below him and above him are littered with rocks in every size, pressed half into the earth like grave markers. Beyond them cliffs have calved off slabs the size of houses.

The HAPPY CHIPS truck disappears around another hairpin. No souls, only a few spindly trees—only boulders and distances. On its pedestal at the museum, the gorgon had seemed huge, big as a dinosaur, but out here the scale of things feels new. What was a dinosaur compared to cliffs like these? Without turning his head Luvo can see ten thousand rocks in which a gorgon might be hidden.

Why did he think he could find a fossil out here? A fifteen-year-old boy who knows only adventure novels and an old woman's memories? Who has never found a fossil in his life?

Luvo eats two pieces of bread and walks slow circles around his sleeping bag, turning over stones with his toes. Splotches of lichen grow on some, pale oranges and grays, and the rocks include grains of color, too, striations of black, flecks of silver. They are lovely but they contain nothing that looks like the fossils in the museum, in Harold's cabinet, in Alma's memories.

All that first day Luvo makes wider and wider circles around his little camp, carrying a bottle of water, watching his shadow slip across the hillsides. Clouds drift above the mountain range at the horizon and their shadows drag across the farms far below. Luvo remembers Harold talking to Alma about time. Younger was "higher in the rocks." Things that were old were deep. But what is higher and lower here? This is a wilderness of rocks. And every single stone Luvo turns over is plain and carries no trace of bone.

Maybe one car comes over the pass every two hours. Three eagles come over him in the evening, calling to one another, never once flapping their wings as they float over the ridge.

The Great Karoo

In dreams Luvo is Alma: a white-skinned estate agent, pain free, well fed. He strides through the Gardens Shopping Centre; clerks rush to help him. Everywhere circular racks gleam with clothes. Air-conditioning, perfumes, escalators. Clerks open their bright, clean faces to him.

His headaches seem only to be intensifying. He has a sense that his skull is slowly being crushed, and that the metallic taste seeping into his mouth is whatever is being squeezed out.

On his second day up on Swartberg Pass, ants chew a hole through one of his bread bags. The sun roasts his arms and neck. Lying there at night Luvo feels as if the gorgon is at the hub of a wheel from out of which innumerable spokes spin past. Here comes Luvo on one spoke, and Roger on another, and Temba on the next, and Pheko and Harold and Alma after that. Everything coursing past in the night, revolving hugely, almost unfathomably, like the wheel of the Milky Way above. Only the center remains in darkness, only the gorgon.

From his memory Luvo tries to summon images of the gorgon at the museum, tries to imagine what one might look like out here, in the rocks. But his mind continually returns to Alma Konachek's house.

Roger is dead. Harold is dead. Alma is either in jail or tucked into a home for the rich and white-skinned. If there's anything left of who she was it's a scrap, a shred, some scribbled note that a cleaner or Pheko has guiltily unpinned from her wall and thrown into the trash. And how much longer can Luvo be any better off, with these ports throbbing in his skull? A few more months?

Here is the surprise: Luvo likes the strange, soothing work of looking into the rocks. He feels a certain peace, clinging to the side of Swartberg Pass: the clouds are like huge silver battleships, the dusks like golden liquids—the Karoo is a place of raw light and monumental skies and relentless silence. But beneath the silence, he's learning, beneath the grinding wind, there is always noise: the sound of grass hissing on the cliffsides and the clattering of Witgat trees tucked here and there into clefts. As he lies in his sleeping bag on his third night he can hear an almost-imperceptible rustling: night flowers unveiling their petals to the moon. When he is very quiet, and his mind has stilled the chewing and whirling and sucking of his fears, he imagines he can hear the coursing of water deep beneath the mountains, and the movements of the roots of the plants as they dive toward it—it sounds like the voices of men, singing softly to one another. And beyond that—if only he could listen even more closely!—there was so much more to hear: the supersonic screams of bats, and, on the most distant tableland, the subsonic conversations of elephants in the game reserves, grunts and moans so deep they carried between animals miles apart, passing through the mountains and then shuttling back.

That night he wakes to the quivering steps of six big antelope, shy and jittery, the keratin of their hooves clacking against the rocks, the vapor of their breath showing in the moonlight as they file past his sleeping bag, not fifty feet away.

On Luvo's fourth morning, wandering below the pass, perhaps a half mile from the road, he turns over a rock the size of his hand and finds pressed into its underside the clear white outline of what looks like a clamshell. The shell is lighter than the stone around it and scalloped at the edges. The name of the fossil rises from some corner of his brain: brachiopod. He sits in the sun and runs the tips of his fingers over the dozens of grooves in the stone. An animal that lived and died eons ago.

Luvo hears Harold Konachek's big, enthusiastic voice: *Two hundred fifty million years ago this place was lush, filled with ferns and rivers and mud.* Flesh washing away, minerals penetrating bones, the weight of millennia piling up, bodies becoming rock.

And now this one little creature had risen to the surface, as the earth was weathered by wind and rain, in the way a long-frozen corpse sometimes bobs to the surface of a glacier after being mulled over in the lightless depths for centuries.

What Endures?

The fifth morning on Swartberg Pass finds Luvo exhausted and hollow and in too much pain to rise from his sleeping bag. He pulls the curled photograph of Harold from his duffel and studies it, running his fingers over the man's features. Pinpoints of sky show through the little holes in each corner.

Luvo tries to cut through his headache, tries to coax his memory back toward the moments before Harold's death. Harold was talking about geology, about death. "What's the one permanent thing in the world? Change!" Wind pumps, sheep pens, a sign that reads SWARTBERGPAS.

Luvo remembers Alma's sandwiches on the dashboard, the wind in the grass beside the road, Harold returning over the apron of the road, staggering as he muttered Alma's name. The pink foam coming out of his mouth. Alma punching telephone buttons in vain. Gravel pushed into Harold's cheek and dust on his eyeballs.

Luvo stares at the photograph of Harold. He has begun to feel as if Alma's wall of papers and cartridges has been reiterated out here a hundredfold on the mountainside, these legions of stones like identical beige cartridges, each pressed out of the same material. And here he is doomed to repeat the same project over and over, hunting among a thousand things for one thing, searching a convoluted landscape for the remains of one thing that has come before.

The shadows turn, shorten; the sun swings up over a ridge. Luvo remembers for the first time something Dr. Amnesty told Alma on one of the cartridges. "Memory builds itself without any clean or objective logic: a dot here, another dot here, and plenty of dark spaces in between. What we know is always evolving, always subdividing. Remember a memory often enough and you can create a new memory, the memory of remembering."

Remember a memory often enough, Luvo thinks. Maybe it takes over. Maybe the memory becomes new again.

In Luvo's own memory a gun explodes. Roger slumps down the stairs and lets out a last breath. A little boy sits in a lounger wrapped in a blanket blinking up at the sky. Alma tears out a page of *Treasure Island* and nails it to a wall. Everything happens over and over and over.

A body, Harold told Alma once, vanishes quickly enough to take your breath away. As a boy, he said, his father would put a dead ewe on the side of the road and in three days the jackals would have reduced it to bones and wool. After a week, even the bones would be gone.

"Nothing lasts," Harold would say. "For a fossil to happen is a miracle. One in fifty million. The rest of us? We disappear into the grass, into beetles, into worms. Into ribbons of light."

It's the rarest thing, Luvo thinks, that gets preserved, that does not get erased, broken down, transformed.

Luvo turns the photograph in his hands and a new thought rises: When Harold was leaning against the Land Cruiser, clutching his chest, his breath coming faster and faster, his heart stopping in his chest, he was not holding his walking stick. The tacky ebony walking stick with the elephant on top. The stick that used to drive Alma mad.

When Harold left the Land Cruiser, he took his walking stick from the back of the truck. And when he returned, a couple of hours later, he no longer had it.

Maybe he'd dropped it on the way back to the Land Cruiser. Or maybe he'd left it in the rocks to mark the gorgon's location. Four years had passed and the walking stick could have been picked up, or washed over a cliff in a storm, or Luvo could be remembering things wrong, but he realizes it had been here once, on the north side of Swartberg Pass, somewhere below the road. Near where Luvo is camped. And it might be here still.

If it's still here, Luvo thinks, it will not be too hard to find. There are no trees up here so big, no branches nearly as long as that walking stick. No wood as dark as ebony.

It's a small thing, perhaps, but it's enough to get Luvo on his feet and start him searching again.

The Gorgon

For that whole day and the next, Luvo walks the sea of stones. He has only one two-liter bottle of water left and he rations it carefully. He works in circles, in rectangles, in triangles. Belts and swaths and carpets of stones. He looks now for something dark, bleached by sun perhaps, a few red beads strung around its handle, the wooden elephant carved on top. Such staffs he has seen sold by children along the airport road and at tourist shops and in Greenmarket Square.

The sixth evening it starts to rain and Luvo drapes his sleeping bag over a bush and crawls beneath it and sleeps a dreamless sleep and around him spiders draw their webs between the branches. When he wakes, the sky is pale.

He stands, shakes the water drops off his sleeping bag. His head feels surprisingly light, almost painless. It's morning, Luvo thinks. I slept through an entire rainstorm. He climbs perhaps fifty feet onto a flat, smooth rock and sits chewing a slice of bread and then sees it.

Harold's walking stick is sticking up from between two boulders two hundred meters away. Even from where he sits Luvo can see the hole almost near the top, a tiny space carved between the elephant's legs.

Every second, walking those two hundred meters, is like leaping into very cold water, like that first instant when the body goes into shock, and everything you are, everything you call your life, disintegrates for a moment, and all you have around you is the water and the cold, your heart trying to send splinters through a block of ice.

The walking stick is sun-bleached and the beads are no longer on the handle but it's still standing upright. As if Harold has left it there for Luvo to find. He stares at it awhile, afraid to touch it. The morning light is sweet and clear. The hillside trickles quietly around him with last night's rain.

There is a carefully stacked pile of stones right beside it and even after Luvo has clawed most of them away, it still takes him a few minutes to realize he is looking down at a fossil. The gorgon is white against the grayer limestone, and the outline of the animal inside seems broken in places. But eventually he can make it out, from one foreleg to the tip of its tail: it is the size of a crocodile, tilted onto its side, and sunk as if into an enormous bathtub of cement. Its big, curved claws are still in place. And its skull sits separate from the rest of the stone entirely, as if it has been set there by the recession of a flood. It is big. Bigger, he thinks, than the one at the museum.

Luvo lifts away more rocks, sweeps away gravel and dust with his hands. The skeleton is fully articulated, looped into the stone. It is perhaps ten feet long. His heart skids.

With the hammer it takes Luvo two hours to break the skull free. Little chips of darker rock fly off as he strikes it and he hopes he is not damaging the thing he has come to find. As big as an old box-television, made entirely of stone, even once it's free of the matrix surrounding it the skull is impossible for him to lift. Even the eye holes and nostrils are filled with rock, a lighter color than the surrounding skull. Luvo thinks: I won't be able to move it by myself.

But he does. He unzips the sleeping bag and folds it over the skull, padding it on all sides, and using the walking stick as a lever, begins to roll the skull, inches at a time, toward the road. It's dark and Luvo is out of water before he gets the skull to the bottom of the retaining wall. Then he goes back to the rest of the skeleton, covers it again with rocks and gravel, marks it with the walking stick, and brings his camp up to the road.

His legs ache; his fingers are cut. Rings of starlight expand out over the ridge-line. The insects in the grass around him exult in their nighttime chorus. Luvo sits down on his duffel bag with the last of his oranges in his lap and the skull waiting six feet below, wrapped in a sleeping bag. He puts on his bright red parka. He waits.

The moon swings gently up over the mountains, huge, green, aswarm with craters.

Return

Three English-speaking Finnish women stop for Luvo after midnight. Two are named Paula. They seem mildly drunk. They ask shockingly few questions about how ragged Luvo looks or how long he has been sitting on the side of one of the most remote roads in Africa. He keeps his hat on, tells them he has been fossil hunting, asks them to help him with the skull. "Okay," they say, and work together, pausing now and then to pass around a bottle of cabernet, and in fifteen minutes have heaved the thing over the wall and made room for it in the back of their van.

They are traveling across South Africa. One of them has recently turned forty and the others are here to celebrate with her. The floor of their camper van is knee-deep with food wrappers and maps and plastic bottles. They pass around a thick, half-hacked-apart shank of cheese; one of the Paulas cuts wedges of it and stacks them on crackers. Luvo eats slowly, looking at his torn fingernails and wondering how he must smell. And yet, there is reggae music washing out of the dashboard, there is the largeness of these women's laughter. "What an adventure!" they say, and he thinks of his paperbacks sitting in the bottom of his duffel. When they stop at the top of the pass and pile out and ask Luvo to take their photograph beside the beaten brown sign that reads DIE TOP, Luvo feels as if perhaps they have been sent to him as angels.

Dawn finds them eating scrambled eggs and chopped tomatoes in the rickety and deserted dining room of the Queens Hotel in a highway town called Matjiesfontein. Luvo drinks an ice-cold Fanta and watches the women eat. Their trip is ending and they show each other photos on the camera's screen. Elephants, wineries, nightclubs.

When he's done with the first Fanta Luvo drinks another one, the slow fans turning above, and the kind, sweaty smiles of the three women turn on him now and then, as if in their worlds black and white are one and the same, as if the differences between people didn't matter so much anymore, and then they get up and pile into the van for the drive back to Cape Town.

One of the Paulas drives; the other two women sleep. Out the windows communication wires sling past in shallow parabolas from pole to pole. The road is relentlessly straight. Paula-the-driver looks back now and then at Luvo in the backseat.

"Headache?" she asks.

Luvo nods.

"What kind of fossil is it?"

"Maybe something called a gorgon."

"Gorgon? Like the Medusa? Snakes for hair, all that?"

"I'm not sure."

"Well, those are the gorgons all right. Medusa and her sisters. Turn you to stone if you look them in the eyes."

"Really?"

"Really," says forty-year-old Finnish Paula.

"This gorgon is very old," says Luvo. "From when this whole desert was a swamp, and big rivers ran all through it."

"I see," says Paula. She drives awhile, tapping her thumb on the wheel in time with the music. "You like that, Luvo? Going out and digging up old things?"

Luvo looks out the window. Out there, beyond the fence lines, beneath the starlit, flat-topped hills, beneath the veld, beneath the dwarf scrub, beneath the endless running wind of the Karoo, what else remains locked away?

"Yes," he says. "I like it."

The Twelve Apostles Hotel

The women walk with Luvo into the museum. Luvo knocks on the door painted the same color as the wall and after a minute, like a miracle, the same Indian man who talked to Luvo eight days earlier steps out. He looks into the back of the camper van with eyes both incredulous and dreamy, as if he is not entirely sure that what is happening is real. He regards the skull and then Luvo and then the women with their matted hair and wrinkled shirts and then puts his hand at his chin for a long time.

They spend the next several hours in the museum with the skull on the floor of a workshop in front of them. The Indian man is a preparator and he telephones the director and the director telephones several more men. Their excitement is obvious. All morning employees come in to look at the skull and the three yawning Finnish women and the strange boy in the wool cap.

Eventually the director, dressed in a trim blue suit, says they can offer 1.4 million rand. The jaws of the Finnish women drop simultaneously. They thump Luvo on the back. They shriek and jump around the preparator's studio. Luvo asks what they can give him now and the director looks at the preparator and says, "Now? As in today?"

"That's what he said," says one of the Paulas. After another hour of waiting they have managed to get Luvo twenty thousand rand and a notarized bill of sale. Luvo asks that the remainder be sent in a complete sum to Pheko Garrett, B478A, Site C, Khayelitsha.

"All of it?" the director asks and Luvo says, "All of it."

Then he says goodbye to the Finnish women, who hug him each in turn and give him their email addresses on little white cards, and one of the Paulas is crying softly to herself as they climb into their rented camper van.

Near the entrance to the Company Gardens is a little English bookshop. Luvo walks inside, his pockets full of money. He finds a paperback of *Treasure Island* and pays for it with a thousand-rand note.

Then he flags down a waterfront cab and tells the driver to take him to the Twelve Apostles Hotel. The driver gives him a look, and the woman at the desk at the hotel gives him the same look, but Luvo has cash and once he has paid she leads him down a hundred-meter-long cream-colored runner of carpet to a black door with the number 7 on it.

The room is as clean and white as it was in Alma's memory. Off the balcony jade-colored waves break onto a golden beach. In the bathroom tiny white tiles line the floor in diamond shapes. Crisp white towels hang on nickel-plated rods. There's a big, spotless, white toilet. White fluffy bath mats lie on the floor. A single white orchid grows from a rectangular vase on the toilet tank.

Luvo takes a forty-five-minute shower. He is somewhere around fifteen years old and he has perhaps six months left to live. After his shower he lies on the perfect white sheets of the bed and watches the huge afternoon sky flow like liquid out the window. Rafts of gulls sail above the beach. Cliffs rise up into the sky. He thinks of Alma's memories, both those carried inside his head and the ones somewhere out in the city—Cabbage will have traded them away by now. He thinks of Alma's memory of this place, of the movie about the fish, gliding out into the great blue. He sleeps.

When he wakes, hours later, he stares awhile into cobalt squares of night outside the windows and then he turns on his lamp and opens *Treasure Island*.

I remember him as if it were yesterday, he reads, *as he came plodding to the inn door, his sea chest following behind him in a hand-barrow; a tall, strong, heavy, nut-brown man...*

The Gorgon

It takes six weeks for a museum crew of twelve people and a telescoping crane to excavate the skeleton. They bring it back to Cape Town in large plastic tubs and send it to an auction house in London. In London it is cleaned, prepared, reassembled, varnished, and mounted on a titanium brace. It sells at auction for 4.5 million dollars, the fourth-highest sum anyone has ever paid for a fossil. The skeleton travels from London on a container ship through the Mediterranean and the Suez Canal and across the Indian Ocean to Shanghai. A week later it is installed on a pedestal in the lobby of a fifty-eight-story office building.

No fake vegetation, no color, just a polyvinyl acetate sprayed along the joints and a Plexiglas cube lowered down over it. Someone sets two big potted palms on either side but two days later the building's owner asks for them to be taken away.

Pheko

Two months pass. Temba is better, his illness a memory. Pheko goes to the post office behind the spaza shop and in his mailbox is a single envelope with his name on it. Inside is a check for almost 1.4 million rand. Pheko looks up. He can hear, all of a sudden, the blood trundling through his head. The ground swivels out from underneath him. Madame Gecelo, behind the counter, looks over at him and looks back at whatever form she is filling out. A bus with no windows passes. Dust rides up over the little post office.

No one is looking. The floor steadies. Pheko peeks again into the envelope and reads the amount. He looks up. He looks back down.

On the subject line the check says *Fossil Sale.* Pheko locks his post-office box and hangs his key around his neck and stands with his eyes closed awhile. When he gets home he shows Temba his two fists. Temba looks at him through his little eyeglasses, then looks back at the fists. He waits, thinking hard, then taps the right fist. Pheko smiles.

"Try the other one."

"The other one?"

Pheko nods.

"You never say to try the other one."

"This time I say try the other one."

"This isn't a trick?"

"Not a trick." Temba taps the left hand. Pheko opens it. "Your train card?" says Temba. Pheko nods.

"Your train card?" repeats Temba.

They stop in the market on the way to the station and buy swimming shorts, each of them, red for Pheko and light blue for Temba. Then they ride the Golden Arrow toward the city. Pheko carries the plastic shopping bag containing the swimming trunks in his right hand but will not let Temba see inside. It is a warm March day and the edges of Table Mountain are impossibly vivid against the sky.

Pheko and Temba disembark at the Claremont stop and walk two blocks holding hands and enter a branch of the Standard Bank of South Africa two storefronts down from Virgin Active Fitness. Pheko opens an account and shows his identification and the clerk spends ten minutes typing various things into his computer and then he asks for an initial deposit. Pheko slides across the check.

A manager shows up thirty seconds later and looks at the check and takes it back behind a glass-walled office. He speaks into a phone for maybe ten minutes.

"What are we doing?" whispers Temba.

"We're hoping," whispers Pheko.

After what seems like an hour the manager comes back and smiles at Pheko and the bank deposits the check.

Alma

Alma sits in the community dining room in a yellow armchair. Her hair is short and silver and stiff. The clothes she is wearing are not hers; clothing seems to get mixed up in this place. Out the window to her left she can see a concrete wall, the top half of a flagpole, and a polygon of sky.

The air smells of cooked cabbage. Fluorescent lights buzz softly in the ceiling. Nearby two women are trying to play rummy but they keep dropping the cards. Somewhere else in the building, perhaps the basement, someone might be howling. It's hard to say. Maybe it's only the air, whistling out of heating ducts.

A ghost of a memory flits past Alma: there, then gone. A television at the front of the room shows a man with a microphone, shows a spinning wheel, shows an audience clapping.

Through the door walks a big woman in a white tank top and white jeans. In the light of the entryway her dark skin is almost invisible to Alma, so that it looks as if a white outfit has become animated and is walking toward her, white pants and a white top and white eyeballs floating. She walks straight toward Alma and begins emptying boxes onto the long table beside her.

A nurse in a flowered smock behind Alma claps her hands together. "Time for arts class, everyone," she says. "Anyone who would like to work with Miss Stigers can come over."

Several people start toward the table, one pushing a walker on wheels. The woman in white clothes is laying out buckets, plates, paints. She opens a big Tupperware bin. She looks over at Alma.

"Hi, sweetheart," she says.

Alma turns her head away. She keeps quiet. A few minutes later some others are laughing, holding up plaster-coated hands. The woman in white clothing sings quietly to herself as she tends to the residents' various projects. Her voice rides beneath the din.

Alma sits in her chair very stiffly. She is wearing a red sweater with a reindeer on it. She does not recognize it. Her hands, motionless on her lap, are cold and look to her like claws.

The woman sings in Xhosa. The song is sweet and slow. In a back room across town, inside a memory clinic in Green Point, a thousand cartridges containing Alma's memories sit gathering dust. In her bedside drawer, among ear plugs and vitamins and crumpled tissues, is the cartridge Pheko gave her when he came to see her, cartridge 4510. Alma no longer remembers what it is or what it contains or even that it belongs to her.

When the song is done a man at the table in a blue sweater breaks into applause with his plaster-coated hands. The piece of sky outside the window is warm and purple. A jetliner tracks across it, winking a golden light.

When Alma looks back, the woman in white is standing closer to her. "C'mon, sweetheart," she says with that voice. A voice like warm butter. "Give this a try. You'll like it."

The woman places a foil pie plate in front of Alma. There is newspaper over the tablecloth, Alma sees, and paint and silk flowers and little wooden hearts and snowmen scattered here and there in plastic bowls. The singing woman pours smooth, white plaster of Paris out of her Tupperware and into Alma's pie plate, wiping it clean with a Popsicle stick.

The plaster of Paris is a beautiful, creamy texture. One of the residents has spread it all over the tablecloth. Another has some in her hair. The woman in white has started a second song. Or perhaps she is singing the first song all over again, Alma cannot be sure. *Kuzo inzingo zalomhlaba*, she sings. *Amanda noxolo, uxolo kuwe.*

Alma raises her left hand. The plaster is wet and waiting. "Okay," she whispers. "Okay."

She thinks: I had somebody. But he left me here all by myself.

Kuzo inzingo zalomhlaba. Amanda noxolo, uxolo kuwe, sings the woman.

Alma sinks her hand into the plaster.

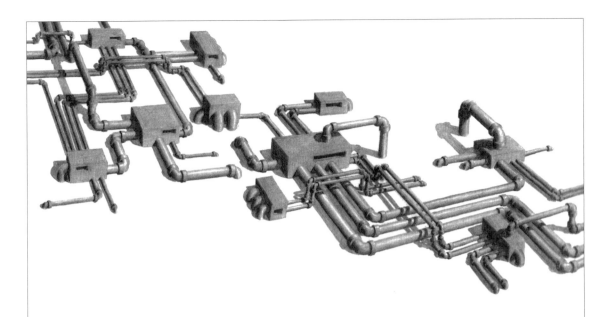

RAW WATER

by WELLS TOWER

"JUST LET ME OUT of here, man," said Cora Booth. "I'm sick. I'm dying."

"Of what?" asked Rodney, her husband, blinking at the wheel, scoliotic with exhaustion. He'd been sitting there for four days, steering the pickup down out of Boston, a trailer shimmying on the ball hitch, a mattress held to the roof of the camper shell with tie-downs that razzed like an attack of giant farting bees.

"Ford poisoning," Cora said. "Truckanosis, stage four. I want out. I'll walk from here."

Rodney told his wife that a hundred and twenty miles lay between them and the home they'd rented in the desert, sight unseen.

"Perfect," she said. "I'll see you in four days. You'll appreciate the benefits. I'll have a tan and my ass will be a huge wad of muscle. You can climb up on it and ride like a little monkey."

"I'm so tired. I'm sad and confused," said Rodney. "I'm in a thing where I see the road, I just don't comprehend it. I don't understand what it means."

Cora rolled down the window to photograph a balustrade of planted organ cactuses strobing past in rows.

"Need a favor, chum?" she said, toying with his zipper.

"What I need is to focus here," Rodney said. "The white lines keep swapping around."

"How about let's scoot up one of those little fire trails," Cora said. "You won't get dirty, I promise. We'll put the tailgate down and do some stunts on it."

The suggestion compounded Rodney's fatigue. It had been a half decade since he and Cora had made any kind of habitual love, and Rodney was fine with that. Even during his teenage hormone boom, he'd been a fairly unvenereal person. As he saw it, their marriage hit its best years once the erotic gunpowder burned off and it cooled to a more tough and precious alloy of long friendship and love from the deep heart. But Cora, who was forty-three, had lately emerged from menopause with large itches in her. Now she was hassling him for a session more days than not. After so many tranquil, sexless years, Rodney felt there was something unseemly, a mild whang of incest, in mounting his best friend. Plus she had turned rough and impersonal in her throes, like a cat on its post. She didn't look at him while they were striving. She went off somewhere by herself. Her eyes were always closed, her body arched, her jaw thrusting up from the curtains of her graying hair, mouth parted. Watching her, Rodney didn't feel at all like a proper husband in a love rite with his wife, more a bootleg hospice man bungling a euthanasia that did not spare much pain.

"Later. Got to dog traffic. I want to get the big stuff moved in while there's still light," said Rodney to Cora, though night was obviously far away, and they were making good time into the hills.

The truck crested the ridge into warm light and the big view occurred. "Brakes, right now," said Cora.

The westward face of the mountain sloped down to the vast brownness of the Anasazi Trough, a crater of rusty land in whose center lay sixty square miles of the world's newest inland ocean, the Anasazi Sea.

Rodney swung the truck onto the shoulder. Cora sprang to the trailer and fetched her big camera, eight by ten, an antique device whose leather bellows she massaged after each use with Neatsfoot Oil. She set up the tripod on the roadside promontory. Sounds of muffled cooing pleasure issued from her photographer's shroud.

Truly, it was a view to make a visual person moan. The sea's geometry was striking—a perfect rectangle, two miles wide and thirty miles long. But its water was a stupefying sight: livid red, a giant, tranquil plain the color of cranberry pulp.

The Anasazi was America's first foray into the new global fashion for do-it-yourself oceans—huge ponds of seawater, piped or channeled into desert depressions as an antidote to sea-level rise. The Libyans pioneered the practice with the great systematic flood of the Qattara Depression in the Cairo desert. The water made one species of fox extinct and thousands of humans rich. Evaporation from the artificial sea rained down on new olive plantations. Villages emerged. Fisherfolk raised families hauling tilefish and mackerel out of a former bowl of hot dirt. American investors were inspired. They organized the condemnation of the Anasazi Trough a hundred miles northwest of Phoenix and ran a huge pipe to the Gulf of Mexico. Six million gallons of seawater flowed in every day, to be boiled and filtered at the grandest desalination facility in the western hemisphere.

A land fever caught hold. The minor city of Port Miracle burgeoned somewhat on the sea's western shore. On the east coast sat Triton Estates, a gated sanctuary for golfers and owners of small planes. But before the yacht club had sold its last mooring, the young sea began to misbehave. The evaporation clouds were supposed to float eastward to the highlands and wring fresh rain from themselves. Instead, the clouds caught a thermal south, dumping their bounty on the far side of the Mexican border, nourishing a corn and strawberry bonanza in the dry land outside Juárez. With no cloud cover over the Anasazi, the sun went to work and started cooking the sea into a concentrated brine. Meanwhile, even as acreage spiraled toward Tahoe prices, the grid spread: toilets, lawns, and putting greens quietly embezzling the budget of desalinated water that should have been pumped back into the sea to keep salt levels at a healthy poise. By the sea's tenth birthday, it was fifteen times as saline as the Pacific, dense enough to float small stones. The desalination plant's reverse-osmosis filters, designed to last five years, started blowing out after six months on the job. The land boom on the Anasazi fell apart when water got so expensive that it was cheaper to flush the commode with half-and-half.

The grocery-store papers spread it around that the great pond wouldn't just take your money; it would kill you dead. Local news shows ran testimonies of citizens who said they'd seen the lake eat cows and elks and illegal Mexicans, shrieking as they boiled away. Science said the lake was not a man-eater, but the proof was in that gory water, so the stories stayed on prime time for a good number of years.

The real story of the redness was very dull. It was just a lot of ancient, red, one-celled creatures that thrived in high salt. The water authority tested and retested the water and declared the microbes no enemy to man. They were, however, hard on curb appeal. When the sea was only twelve years old, the coastal population had dwindled to ninety-three, a net loss of five thousand souls no longer keen on dwelling in a case of pinkeye inflamed to geologic scale.

The story delighted Cora Booth as meat for her art. She'd long been at work on a group of paintings and photographs about science's unintended consequences: victims of robot nanoworms designed to eat cancer cells but which got hungry for other parts, lab mice in DNA-grafting experiments who'd developed a crude sign language using the hands of human infants growing from their backs. Once the tenants had fled and the situation on the sea had tilted into flagrant disaster, Cora banged out some grant proposals, withdrew some savings, and leased a home in Triton Estates, a place forsaken by God and movie stars.

Salvage vandals had long ago stolen the gates off the entrance to the Booths' new neighborhood, but a pair of sandstone obelisks topped with unlit gas lamps still stood there, and they still spelled class. Their new home stood on a coastal boulevard named Naiad Lane, a thin track of blond scree. They drove slow past a couple dozen homes, most of them squatly sprawling bunkerish jobs of off-white stucco, all of them abandoned, windows broken or filmed with dust; others half-built, showing lath, gray bones of sun-beaten framing, pennants of torn Tyvek corrugating in the wind. Rodney pulled the truck into the driveway at number thirty-three, a six-bedroom cube with a fancy Spanish pediment on the front. It looked like a crate with a tiara. But just over the road lay the sea. Unruffled by the wind, its water lay still and thick as house paint, and it cast an inviting pink glow on the Booths' new home.

"I like it," said Cora, stepping from the truck. "Our personal Alamo."

"What's that smell?" said Rodney when they had stepped inside. The house was light and airy, but the air bore a light scent of wharf breath.

"It's the bricks," said Cora. "They made them from the thluk they take out of the water at the desal plant. Very clever stuff."

"It smells like, you know, groins."

"Learn to love it," Cora said.

When they had finished the tour, the sun was dying. On the far coast, the meager lights of Port Miracle were winking on. They'd only just started unloading the trailer when Cora's telephone bleated in her pocket. On the other end was Arn Nevis, the sole property agent in Triton Estates and occupant of one of the four still-inhabited homes in the neighborhood. Cora opened the phone. "Hi, terrific, okay, sure, hello?" she said, then looked at the receiver.

"Who was that?" asked Rodney, sitting on the front stair.

"Nevis, Arn Nevis, the rental turkey," said Cora. "He just sort of barfed up a dinner invitation—*Muhhouse, seven-thirty*—and hung up on me. Said it's close, we don't need to take our truck. Now, how does he know we have a truck? You see somebody seeing us out here, Rod?"

They peered around and saw nothing. Close to land, a fish or something buckled in the red water, other than themselves the afternoon's sole sign of life.

But they drove the Ranger after all, because Rodney had bad ankles. He'd shattered them both in childhood, jumping from a crabapple tree, and even a quarter mile's stroll would cause him nauseas of pain. So the Booths rode slowly in the truck through a Pompeii of vanished home equity. The ride took fifteen minutes because Cora kept experiencing ecstasies at the photogenic ruin of Triton Estates, getting six angles on a warped basketball rim over a yawning garage, a hot tub brimming and splitting with gallons of dust.

Past the grid of small lots they rolled down a brief grade to number three Naiad. The Nevis estate lay behind high white walls, light spilling upward in a column, a bright little citadel unto itself.

Rodney parked the truck alongside an aged yellow Mercedes. At a locked steel gate, the only breach in the tall wall, he rang the doorbell and they loitered many minutes while the day's heat fled the air. Finally a wide white girl appeared at the gate. She paused a moment before opening it, appraising them through the bars, studying the dusk beyond, as though expecting unseen persons to spring out of the gloom. Then she turned a latch and swung the door wide. She was sixteen or so, with a face like a left-handed sketch—small teeth, one eye bigger than the other and a half-inch lower on her cheek. Her outfit was a yellow towel, dark across the chest and waist where a damp bathing suit had soaked through. She said her name was Katherine.

"Sorry I'm all sopped," she said. "They made me quit swimming and be but-
ler. Anyway, they're out back. You were late so they started stuffing themselves."
Katherine set off for the house, her hard summer heels rasping on the slate path.

The Nevis house was a three-wing structure, a staple shape in bird's-eye view. In the
interstice between the staple's legs lay a small rectangular inlet of the sea, paved and
studded with underwater lights; it was serving as the family's personal pool. At the
lip of the swimming area, a trio sat at a patio set having a meal of mussels. At one
end of the table slouched Arn Nevis, an old, vast man with a head of white curls,
grown long to mask their sparseness, and a great bay window of stomach overhang-
ing his belt. Despite his age and obesity, he wasn't unattractive; his features bedded
in a handsome arrangement of knobs and ridges, nearly cartoonish in their prominence. Arn was in the middle of a contretemps with a thin young man beside him.
The old man had his forearms braced on the tabletop, his shoulders hiked forward, as
though ready to pounce on his smaller companion. On the far side of the table sat a
middle-aged woman, her blouse hoisted discreetly to let an infant at her breast. She
stroked and murmured to it, seemingly unaware of the stridency between the men.

"I didn't come here to get hot-boxed, Arn," the smaller man was saying, staring
at his plate.

"Hut—hoorsh," stuttered Nevis.

"Excuse me?" the other man said.

Nevis took a long pull on his drink, swallowed, took a breath. "I said, I'm not
hot-boxing anybody," said Nevis, enunciating carefully. "It's just you suffer from a
disease, Kurt. That disease is caution, bad as cancer."

The woman raised her gaze and, seeing the Booths, smiled widely. She introduced herself as Phyllis Nevis. She was a pretty woman, though her slack jowls
and creased dewlap put her close to sixty. If she noticed her visitors' amazement at
seeing a woman of her age putting an infant to suck, she didn't show it. She smiled
and let a blithe music of welcome flow from her mouth: Boy, the Nevises sure were
glad to have some new neighbors here in Triton. They'd met Katherine, of course,
and there was Arn. The baby having at her was little Nathan, and the other fellow was Kurt Hackberry, a business friend but a real friend, too. Would they like a
vodka lemonade? She invited the Booths to knock themselves out on some mussels,

tonged from the shallows just off the dock, though Cora noticed there was about a half a portion left. "So sorry we've already tucked in," Phyllis said. "But we always eat at seven-thirty, rain or shine."

Katherine Nevis did not sit with the diners but went to the sea's paved edge. She dropped her towel and slipped into the glowing water without a splash.

"So you drove down from Boston?" Hackberry asked, plainly keen to quit the conversation with his host.

"We did," said Rodney. "Five days, actually not so bad once you get past—"

"Yeah, yeah, Boston—" Nevis interrupted with regal vehemence. "And now they're here, sight unseen, whole thing over the phone, not all this fiddlefucking around." Nevis coughed into his fist, then reached for a plastic jug of vodka and filled his glass nearly to the rim, a good half-pint of liquor. He drank a third of it at one pull, then turned to Cora, his head bobbing woozily on his dark neck. "Kurt is a Chicken Little. Listens to ninnies who think the Bureau of Land Management is going to choke us off and starve the pond."

"Why don't they?" Cora asked.

"Because we've got their nursh—their nuh—their nads in a noose is why," said Nevis. "Because every inch of shoreline they expose means alkali dust blowing down on the goddamned bocce pitches and Little League fields and citrus groves down in the Yuma Valley. They're all looking up the wrong end of a shotgun, and us right here? We're perched atop a seat favored by the famous bird, if you follow me."

Nevis drained his glass and filled it again. He looked at Cora and sucked his teeth. "Hot damn, you're a pretty woman, Cora. Son of a bitch, it's like somebody opened a window out here. If I'd known you were so goddamned lovely, I'd have jewed them down on the rent. But then, if I'd known you were hitched up with this joker I'd have charged you double, probably." He jerked a thumb and aimed a grin of long gray teeth at Rodney. Rodney looked away and pulled at a skin tab on the rim of his ear. "Don't you think, Phyllis?" said Nevis. "Great bones."

"Thank you," Cora said. "I plan to have them bronzed."

"Humor," Nevis said flatly, gazing at Cora with sinking red eyes. "It's that actress you resemble. Murf. Murvek. Urta. Fuck am I talking about? You know, Phyllis, from the goddamn dogsled picture."

"Drink a few more of those," said Cora. "I'll find you a cockroach who looks like Brigitte Bardot."

"Actually, I hate alcohol, but I get these migraines. They mess with my speech, but liquor helps some," Nevis said. Here, he sat forward in his chair, peering unabashedly at Cora's chest. "Good Christ, you got a figure, lady. All natural, am I right?"

Rodney took a breath to say a hard word to Nevis, but while he was trying to formulate the proper phrase Phyllis spoke to her husband in a gentle voice.

"Arny, I'm not sure Cora appreciates—"

"An appreciation of beauty, even if it is sexual beauty, is a great gift," said Nevis. "Anyone who thinks beauty is not sexual should picture tits on a man."

"I'm sure you're right, sweetie, but even so—"

Nevis flashed a brilliant crescent of teeth at his wife and bent to the table to kiss her hand. "Right here, the most wonderful woman on earth. The kindest and most beautiful and I married her." Nevis raised his glass to his lips. His gullet pumped three times while he drank.

"His headaches are horrible," said Phyllis.

"They are. Pills don't work but vodka does. Fortunately, it doesn't affect me. I've never been drunk in my life. Anyway, you two are lucky you showed up at this particular juncture," Nevis announced through a belch. "Got a petition for a water-rights deal on Birch Creek. Hundred thousand gallons a day. Fresh water. Pond'll be blue again this time next year."

This news alarmed Cora, whose immediate thought was that her work would lose its significance if the story of the Anasazi Sea ended happily. "I like the color," Cora said. "It's exciting."

Nevis refilled his glass. "You're an intelligent woman, Cora, and you don't believe the rumors and the paranoia peddlers on the goddamned news," he said. "Me, I'd hate to lose it, except you can't sell a fucking house with the lake how it is. Of course, nobody talks about the health benefits of that water. My daughter?" He jerked his thumb at Katherine, still splashing in the pool, and lowered his voice. "Before we moved in here, you wouldn't have believed her complexion. Like a lasagna, I'm serious. Look at her now! Kill for that skin. Looks like a marble statue. Hasn't had a zit in years, me or my wife neither, not one blackhead, nothing. Great for the bones, too. I've got old-timers who swim here three times a week, swear it's curing their arthritis. Of course, nobody puts that on the news. Anyway, what I'm saying is, buy now, because once this Birch Creek thing goes through, this place is going to be a destination. Gonna put the back nine on the golf course. Shopping district, too, as soon as Kurt and a few other moneymen stop sitting on their wallets like a bunch of broody hens."

Nevis clouted Hackberry on the upper arm with more force than was jolly. Hackberry looked lightly terrified and went into a fit of vague motions with his head, shaking and nodding, saying "Now, Kurt, now, Kurt" with the look of a panicked child wishing for the ground to open up beneath him.

When he had lapped the fluid from the final mussel shell, Arn Nevis was showing signs of being drunk, if he was to be taken at his word, for the first time in his life. He rose from the table and stood swaying. "Clothes off, people," he said, fumbling with his belt.

Phyllis smiled and kept her eyes on her guests. "We have tea, and we have coffee and homemade peanut brittle, too."

"Phyllis, shut your mouth," said Nevis. "Swim time. Cora, get up. Have a dip."

"I don't swim," said Cora.

"You can't?" said Nevis.

"No," said Cora, which was true.

"Dead man could swim in the water. Nathan can. Give me the baby, Phyllis." He lurched for his wife's breast, and with a sudden move, Phyllis clutched the baby to her and swiveled brusquely away from her husband's hand. "Touch him and I'll kill you," Phyllis hissed. Nathan awoke and began to mewl. Nevis shrugged and lumbered toward the water, shedding his shirt, then his pants, mercifully retaining the pair of yellowed briefs he wore. He dove messily but began swimming surprisingly brisk and powerful laps, his whalelike huffing loud and crisp in the silence of the night. But after three full circuits to the far end of the inlet and back, the din of his breathing stopped. Katherine Nevis, who'd been sulking under the pergola with a video game, began to shriek. The guests leaped up. Arn Nevis had sunk seven feet or so below the surface, suspended from a deeper fall by the hypersaline water. In the red depths' wavering lambency, Nevis seemed to be moving, though in fact he was perfectly still.

Rodney kicked off his shoes and jumped in. With much effort, he hauled the large man to the concrete steps ascending to the patio and, helped by Cora and

Hackberry, heaved him into the cool air. Water poured from Rodney's pockets. He put his palms to the broad saucer of Nevis's sternum and rammed hard. The drowned man sputtered.

"Wake up. Wake *up*," said Rodney. Nevis did not answer. Rodney slapped Nevis on the cheek, and Nevis opened his eyes to a grouchy squint.

"What day is it?" asked Rodney. By way of an answer, Nevis expelled lung water down his chin.

"Who's that?" Rodney pointed to Phyllis. "Tell me her name."

Nevis regarded his wife. "Big dummy," he said.

"What the hell does that mean?" Rodney said. "Who's that?" He pointed at Nevis's infant son.

Nevis pondered the question. "Little dummy," he said, and began to laugh, which everybody took to mean that he had returned, unharmed, to life.

Kurt Hackberry and Katherine led Arn inside while Phyllis poured forth weeping apologies and panting gratitude to the Booths. "No harm done. Thank God he's all right. I'm glad I was here to lend a hand," Rodney said, and was surprised to realize that he meant it. Despite the evening's calamities, his heart was warm and filled with an electric vigor of life. The electricity stayed with him all the way back to number thirty-three Naiad Lane, where, in the echoing kitchen, Rodney made zestful love to his wife for the first time in seven weeks.

Rodney woke before the sun was up. The maritime fetor of the house's salt walls and recollections of Arn Nevis's near death merged into a general unease that would not let him sleep. Cora stirred beside him. She peered out the window, yawned, and said that she wanted to photograph the breaking of the day. "I'll come with you," Rodney said, and felt childish to realize that he didn't want to be left in the house alone.

Cora was after large landscapes of the dawn hitting Triton Estates and the western valley, so the proper place to set up was on the east coast, in Port Miracle, with the sun behind the lens. After breakfast they loaded the Ford with Cora's equipment and made the ten-minute drive. They parked at the remnant of Port Miracle's public beach and removed their shoes. Most of the trucked-in sand had blown away, revealing a hard marsh of upthrust minerals, crystalline and translucent, like stepping on warm ice. Rodney lay on the blanket they had brought while Cora took some exposures of the dawn effects. The morning sky involved bands of iridescence, the lavender-into-blue-gray spectrum of a bull pigeon's throat. Cora made plates of the light's progress, falling in a thickening portion on the dark housekey profile of the western hills, then staining the white homes scattered along the shore. She yelled a little at the moment of dawn's sudden ignition when red hit red and the sea lit up, flooding the whole valley with so much immediate light you could almost hear the *whong!* of a ball field's vapor bulbs going on.

"Rodney, how about you go swimming for me?"

"I don't have a suit."

"Who cares? It's a ghost town."

"I don't want to get all sticky."

"Shit, Rodney, come on. Help me out."

Rodney stripped grudgingly and walked into the water. Even in the new hours of the day, the water was hot and alarmingly solid, like paddling through Crisco. It seared his pores and mucous parts, but his body had a thrilling buoyancy in the thick water. A single kick of the legs sent him gliding like a hockey puck. And despite its lukewarmth and viscosity, the water was wonderfully vivifying. His pulse surged. Rodney stroked and kicked until he heard his wife yelling for him to swim back into camera range. He turned around, gamboled for her camera some, and stepped into the morning, stripped clean by the water, with a feeling of having been peeled to new young flesh. Rodney did not bother to dress. He carried the blanket to the shade of a disused picnic awning. Cora lay there with him, and then they drowsed until the sun was well up in the sky.

Once the drab glare of the day set in, the Booths breakfasted together on granola bars and instant coffee from the plastic crate of food they'd packed for the ride from Massachusetts.

Cora wished to tour Port Miracle on foot. Rodney, with his bad ankles, said he would be happy to spend the morning in his sandy spot, taking in the late-summer sun with a Jack London paperback. So Cora went off with her camera, first to the RV lot, nearly full, the rows of large white vehicles like raw loaves of bread. She walked through a rear neighborhood of kit cottages, built of glass and grooved plywood and tin. She photographed shirtless children, Indian brown, kicking a ball in a dirt lot, and a leathery soul on a sunblasted Adirondack chair putting hot sauce into his beer. She went to the boat launch where five pink women, all of manatee girth, were boarding a pontoon craft. Cora asked to take their picture but they giggled and shied behind their hands and Cora moved on.

At the far end of town stood the desalination facility, a cube of steel and concrete intubated with ducts and billowing steam jacks. Cora humped it for the plant, her tripod clacking on her shoulder. After calling into the intercom at the plant's steel door, Cora was greeted by a gray-haired, bearded man wearing something like a cellophane version of a fisherman's hard-weather kit. Plastic pants, shirt, hat, plus gloves and boot gaiters and a thick dust mask hanging around his neck. His beard looked like a cloudburst, though he'd carefully imprisoned it in a hairnet so as to tuck it coherently within his waterproof coat.

"Whoa," said Cora, taken aback. Recovering herself, she explained that she was new to the neighborhood and was hoping to find a manager or somebody who might give her a tour of the plant.

"I'm it!" the sheathed fellow told her, a tuneful courtliness in his voice. "Willard Kamp. And it would be my great pleasure to show you around."

Cora lingered on the threshold, taking in Kamp's protective gear. "Is it safe, though, if I'm just dressed like this?"

"That's what the experts would tell you," said Kamp, and laughed, leading Cora to a bank of screens showing the brine's progress through a filter-maze. Then he ushered her up a flight of stairs to a platform overlooking the concrete lagoons where the seawater poured in. He showed her the flocculating chambers where they added ferric chloride and sulfuric acid and chlorine and the traveling rakes that brought the big solids to the surface in a rumpled brown sludge. He showed her how the water traveled through sand filters, and then through diatomaceous earth capsules to further strain contaminants, before they hit the big reverse-osmosis trains that filtered the last of the impurities.

"Coming into here," Kamp said, slapping the side of a massive fiberglass storage tank, "is raw water. Nothing in here but pure H's and O's."

"Just the good stuff, huh?" Cora said.

"Well, not for our purposes," Kamp said. "It's no good for us in its pure form. We have to have to gentle it down with additives, acid salts, gypsum. Raw, it's very chemically aggressive. It's so hungry for minerals to bind with, it'll eat a copper pipe in a couple of weeks."

This idea appealed to Cora. "What happens if you drink it? Will it kill you? Burn your skin?"

Kamp laughed, a wheezing drone. "Not at all. It's an enemy to metal pipes and soap lather, but it's amiable to humankind."

"So what's with all the hazmat gear?" asked Cora, gesturing at Kamp's clothes.

Kamp laughed again. "I'm overfastidious, the preoccupation of a nervous mind."

"Nervous about what?"

His wiry brow furrowed and his lips pursed in half-comic consternation. "Well, it's a funny lake, isn't it, Cora? I am very interested in the archaebacteria, the little red gentlemen out there."

"But it's the same stuff in fall foliage and flamingos," Cora said, brandishing some knowledge she'd picked up from a magazine. "Harmless."

Kamp reached into his raincoat to scratch at something in his beard. "Probably so. Though they're also very old. Two billion years. They were swimming around before there was oxygen in the atmosphere, if you can picture that. You've heard, I guess, the notion that that stuff in our pond is pretty distinguished crud, possibly the source of all life on earth."

"I hadn't."

"Well, they say there's something to it," said Kamp. "Now, it's quite likely that I haven't got the sense God gave a monkey wrench, but it seems to me that a tadpole devious enough to put a couple of million species on the planet is one I'd rather keep on the outside of my person."

Of Port Miracle's eighty dwellers, nearly all were maroon ancients. They were unwealthy people, mainly, not far from death, so they found the dead city a congenial place to live the life of a lizard, moving slow and taking sun. But they were not community-center folk. Often there was public screaming on the boulevard, sometimes fights with brittle fists when someone got too close to someone else's wife or yard. Just the year before, in a further blow to the Anasazi's image in the press, a retired playwright, age eighty-one, levered open the door of a Winnebago parked on his lot and tortured a pair of tourists with some rough nylon rope and a soup-heating coil.

According to the rules of the Nevis household, young Katherine was not permitted past the sandstone obelisks at the neighborhood's mouth. But the morning after the dinner party her father was still abed with a pulsing brain, and would likely be that way all day. Knowing this, Katherine slipped through the gate after breakfast, wheeled her little 97cc minibike out of earshot, and set a course to meet two pals of hers, Claude Hull and Denny Peebles, on the forbidden coast.

She found them by the public pier, and they greeted her with less commotion than she'd have liked. They were busy squabbling over some binoculars through which they were leering at the fat women out at sea on the pontoon barge.

"Let me look," Claude begged Denny, who had snatched the Bausch & Lombs, an unfair thing. The Bausch & Lombs belonged to Claude's father, who owned Port Miracle's little credit union and liked to look at birds.

Denny sucked his lips and watched the women, herded beneath the boat's canopy shade, their bikinis almost wholly swallowed by their hides. They took turns getting in the water via a scuba ladder that caused the boat to lurch comically when one of them put her bulk on it. The swimming lady would contort her face in agonies at the stinging water while her colleagues leaned over the gunwale, shouting encouragement, bellies asway. After a minute or two, the others would help the woman aboard and serve her something in a tall chilled glass and scrub at her with implements not legible through the Bausch & Lombs. The women were acting on a rumor that the sea's bacteria devoured extra flesh. It had the look of a cult.

"Big white witches," whispered Denny.

"Come on, let me hold 'em, let me look," said Claude, a lean, tweaky child whose widespread eyes and bulging forehead made it a mercy that he, like the other children who lived out here, attended ninth grade over the computer. Denny, the grocer's child, had shaggy black hair, a dark tan, and very long, very solid arms for a boy of fourteen. "Fuck off," said Denny, throwing an elbow. "Get Katherine to show you hers. You'll like 'em if you like it when a girl's titty looks like a carrot."

"I'm not showing Claude," said Katherine.

In the sand beside Denny lay a can of Scotchgard and a bespattered paper bag. Katherine reached for it.

"Mother may I?" Denny said.

"Bite my fur," said Katherine. She sprayed a quantity of the Scotchgard into the bag, then put it to her mouth and inhaled.

"Let me get some of that, Kathy," Claude said.

"Talk to Denny," said Katherine. "It's not my can."

"Next time I'm gonna hook up my camera to this thing, get these puddings on film," said Denny, who was lying on his stomach in the sand, the binoculars propped to his face. "Somebody scratch my back for me. Itches like a motherfucker."

"Sucks for you," said Katherine, whose skull now felt luminous and red and full of perfect blood.

"You scratch it for me, Claude," said Denny. "Backstroke, hot damn. Look at those pies. Turn this way, honey. Are you pretty in your face?"

Just last week, for no reason at all, Denny Peebles had wedged Claude Hull's large head between his knees and dragged him up and down Dock Street while old men laughed. Claude loved and feared Denny, so he reached out a hand and scratched at Denny's spine.

"Lower," Denny said, and Claude slid his hand down to the spot between Denny's sacral dimples, which were lightly downed with faint hair. "Little lower. Get in the crack, man. That's where the itch is at."

Claude laughed nervously. "You want me to scratch your *ass* for you?"

"It itches, I told you. Go ahead. It's clean."

"No way I'm doing that, man. You scratch it."

"I can't reach it. I'm using my hands right now," said Denny. "I'm trying to see these fatties."

Katherine sprayed another acrid cloud into the bag and sucked it in. Dust clung in an oval around her mouth, giving the effect of a chimpanzee's muzzle.

"Just do it, Claude," Katherine said. "He likes it. He said it's clean. You don't believe him?"

Denny took the glasses from his face to look at the smaller boy. "Yeah, you don't believe me, Claude? What, I'm a liar, Claude?"

"No, no, I do." And so Claude reached into Denny's pants and scratched, and this intimate grooming felt very good to Denny in a hardly sexual way, so to better concentrate on the sensation, he rested the binoculars and held his hand out for the can of Scotchgard and the paper bag.

After an hour on the beach, Rodney put a flat stone in his paperback, retrieved his pants, and got up to stretch his legs. He had the thought that strolling through the still water might cushion his ankles somewhat, so he waded in and set off up the cove. Forbidding as the water looked, it teemed with life. Carp fingerlings nibbled his shins. Twice, a crab scuttled over his bare toes. He strolled on until he reached the pier, a chocolate-colored structure built of creosoted wood. Rodney spied a clump of shells clinging to the pilings. These were major oysters, the size of cactus pads. He tried to yank one free, but it would not surrender to his hand. It was such a tempting prize that he waded all the way back to the truck and got the tire iron from under the seat. Knee-deep in the water, he worked open a shell. The flesh inside was pale gray and large as a goose egg. That much oyster meat would cost you thirty dollars in a Boston restaurant. The flesh showed no signs of dubious pinkness. He sniffed it—no bad aromas. He spilled it onto his tongue, chewing three times to get it down. The meat was clean and briny. He ate two more and felt renewed. Wading back to shore, a few smaller mollusks in hand, he peered under the wharf and spotted Katherine Nevis on the beach with her friends. The desolation of the town had cast a shadow on the morning, and it cheered Rodney to see those children out there enjoying the day. It would be unneighborly, Rodney thought, not to say hello.

When Rodney got within fifty yards, Denny and Claude looked up, panicked to see a shirtless fellow coming at them with a tire iron, an ugly limp in his gait. They took off in a kind of skulking lope and left Katherine on the beach. Obviously Rodney had caught them in the middle of some teenage mischief, and he chuckled to see the boys scamper. Katherine cupped a hand over the beige matter on her face and looked at her toes as Rodney approached. He wondered about the grime, but instead asked after her dad. "I dunno," she said. "I'm sure he's doing awesome."

Rodney nudged the Scotchgard can with his foot. "Stainproofing the beach?" he asked. Katherine said nothing. "Whatever happened to just raiding your parents' booze?"

"He has to drive all the way to Honerville to get it," she said. "He keeps it locked up, even from my mom."

Rodney put the tire iron in his belt and dropped his oysters. He took out his handkerchief and reached for her, thinking to swab her face. She shrank away from him. "Don't fucking touch me," she said. "Don't, I swear."

"Easy, easy, nobody's doing anything," Rodney said, though he could feel the color in his cheeks. "It's just you look like you need a shave."

Cautiously, a little shamefully, she took the handkerchief and daubed at her lips while he watched. The girl was conscious of being looked at, and she swabbed herself with small ladylike motions, making no headway on the filth.

"Here," said Rodney, very gently, taking the hanky from her damp hand. He sucked awhile at the bitter cloth, then he knelt and cradled the girl's jaw in his palm, rubbing at her mouth and chin. "Look out, you're gonna take off all my skin," she said, making a cranky child's grimace, though she didn't pull away. He heard her grunting lightly in her throat at the pleasure of being tended to. A smell was coming off her, a fragrance as warm and wholesome as rising bread. As he scrubbed the girl's dirty face, he put his nose close to her, breathing deeply and as quietly as he could. He had mostly purged the gum from Katherine's upper lip when she jerked away from him and hearkened anxiously to the sound of a slowing car. Arn Nevis's eggnog Mercedes pulled into the gravel lot. He got out and strode very quickly down the shingle.

"Hi, hi!" Nevis cried. His hair was in disarray, and his hands trembled in a Parkinsonian fashion. In the hard noonday light, he looked antique and unwell. Rodney saw, too, that Nevis had a fresh pink scar running diagonally across his forehead, stitch pocks dotting its length. Rodney marveled a little that just the night before, he'd felt some trepidation in the big man's presence. "Kath—Kuh, Kutch." Nevis stopped, marshaled his breathing, and spoke. "Kuh, come here, sweetie. Been looking for you. Mom's mad. Come now, huk—honey. See if I can't talk your mom out of striping your behind."

In his shame, Arn did not look at Rodney, which at once amused and angered the younger man. "Feeling okay, there, Arn?"

"Oh, shuh-sure," Nevis said, staring at a point on Rodney's abdomen. "Thank God it's Friday."

"It's Thursday," Rodney said.

"Oysters," the old man said, looking at Rodney's haul where he'd dropped it on the ground. "Oh, they're nice."

Rodney crouched and held them out to Nevis in cupped hands. Nevis looked at the oysters and then at Rodney. His was the manner of a craven dog, wanting that food but fearing that he might get a smack if he went for it. "Go on," said Rodney.

With a quick move, Nevis grabbed a handful. His other hand seized Katherine's arm. "Alrighty, and we'll see you soon," said Nevis over his shoulder, striding to his car.

*   *   *

The days found an agreeable tempo in Cora and Rodney's new home. Each morning they rose with the sun. Each morning, Rodney swam far into the sea's broads, then returned to the house, where he would join Cora for a shower, then downstairs to cook and eat a breakfast of tremendous size. When the dishes were cleared, Cora would set off to gather pictures. Rodney would spend two hours on the computer to satisfy the advertising firm in Boston for which he still worked part-time, and then he'd do as he pleased. His was a life any sane person would envy, yet Rodney was not at ease. He felt bloated with a new energy. He had never been an ambitious person, but lately he had begun to feel that he was capable of resounding deeds. He had dreams in which he conquered famous wildernesses, and he would wake up with a lust for travel. Yet he was irritable on days when he had to leave the valley for provisions not sold in Port Miracle's pitiable grocery store. One day he told Cora that he might quit his job and start a company, though he grew angry when Cora forced him to admit that he had no idea what the company might produce. For the first time in his life, he resented Cora, begrudged the years he'd spent at her heel, and how he'd raised no fuss when she'd changed her mind after five years of marriage and said she didn't want children after all. His mind roved to other women, to the Nevis girl, a young thing with a working womb, someone who'd shut up when he talked.

When Cora left him the truck, he often went fishing off the wharf at Port Miracle, always coming home with several meals' worth of seafood iced down in his creel. He would wait until he got home to clean the catch so that Cora could photograph the haul intact.

"Ever seen one of these?" Cora asked him one night. She was sitting at the kitchen table with her laptop, whose screen showed a broad fish ablur with motion on the beach. "This thing was kind of creeping around in the mud down by that shed where the oldsters hang out."

"Huh," Rodney said, kissing Cora's neck and slipping a hand into her shirt. "Snakehead, probably. Or a mudskipper."

"It's not. It's flat, like a flounder," she said. "Quit a second. I wish I could have kept it, but this kid came along and bashed it and took off. Look."

She scrolled to a picture of Claude Hull braining the crawling fish with an aluminum bat.

"Mm," said Rodney, raising his wife's shirt and with the other hand going for her fly.

"Could you quit it?"

"Why?"

"For one thing, I'm trying to deal with my fucking work. For another, I'm kind of worn out. You've gotten me a little raw, going at me all the time."

Sulking, he broke off his advances and picked up his phone from the counter. "Tell you what," he said. "I'll call the neighbors. Get them over here to eat this stuff. We owe them a feed."

He stepped outdoors and called the Nevises, hoping to hear Katherine's hoarse little crow timbre on the other end. No one answered, so Rodney phoned two more times. He had watched the road carefully that morning and knew the family was home.

In fact, Katherine and her mother were out on a motorboat cruise while Arn Nevis paced his den, watching the telephone ring. He did not want to answer it. His trouble with words was worsening. Unless he loosened his tongue with considerable amounts of alcohol, the organ was lazy and intractable. In his mind, he could still formulate a phrase with perfect clarity, but his mouth no longer seemed interested in doing his mind's work and would utter a slurring of approximate sounds. When Nevis finally answered the telephone and heard Rodney's invitation, he paused to silently rehearse the words *I'm sorry, but Phyllis is feeling a bit under the weather*. But Nevis's tongue, the addled translator, wouldn't take the order. "Ilish feen urtha" and then a groan was what Rodney heard before the line went dead.

Until recently, the headaches Arn Nevis suffered had been slow pursuers. A stroll through the neighborhood would clear the bad blood from his temples and he'd have nearly a full day of peace. But lately, if he sat still for five minutes, the glow would commence behind his brow. He would almost drool thinking about a good thick augur to put a hole between his eyes and let the steam out of his head. After five minutes of that, if he didn't have a bottle around to kill it, white pain would bleach the vision from his eyes.

The pain was heating up again when he hung up on Rodney Booth, so he went out through the gate and strolled up to the dry tract slated to become nine new putting greens once the water lease on Birch Creek went through. He set about measuring and spray-painting orange hazard lines in the dirt where a ditcher would cut irrigation channels. Nevis owned most of this land himself, and he was tallying his potential profits when motion in the shadow of a Yerba Santa bush caught his eye. Scorpions, gathered in a ring, a tiny pocket mouse quaking at the center of them. The scenario was distasteful. He raised his boot heel and made to crush the things, but they nimbly skirted the fat shadow of his foot. The circle parted and the mouse shot out of sight.

He glanced at his watch. Four-thirty. In half an hour, he had an appointment to show number eight Amphitrite Trail to a prospective buyer. The flawless sky and the light breeze were hopeful portents. Arn felt confident that on this day, he would make a good sale. To celebrate the prospect, Arn took the quart of peppermint schnapps from his knapsack, but then it occurred to him to save it, to drink it very quickly just before the client's arrival for maximum benefit to his difficult tongue.

Eight Amphitrite was a handsome structure, a three-thousand-square-foot Craftsman bungalow, the only one like it in the neighborhood. The plot was ideally situated, up on high ground at the end of the road with no houses behind it. Sitting there on the front steps, Nevis felt a particular comfort in the place, an enlargement of the safe feeling he experienced in restaurants when he found a spot with his back to the wall and a good view of the door. Nevis checked his watch. Ten of five. He opened the bottle and tipped it back. He stretched his tongue, whispering a silent catechism: "Radiant-heat floors, four-acre lot, build to suit."

Arn had just finished the last of the schnapps when a Swedish station wagon pulled into the drive. A young man got out, tall, with soft features, combed sandy hair, and a cornflower-blue shirt rolled to the elbows. He watched Arn Nevis pick himself up off the stairs and come toward him with his hand out. "Mr. Nevis?" the young man had to ask, for Arn did not much resemble the photograph on his website. His white shirt was badly wrinkled and yellowed with perspiration stains, and his hair looked like a patch of trodden weeds. His left eye was badly bloodshot and freely weeping.

"Urt! Guh," Arn Nevis said, then paused in his tracks, opening and closing his mouth as though priming a dry pump. The client watched him, aghast, as though Nevis was some unhinged derelict impersonating the man he'd come to meet. "Guh—good day!" Nevis said at last, and having expelled that first plug of language, the rest flowed out of him easily. "Mister Mills? It's an absolute delight, and I'm so glad you could pay us a visit on this fabulous day."

"Daniel, please," the young man said, still looking guarded. But the anxiety slowly drained from Mills's features as Nevis rolled into a brisk and competent disquisition on eight Amphitrite's virtues. "That nice overlay on the foundation? That's not plastic, friend. It's hand-mortared fieldstone harvested out of this very land. Clapboards are engineered, and so's the roofing shake, so eat your heart out, termites, and fifteen years to go on the warranty on each."

Nevis was ushering Mills over the threshold when his pitch halted in midstream. Nevis gaped at the empty living room, his mouth open, his eyes stretched with wonder. "My gosh," he said.

"What?" asked Daniel Mills.

"My gosh, Ted, this is that same house, isn't it?" Nevis said, laughing. "From Columbus. When you and Rina were still married."

Mills looked at Arn a moment. "It's Daniel. I—I don't know any Rina."

Nevis's eyes moved in their sockets. He began to laugh. "Jesus Christ, what the hell am I saying?" he said. "My apologies. I've had this fever."

"Sure," said Mills, taking a step back.

"So over yonder is a galley kitchen," said Nevis, leading the way. "Poured concrete counters, and a built-in—"

"Excuse me, you've got something here," murmured Mills, indicating Nevis's upper lip. Nevis raised a finger to his face and felt the warm rush of blood pouring from his nose, dripping from his chin, landing in nickel-size droplets on the parquet floor.

By his sixth week in Triton Estates, an exuberant insomnia assailed Rodney Booth. While his wife snored beside him, Rodney lay awake. His body quivered with unspent energy. His blood felt hot and incandescent. With each stroke of his potent heart, he saw the red traceries of his arteries filling with gleeful sap, bearing tidings of joy and vigor to his cells. His muscles quaked. His loins tittered, abloat with happy news. His stomach, too, disturbed his rest. Even after a dinner of crass size, Rodney would lie in bed, his gut groaning as though he hadn't eaten in days. He would rise and go downstairs, but he could not find foods to gratify his hunger.

Whether cold noodles, or a plate of costly meats and cheeses, all the foods in his house had a dull, exhausted flavor, and he would eat in joyless frustration, as though forced to suffer conversation with a hideous bore.

Exercise was the only route to sleep for Rodney. His ankles plagued him less these days, and after dinner he would rove for hours in the warm autumn dark. Some nights he strolled the shore, soothed to hear the distant splashes of leaping night fish. Sometimes he went into the hills where the houses stopped. The land rose and fell before him, merging in the far distance with the darkness of the sky, unbroken by lights of civilization. A feeling of giddy affluence would overtake Rodney as he scrambled along. All that space, and nobody's but his! It was like the dream where you find a silver dollar on the sidewalk, then another, then another, until you look up to see a world strewn with free riches.

On these strolls, his thoughts often turned to Katherine Nevis, that fine, wretched girl imprisoned at the end of Naiad Lane behind the high white wall. He recalled the smell of her, her comely gruntings that day on the shore, the tender heft of her underjaw in his palm. One evening the memory of her became so intolerable that it stopped him in his tracks, and he paused between the dunes in an intimate little hollow where dust of surprising fineness gathered in plush drifts.

Rodney stooped to caress the soft soil, warm in his hand. "Listen, you and me are in a predicament here, Katherine," he explained to the dust. "Oh, you don't, huh? Fine. You stay right there. I'll get it myself."

With that, he unbuckled his pants and fell to zealously raping the dirt. The sensation was not pleasurable, and the fierceness of the act did not sit right with Rodney's notion of himself, but in the end he felt satisfied that he had completed a job of grim though necessary work.

Floured with earth, he made his way to the water and swam vigorously for twenty minutes. Then he crawled into bed beside his wife and slept until the sun rose, minding not at all the pricking of the soft sheets against his salty skin.

The following night Rodney ranged along the shore and back up into the hills, yet his step was sulky and his heart was low. As with the pantry foods he did not care to eat, that evening the great open land had become infected with a kindred dreariness. Squatting on a boulder, Rodney gazed at the column of clean light spilling from the enclosure of the Nevis home. A breathless yearning caught hold. The desert's wealth of joy and deliverance seemed to have slipped down the rills and drainages, slid past the dark houses, leached south along the hard pink berm, and concentrated in the glare above the one place in the Anasazi Basin where Rodney was not free to roam. He stood and walked.

Rodney told himself he would not enter the Nevis property. The notion was to loiter at the gate, have a glimpse of the courtyard, sport a little with the pull of the place, the fun of holding two magnets at slight bay. And perhaps Rodney would have kept his promise to himself had he not spotted, bolted to the top of a length of conduit bracketed to the wall, a fan of iron claws, put there to discourage shimmiers. The device offended Rodney as an emblem of arrogance and vanity. Who was Arn Nevis to make his home a thorny fort? The spikes were pitiful. A determined crone could have gotten past them. Rodney jumped and grasped in either hand the two outermost claws. With a strength and ease that surprised him, he vaulted himself over the hazard and onto the lip of the wall.

He dropped onto the flagstones and the agony in his ankles caused his lungs to briefly freeze with pain. Rodney held his breath, waiting to hear a barking dog or an alarm, but heard nothing. Beyond the batteries of floodlights, only a single window glowed in the far corner of the house. Rodney waited. Nothing stirred.

Crouched in the courtyard, a new oil seemed to rise in Rodney's joints. His body felt incapable of noisy or graceless moves. He removed the screen from an open window and found himself in the Nevises' living room. He paused at a grand piano and rested his fingers in a chord on the sheeny keys. The temptation to sound the notes was strong, so electrified was Rodney that the house was under his authority. The fragrance in the room was distasteful and exciting—an aroma of milk and cologne—and it provoked in him an unaccountable hunger. He padded to the Nevises' kitchen. In the cold light of the open refrigerator, Rodney unwrapped and ate a wedge of Gruyère cheese. Then he had a piece of unsweetened baking chocolate, which he washed down with a can of Arn's beer. Still, his stomach growled. Under a shroud of crumpled tinfoil, he found a mostly intact ham, and he gnawed the sugary crust and then went at it with his jaws and teeth, taking bites the size of tennis balls, glutting his throat and clearing the clog with a second, then a third can of his neighbor's beer.

When he had at last had all he wanted, Rodney's breathing had become labored.

He was dewed in hot sweat. His bladder, too, was full, but his feeling of satiety there in the kitchen was so delicate and golden that he did not feel like shifting an inch to find a toilet. So he lowered his zipper and relished the sound of fluid hitting terra-cotta tiles, which mingled with the keen scent of his own urine in a most ideal way.

He had only just shut the refrigerator door when a white motion in the window caught his eye. Who was it but Katherine Nevis, the darling prisoner of the house? She plodded across the rear courtyard, on flat, large girl's feet, heading for the little inlet. She shed her robe, and Rodney was unhappy to see that even at that private hour of the evening, she still bothered to wear a bathing suit. She dove, and the water accepted her with the merest ripple. For many minutes, Rodney watched her sporting and glorying in the pool, diving and breaching, white, dolphinlike exposures of her skin bright against the dark red tide. When he could put it off no longer, Rodney stepped through the sliding door and went to her.

"Howdy!" he called, very jolly. She whirled in the water, only her head exposed. Rodney walked to the edge of the pool. "Hi there!" he said. She said nothing, but sank a little, gathering the water to her with sweeping arms, taking it into her mouth, pushing it gently over her chin, breathing it, nearly. She said nothing. Rodney put his fists on his hips and grinned at the surveillant moon. "Hell of a spotlight. Good to swim by, huh?"

Her eyes were dark but not fearful. "How'd you get in here?" the girl said wetly.

"Oh, I had some business with your dad," he said.

"My dad," she repeated, her face a suspicious little fist.

"Maybe I'll get in there with you," Rodney said, raising his shirt.

"Do what you like," the girl said. "I'm going inside."

He put a hand out. She took it and pulled herself into the night air. He picked up her robe. Draping it on her, he caught her sourdough aroma, unmasked by the sulfur smell of the sea. His heart was going, his temples on the bulge.

"Stay," he said. "Come on, the moon's making a serious effort here. It's a real once-in-a-month kind of moon."

She smiled, then stopped. She reached into the pocket of her robe and retrieved and a cigarette. "Okay. By the way, if I yelled even a little bit, my mom would come out here. She's got serious radar. She listens to everything and never sleeps. Seriously, how'd you get through the gate?"

Rodney stretched his smile past his dogteeth. A red gas was coming into his eyes. "She's one great lady, your mom." He put a hand on the girl's hip. She pushed against it only slightly, then sat with her cigarette on a tin-and-rubber chaise longue to light it. He sat beside her and took the cigarette, holding it downwind so as to smell her more purely. He made some mouth sounds in her ear. She closed her eyes. "Gets dull out here, I bet," he said.

"Medium," she said. She took back the ocher short of her roll-your-own. He put his hand on her knee, nearly nauseated with an urge. The girl frowned at his fingers. "Be cool, hardcore," she said.

"Why don't you... how about let's... how about..."

"Use your words," she said.

He put his hand on the back of her head and tried to pull her to his grasping lips. She broke the clasp. "What makes you think I want to kiss your mouth?"

"Come on," he groaned, nearly weeping. "God*damn*, you're beautiful."

"Shit," the girl said.

"You are a beautiful woman," said Rodney.

"My legs are giant," she said. "I've got a crappy face."

"Come here," he said. He lipped some brine from her jaw.

"Don't," she said, panting some. "You don't love me yet."

Rodney murmured that he did love Katherine Nevis very much. He kissed her, and she didn't let him. He kissed her again and she did. Then he was on her and for a time the patio was silent save the sound of their breath and the crying of the chaise's rubber slats.

He'd gotten her bikini bottoms down around her knees when the girl went stiff. "Quit," she whispered harshly. He pretended not to hear her. "Shit, goddammit, stop!" She gave him a hard shove, and then Rodney saw the problem. Arn Nevis was over by the house, hunched and peering from the blue darkness of the eave. Nevis was perfectly still, his chin raised slightly, mouth parted in expectancy. His look changed when he realized he'd been spotted. From what Rodney could tell, it wasn't outrage on the old man's features, just mild sadness that things had stopped before they'd gotten good.

Three mornings later, Rodney Booth looked out his bedroom window to see a speeding ambulance dragging a curtain of dust all the way up Naiad Lane to the

Nevis home. He watched some personnel in white tote a gurney through the gate. Then Rodney went downstairs and poured himself some cereal and turned the television on.

Later that afternoon, as Rodney was leaving for the wharf with his fishing pole and creel, Cora called to him. She'd just gotten off the phone with Phyllis Nevis, who'd shared the sad news that her husband was in the hospital, comatose with a ruptured aneurysm, not expected to recover. Rodney agreed that this was terrible. Then he shouldered his pole and set out for the wharf.

The day after the ambulance bore Arn Nevis away, Rodney began to suffer vague qualmings of the conscience relating to the Nevis family. He had trouble pinpointing the source of the unease. It was not sympathy for Nevis himself. There was nothing lamentable about an old man heading toward death in his sleep. And his only regret about his tender grapplings with the sick man's daughter was that they hadn't concluded properly. Really, the closest Rodney could come to what was bothering him was some discomfort over his behavior with Phyllis Nevis's ham. He pictured mealtime in her house, the near widow serving her grieving children the fridge's only bounty, a joint of meat, already hard used by unknown teeth. The vision made him tetchy and irritated with himself. He felt the guilt gather in his temples and coalesce into a bothersome headache.

That afternoon, Rodney harvested and shucked a pint or so of oysters. He packed in ice three pounds of fresh-caught croaker filets. He showered, shaved, daubed his throat and the line of hair on his stomach with lemon verbena eau de cologne. In the fridge he found a reasonably good bottle of Pouilly-Fuissé, and he set off up Naiad Lane.

Phyllis Nevis came to the gate and welcomed him in. "I brought you something," Rodney said. "It isn't much."

She looked into the bag with real interest. "Thank you," she said. "That's very, very kind."

"And the wine is cold," said Rodney. "Bet you could use a glass."

"I could," said Phyllis quietly.

Together they walked inside. Rodney put the fish in the refrigerator. He opened the bottle and poured two large glasses. Phyllis went upstairs and then returned with her baby, Nathan. She sat on the sofa, waiting for Rodney, giving the infant his lunch.

Rodney gave the woman a glass and sat close beside her.

"Thank you," said Phyllis, tears brightening her eyes. "One week, tops. That's what they said."

"I'm so, so sorry," Rodney said. He put his arm around her, and while she wept, she allowed herself to be drawn into the flushed hollow of Rodney's neck. The infant at her breast began to squeal, and the sound inflamed the pain in Rodney's temples, and he had an impulse to tear the baby from her and carry it out of the room. Instead, he swallowed his wine at a gulp. He poured himself a second glass and knocked it back, which seemed to dull the pain a little. Then he settled against the cushion and pressed Phyllis's tearful face into his neck. While she quaked on him, Rodney stroked the tender skin behind her ears and stared off through the picture window. Far above the eastern hills, a council of clouds shed a gray fringe of moisture. The promise of rain was a glad sight in the mournful scene, though in fact this was rain of a frail kind, turning to vapor a mile above the brown land, never to be of use to women and men on earth.

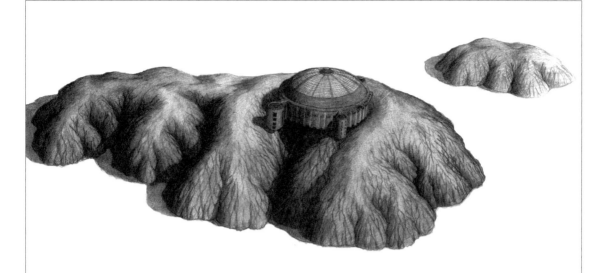

EIGHTH WONDER

by CHRIS BACHELDER

1

HEN THEY CAME they destroyed.

2

They came swimming, paddling, rowing with lumber. Shocked by storm, they rushed in like the water. They broke the locked doors of offices, closets, skyboxes. They splintered wood and smashed glass. The dome roared with de-creation. Bodies floated in the water. Blood tarnished the handles of doors. Drawings and messages covered the walls. Prayers and threats. Parents searched for their children and children searched for their pets. The nights were worse than the days. They rose to the upper decks and hid from one another in the dark. They took refuge. All night there was crying and barking and the squeak of wet soles running. There was a storm outside the dome and a storm inside. The water, all day and night, splashed softly down the concrete stairs. Fifty thousand seats encircled the calm, dark lake.

3

It was a Fast Fact that the level of the dome floor was lower than the level of the street. It was a Fun Trivia that the game scheduled for June 15, 1976 was postponed because of a flood.

4

It was early spring. The last of the four storms stalled, churned, departed slowly. Some swam away from the dome but many stayed. They formed clans along the club level. Clan membership provided protection but required precious supplies. The food that was found was eaten. The water that was found was drunk. They left the dome for food and supplies but often did not return. There were pirates on Kirby, on 610. There were pirates on the Old Spanish Trail. Swimming was perilous. They still thought of themselves as refugees. The dome, and life itself, seemed temporary.

5

What are human beings like? How are they inclined to act? These humans ate dogs, stole one another's shoes, struck each other with the sharpened legs of chairs. They were vicious and frightened. They drank urine and salt water. They lost their minds with grief and despair and privation. They walked the narrow catwalks along the roof of the dome and then jumped. It was a Fast Fact that it was like jumping from an eighteen-story building. Beneath the dark, shallow water was concrete, ruined turf. These humans took care of their babies. They gave food and solace to strangers. They made a chapel in Section 749, an infirmary in Section 763, a nursery in Section 733. They built a long, fast waterslide in one of the external pedestrian ramps. The children waited in line, then slid, screaming.

6

They sat in colorful seats and looked down at the event of the water. They lived in the air, and they felt themselves perched high in the heavy dome, suspended by it. They had dim light but no sun. Their skin grew waxy and pallid; their eyes ached with strain. The water did not recede, as the refugees believed it would. This would take some time to understand. They thought the water concealed the damage. But the water was the damage.

7

It was a Fast Fact that the dome covered nine and a half acres, and yet the sound of the violin carried through the darkness to each section and level. Every night it was clear and distant. The people cursed and shouted for it to stop. They lay in nests and strained to hear it. Then one night it stopped. Many days passed. It was not difficult for the people to imagine the destruction of the violin, so small and fragile. Another dead and broken thing, floating. But after a time it began again, just as suddenly as it had ceased, the same violin or perhaps another one, a small sound expanding to fill its container. A pulse, resuming.

8

In Section 435, near the water, the electrician lay in the dark and imagined. In the mornings he woke early and walked the dome, learning it. He passed through even the dangerous sections. He moved lightly, like a thought. He was tall, thin, quiet. His large hands hung nearly to his knees. He did not seem quite real and so no violence came to him. He carried a notebook and a pen. His books were stashed in secret places. Like all electricians, he was awake to the power of the invisible.

9

They were still refugees, not residents, so the dome was squalid. The hallways were strewn with trash, excrement, the bones of animals. The still heat was horrible, the stench was worse. The street-fed lake beneath them was filled with broken furniture, rusted metal, floating fish. Boys dropped heavy things from the low sections, hooted at the splash. Some even dived. They swam to the bottom, looking for treasure. Every room had been turned over. In many places the electrician found slashed cardboard boxes spilling glossy programs. He took them, organized them, stashed them. He created a library. He read them at night with a candle he received in exchange for a candy bar. He read the Fast Facts, the Fun Trivia, the Dome History.

It was a Dome History that Judge Roy Hofheinz enjoyed watching minor-league baseball with his daughter Dene. After a rainout in the summer of 1952, the disappointed girl asked her father, Why can't they play baseball inside? Hofheinz, the son of a laundry-truck driver, was inspired by the Colosseum in Rome, the enormous velaria that protected spectators from the sun. The dome was completed in November 1964. It was the first of its kind. The Eighth Wonder of the World, Hofheinz called it. The electrician blew out his candle. He did not clutch a weapon. Before sleep he tried to make his mind as large as the dome. The ceiling was 710 feet in diameter. He tried to make the space where something might occur. He had noticed the catwalks. He had noticed the rising water, halfway up the doors of the lobbies, flowing through the hallways of the first level and down the concrete stairs to the dark lake.

10

Parents brought their sick children to the infirmary. This is not the infirmary, they were told. The infirmary is in Section 763. The parents looked about. They turned to leave, then turned back. Then what is this, they asked. This is the nursery, they were told.

11

Other instruments joined the violin at night. A flute, a clarinet, a French horn. They tried to make something simple and beautiful, but there was too much acreage. Their music converged too slowly. They could not synchronize. The concerts were discordant, disconcerting. The electrician lay still and considered it. The musicians stopped or were stopped.

12

Others must have read what the electrician read. The soggy programs were scattered throughout the dome. It was a Dome History that the original floor was dirt, the playing field was grass. It was Tiffway-419 Bermuda. The grass had been tested in a specially constructed greenhouse at a university. The ceiling was made of 4,796 semitransparent plastic panels to allow for sunlight. Grass grew in the dome. The fielders could not catch fly balls because of the glare. Outfielders wore sunglasses and batting helmets. Orange baseballs did not solve the problem. The team went on a long road trip while workers painted the ceiling panels a translucent white. The glare was reduced, but the grass died. The team played on dirt that was painted green. The baseballs rolled through the outfield and turned green. A chemical company invented grass made of nylon. The team went on a long road trip while workers installed it over the dirt. The electrician carefully removed the pages and hid them. He had a deep gash across his palm. He tried to keep it clean and wrapped. He blew out his candle. He understood that the dome was the space where the dome could be dreamed.

13

Birds lived there, too, in the spaces between beams. They flew through the deep, sunless sky. People looked up to watch, but they grew dizzy and had to sit.

14

The dome had its first baby. Everyone could hear the birth in the skybox and they felt like part of it. There were plenty of doctors. Gifts arrived. Someone made a sturdy crib. Someone made a mobile of feathers. For two days nobody leaped, nobody fired a gun. Something was wrong with the baby. It didn't make a sound. It was small and its color was wrong. When it died, even the doctors went to stare into the lake. They had strong assumptions about human life, which they were prepared to have confirmed. Other babies were born and others were conceived. This was either heroic or foolish, and the parents had no way, except time, to know which. For the babies the dome was home. At night, between fitful naps, the electrician sketched the dome, the gentle curve of the roof, the crosshatch of catwalk. To save candles he occasionally drew in the dark, blind, and he awoke in the light to odd lines, impossible arcs. It was a Dome History that people wondered whether clouds would form beneath the roof. He stashed his notebook, ate crackers from plastic packages. He walked, searching for a shoelace, a belt.

15

The electrician found a discarded weapon, a hollow metal pole, roughly three feet long, roughly three inches in diameter at its ends. For one day he pounded the end of the pole with the marble base of a trophy he found in an office closet. The top of the trophy was a gold man riding a gold bull. The end of the pole became flat and sharp. The electrician took the pole and climbed the catwalk to the top of the ceiling. The catwalk was narrow, its railings low. The electrician's legs grew weak and he struggled for air. He lay down and closed his eyes. He crawled, trying not to look at the water below. Near the top he saw the leapers' tokens, the notes and letters, photographs, keys, gold bands. A hat, a doll, a child's shoe. The electrician was careful not to disturb the objects. When he got to the top of the dome, he lay on his back and looked up at the skylight panels. The ceiling side had not been painted. There was a short ladder leading to a small hatch in the roof, just as the electrician knew there would be. He climbed the ladder, opened the hatch, and emerged onto the roof of the dome, squinting. The sun was too bright, too close, too hot. He had not been outside since arriving. He was on top of the sky and beneath it. He did not see another person. The water extended to every horizon. Beside the dome, to the west, was the other stadium, its light stanchions snapped or swaying. In the distance, to the north, was downtown, silver buildings rising from the water, their windows glowing with sun. To the east was ocean, dotted with billboards. Out near Fannin the electrician could see the large helicopter of a relief organization, capsized and nearly submerged. To the south, the overpasses on 610 arched over the flood, crowded with abandoned cars. He walked out onto the roof, onto a rectangular panel, roughly six feet by four feet. The pitch was less steep than the electrician had imagined, though he knew the Fast Fact that the roof of the dome, the dome itself, was built flatter than its original plans. The electrician squatted, and with the flat, sharp end of his metal pole he began scraping the surface of the white panel. The paint did not peel or chip. He stood and moved to another panel. He squatted and scraped. He moved to another panel. He stood in the heat and wiped his face with his shirt. It was a Dome History that a man on a motorcycle jumped over thirteen cars on January 9, 1971. That a woman beat a man in tennis on September 20, 1973. The electrician returned to the original panel. He went to his hands and knees. Eventually he scraped up a thin white layer of dust. He leaned down and blew it away. The electrician's body remembered working on his grandfather's house, twenty years earlier. The same motion, sound. The same patience. Eventually the tool created a small hole in the paint. He had scraped down to the transparent plastic panel. This—it was a Fast Fact—was Lucite. He put his forehead on the panel and cupped his hands around his eyes. He peered through the small hole into the dome, but could only make out a dark blur. He scraped from inside the hole, working outward, making it larger, chipping away larger pieces of paint from the plastic panel. It occurred to him that it would be useful to have a set of scrapers of various widths. He had to squint against the glare. He saw spots. He could feel the sun burning the back of his neck. His sweat dripped into his work. He had no water for his thirst. He smacked mosquitoes, smeared his own blood across his skin. In three hours he had finished a panel. He was dizzy, delirious. The pole slipped from his hands. Later he would not remember climbing back into the hatch, walking the catwalks. That night he lay in his nest, shivering and vomiting. He awoke in the infirmary, staring at the ceiling.

16

Many of the poems survive. The poetry of the dome is distinguished by its resignation, its rejection of nostalgia, its ambivalence toward the structure, the treatment of humans as animals, and its careful observation of startling juxtaposition and conjunction.

17

The electrician returned to the roof. He worked in the mornings and evenings. In a week he had scraped eight panels. His hands were blistered. The gash in his palm had reopened, bloodying the rags he bound it with. The dome leaked light. A beam moved daily down the seats, across the water, up the seats. It marked the days, it returned the dome to the natural world. The beam was salutary. People sat in the hot, bright seats, eyes closed. Others looked upward for the source, squinting and shading their eyes. Many took credit for the sun. The electrician hunted for metal to make more tools. He pounded flat, sharp ends until his neighbors hollered. He was regarded as suspicious, dangerous, making so many sharp things. He stashed the tools with his books and programs. When he visited the clans along the club level, his voice was too quiet. They asked him to speak louder and when he did, they laughed or shouted threats. He wore a yellow construction helmet. He cupped his hands in front of him as he spoke, as if holding something that might leap out. He walked a circle around the dome.

18

One morning at dawn three men were waiting on the roof when the electrician emerged through the hatch. The men held clubs and knives. The catwalk was the electrician's only escape, but the height still terrified him. He often had to lie down, crawl. He would not be able to run. He was surprised by his terror, his attachment to this life. Please, he said quietly, I just want to work. In the dim light he could not see them well. What he had thought to be clubs and knives were tools. The next morning there were nine more, six men and three women. One of the workers attached a wooden handle to his metal scraper, then held the scraping end in the flame of a torch. Others constructed large screens to block the sun. Velaria, thought the electrician. More workers arrived each day. They emerged through the hatch like ants from an anthill. Many did not even know why they were scraping, what they were building, nor did they care. They were happy to feel useful. Many had worked for years before the water and had never felt useful. One good worker could finish two to three panels per day. Several workers were burned by hot steel, several collapsed in the heat, several were sliced by splinters of wood or metal. One man lost an eye. Fights erupted and workers were badly injured by the scrapers. The paint dust blew across the roof and covered their skin and clothes. Those who scraped paint by day could be heard coughing at night. It was a Fast Fact that one worker had died constructing the dome. The poets wrote about Michelangelo on his scaffold. Rain came and washed away the dust and chips of paint. The electrician watched the water flow down the panels of the roof. The panels gradually became clearer, and the dome filled with light.

19

The yacht salesman stared at the electrician's drawings of the platform. He nodded, though the sketch was poor and implausible. He left the dome, scouting wood in a yellow raft. He paddled past the other stadium, then north along Kirby.

When he tied his raft to a telephone pole, he got a splinter in the tip of his finger. He pulled out the splinter and then looked up at the pole. They were everywhere, they stretched away forever, and yet they had been invisible to him. The heat was nearly unendurable. Paddling back, the yacht salesman saw the dome in the distance behind the other stadium. He saw the workers spread out across the white hemisphere of the roof. The workers heard a distant buzz in the sky. They all stood, shielded their eyes with their dusty hands. They saw the speck of the airplane to the west. Then it was gone and they knelt again on the panels.

20

It was a Fast Fact that the dome's air-conditioning system could circulate 2.5 million cubic feet of air per minute. It was a Fun Trivia that dome engineers claimed they could make it snow.

21

The electrician often could not sleep. One night, after meeting with the yacht salesman and the translator, he sat in Section 452, low down by the lake, listening to the soft splash and trickle, the cries of babies. Above, the disk of the full moon was fuzzy through the Lucite. Upper-deck candles looked like stars. There was movement on the catwalk, near the hatch. He thought he saw the hatch open. When he crawled through, clutching a scraper, there was nobody there. Then, in the light of the moon, he saw a head above the distant slope of the roof. For a week someone had been darkening the panels. Everyone had assumed that the vandal was a teenage boy, or a group of teenage boys. But here was a man in his fifties, a former librarian, rubbing a panel with sticky black syrup. He looked up at the electrician but did not stop until he'd finished the panel. He had covered four. The black material, when dry, had proven more difficult to scrape than the white paint. The librarian stood and said, There. The electrician said, That's enough. The librarian said, I hate watching you fools. I can't stand it. All you busy fools. The electrician did not say anything. He led the librarian back to the hatch and down. He speculated that the librarian had had a good life before the water. It was those who had been content that had the most trouble in the dome.

22

The summer storms came without warning or names. Lobby doors collapsed and the dark lake grew deeper. Stores of food grew thin. The sun's heat entered the dome and did not leave. Its light was too bright off the water. Those in the upper decks descended because of the heat. Those on the lower decks rose because of the water. The club level became crowded, loud, filthy. The infirmary filled, expanded. The sick sat in cushioned seats or lay on thin sheets on the concrete. Through their dry lips they cursed the electrician.

23

Beyond Dome History, after it, the dome was empty. A new stadium was built beside it. The dome was a problem. It could become something or nothing. It could be a shopping center, a parking garage, a museum. It could be demolished. It could implode, crumble in on itself. The pieces could be hauled away to make a parking lot. A monument could be erected there. Engineers worried that even the most cautious demolition might harm surrounding structures. It could be a movie studio, a luxury hotel.

24

The yacht salesman led six boats out on Fannin, steering a line beneath the thick wires strung between telephone poles. Their boats were made from conference tables and large blocks of Styrofoam. The world outside was still and flat and quiet. Faded pictures of food peeled away from half-submerged billboards. The sailors used long poles and makeshift oars to guide the boats along the street. On low rooftops they could see scattered clothes, plastic bags, suitcases. Some thought they saw faces from the second-story windows of stores and offices. They turned occasionally to look back at the dome behind them. It seemed to float or hover like a ghost ship. It was a Dome History that a press release in 1965 compared the dome to the Eiffel Tower. The yacht salesman stopped and pointed up at a telephone pole. The other boats kept their distance, spread out, kept watch. One sailor climbed up the pole. With a rope he pulled up a rusty saw. He hesitated before cutting the wires. Zap, the sailors yelled, laughing. The sailor on the top of the pole did not laugh. His hand was shaking. He cut through the wires, lowered the saw, climbed down. Three sailors took turns swinging the ax at the telephone pole. When it fell the pole shattered a streetlight, nearly cleaved the yacht salesman's boat. The waves rocked the boats, soaked the sailors. They cheered and slapped each other's backs. They took down another, then tied ropes to the poles. The six boats turned back to the dome, dragging the lumber. There was a loud shot and a sailor fell, bleeding from the shoulder. The sound did not fade from the air. Leave the poles, the yacht salesman shouted. The sailors paddled back to the dome, their boats nearly full of water. The injured sailor was carried to the infirmary. The other sailors were concerned but not surprised. They had all felt, so recently, the impulse to unmake.

25

It was either a Fast Fact, a Fun Trivia, or a Dome History that a no-hitter was thrown on September 25, 1986. Only three balls were hit out of the infield. Only three players reached base. The yacht salesman had been there with his uncle. The old scoreboard, nearly five hundred feet wide, showed fireworks and six-shooters. The ticket stub was still in the yacht salesman's wallet but his wallet was long lost.

26

The platform would require miles of telephone poles. The yacht salesman and the banker took the sailors back out. Each boat had a gun, each gun pointed at passing windows, rooftops. One morning a sailor crawled through the second-floor window of a small office building. He was gone a long time. The yacht salesman considered whether to leave or to send someone after him. Then the man was at the window, beckoning the others to come in. They tied their boats to gargoyles and ducked through the window. The sailor led them down a hallway, through a smashed door, and into a large, carpeted room with couches and chairs. On a bar there were a dozen large bottles. They drank all day. They ate food from small plastic pouches. They saved nothing. They cleared a space in the middle of the room to dance and wrestle, then they fell asleep on the couches and the carpet.

27

New people arrived at the dome daily, bringing ideas, guns, illness, strength, food, and hunger. The electrician rowed a small raft around the perimeter of the dome. He saw them coming. He saw them swimming or paddling their leaky boats. Go away, he thought. Please go. Often they were injured. Often their eyes did not work anymore except to see. He helped them into the lobbies and up the ramps to dry ground. The lobbies had become treacherous with water and flotsam. The electrician walked circles around the dome, ducking beneath the clotheslines. Frequently his arms and cheeks brushed the hanging clothes, the cotton and polyester, cool and damp against his skin. The electrician stared up and back down. He opened his notebook. They could use dome-made sledgehammers to smash holes on the second level of the external pedestrian walkways. The holes would need to be large enough to load in the wood, the soil. They could build floating docks for boats. The docks could rise with the water and so, for a time, could they. It was a Dome History that the dome's original name was the Harris County Domed Stadium. The electrician admired that name for its modesty, its accuracy. It seemed to him a true and accommodating name.

28

Boys fished the dome lake. One of them caught a giant turtle. There was great commotion as they pulled it in, placed it on its back, argued about the best way to destroy it. With plywood scraps the boys built a ramp down the stairs between Sections 259 and 260. They took turns riding the two bicycles down the ramp and into the water. The bicycles rusted, their tires went flat, the wheel rims bent. The translator watched the boys from a skybox. The boys were her problem. The lake had to be cleaned before the platform could be built. If you clear the lake, the translator said to the boys, I'll get you another bike. The boys looked as if they might set upon her. They were barefoot, shirtless, and they dripped water onto the concrete. A few had patchy beards. Five bikes, one said. Four, she said. The boys called and whistled as she walked away. They swam into the water and began to haul out the suitcases, tires, chairs, bottles, cans, knives, clothing, birds, stuffed animals, flashlights, books, programs, boxes, computers, phones, strollers, blankets, guns, dogs. Two boys swam down to tie a rope around a heavy wooden box resting on the turf. Five boys pulled the box up out of the lake. Inside the box were hundreds of little domes.

29

There once had been (Fun Trivia) shoeshine stands located on the lower level behind home plate. The children who heard the story could not understand it. Shiny shoes. Shoeshine. The world before seemed strange to them. Snow in the dome, and grass, and men who walked on shoes that shone. They played games, knelt at each other's feet, pretended they had shoes, pretended their shoes were too bright to behold.

30

The yacht salesman's dreams were horrors. He stayed awake for days, until his waking life was a dream, and then he swam away from the dome.

31

The banker went out at dawn with eight boats. He had grown up on a lake. He remembered the sudden plunge of the bobber, the dragonflies that settled on the ends of the rods. He lived in a skybox (19) and the sailors did not like him, but they did what he said. They brought down more telephone poles, cut two-by-fours and two-by-sixes out of stores and houses, pulled plywood from storm-boarded offices. The lumber for the platform was stored in dry passageways above the lower level. Late at night one of the guards would allow the insurance executive and his daughter to take pieces of wood to build coffins. The coffins were flat, crude boats with small ornate boxes for candles, dried flowers, letters, toys, or jewelry. The coffins were stacked, large to small, several levels up in an external pedestrian walkway. The banker noticed the missing wood. One night he hid in the passageways. He saw the insurance executive nod to the guard. He saw him select his pieces and carry them, with his daughter, back to the pedestrian walkway. They walked quickly through the dark. The banker followed them up the ramps. He lit a torch and walked along the long row of stacked coffins, touching them lightly. He knelt down to look at some unfinished boxes. He picked up the woodworking tools and held them close to his face. The insurance executive and his daughter sat in the shadows. The banker stood and walked back down the ramps.

32

Whatever story the poets wanted to tell, the dome contained it. Nature was proven, and so was nurture. Altruism and selfishness were proven. Community and individual, chaos and order, art and shit, tool and weapon, freedom and gene, God and void— everything was proven and true, filling the dome like music. And every person was a dome, too. But won't the telephone poles float? asked the limousine driver. The electrician stared at him. I need you to figure that out, he said. The limousine driver sat and thought for days. Once the platform was built, the poles would be weighted down, but the problem was how to begin, how to plant and secure the poles in the turf, partially submerged in the water. When his son would not stop crying, the limousine driver held the infant up by his ankle and shook. He climbed to Section 909, high above the lake. His notebook was full of strange sketches, smudged by his sweat. He felt constrained by the elements and conditions of the dome, the physical laws of the planet. He stared across the dome at tattered clothes on taut lines. There was nothing and then from nothing there was something, elegant and correct. He would need some kind of drill and great lengths of strong cable.

33

What are the rights of humans? One morning the boys caught the librarian urinating in the lake. They had all urinated in the lake many times, occasionally as a contest. When they ran at him, he did not try to escape. They picked him up and threw him into the water. Broken-necked, he floated, and the boys swam in to pull his body out.

34

The platform was a large rectangle of plastic-wrapped plywood sheets resting on top of hundreds of telephone poles cut to the same length. It stood ten feet above the water, centered in the lake. The platform workers were vulnerable to objects dropped from the catwalks. In late fall and winter the dome cooled. The platform workers erected tall, thick sides around the perimeter of the platform. The outside of the platform walls had painted messages from the city from long ago. HELP. NEED WATER. NEED INSULIN. TIMMY WAIT HERE. THIS BUILDING PROTECTED BY GUN. GOD IS WATCHING. EAT ME. SAVE ME NASA. There were three kinds of workers: those who deliberately concealed the writing by facing it inward, those who deliberately displayed the writing by facing it outward, and those who both concealed and displayed because they did not notice or care about the writing. There were arguments and all of the positions were sound. Wooden walkways spanned the water between the platform and the sections of the lower deck.

35

Twenty-one boats sailed northeast, over the Old Spanish Trail, past the medical center, until they saw Sam Houston's horse standing on the water. That was Hermann Park. Then it was slow and dangerous, diving to bring up soil in buckets, baskets, boxes, hands. At the end of the day, tiny piles dotting the enormous platform. How many days just to cover the platform floor. The carts, barrows, and chutes. The soccer coach didn't believe in it. He dreamed of killing the electrician, burying him alive, but he kept sailing to the park, diving for dirt. When others complained, he talked them into believing in something foolish. He stood in his wobbly boat and exhorted. Let's go, the soccer coach shouted. What's your plan? That's what I thought. It's a bountiful planet. It gives and gives. Bring it out of the water. We're soil men. Brown gold. Come on. Get the dirt.

36

It was a Fun Trivia that the dome was, at the millennial turn, the nation's 134th-favorite structure.

37

Even the pirates had given up. The soilers could work all day. They took dirt from the Japanese Gardens, the golf course. Twice a day the soccer coach would take off his shirt and dive with the others. When he came back up, he tipped his small load into the dirt raft and sat on the edge of the boat with his feet in the water. He could not see his toes. He did not know what month it was. The sun dried his back and hair. If he had cigarettes, he would hand them out, one each. They would all sit, still breathing heavily, staring into the water. If the dirt raft was more than half full, someone might say something. The water's warm. Like it is in the Gulf. Like it was. The soccer coach would nod. He had lain on a raft, his arm dangling over the edge. He had gotten stung by something. All he had seen was a dark ripple. Others nodded and pointed to places on their bodies. Most of them had been stung long ago by something in the Gulf.

38

The historian says, They brought soil to the dome, filled the platform. The sentence makes a bridge over time. Beneath the bridge are the minutes, the bodies, the glare off the water, the dead cranes floating. The golf balls and dark quarters the divers brought back for children. The aching lungs, flaking skin, the infections that never healed. Someone had painted the flank of Sam Houston's horse. It said PTSD DADDY. One day a soiler, catching his breath, pointed at the statue and said, He's the only person ever to serve as governor of two different states. The soccer coach was up on the horse with Sam Houston like a lifeguard or emperor. Let's go now, he said. Come on. Cut the small talk. Soil time.

39

The veterinarian, the florist, the animal researcher, the data enterer, the consultant, the editor, the lab technician, the classics professor, the actuary, the hotline volunteer, the sculptor, the traffic engineer, the detective, the door and window installer, the plumber, the landscaper, the gambler, the architect, the quilter, the taxidermist, the nurse, the accountant—none of them returned with seeds. The mechanic thought he had something, but it turned out he did not. The historian builds a bridge over a year, says That was the worst time imaginable. The storms came, the food ran out, the heat increased, the water rose. Despair became violence. Many died and many swam away. The boys tore down the walls of the platform and soil slid into the lake. The coffin-maker's hands were swollen and splintered. His daughter died and he pushed her lightly from the floating dock. The violin stopped and did not start again. The historian knows how it turned out. The people in the dome did not know. This is the end of the story because they considered it the end, the very worst they could imagine.

40

They would eventually find seeds. Eventually there would be vegetables, rice, cotton, but initially wheat and corn. They repaired the wooden walls of the farm, replaced the lost soil. They planted and waited. They gripped the sides of the platform, peeking over. The sunlight through the roof coated the soil, turned it gold. Then the tiny green stalks pushed through the dirt and into the dome. One morning the electrician woke up early. He saw a sleeping guard, a deer in the corn. It looked like a dream, but it wasn't. He watched it for some time. The electrician would have a life precisely bisected. The harvest would be meager, the corn salty. They would fry fish, dance, play music. They would have a feast beneath the blurry moon. They would plant again, rotate crops, trap rainwater on the roof. The electrician would walk circles around the dome, listening. His hand would be amputated. He would meet with the residents one section at a time. We could try to remove some of the ceiling panels to allow sunlight and rain, a woman in Section 433 would say. We could use gutters and spouts to funnel rainwater down into the dome, a man in Section 638 would say. We could plant saltbush to desalinate the soil, an elderly man in Section 928 would say. We'll have to raise and extend the platform, a woman in Section 767 would say. We have to get air in here, a man in Section 722 would say. A boy in Section 600 would stand and speak quietly. Louder, son, people would say. Why can't this whole dome float, the boy would repeat. The electrician would stare at the boy's drawing. Some of the residents would laugh but many of the residents would not.

THE BLACK SQUARE

by CHRIS ADRIAN

HENRY TRIED TO PICK OUT the other people on the ferry who were going to the island for the same reason he was. He wasn't sure what to look for: black Bermuda shorts, an absence of baggage, too-thoughtful gazing at the horizon? Or just a terminal, hangdog look, a mask that revealed instead of hiding the gnarled little soul behind the face? But no one was wearing black, or staring forlornly over the rail. In fact, everyone was smiling. Henry looked pretty normal himself, a man in the last part of his young middle age dressed in plaid shorts and a T-shirt, a dog between his legs and a duffel bag big enough to hold a week's clothes at his side.

The dog was Bobby's, a black Lab named Hobart, borrowed for the ostensible vacation trip to make it less lonely. It was a sort of torture to have him along, since he carried thoughts of Bobby with him like biting fleas. But Henry loved Hobart as honestly as he had ever loved anything or anybody. And, in stark opposition to his master, the dog seemed to love Henry back. Henry was reasonably sure he would follow him, his paws fancy-stepping, through the black square. But he wasn't going to ask him to do that. He had hired an old lady to bring Hobart back to Cambridge at the end of the week.

He reached down and hugged the dog around the neck. Hobart craned his neck back and licked Henry's face. A little girl in enormous sunglasses, who'd skibbled over twice already since they'd left Hyannis, did it again, pausing before the dog and holding out her hand to him. "Good holding out your hand for the doggie to sniff!" her mother called out from a neighboring bench, and smiled at Henry. "What's his name?" the girl asked. She hadn't spoken the other two times she'd approached.

"Blackheart's Grievous Despair," Henry said. Hobart gave up licking her hand and started to work on her shoe, which was covered in the ice cream she'd been eating a short while before.

"That's stupid," the girl said. She was standing close enough that Henry could see her eyes through the sunglasses, and tell that she was staring directly into his face.

"So are you," he said. It was one of the advantages of his present state of mind, and one of the gifts of the black square, that he could say things like this now, in part because his long sadness had curdled his disposition, and in part because all his decisions had become essentially without consequence. He wasn't trying to be mean. It was just that there wasn't any reason anymore not to say the first thing that came into his mind.

The little girl didn't cry. She managed to look very serious, even in the ridiculously oversized sunglasses, biting on her lower lip while she petted the dog. "No," she said finally, "I'm not. *You* are. You are the *stupidest*." Then she walked away, calmly, back to her mother.

He got surprises like this all the time these days, ever since he had decided to give up his social filters. A measured response from a five-year-old girl to his little snipe, a gift of flowers from his neighbor when he'd told her he didn't give a flying fuck about the recycling, a confession of childhood abuse from his boss in response to his saying she was an unpleasant individual. The last was perhaps not so surprising—every unpleasant individual, himself included, had a bevy of such excuses that absolved them of nothing. But there was something different about the world ever since he had discovered the square and committed himself to it. *People go in*, someone had written on the Black Square Message Board, which Henry called up over his bed every night before he went to sleep, *but have you ever considered what comes OUT of it?* Most of those who wrote there were a different sort of freak from Henry, but he thought the writer might mean what he wanted him to mean, which was those sort of little daily surprises, and more than that a funny sense of carefree absolution. Once you had decided to go in (he didn't subscribe to the notion, so popular on the board, that the square called you or chose you) things just stopped mattering in the way that they used to. With the pressure suddenly lifted off of every aspect of his life, it had become much easier to appreciate things. *So many wonderful things have come to me since I accepted the call*, someone wrote. *It's too bad it can't last.* And someone replied, *You know that it can't.*

The girl's mother was glaring now, and looked to be getting ready to get up and scold him, which might possibly have led to an interesting conversation. But it didn't seem particularly likely, and one surprise a day was really enough. Henry got up and walked to the bow of the ferry. Hobart trotted ahead, put his paws up on the railing, and looked back at him. The island was just visible on the horizon. Henry sat down behind the dog, who stayed up on the rail, sniffing at the headwind and looking back every now and then. Henry laughed and said, "What?" They sat that way as the island drew nearer and nearer. The view was remotely familiar—he'd seen it countless times when he was a little boy—though it occurred to him as he stared ahead that he had the same feeling, coming up on the island, that he used to get facing the other way and approaching the mainland: he was approaching a place that was strange, exciting, and a little alien, though it was only the square that made it that way now. Nantucket in itself was ordinary, dull, and familiar. *You are especially chosen*, a board acquaintance named Martha had written, when he'd disclosed that he had grown up on the island. *Fuck that*, he had written back. But as they entered the harbor, he hunkered down next to the dog, who was going wild at the smells rolling out from the town and the docks. "Look, Hobart," he said. "Home."

Those who ascribed a will or a purpose to it thought it was odd that the square should have chosen to appear on Nantucket, one of the least important places on the planet, for all that the island was one of the richest. Those same people thought it might have demonstrated a sense of humor on the square's part to appear, of all the places it could have, in the middle of a summer-mansion bathroom, where some grotesquely rejuvenated old lady, clinging to her deluxe existence, might have stepped into it accidentally on her way out of the tub. But it had appeared on the small portion of the island that was still unincorporated, in a townie commune that had been turned subsequently into a government-sponsored science installation and an unofficial way station for the ever-dwindling and ever-renewing community of people who called themselves Black Squares.

Every now and then someone posted a picture of a skunk or a squirrel on the board, with a caption naming the creature Alpha or Primo or Columbus, and calling it the first pioneering Black Square. It was true that a number of small animals, cats and dogs and rabbits and even a few commune llamas, went missing in the days before the square was actually discovered by a ten-year-old boy who tried to send his little sister through it. Around her waist she wore a rope that led to her brother's hand; he wasn't trying to kill her. He had been throwing things in all day, rocks and sticks and one heavy cinderblock, and finally a rabbit from the eating stock. His mother interrupted him before he could send his sister through. He had put a helmet on her, and given her a flashlight, sensing, as the story went on the board, that there was both danger and discovery on the other side.

There followed a predictable series of official investigations, largely muffled and hidden from the eyes of the public, though it seemed that from the first missing rodent there was mention of the square on the boards. The incorporated portion of the island wanted nothing to do with it. Once the government assured them that it would be a very closely supervised danger, they more or less forgot about it, except to bemoan the invasion of their island by a new species of undesirable, one that didn't serve them in their homes or clubs. The new arrivals had a wild, reckless air about them, these people who had nothing to lose, and they made one uncomfortable, even if they did spend wildly and never hung around for very long. The incorporated folks hardly noticed the scientists, who once the townies had been cleared out never left the compound until they departed for good within a year, leaving behind a skeleton crew of people not bothered by unsolvable mysteries.

By then it had become obvious that there was nothing to be learned from the square—at least nothing profitable in the eyes of the government. It just sat there, taking whatever was given to it. It refused nothing (*And isn't it because it loves everyone and everything perfectly, that it turns nothing and no one away?* Martha wrote), but it gave nothing back. It emitted no detectable energy. No probe ever returned from within it, or managed to hurl any signal back out. Tethers were neatly clipped, at various and unpredictable lengths. No official human explorer ever went through, though an even dozen German shepherds leaped in obediently, packs on their backs and cameras on their heads. The experiments degraded, from the construction of delicate listening devices that bent elegantly over the edge of the square to the government equivalent of what the boy had been doing: tossing things in. The station was funded eventually as a disposal unit, and the government put out a discreet call across the globe for special and difficult garbage, not expecting, but not exactly turning away, the human sort that inevitably showed up.

Henry had contracted with his psychiatrist not to think about Bobby. "This is a condition of your survival," the man had told him, and Henry had not been inclined to argue. There had been a whole long run of better days, when he had been able to do it, but it took a pretty serious and sustained effort, and exercised some muscle in him that got weaker, instead of stronger, the more he used it, until he succumbed to fatigue. Now it was a sort of pleasure not to bother resisting. It would have been impossible, anyway, to spend time with Bobby's dog and not think of him, though he loved the dog quite separately from Bobby. It was a perfectly acceptable indulgence, in the long shadow of the square, to imagine the dog sleeping between them on their bed, though Hobart hadn't been around when they were actually together. And it was acceptable to imagine himself and Bobby together again—useless and agonizing, but as perfectly satisfying as worrying a painful tooth. It was even acceptable to imagine that it was he and Bobby, and not Bobby and his Brazilian bartender husband, who were about to have a baby together, a little chimera bought for them from beyond the grave by Bobby's fancy dead grandma.

Yet Bobby wasn't all he thought about. It wasn't exactly the point of the trip to torture himself that way, and whether the square represented a new beginning or merely an end to his suffering, he wasn't trying to spend his last days on the near side of the thing in misery. He was home, after all, though Nantucket Town did not feel much like home, and he didn't feel ready, at first, for a trip to the old barn off Polpis Road. But there was something—the character of the light and the way the heat seemed to hang very lightly in the air—that though unremembered, made the island feel familiar.

He showed the dog around. It was something to do; it had never been his plan to go right to the square, though there were people who got off the ferry and made a beeline for it. Maybe they were worried that they might change their mind if they waited too long. Henry wasn't worried about changing his mind or chickening out. The truth was he had been traveling toward the thing all his life, in a way, and while the pressure that was driving him toward it had become more urgent since he came to the island, he still wasn't in any particular hurry to jump in. There were things to say goodbye to, after all; any number of things to be done for the last time. He had spent his last sleepless night in Cambridge in a bed-and-breakfast down the street from where Bobby lived with his bartender, lying on the bed with his hands behind his head, staring at the ceiling and enumerating all those things he'd like to do one last time. He wasn't organized enough to make a list, but he'd kept a few of them in his head. It turned out to be more pleasant to do them with the dog than to do them alone, and more pleasant, in some ways, to do them for the dog instead of for himself. Last meals were better enjoyed if Hobart shared them with him—they ate a good deal of fancy takeout in the hotel room, Henry sitting on the floor with his back against the bed, Hobart lying on his belly with his face in a bowl resting between his legs. Henry made a tour of some dimly remembered childhood haunts, rediscovering them and saying goodbye to them at the same time: a playground on the harbor, a pond that he thought was Miacomet but might have been Monomy, and finally the beach at Surfside.

He had pictures of himself at that beach on his phone, taken by his father during Henry's very well-documented childhood. He was his father's last child, and the only one from his second marriage. His brothers were all much older than him, born when their father had been relatively poor, when he still made his living, despite his Haverford education and his well-received first book, playing piano in bars. Henry came in well after that, when there was money for cameras and camcorders and time, attention, and interest to take a picture of the baby every day. He had thumbed through them in bed the night before, showing them to Hobart, who somehow got conditioned to yawn every time he saw a picture of Henry at the beach with a bucket and a shovel. It was a less melancholy pastime, and less pathetic, to look at old pictures of himself, instead of pictures of himself and Bobby, though he did that, too, late into the night, with Hobart's sleeping head on his chest.

They spent the morning making their way slowly down the beach by throws of a rubber football the size of a child's fist. Henry had a reasonably good arm: once or twice he threw the ball far enough that Hobart disappeared around a dune to go in search of it. He daydreamed considerably as they went, and thought indulgently of Bobby as Hobart leaped and galumphed and face-planted into the sand. He had to be persuaded every time to give up the ball, running back as if to drop it at Henry's feet, then veering away and playing a prancing, high-stepping keep-away until

Henry caught him around the neck and pulled open his jaws. It made him a defective sort of retriever, and it doubled the work of play with him, but Henry didn't mind it.

He laughed at the dog, and thought of his father laughing behind the camera at him, and thought of something Bobby had said to him more than once. He'd accused Henry of being unable to delight in him, and had said that this was part of the reason that Henry had never been properly able to love him, or anybody, really. Bobby had said deflating things like that all the time—he'd kept an arsenal of them always at hand and ready to spoil any occasion—and the Bobby in Henry's head still kept up a running commentary years after they broke up. But it had been fair, for Bobby to say he was delightless, a million years before, when Henry had been an entirely different person, selfish and self-loathing and more in love with his own misery than with the man who wanted to marry him.

All that had changed. It was far too late to make any difference with Bobby, but now he was the sort of person who couldn't help but take pleasure in the foolish exuberance of a clumsy black Lab. "Look, Bobby," he said quietly as Hobart raced after the football. "Look at him go." He shook his head at himself, and sat down, then lay down on his back with his knees bent and his arms thrown out at his sides, staring up at the sky for a while before he closed his eyes. "I'm tired, Hobart," he said, when the dog came back and started to lick his face. "Sit down and relax for a minute." But the cold nose kept pressing on his eyelids, and the rough tongue kept dragging across his cheek and nose and lips. He swatted at the dog's head, and grabbed his collar, and reached with his other hand to scratch the Lab's neck.

In another moment his face was being licked from the other side. When Henry opened his eyes he discovered that this was Hobart. The dog he had been petting was someone else entirely, another black Lab, but with a face that was much pointier (and frankly less handsome) than Hobart's. The owner came trotting up behind him. He was standing in front of the sun. Henry only registered his hairy chest and baseball cap before the man asked him, "Why are you making out with my dog?"

One heard various stories about Lenny. He was alternately from San Francisco, or Houston, or Pittsburgh, or Nantucket, or someplace no one had ever heard of. He was a teenager, or an old man, or in his middle age. He was perfectly healthy, or terminally ill. He was happily married, or heartbroken and bereft. He was a six-foot-eight black man or he was a diminutive honky. He might not even have been the first one to go through. It was only certain that he'd been the first to announce that he was going, and the founding poster on what became the Black Square Message Board. As the first official Black Square (the anonymous individuals who might have passed in before him, as well as the twelve German shepherds, together held that title unofficially) he had become something of a patron saint for everyone who proposed to go after him. *Lenny knows* was a fairly common way to preface a platitude on the board, and his post, *this is not a suicide*, had become a motto of sorts for the whole group. The post had a *ceci n'est pas une pipe* quality about it, but it was consistent with what became the general attitude on the board, that the square offered an opportunity to check into another universe as well as the opportunity to check out of this one. *He should have said, This is not MERELY a suicide*, Martha wrote. Not everything she wrote was stupid, and Henry was inclined to agree with her on this count. There was an element of protest to Lenny's leap into the square: it was a fuck-you to the ordinary universe the likes of which it had not previously been possible to utter. By entering into the square you could express your disdain for the declined world, so far fallen, to some people's minds, from its potential for justice and beauty, as effectively as you could by blowing your head off, but instead of just dying, you might end up someplace else, someplace different—indeed, someplace full of people just like you, people who had leaped away from their own declined, disappointing lives.

The pointy-nosed Lab's name was Dan; his master's name was Luke. Henry ought not to have talked to him beyond saying "Sorry!" Meeting yet another handsome, witty, accomplished fellow who was utterly uninteresting on account of his failure to be Bobby was not part of the plan for his last days on the near side of the square. Henry tried to walk away, but the dogs were already fast friends, and Hobart wouldn't come. The man was smiling and looking at Henry in a particular way as Henry tugged on Hobart's collar. He was short and muscled-up and furry, and had a pleasant, open face. Henry was trying to think of something inappropriate to say, but nothing was coming to mind. The man stuck out his hand and introduced himself. Henry, his left hand still on Hobart's collar, stuck out his own, shifting his balance as he did, so when Hobart lunged at his new friend he pulled Henry over. Henry ought to have let go of the stranger's small, rough, appealing palm—he thought as he squeezed it harder that it felt like a blacksmith's palm, and that it went along nicely with the man's blacksmith build—but he gripped it harder as he fell, and pulled the other man over on top of him. They were momentarily a pile of bodies, human and canine, Luke on Henry on Hobart, with Dan on top of all of them. Henry got a paw in his face, and a dog nail scratched his cheek, and his face was pressed hard into Luke's chest. Luke smelled like coffee and salt, and tasted salty too, when Henry thought he had accidentally tasted the sweat on the man's hairy chest, but it turned out that it was his own blood on his lip, trickling from the scratch.

The injury, though it wasn't totally clear which dog had inflicted it, prompted profuse apologies and an invitation to dinner. Henry felt sure he should have declined. All his plans aside, he knew that he wasn't going to be interested in this man as certainly as he knew that the sun got a little colder every day, or that eventually the whole island would be incorporated as surely as Hilton Head or Manhattan, and that the rich folk would have to ferry in their household help from Martha's Vineyard. It was inevitable. But he considered, as he wiped the blood off his face and listened to Luke apologize, that he might be overlooking another gift of the square, and that it didn't matter that loving Bobby had ruined him, and smothered in the cradle any possible relationship with any other man. He had no future with anyone, but he had no future at all. That took the pressure off of dinner. And it was something else to say goodbye to, after all: dinner with a handsome man.

"Sometimes I kind of like being the only homo in a ten-mile radius," Luke said while they were eating. "Or almost the only one." Henry had asked what had possessed him to come to Nantucket for a vacation. When Henry cocked his head at that, Luke asked him the same question.

"Something similar," Henry said, reaching down to pet Hobart's head, a gesture that was becoming his new nervous tic. They were sitting outside at a restaurant in 'Sconset, both dogs at their feet and a bowl of clams between them. Dan was just as well-behaved as Hobart was. They both sat staring up at the sky or at another table, or staring intently into each other's eyes, leaning forward occasionally to sniff closer and closer, touching noses and then touching tongues before going back to looking distracted and disinterested until they started it all over again with a sudden glance. Henry and Luke took turns saying "I think they like each other."

"I was born here," Henry added. Luke was smiling at him—he seemed to be one of those continuous smilers, the sort of people that Henry generally disliked (Bobby, until he had left, had always appeared perpetually troubled), but there was something sad, or at least resigned, in Luke's smile that Henry found appealing.

"I didn't think anybody was born on Nantucket," Luke said. "I thought people just magically appeared here once they made enough money."

"They do," Henry said. "Sort of. There's a ceremony. You claw your way naked through a pool of coins and they drape you in a white robe and everyone chants, 'One of us! One of us!' But if you're poor you just get squeezed out of a vagina and they put your name on a plaque in the hospital."

"You have a plaque?"

"Sure. Henry David Conroy. May 22, 1986."

"I figured you were special," Luke said, managing to smile differently, more warmly and more engagingly and more attractively. Henry looked away. It was part of his problem that flattering attention from handsome men only made him more sad, and made him feel Bobby's rejection more achingly and acutely. The handsomer the man, and the more flattering the attention, the greater his sadness. To date, anybody else had only discovered in miserable degrees how thoroughly and hopelessly they were not Bobby. But there was always that homunculus in Henry, weakly resistant to the sadness, that protested in a meek little voice whenever he said goodbye early, or declined an invitation up to someone's apartment. Proximity to the square made it a little bolder, and Henry thought he could hear it shouting something about saying goodbye to sucking on a nice cock.

Henry took a clam and looked at the dogs. They were looking away from each other now, but he said it anyway. "Look at that. They really like each other, don't they?"

"They sure do," Luke said.

Because of my mother, somebody wrote. Half the messages on the farewell board were unsigned. You were only supposed to post your final notes there, but this was a rule that was impossible to enforce, since anybody could retire one ID and come back with a new one. And you were supposed to limit yourself to just one reason, either by prioritizing, or, more elegantly, by articulating a reason that contained all other possible reasons. While *Because of my mother* could be unpacked at length, there was something crude, or at least unsophisticated, about it. *Because of incorporation* was its political equivalent: it contained a multitude of reasons, all the accumulated disappointments of the past decade for the people who cared to mourn the dashed hopes of the early part of the century. But it was less subtle and less mysterious than *Because I believe*, into which one could read a richer sort of disappointment, one that was tempered with hope that something besides oblivion lay on the other side of the square. This sort of post could be crude as well: *Because I want to see Aslan* was its own common type. Still, there was something pleasing about these notes which looked forward through the square and saw something or someone waiting there, Aslan in Narnia, Dejah Thoris on Barsoom, or more private kings in more particular kingdoms. *Because I have suffered enough* was less appealing than *Because I wish to suffer differently*.

Most mysterious and most mundane of all were the last posts of the lovelorn. They were neither necessarily hopeful nor despairing. *Because of Alice* could mean anything in a way that *Because of my mother* generally could not—Alice might be hero or villain, after all, but all mothers were villains on the Board. *Because of Louise, Because of Juliet, Because of John, Because of Alan and Wanda and Bubbles*—that one seemed like cheating to Henry, though he liked it for the possibility that Bubbles might be a chimpanzee, and for the likelihood that the circumstances driving the poster through the square must be uniquely weird and horrible. *Because of George, Because of Althea, Because of you. Because I broke his heart, Because she broke my heart. Because of Bobby.*

Henry took Luke and the dogs out to the old barn. There were pictures of that, too, taken back when it had been Henry's home. Henry had called them up on the ceiling and they had all looked at them, even the dogs. It was hardly a first-date activity, to share your distant past this way, though he'd done it with Bobby, the two of them sitting in an overpriced café in Cambridge with their phones on the table, excitedly trading pictures of their dead brothers and fathers. That had felt like showing each other their scars, part of the process of recognition by which they came independently to understand that, while it was probably too early to say they were meant for each other, they were at least very lucky to have collided. It was a less intimate revelation to show pictures of himself at five years old, naked except for a little cowboy hat and boots, to a man he had fucked three times in the twelve hours he had known him, but it was still a startling bit of progress. He hadn't been interested in that sort of thing—the moving-on that his friends and shrinks and Bobby himself had encouraged him to do—largely because it seemed both impossible and unnecessary. Trying to not be in love with Bobby was like trying to not be gay anymore, or like annulling the law of gravity by personal decree. It was ridiculous to try, and anyway gayness and gravity, for whatever sadness or limitation they might generate, felt right. Henry still wasn't interested in moving on, but there was something about his pending encounter with the square that made it feel like this was something else, similar in form but not in substance to getting over it at last, since he was about to make a permanent attestation to his devotion to Bobby, and to his objection to the end of their relationship.

"This is okay," he said to Hobart, the only other one of the four still awake after the slide show. Luke and his dog had fallen asleep before it finished, and now the man's head was on Henry's chest. "This is okay," Henry said again, staring down his nose at Luke's face. He was doing a whistling sort of snore, in through the nose, out through the mouth. "I'm not making out with your dog," Henry said quietly. "He's throwing up into my mouth." He wondered why he couldn't have thought to say that two days before. Hobart crawled up the bed and added his head to the empty side of Henry's chest. It was a little hard to breathe, but he still fell asleep that way.

The barn was in as much of a state of ruin as the law would allow. No one had lived there for five years, and no one sanely inclined to keep it up had lived there for fifteen. A friend of his father's, a crazy cat lady who kept birds instead of cats, had moved in after his father had died, and after she died Henry had left it empty, never visiting and only paying now and then to have it painted when the nearest neighbor complained that it was starting to look shabby in a way that was no longer picturesque. All the nearest neighbors were eventually eaten up by incorporation, and there were mansions all around now in the near distance, but Henry had never sold the place in spite of offers that grew both more generous and more threatening. He'd left it to Bobby with instructions never to sell, which he probably wouldn't— Bobby was not exactly a friend of incorporation—but who knew. Maybe he and the Brazilian would want to make another baby together, and Bobby's grandma had only been good for one.

*　　*　　*

"You used to live here?" Luke asked in the morning. "All the time?"

"All the time," Henry said. "It's why my manners are so atrocious." They were standing in what remained of the living room. A pair of squirrels were staring at them from a rafter above. The dogs were staring back. "It was fine," Henry said. "It was great, actually. As much as I remember. It doesn't have anything to do with… it."

"Yeah. Mine neither," Luke said. They had started talking about the square during breakfast. Henry wasn't the one to bring it up. Out of nowhere and all of a sudden Luke had asked him what he was going to wear when he went through. "Shorts," Henry had said, not thinking to deny it, or even ask how Luke knew he was a Square.

"I brought a parka," Luke said.

"Because you think it will be cold?" Henry asked.

"Because I like the parka," Luke said. "It's my favorite piece of clothing. It's puffy but not too puffy." A silence followed, not entirely awkward. They were eating in the room, on the bed, and had just moved the plates to the floor for the dogs to finish up. Henry was still trying to decide what to say next when Luke reached over for his cock, and what followed felt like a sort of conversation. Henry had always thought that having someone's cock in your mouth ought to provide you with some kind of insight on them, though this hadn't ever been the case. Staring into someone's eyes while he pounded on their ass made him feel infinitely remote from them, except of course for Bobby, and maybe it was the extraordinary intimacy he had achieved doing such things with Bobby that spoiled it with everyone else. But there was something revealing in the exchange between him and Luke. Luke was holding on to him too tightly, and he was holding on too tightly to Luke, and Henry thought he heard notes of agonized sadness in both their voices when they cried out at each other as they came. By the end of it Henry felt as if they had communicated any number of wordless secrets, and that he had a deep, dumb understanding of why Luke was going through the square, and felt sure that Luke felt the same way, and it seemed all of a piece with the whole process that it would fuck things up by asking if this was true.

"I was such a happy kid," Luke said. "Not one single thing about my childhood was fucked up. I always wanted to put that on my gravestone, if I was going to have a gravestone."

"Mine would say..." Henry started, and then thought better of it.

"What?" He had been going to say, *He made bad choices.*

"*Poodle,*" he said. "Just, *Poodle.* And let people wonder what that meant, except it wouldn't mean anything." Luke put an arm around him.

"I like you," he said. "I *like* you." The way he stressed the *like* made it sound as if he hadn't liked anybody for a while.

"I like you, too," Henry said, feeling stupid and exalted at the same time. It changed nothing, to like somebody. It didn't change anything at all about why he was here, or what he was going to do. He could like somebody, and say goodbye to liking somebody, in the same way he was saying goodbye to ice cream and ginger-snaps and blow jobs and the soft fur on the top of Hobart's head. It didn't change the past, or alter any of the choices he had made, or make him into a different person. It didn't change the fact that it was too late to do anything but proceed quietly and calmly through the square.

The dogs were taking turns leaping and barking uselessly at the squirrels. "I *like* you," Henry said again, trying to put the same charming emphasis on the word that Luke had, but it only came out funny, his voice breaking like he was thirteen, or like he was much sadder or more overcome than he actually was. Luke gathered him closer in his arms, and pressed his beard against Henry's beard, and Henry was sure this man was going to say something that would be awkward and delightful and terrifying, but after five minutes of squeezing him and rubbing their faces together but never quite kissing all he said was "You're *cuddly.*"

Some days I'm INTO, Martha wrote, *and some days I'm* THROUGH. *But I'm never not going.* Everybody had those days, when the prospect of going into the square, with no expectation of anything but oblivion on the other side, was more appealing than the prospect of passing through it to discover a new world where pain was felt less acutely, or less urgently, or even just differently, although most people liked to pretend that they were only interested in the latter destination. These were not suicides, after all. But how many people would pass through, Henry wondered, if it were in fact a guaranteed passage to Narnia? He wasn't sure that nuzzling with Aslan would make him any less troubled over Bobby, or that topping Mr. Tumnus's hairy bottom would dispel any unwanted memories. Living beyond Bobby, beyond the pain and delight of remembering him, beyond the terrible ironies of their failed almost-marriage, required something more than the promise of happiness or relief. It could only be done someplace farther away than Narnia, and maybe even someplace farther away than death, though death, according to the deep illogic that had governed all Henry's actions since he and Bobby had broken up beyond any hope of reconciling, was at least a step in the right direction. When he had made his drunken attempt to hang himself all Henry had been thinking about was getting away from Bobby, from loving him and hurting over him and from the guilt of having hurt him, but when he actually settled his weight down on the telephone cord around his neck and let himself begin to be suspended by it, some monstrously naive part of him felt like he was accelerating back toward his old lover. Killing himself, as he tried to kill himself, felt like both a way forward and a way back.

He blacked out ever so gently—he'd chosen to hang himself for the sheer painless ease of it—and he felt sure that he was traveling, felt a thrill at having made what seemed like a reportable discovery, that death was falling. This seemed like tremendously important news, the sort of thing that might have validated his short-lived and undistinguished scientific career. He thought how sad it was that he wasn't going to be able to tell Bobby—It's all right after all, he would have said, that our brothers are dead and our fathers are dead because death is only *falling*. And at the same time he thought, I'll tell him when I see him.

He woke up with a terrible headache, lying among the shoes on his closet floor, all his neatly pressed work clothes on top of him and splinters from the broken closet bar in his hair. He spent the night there because it seemed like this was the place he had been heading all his life, and the dreary destined comfort of it gave him the best night's sleep he'd had in months. When he woke again all the desperate intoxications of the night before had worn off, and he only felt pathetic, failed suicides being the worst sort of losers in anybody's book, his own included. He stayed in there through the morning—he'd wet himself as he lay unconscious, and did it again without much hesitation—feeling afraid to go out into what seemed now like a different world. It was early evening before growing boredom forced him to look at his phone. He'd sent a text to Bobby—*I'm so sorry*—and received no reply.

* * *

Henry went walking at dusk with Luke along the fence around the station where the square was housed. The dogs went quietly before them, sniffing at the grass that poked around the chain-link but neither one ever finding a place to pee. When they came into view of the concrete shed, Dan barked softly at it, but Hobart only lay down and appeared to go to sleep. Henry and Luke stared silently for a while, holding hands.

"How did you know I came to Nantucket for this?" Henry asked.

"I don't know," Luke said. "Same way I knew you were gay, I guess. Squaredar."

"Huh," Henry said. "I didn't know with you until you asked. And then I knew." This seemed like a terribly lame thing to say. He was reminded of all his late conversations with Bobby, before Bobby had ended their long fruitless talk about whether or not they should try being together again by marrying the Brazilian, when hapless unrequited love of the man had kept Henry from making a single articulate point.

"And you didn't know I was gay until I came in your mouth."

"I'm slow," Henry said. "But that doesn't make you gay. Hundreds and hundreds of straight guys have come in my mouth. Hundreds and hundreds and hundreds." It suddenly occurred to him that holding hands they would be too big to fit through the square.

They were quiet for a little while, until Luke heaved a big sigh and said, "There it is." His tone was somehow both reverential and disappointed.

"You couldn't have thought it would be bigger," Henry said. "Everybody knows how big it is."

"No. I just thought I would feel something… different. If I close my eyes I can't even tell it's there."

"Well," Henry said. "Maybe it's just a hole."

Luke shook his head. "Look," he said, and pointed. Someone was approaching the shed. Luke raised a little pair of binoculars to his eyes and made an odd noise, a grunt and a laugh and also something sadder than either of those noises, and handed the glasses to Henry. It was a woman wearing in a short, sparkling dress. "I don't think it's very practical to go through in heels," Henry said.

"Makes it difficult to leap properly," Luke said. "She's probably just going to fall in, which isn't right at all."

Henry put the binoculars down. "Why do you think she's going?"

Luke shrugged. "'Cause she's too pretty for this world." He took the glasses back from Henry, who gave them up gladly, not wanting to watch her pass through the door.

"Let's go," Henry said.

"Hold on," Luke said, still watching. "She's stranded here from another dimension, and thinks this might be the way back."

"Or some dead person told her to do it," Henry said. "To be with them again. Let's go."

"Just a minute," Luke said, and lifted his head like Hobart sniffing at the harbor smells, cocking his head and listening. Henry turned and walked away, whistling for Hobart to follow him, but the dogs stayed together, sitting next to Luke, all of them sniffing and listening. Henry kept walking, and shortly they all came bounding up behind him. Luke caught him around the shoulders and pulled him close. "She's gone," he said matter-of-factly. "Did you feel it?"

All through dinner Henry wanted to ask the question that he knew he shouldn't, the question that probably didn't need to be answered, and the one that he felt intermittently sure would be ruinous to ask. But it wasn't until later, as Luke lay sweating on top of him, that he couldn't resist anymore, and he finally asked it. "How come?" he said into Luke's shoulder.

"What?"

"How come you're going through?"

"It's complicated," he said. "Why are you going?"

"It's complicated," Henry said.

"See?"

"Yeah. Dumb question," Henry said. Though in fact his reason for going through no longer seemed very complicated at all. If it was simple that didn't make it any less powerful, but crushing hopeless loneliness was something Henry suddenly felt able to wrap his arms around even as he wrapped his arms around Luke. "I'm lonely" did no sort of justice to what he'd suffered in the past two years, and yet he could have said it in answer and it would have been true. It seemed suddenly like it might be possible that loneliness did not have to be a crime punishable by more and more extreme loneliness, until a person was so isolated that he felt he was being pushed toward a hole in the world.

"Not dumb. Not dumb." Luke kissed the side of Henry's neck each time he said it. "You're *cuddly*."

"I was going to go tomorrow," Henry said. "That was my date. That's what I paid for. But I was thinking of changing it."

"Really?"

"Really. It's not going anywhere, right? It'll be there next week. And the next week. It's kind of nice, you know, how it's always there, not going anywhere. Nice to know you could always just go in, whenever you want. But that you don't have to, yet, if you want to go to the beach tomorrow instead. Or if you want to play tennis, instead, or before. Tennis, and then in you go. Unless you want to make pancakes first."

"I don't think Hal gives refunds," Luke said. Hal was the guard who took semi-official bribes to look the other way while people took one-way trips into the shed.

"I don't mind," Henry said. "It's just money. When were you going?"

A long silence followed. Henry was afraid to ask again, because he couldn't imagine that Luke hadn't heard him. But Luke only lay there, dripping less and less and breathing more and more deeply, until Henry decided that he was asleep. Henry was almost falling asleep himself, for all that the unanswer was a disappointment, when Luke spoke, not at all sleepily, into his shoulder. "Next week," he said. "Around then."

Then he really did fall asleep, and Henry stayed awake, thinking of the week to come, and the one after that, and the one after that, and of repairs to the barn, and sex among the power tools, and the dogs frolicking, and of Bobby wondering what happened to his wonderful fucking dog, and whether Hobart would be sad if he never went back to Cambridge. Henry fell asleep not any less sad, or any less in love with Bobby, but surprised in a way that did nothing to satisfy his cynicism. Nantucket, he thought before he slept, and two dogs, and a good man asleep on him. It was all relatively all right.

How a two-hundred-pound man could roll off of him and get dressed in the dark and take his parka out of a closet full of rattling wire hangers without waking him up Henry never could figure. He left a note. *You are lovely but the square is lovelier.* It was pinned to Dan's collar. Both dogs stared at Henry impatiently while he sat on the bed with the note in his hands, probably wondering when they were going to go out, or be fed, or be played with, or even acknowledged when they licked his hands or jumped up on the bed to nuzzle his chest. Dan eventually peed in the corner, and then joined Hobart to lay at Henry's feet, both of them wagging their tails, then staring up at him with plaintive eyes, then eventually falling asleep as the morning turned into the afternoon. Henry finally dozed himself, the note still in his hand, maintaining the posture of sad shock he felt sure he was going to maintain forever, and did not dream of Bobby or Luke or the square or his brother or his father or the frolicking dogs or of the isle of Nantucket sinking into the sea. When he woke up he stood and stretched and rustled up his phone from where it had got lost amid the sheets. Then he called the old lady, sure he was going to tell her there was an extra dog for her to bring to Cambridge until he left her a message saying he would bring Hobart back himself.

OBLAST

by J. ERIN SWEENEY

BAKU, ON THE COAST of the Caspian Sea. A pier between the cold, polluted deep and the early-morning light of an ancient, weary city undergoing a shift, an awakening of sorts, accompanied by a surge of interest in reality television, tiny dogs, and poetry. The seal team boards the ship, supervising the loading of four crates the size of industrial freezers, each one strapped into a wooden frame and secured by heavy nylon belts.

Jones and Lavecchia are still reviewing paperwork. There is no end to the forms they must read and sign and produce when asked. They each carry flat black bags heavy with various documents. They do everything with clipboards and manila folders now—their computers have been temporarily confiscated and will be handed back later, below decks. The official on the pier takes Lavecchia's arm and leans toward her in a paternal way. He seems to be warning her about something. She humors him, uninterested in delays.

Mills and Yin watch from the deck of the boat. They have already been processed, and have done everything they can do until the seal crates are on board. They're ready to go.

"What do you think he wants?" says Mills.

"I don't know. Stop fidgeting like that."

"Like what?"

"You look nervous."

"Whatever. This is taking forever."

"Relax."

"They can hardly move in there."

"Just relax, I said."

One week earlier. Nikolay is running through a shopping mall, past well-dressed headless mannequins and advertisements for products that are still not quite familiar. He murmurs apologies as women move out of his way. His school uniform is askew.

Niko and his younger brother have been attending an ivy-entwined boarding school in Philadelphia for three months, and except for moments like this one they have been under constant surveillance during this time. The headmaster always knows Niko's whereabouts, and so does his host family, an elegant pair of retired diplomats who live in a gated community near the school. They check in with him every day.

He has been treated with kindness, so far. Mostly he's been left alone. His brother has not been so lucky and is making enemies, but Niko keeps Gevy close and counsels him when he can. He pays careful attention in class and encourages Gevy to do the same, since he doesn't know how long they will have to stay here. He has asked where his sister is, but he has not been told. This is Niko's only complaint and he keeps it to himself. He tries not to feel anything regarding his father.

Weeks of order and routine have passed quietly for Niko. But this morning, when he made his way to his brother's dormitory to visit Gevy before class, Gevy was not there. This is how Niko has found himself in a shopping mall at eleven a.m. instead of in his own classes. In the dorm he interrogated one young boy and then another and now he has reason to suspect that Gevy has gone on the lam and come here with some of his companions. His truancy is not unusual, but the shopping complex is four miles from the school grounds, and Gevy has left no message. This angers Niko, but it also swells his heart.

Before arriving here, Niko and Gevy had never been outside their own country. They were born in Nagorno-Karabakh, a piece of land broken away from Armenia by cartographers in a previous decade and set adrift entirely inside the borders of Azerbaijan. Cut off from their homeland and surrounded by unsympathetic neighbors, the inhabitants of Karabakh established a new republic, a tiny and fully independent state. But a year ago its nascent government was shattered by a rigged election, and the new regime was diplomatically isolated by Karabakh's most powerful allies. The vulnerable young nation, having nearly lost its footing, was finally betrayed by two of its own administrators, and has since endured what media outlets across the United States and Europe have characterized as "a wave of bloodshed."

The more influential of the men behind these events, and the more calculating, is Niko's father. According to the news reports Niko is encouraged not to read, his father is responsible for the worst massacre the region has endured in this century.

Now Niko is here in an American shopping complex, checking the video-game stores and the food counters, describing his brother to clerks and watching as they shrug and shake their heads. He pushes through crowds in some places and makes his way down desolate aisles in others, between shelves lined with plastic clocks and plastic trees in plastic pots.

Finally a man calls out to him from behind.

He is outside now, standing in a concrete corridor between two buildings connected by an enclosed walkway that arches above him. He does not know where to go next.

"Excuse me," says the man. "Are you looking for your brother?"

"Yes," says Niko.

"A small boy, about like this?"

The man holds his hand out, palm downward. Niko studies the hand for a moment. He considers the height of his brother's uncombed head. On a summer night three months ago, just before their father disappeared, Niko and his brother were dragged from their beds and hurried into a car. They were thousands of miles away by morning, Gevy still wearing his pajamas. Niko had to ask five times before being told what continent they were on.

More people are appearing around him now.

He hasn't decided how to feel about this or what to do about it.

The man says, "You should come with us, please."

This is delivered politely. Otherwise, Niko would still go, but in a different state of mind.

*　*　*

Philadelphia. At the zoo. The seal building is busier than ever, though many of the seals are already gone. The enclosures are being evacuated. Taking advantage of a quiet moment, Dr. Yin, the CS evacuation team leader, is alone in a room adjacent to a pool lined with artificial rock formations. She is checking the crates.

Dr. Yin's team is overseeing the preparation of CS 1, 2, 3, and 4 for life in the wild. These are Caspian seals, functionally extinct outside of the forty that remain in captivity worldwide. Of these forty, at least thirty-five will be released into the open sea by year's end, in compliance with a series of international agreements established for their protection.

They will be carried back to an area of the Caspian Sea near the mouth of the Volga River, to an archipelago of rocky haul-outs recognized as the traditional breeding grounds of their kind. There they will be left. Their crates will be opened, and after they shimmy out they will be observed for a few hours and then abandoned.

Recent events have demonstrated that there is no longer any hope for a seal kept in captivity. Eight months ago, a poorly understood zoonotic flu virus began to pass between humans and pinnipeds, causing humans to experience mild symptoms and killing seals and sea lions within days. This being the case, all captive seals, prepared or otherwise, are being returned to the wild. Highest on the list of evacuees are the rarest. And none are rarer, or more in peril, than CS 1 through 4 and their thirty-six brethren in zoos from South Africa to Iceland. On timetables dictated by the laws of their own nations, most of them will be carried back to the Caspian within a few months.

Already they are for all practical purposes gone from the world. Even if they live, they may not breed. And even if they breed, inbreeding will further jeopardize the chances of those pups lucky enough to be carried to term and born into mercury-laced waters where black markets can still offer more than ten thousand U.S. dollars for a handkerchief-size swatch of their skins. But. A series of international agreements is a series of international agreements. CS 1, 2, 3, and 4 have been trained to hunt for themselves, and now the evacuation team will oversee their release.

These four seals have lived their entire lives (the youngest is two months old; the oldest is thirty-two) here in the zoo, under the watchful eye of the public, cared for by an international team of veterinarians and meriting the foundation of a

Caspian Seal Society and a few spinoff groups, including the Philadelphia Caspian Seal Conservation Society. The older seals, especially, have been difficult to acclimate to life in the open sea; they have been slower in their progression from kibble, to dead fish, to dead fish dragged on a string, to live fish. But Dr. Yin isn't worried about this, not right now.

The technical term for what bothers her is "arrival failure." Seals can disappear into an airplane or ship and not reappear at the intended destination for a variety of reasons, the number of reasons increasing as the black-market value of the species rises. According to the patchwork of international agencies involved, cadavers are to be supplied to the nearest designated research facility for further study if a seal dies en route. But compliance isn't always practical. And certain member states are exempt from certain rules under certain circumstances. Hijacking and theft are not unheard of either.

It is problems like these that concern Dr. Yin as she checks and rechecks the integrity of the four big crates, crawling into and under them with wrench in hand. She removes a metal plate at the base of one of the crates, revealing a hidden latch. The latch lifts easily and the bottom of the crate slides out, a floor under the floor, gliding on silent Teflon-coated rails like a well-designed drawer. Dr. Yin is pleased. She opens and closes the big drawer several times. She stops when she hears someone coming. She slides the drawer closed and covers the latch again.

Niko has been detained in a hotel and closely guarded for almost three days now. On the first day he asked the uniformed woman watching over him, Mary, if that was her real name. She said no. He asked her for her real name and instead of answering she asked him if he wanted anything. Books? Anything to eat? She has been kind, but she expresses her kindness only by feeding him and bringing him things.

Niko does not want things. He only wants his brother and sister. He wants them safe. Beyond this, he has placed all of his desires on indefinite hold and hasn't examined them in years.

Mary says his brother and sister may be joining him before he reaches his destination but she can't promise anything. She is doing all she can to make sure the three of them arrive together. Niko believes this. He likes Mary and trusts her, though his destiny would be little altered if he didn't. He is the child of a monster, a monster who has vanished and effectively abandoned him, and as such he is in the hands of the world now. The world will decide how to deal with him.

Every morning and night Niko examines his fear levels. He hasn't tried to explain this to Mary, but he is making an effort to surrender his life to God. Wherever God sends him, that is where he will go with dignity. This is his project.

On the third day, just before they leave, he and his brother are brought together again. Mary steps aside to let them talk.

"I'm not getting in there," says Gevy.

"What?" says Niko. "Are you afraid?"

"No."

"Then what?"

"This is stupid. This is a stupid plan."

"What would you prefer?"

Niko works to keep the urgency out of his voice. He knows his brother. Gevy has been difficult for these people to manage, Niko is sure. He has no doubt been spitting at them, biting, making threats, and demanding phones since he left Niko's sight three days ago. But Niko also knows that if Gevy refuses to cooperate on this last step, he will be left behind. No one will coerce or hurt him. He will be abandoned to his own devices, that's all, and this is not acceptable. Niko doesn't know what could happen should his brother be left without a family, without a country, without protection of any kind. He only has an imagination, and his imagination gives him some idea of what it means to be truly alone in the world. To slip through the cracks, so to speak, and fall down into whatever lies underneath all of this, into that dark wilderness.

"You'll get in, I think," he says.

"Maybe," says his brother.

"If not, then not."

"I'll do what I choose," says Gevy.

It's the best he can expect. Niko is satisfied.

"Okay," he says.

"What *I* choose."

"Of course you will," says Niko.

He notices that Gevy's face is red. He feels okay, or so he says, but he looks flushed. Niko will keep an eye on this.

*   *   *

For the first few hours at sea, everything goes according to plan. The ship is a coaster, a small cargo ship with a crew of six, plus the seal team, plus the cargo, plus the seals. The seal crates are kept in a room below the rear deck and are held under quarantine, as much as they can be under these circumstances, which is not much. No humans are permitted to interact with the seals or approach within ten yards of the crates except the seal team, and every member of the team has received a compound cocktail of flu vaccines, whereas the rest of the crew has received only the standard dose. The team members open the seal crates once a day to feed and check the health of their charges. Otherwise all elements of the room—temperature, light, and air quality—are controlled remotely and by timers. Cameras in each tank transmit a visual feed of the seals to monitors elsewhere in the ship, where they're watched by the seal team at all times. The Azerbaijani crew shows little interest in the seals, so enforcing compliance with the quarantine is not difficult.

At this point the seals do nothing except eat, paddle in the shallow pools of water at the end of their crates, and bark at one another through their ventilation slats. None of them has yet shown signs of declining health. These four have been very lucky. But at any moment their luck is expected to run out.

All over the northwestern United States, across Canada, northern Europe, and anywhere else that seals and people come in contact, dead pinnipeds have been washing up on shores in decaying, bloated heaps, astonishing the residents of coastal towns who never believed the sea could hold so many seals, and certainly never imagined that this entire unseen population could be heaved up from its unseen civilization and discarded along miles of shoreline like so much slick-furred, glistening detritus. In some places the bodies have become a serious municipal problem.

But the ones washing up on those shores are common species, mostly crabeater and harbor seals. As devastated as their numbers may become before the epidemic is contained, they still don't warrant the same concern as the more endangered animals, the giant walruses and the Steller sea lions and of course the Caspian seals.

The sea is a dangerous world. Its pleasures are few and its difficulties are many, but it's where they belong. Complete international agreement has been secured on this matter from all parties involved. Except of course from the seals themselves, who don't know anything about it.

*   *   *

Mills was transferred to the Philadelphia seal team in July, after the closing of a small animal show in northern Idaho. The ten trained California sea lions featured in the show were loaded into rented vans and released from an island off the coast of Seattle. Mills was an outside specialist on that project, a hired biologist-consultant employed by UMG Biological Consulting Services, which may or may not technically exist. The show in Idaho never existed either, but this background information was not thoroughly checked by the zoo, if it was checked at all. The seals are a liability, and the zoo wants to be rid of them. Now that the task has been handed off to the EPA, which subcontracts the releasing work, and the seals are gone, the zoo can rest easy. Mills showed up in Philadelphia on a Thursday and was gone a month later, onto a plane with the seals and now onto a boat, where his references are no longer a concern to anyone. Except of course to Dr. Yin, sent by the EPA, who is not really a doctor of anything.

When evening arrives Dr. Yin calls the team together for a meeting. They are in a room in the forecastle of the boat, seated on two sides of a table that unfolds from a wall.

"Can you tell us now why we're here, for real?" says Lavecchia.

Jones interrupts before Yin can answer.

"We're here for the seals," says Jones.

The objective of their mission seems to be changing shape from one minute to the next, but even as this happens Jones has stubbornly maintained that the seals come first. He has worked closely with the seals for eight years, is the vice president of the Philadelphia Caspian Seal Conservation Society, and loves CS 1 through 4 more than he has loved most people in his life.

"We're here for the seals," says Dr. Yin. "Yes. But these are complicated times. And as you now know, we have two additional passengers on board."

She says she will introduce Niko and Gevy after the two of them have finished the chicken stew and corn cake they are eating in the galley with the cook standing by. They have not had a proper meal since the night before.

"We'll have them with us for a few days," says Mills.

"And then what?" says Lavecchia.

"Then we won't anymore."

A few hours earlier, as the ship left the harbor and the cameras were turned on,

Mills went belowdecks to the seal room. There he slid open the big drawer under CS 2 and helped Niko out by the arm. From the drawer under CS 3 he extracted Gevy, who swore and insisted that his arms and legs and hands and feet had all fallen asleep. Mills was relieved to see Gevy unharmed. Mills likes Gevy. Mills always likes difficult children.

Jones and Lavecchia are debriefed on everything they need to know, which is not much. They are given the schedule details for that night and the next morning. Then they are dismissed.

The two of them are standing on the deck a few minutes later. They share a flask and stare at the sea, which is to say, at nothing.

Jones rubs his beard with the back of his hand.

"Can you believe this shit?" he says.

Lavecchia can believe it. Of course she can. This kind of thing has happened on several of these missions, as far as she is aware. Just never on hers.

"We're like secret agents or something," she says. "Just think of it that way."

"Not us," says Jones.

"Nothing is ever easy," Lavecchia says.

Night falls. The moon rises over the sea. The lights of Baku are fading, but the clouds in that part of the sky still glow from beneath.

Dr. Yin has seen the children to their bunks and joined Mills for a conference call from the radio room. Now Mills has left for bed as well and she is alone in the room typing notes.

The children will be bored for a few days, but she is prepared for this. If they can be kept out of trouble, they will not need to be confined to one part of the ship. She wants to avoid any suffering on their part or any suggestion of coercion or mistreatment. So long as they do not interfere with the seal project or the functioning of the ship, they will do as they like. The older one seems well-behaved and the younger one has not been unmanageable.

Dr. Yin has a responsibility. According to the laws by which she lives, responsibility is paramount, and she is now delivering two children to sanctuary and thus playing a small role in the protection of relations between the U.S. and a tiny de facto nation until recently unrecognized by the Western world.

She is taking the two of them to a cargo pier in Kazakhstan. There they will be handed over to someone else, who will put them on a private plane to Rostov. At that point, if the Russians honor their commitments, they will be safe, presumably. At least for a while, and at least safer than they are now.

They were relocated to the United States first, but they've been unable to gain permanent legal asylum there. It's been determined that the appearance of U.S. partiality would strain fragile diplomatic relations across the oil-rich Transcaucasus, and the risk is untenable. Denial of asylum has left the children with no options but deportation back to their own country, where Yin's handlers believe that the populace would not respond well to their presence. So, to avoid this, they have been transported out of the U.S. in secret compartments hidden under the rarest animals in the world, animals who receive deference as they cross international borders, it being assumed everywhere the seals travel that science serves a higher purpose than politics.

As far as most people who knew them know, they have simply disappeared. The school has a cover story to provide to those who ask. The host family has its own role to play. Disappearance is not so unusual; Yin knows this. It happens more often than one might think. The puzzled outcry over Niko and Gevy, if it happens at all, will be minimal.

Their father has disappeared as well, and in his case the puzzled outcry has led to an international manhunt. These days, self-governing nations everywhere voice strong support for the small country he nearly destroyed. They invest great capital in the belief that if everyone approaches the democratic experiment in good faith, then even in a place like Karabakh—especially in places like Karabakh—peace will always prevail. Though the country exists on ancient soil and its people embrace ancient traditions, it is nevertheless very young. Like all youthful things, it is beamed upon. And as long as the energy for ferocity holds out, its detractors are pursued ferociously.

But. Both inside and outside of these kinds of metaphors, children are still children. The two on this boat will be granted respect for their vulnerability and lack of involvement. Dr. Yin will see to this. In the general sense, she is helping a fragile young democracy find its footing, tempering the escalation of its troubles. And in the specific sense, she is sending the nonimplicated children of a warlord, a murderer, and the betrayer of a nation to safety and some version of a normal life.

Her mission is just and correct—she wouldn't be doing it otherwise. At least, she likes to think she wouldn't. Everyone has a job to do in this world. Everyone has a purpose. She is their shepherd. She closes her files and brings the day to an end.

The Azerbaijani crew members are playing cards elsewhere on the ship, and Yin can hear them through the walls. One of them is shouting, he's on some kind of rant, and the others are laughing as they calm him.

In the morning, the children are introduced to the seals through the monitors in the observation room. Niko listens with fascination to the story of each one, to the details of their histories and personalities. They are like dogs, he decides. Like fat, happy dogs with flippers instead of legs. He watches them flail and bark and mug at the cameras. They even have tails, little dog tails, which he hadn't known until now.

Jones is sitting in a chair beside him, telling him what the seals eat and what they like and what they do. On the screen, they can see Lavecchia opening one of the crates and reaching her gloved arms in. She seizes a flipper and takes a pulse and then a blood sample. She pauses in her work to give the camera a thumbs-up. She is wearing a mask, but under the mask she's probably smiling. Niko smiles back even though she can't see him.

These are not Azerbaijani seals. They are not Iranian seals, either, or Russian seals. They are American seals. They have been in Philadelphia for every day of their lives, splashing in a glass tank and hauling themselves out of the water onto fiberglass rocks. They know one home. They speak one language. They have never been hurt. They have never gone hungry. And they have never, even for one day, been alone. Jones says this with gravity.

"They don't know what it's like," he says, "not to be cared for. They don't know what they're supposed to do. They probably don't even know exactly what they are."

"They don't know what they are?" says Gevy. "That's stupid. They're seals."

Jones nods absently.

"That's true. But it never mattered to them before. Now they have to figure that out, and do it quick, or they'll die."

"Can we pet them?" says Gevy.

"Oh, no. They've been too close to you already. From now on, it's just us in there. Sorry."

Gevy loses interest. He wants to explore more of the ship. Niko follows him out of the room.

"Thanks," he says to Jones on his way out the door.

Jones doesn't look up from the monitor. He does not appear to have heard.

Later that afternoon, Niko goes belowdecks for a while. He is looking for a quiet place to do some writing. He has some half-finished things that he would like to work on, and now he walks along a slim corridor holding the pads of paper and the pen provided to him earlier by Mary.

His poems have been about destiny and grand things lately, and the idea of a life with purpose. But Niko is having trouble shaping these themes to his satisfaction. This is probably because he expects to die soon. He has felt this way since he left for the United States; each passing day has not diminished the feeling. If he does not die, then he will have to do something else, and he has no idea what that might be. But it should be something important. He is fascinated by important things, important lives. Who isn't?

He flips his pen around his fingers, then attempts to do it again and drops the pen.

When he reaches down to retrieve it, he feels a rush of nausea. The feeling does not subside immediately.

Some time passes and it becomes evident to Niko that something is wrong with him. There is a tightness and a grimness clenching the hinge of his jaw and exhausting him beyond all hope of restoration.

His heart is troubled, he decides. The time rolls out in front of them now, after all, a new terror waiting within every hour. He and Gevy are on a boat in the sea, small and exposed, and the world is four shades of gray extending in all directions to eternity.

Niko worsens. He begins to feel as if he will never want food again.

He throws up several times. The scientists check in on him. They think he is seasick. And maybe he is. He's never been at sea this long. His country is landlocked.

* * *

A few hours pass, and Niko recovers. Eventually he can move again. This mystifies and pleases him. With slow steps at first, he makes his way out onto the deck. The sun feels good.

He sees his brother leaning against a rail at the edge, spitting and then following the spit with his eyes, squinting in the wind. Mills stands at the rail next to Gevy, leaning and squinting also.

"You know," Niko overhears him say, "when I was your age, we used to spit forward into the wind. When we were on boats. Then we would dodge the spit."

Gevy is uninterested.

"Yeah," he says. "That's... great."

Mills shrugs under this rejection and soldiers on.

"Well, we liked it. It was fun."

A few times now Mills has invested short bursts of effort into befriending Gevy. Mills seems to like the idea of making a difference in the life of a child, especially a bad child. Imparting wisdom and judgment and leaving the child with a character altered for the better. It appears that Mills does not have children of his own.

Niko does not interfere with his efforts. He walks past the two of them on his way to the observation room. He finds Lavecchia there.

She waves him over as he comes in.

"Is anything happening?" he says.

Lavecchia points to the screen.

CS 4, the pup, is mouthing the curved wrist of his left flipper. He muddles the flipper between his whiskery lips, soaking the fur with drool. Then he switches to the right flipper and gives it the same treatment.

"Flipper sucking," says Lavecchia.

"What does it mean?"

"It's a sign of stress. Especially in pups."

"Is he sick?" says Niko. He feels a new sympathy for the sick.

"No, it's not that, thank God," says Lavecchia. "Only what you would expect. Anxiety. He's comforting himself."

Lavecchia and Niko watch the seal in silence for a while. The camera is attached to a microphone, and they can hear the soft sound of CS 4's mournful, repetitive slurps.

"I wish we could always watch them like this," says Niko. "I mean, it would be good to know if they survive or not."

"Oh, we can do that," says Lavecchia.

"How?"

Lavecchia glances up at him and then back at the screen before answering.

"They have satellite tracking devices implanted in them. Subcutaneously. As long as we have all four tracking signals, we know where they are. We can't do anything for them, but at least we know."

"I thought that was illegal," says Niko.

"It is," says Lavecchia. "Jones and I did it ourselves. As long as we're the only ones who know the tracking signatures, it can't hurt anything."

"But what if poachers get a hold of the signatures or something? They're worth a lot of money, aren't they?"

"We decided it's a risk we're willing to take," says Lavecchia.

"Just the two of you?"

"Yeah."

"No one else knows?"

"Nope."

Niko watches Lavecchia's expression in the glow of the screen. She is casual about this defiance of international law. Contemptuous, even. But she hasn't made the decision lightly. This is clear.

Niko shrugs. It is not his business. Besides, he likes Lavecchia, and if he feels anything, it is pleasure that she trusts him with this secret.

"Two more days," she says to the video monitor. "Not much longer now, little friend."

CS 4 is back at work on his right flipper. The repetitive sucking sound is broken only by soft little sniffs and growls, a lonely conversation with himself in the quiet of his crate.

Evening, and the off-duty crew members have been enticed into a game of nines and sevens with the scientists and Niko and Gevy. The cards have been dealt and a stereo in the corner plays the first album, a local classic, by Hovhanisyan-B, the rising Armenian rap star. It is wild music for such a small, close room. Niko has not been drinking, but most of the others have. Gevy looks over Niko's shoulder and comments on his hand. Niko pulls the hand away.

Lavecchia begins the round by laying down four eights. Mills raises an eyebrow and trumps her hand by picking up two of the four and laying down three other cards, which causes a howl among the crew members. Gevy is next and lays down a five. Yin hands it back to him, explaining that fives are silver. He can lay a nine if he has one—nines are gold. Does he have a nine? Gevy's forehead furrows. The rules of this game are complicated. He is already losing, and he's getting embarrassed and angry.

"Don't worry," says Niko. "You can collect the stack later if you pass on this round."

Gevy passes, appeased. The tattooed second mate with one ear is up next. He shows his nine and gathers all the cards, winking at Lavecchia. Everybody laughs except Gevy.

An hour passes and then another. Gevy nearly wins the third round but falters on his last turn and Mills takes the cards that would have been his. The adults in the room are gentle with Gevy, of course, but Niko recognizes the black cloud gathering over his brother and knows it will soon be time to excuse themselves and go to bed.

As he is considering this and the next set of cards are skimming around the table, Gevy coughs.

It happens just once, and it is quick and dry, more like a nervous tic than a cough. But silence falls over the room.

"What do you think?" Yin asks Lavecchia after a minute.

"We'll keep an eye on it," says Lavecchia. "If it happens again, we have a mask he can wear. He'll keep his hands clean. He's already been vaccinated. Not much more we can do, I think. At least until tomorrow."

"We can do more."

"Yes," says Lavecchia. "But it could be anything. We'll worry about it if it happens again. Jones would have a heart attack, but Jones isn't here."

Jones is in the observation room, where he spends almost all of his time now. He leaves the room only to eat and sleep.

"Make sure he stays clean," says Lavecchia to Niko.

Gevy cringes at this, and Niko wishes it had not been said.

"Right," he says.

It is time for the evening to end.

*   *   *

It is dark in the bedroom except for the glowing numbers of the digital clock. Niko, sleeping until just now, is awake. The bunk above him is silent, and as he thinks about it he recalls the sound of Gevy climbing down a moment ago and putting on his shoes.

His bed is comfortable and the air is cold. But as he has done many times before and knows he must do again, Niko drags himself from comfort and goes forth to follow his brother out into the dark world, to find out what he is doing and set right whatever has gone wrong during Niko's lapse of vigilance.

His instincts lead him to the seal room. He finds Gevy there, standing by the door.

"Come on," Niko says simply. "Let's go."

"I want to pet them," says Gevy.

"What?"

"I want to pet them. Before they're gone."

"Gevy," says Niko.

"What?"

"Leave the door alone. Go back to bed."

"No. I want to see them at least."

"It would kill them. You know that. Besides, you don't know the door code."

As he says this, Gevy bends down and pokes at the keypad. The door clicks open.

Niko is a few yards away from his brother. He could close the distance quickly. But if he makes a sudden move Gevy will be inside the room by the time Niko reaches him. And then Gevy is in the room.

Niko follows. In the altered light he sees something he didn't see before.

"What's that?"

"What?"

"In your hand. Is that meat?"

There is something wrapped inside the meat, some sharp thing like wire.

"It's nothing."

Gevy is smiling at CS 2 now, who lies belly up, awake. One clawed flipper is scratching an itch on CS 2's speckled chest. The other is suspended at his side as if he's making a lazy point.

CS 2 rolls over and looks up hopefully at the object in Gevy's hand. He presses his whiskered snout against the slats of his crate. His eyes are black pools, deep and wet and featureless.

Niko reviews his options.

Years ago, Niko and Gevy sat on the terrace of their villa watching a cat dismember a mouse, a process that took some time. The cat's head inclined aristocratically. She was a picture of casual grace. The mouse ran out from under her paw and she brought it back twice and then a third time, more grievously injured at each repetition. And then the real work began.

It took some disturbing incidents over the course of the next few weeks for Niko to process this episode for little Gevy. Gevy didn't understand that what is reasonable behavior for an animal is not reasonable for a person. He could not see how a cat stands above and apart from himself, and how power and nature hold their form in one place and elsewhere are not transferable.

Their conversations on the subject were thoughtful and structured, and Niko remembers them as a kind of poetry. Niko has considered this several times since then while at work on his own poems. He does not want the lines he writes to be so heavily weighed down with children—how we teach our children about the world and things like that. But then, he is asking himself now, what else is poetry for?

Niko speaks to Gevy in their own language.

"You aren't really like this," he says.

"Whatever."

"You aren't this kind of person."

"How do you know?"

"And besides, you get nothing out of it."

"Who cares what I get out of it?"

"I do."

As they speak, the door stands open. Niko wonders how many air molecules cross the threshold per second. A hundred million? He reaches for a point of reference. There are three quarters of a million people in his country.

It occurs to him, as it often does, that his father has looked into the eyes of many of these men and women, looked right into their eyes. And still things went the way they did. Nothing intervened. Nothing stepped forward to complete that broken circuit of recognition.

Niko has had enough.

He says his brother's full name, including the parts of the name that they share. He says it is time to walk away now.

And of course, Gevy does. Niko observes this ordinary miracle with the same wonder and amusement that he has felt a hundred times before, always at the moment when his brother abandons some sadistic project and comes unexpectedly to heel. Gevy presses the meat into Niko's extended hand and ambles back down the hall, finished with this adventure and ready for sleep.

Niko has suspected before, and he knows now—he knows this for sure now that they are on their own—that he is on this earth for a reason. The person beside him is his holy charge. He may have no other holy charge as long as he lives. And if so then so. Everybody has a job to do in this world. Everybody has a purpose.

Gevy trots down the corridor a few steps ahead of him like a shaggy pony, back to bed, and Niko follows behind. Just as he will tomorrow, and the next day, and the day after that. If they live, which they will. They will live and live and live. He knows this now, and he is prepared.

Not everyone on the boat is asleep. Mills and Jones are standing on the foredeck, the card game over and Jones having completed the last of his paperwork for the night. These two have little common ground on which to build a conversation, and so they have moved in some odd directions over the last few minutes. They have discussed the difficulty of predicting the weather, then the importance of family, and now they are reviewing the season's prospects for Manchester United. Jones is trying to be personable, but he is wondering why Mills continues to stand here casting about for conversation instead of going to bed.

Not that he minds. If not for this encounter, he would probably be out here pacing the deck alone.

"How's that pup?" says Mills, finally.

He has been leading up to this for some time, Jones suspects, moving by degrees toward the seals. What else is there to talk about? The seals are the obvious object of Jones's preoccupation. He can't help it. It's his job.

"4? He'll be okay," says Jones. "They're sensitive to stress at that age."

"Sure, oh sure," says Mills.

And then Mills says an unexpected thing. He says that he and Yin know about the devices implanted in the seals. They know about them, but they don't intend to report them. What's done is done. The devices can't be taken out, and soon it won't matter anyway.

Jones tries to control the expression on his face. He affects only the mildest of interest.

"Great," he says. "That's great. Thanks."

"But you should know," Mills says, "what you've done here. I mean, you should know the full extent of it. The danger you're putting them into. And us, in the meantime. The kids."

"We're the only ones that have the tracking signatures," says Jones.

"Listen," says Mills. "This kind of technology—we're familiar with it. It's not as difficult to crack as you might think."

Jones shrugs. He doubts this. But he's not surprised to hear it, coming from Mills.

Of course Mills is familiar with this kind of technology. Of course. He's only known Mills for a few weeks, but during that time it's become evident that for a secret agent or whatever he is, Mills has a great deal to say about the things he knows and what he knows about them. Right now he's also slightly drunk, and he looks like he might reach out at any moment and pat Jones on the back. Jones is becoming annoyed.

There's something sad and clownish about Mills. It's clear that he's a company man, and to Jones his loyalty to his organization is embarrassing. Underneath the self-important secrecy, Mills doesn't really seem to know why he's out here ferrying these kids around and preempting everything Jones has worked for all his life. If he did, it would show.

"Yes, well," says Jones. He rubs his beard. "Being unlikely to ever have another chance, we decided it was for the best. Besides, what do you care? As soon as we drop them off, they're gone. Not your concern anymore. The kids are safe. Everybody's safe. We each have our jobs to do out here and this isn't really yours, right?"

"True," says Mills.

"We're biologists," says Jones. "Real ones."

"Sure. I get that."

They are silent for a while.

Then Mills says, "We just thought you could help us to help you."

"What?" says Jones.

"In exchange for us keeping it quiet, I mean."

"Oh," says Jones. "I see. Right. No. Of course not."

"Well. Think it over. We could do a lot with that information. A lot of good."

"Like what?"

"Well—that's not really our area. But it could be used to find poachers, and… apprehend them. Not by us, per se, but we would pass it along to the divisions that would be able to—"

"Please. Don't patronize me. And if it's so easy, why don't you crack it yourselves?"

"You could save us the trouble."

"Right. Okay."

"Look—the more control we have over these kinds of things, the more information we have, the better it works out for everyone."

"Plus there's all the money."

"That's not what I'm about."

"I didn't say it was."

Mills removes a knit cap from his coat pocket, a longshoreman's hat. He fidgets with it before pulling it on over his head.

"Let me put it like this," he says. "Say you had the ability to negotiate with some very bad people. Like you had something to offer them in exchange for information that might—let's say it would stop a boatload of heroin from reaching shore. You would do it, right?"

"So that's your plan? Trading them for something else?"

"No. There's no plan. And I'm asking you as a favor."

"Are you finished?"

"I'm just saying. If there's anything you can do to help us out, you should do it."

"No thanks."

"And this could help us out."

"I said no."

Mills, in his bed a while later, does not sleep well.

He is cold. Also his back hurts. And when he does drift off for a few minutes at a time, he has bad dreams. Mills does not believe his dreams have anything to tell him—no grim angels are actually standing over his bed staring down at him while he sleeps. He's just cold. He studies the ceiling light fixture, which sways with the motion of the ship. In this place, nothing is ever perfectly still.

When Mills first began this assignment he identified strongly with Gevy, which made the work easier and also more difficult. Gevy was fully formed in his passionate, snarling little way, and something about him made Mills feel protective.

But Mills has come a long way since then. He can't afford to be one of these people like Jones, these irritating people who don't know how to separate one thing from another, who feel responsible for the fate of the universe and think it all sits on a single pin. Mills lets go of things when it's time to let go.

It's better this way. He's a realist.

The following morning. The team meets for a status update. Lavecchia reports that the pup is showing signs of congestion. His nose and tear glands appear to be emitting the telltale fluid that signifies influenza.

Yin solicits recommendations. Jones and Lavecchia suggest an extension of the observation period. The adult seals can be released this afternoon as planned and the pup can be kept onboard for an additional day or so in case the symptoms progress.

Yin says no.

"What's the problem?" says Lavecchia. "We're ahead of schedule."

"Your tracking devices are the problem," says Yin. "We need to let go of these animals and get away from them as soon as possible. I'm sorry about the pup, but we have other things to take into account."

"Are you serious?"

"Yes."

"We're not dropping a sick seal into the ocean and driving away."

"Look," says Mills. "Don't make this into a crusade. It's better for everyone if you don't do that."

"Nobody's coming after us," says Lavecchia. "We would have seen them by now."

"It's not a risk we can take. Do you realize what these people have been through?"

"Do I—look, if this one lives, that improves the odds for the whole species by about three hundred percent. If it dies, that's the end. It's extinction."

"Stop saying that."

"Stop sabotaging our work!"

The intercom in the room clicks on.

"There's a boat," says the captain.

Silence follows. The captain is a man of few words.

Yin reaches for the button on the intercom.

"What?" she says.

"There's a boat here," says the captain again. "You should probably come up."

When the four of them reach the control room, they find the captain there. Niko and Gevy are there as well. They are gazing through the window and across the bow of the coaster through a pair of binoculars passed between them.

Sure enough, beyond the haul-out where they intend to release the seals, there is a dhow, a small one. They have not seen another vessel in this part of the sea for quite some time.

"Can you radio them?" says Yin.

"Ah. If you mean call them on the BOS transmitter, then yes. But they are not responding. They are just sitting there."

"Are they fishing?"

"No."

"Well, we can't put the seals down with them sitting right there."

"No."

"But we don't have the authority to move them."

"Okay."

The captain shows no expression. The children are shifting from foot to foot, and Jones and Lavecchia are conversing in the silent language they must have learned from so many years working with animals who communicate underwater.

"We'll just... wait them out. For now."

"For now, we wait. Okay."

An hour passes. Scudding clouds move by overhead.

Jones decides that the end of the world is always here, all the time, in one way or another. There are always a few people who get to see it before it goes. Some people who are luckier than others.

The smaller boat motors off by a few hundred yards. It stays there for a while, and then it motors back.

"You have guns and stuff, right?" he says to Yin.

"Not really, no."

"I thought you were… special forces or something."

"We aren't that kind."

"Then what kind are you?"

"Not that kind."

Again and again Yin decides to move forward with this project, and then she hesitates. In a quiet, wide-open place like this it's often easier to wait than to do.

What if the seals, as a species, can't be saved? What if a small nation falters and its name becomes a geographic distinction rather than a political one? What if long ago her life had taken an entirely different turn? What if not one thing in the world can be predicted and not one element of this scenario makes any goddamn sense at all?

The last question is her favorite.

She looks at the sky, like Jones is doing. She tries to follow his eyes to whatever he is staring at. There it is, far up there. Some kind of bird.

It is Gevy who breaks the longest of the silences.

"I don't think they're moving," he says. "I think they're waiting for us."

Yin agrees. She asks the biologists what they would like to do.

All eyes turn to Jones.

"We'll let them go," he says. "If it's too late, it's too late."

"We can stay for a little while," says Yin, "before we move on. It will give them a chance to swim away, at least. For what it's worth."

"Okay then," says Lavecchia, looking to her partner. "Let's go."

A half an hour later, a small motorboat has been lowered into the water. Four cages have been placed on its floor, and in each cage is a seal. Masked and gloved, Jones and Lavecchia take their places in the boat, and then the motor buzzes to life. A wake of froth takes shape behind them as they plow through the water and away to the distant rocks of the haul-out.

The rest is visible only through binoculars.

Niko watches the biologists lift the cages out and place them on the ground. Gevy watches, silent. The ship crew and Mills and Yin watch. From the fishing boat, it is clear that someone else is watching as well. And this is the last any of them will see of the Caspian seals, singular among all life in the known world.

Before the plane reached Baku a few days ago, Yin looked down from the window at Mount Ararat, the landing place of Noah's ark. After decades on the other side of the Turkish border, it belongs to Armenia now. Karabakh is independent, with all the burdens of independence. Azerbaijan is hosting an international conference this year on zoonotic pathogens. She never thought this world would occur in her lifetime, but here it is.

The seals wubble out of their crates, one by one, and gaze to the left and the right. Then two of them, 1 and 3, head for the water as if they know exactly what to do. The other two are slower. They dip their flippers in first, just like people. But soon they are immersed and their confused heads are rising from the surface of the water like nothing so much as seal heads rising from the surface of water. They move up and down with the rhythm of the waves as smoothly as if they were attached to pistons. It is impossible to tell if they are happy. Then they are gone.

Gevy searches the sea, waiting for the seals to reappear, then turns to Niko and says something. Niko holds the binoculars for him with one hand and points with the other. For a moment, they could be any ordinary children. This is how Yin would like to remember them.

All favors have ended now and so have all obligations. This is not the way the world works, but then sometimes it is, Yin decides. Not everything is connected. It is a relief, in some ways, to decide this.

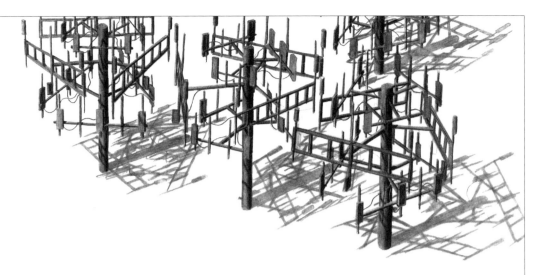

THERE IS NO TIME
IN WATERLOO

by SHEILA HETI
conceived with MARGAUX WILLIAMSON

EVERYONE IN WATERLOO was an amateur physicist, and they endlessly
bugged the real physicists as the physicists sat in cafés talking to each
other. The amateurs would approach and put questions to them; simple
questions, obvious ones. Or else they asked questions that even a physicist couldn't
answer, or questions that weren't in the realm of physics at all, but had more to
do with biology or straight computation. People who know almost nothing about
what they're talking about are often more enthusiastic than the ones who know a
lot, so they do all the talking, while the ones who know their stuff stay silent and
get red in the face.

Whenever a real physicist would start to correct or explain a point, the amateur would smile and nod, and loudly proclaim that they'd read something about
that in a magazine or a book recently. Then they would start to explain and the
physicist would listen, tight-lipped, or else abruptly put an end to the conversation in frustration.

Then the physicist would return to the Perimeter Institute, which was built on
the top of a gently sloping hill, and sigh in relief to be home again, standing at the
chalkboard, working out equations.

*   *   *

One afternoon in March, a rumor went around town that some boy's Mothers had predicted that a kid was going to blow up the mall on the left side of town, so all the teenagers got on their scooters and sped off toward the parking lot there.

As Sunni was leaving her apartment, her mother called out from her usual place on the couch and asked where she was going. Sunni returned and explained about the rumor, and admitted that she was really eager to see the mall be blown up; that she and her friends had so much pent-up energy—they were wild with energy, and simply couldn't wait.

Sunni's mother felt a bit of regret that Sunni was going to watch the mall explode, but she didn't object; after all, if that was Sunni's destiny, who was she to interfere?

At the mall the teenagers spoke excitedly with each other, drawing together and apart, eager for the show to begin. They asked around to discover whose Mothers had predicted the explosion, but no one seemed to know. When, after an hour and a half, the mall remained standing, undisturbed, they started checking their Mothers to see if they were the one destined to blow it up. It appeared that none of them were.

Now they began to grow tense and upset. It was not the first time something like this had happened. The week before, some boy's Mothers had predicted a fight, but no one had thrown the first punch. A month ago, there was supposed to have been an orgy in the back of the other mall, the nice one, but after standing around awhile they had checked their Mothers and learned that the probability of their participating in an orgy was really low.

It started to rain, as a weatherman had predicted. Dispirited, the teenagers began to drift off. Only Sunni and a few of her friends remained, to finish the conversation they'd been having about film. They each had their own distinct opinions about art, but came together in agreement that drama was an inaccurate reflection of life; the best stories followed the path of greatest likelihood. Indeed, when you thought about the best stories down through time, their greatness and terror came from the fact that the most predictable and most probable thing always occurred.

"Like in Oedipus," Sunni said. And in that moment, one of Sunni's friends tossed a match into the air, having just used it to light his cigarette. It landed smack on Sunni's Mothers, igniting a little flame.

"Oh, *fuck!*" Sunni cried, batting her Mothers into the air. It arced, smoking, and dropped onto the pavement.

"Oh my God, Sunni—is your Mothers dead?" Danny gasped.

"Nope! Nope! Luckily no!" Sunni replied, picking it up. It was burning hot, and she tossed it from hand to hand. Looking down at it as it cooled, she saw that the screen had been melted into a squinty little eye. The keys were matted down to their wires, and the casing was tarry and charred.

"Still works!" Sunni announced. Then she got onto her scooter, feeling like she was about to faint, and rode to the parking lot around the other side of the mall, her Mothers propped up against the windshield. She kept glancing down at it, but no glance transformed it from the twisted, charry mess it had been in the glance before.

In the back parking lot, she stopped her scooter and got off and doubled over, hyperventilating a bit, then ran a distance to throw up. When she returned to her scooter and saw her Mothers there, she was overtaken by another spell of dizziness. It wasn't clear yet whether this was the worst, most tragic thing that had ever happened to her, or if this was the most exciting moment of her life. She only knew that she had never felt such vertigo before, and upon asking herself what to do now, then glancing down reflexively at her Mothers for the answer, she was overwhelmed by vertigo once more.

Twenty years earlier, the citizens of Waterloo had become enthralled by a book written by a physicist who had been invited to spend some time working at Perimeter. The book was called *The End of Time*, and its author, Julian Barbour, had argued in a persuasive and beautiful way that time did not exist; that the universe was static. There were a slightly less than infinite number of possible futures hanging about, like paintings in an attic, all real but out of reach, and each person's destiny was nothing more and nothing less than the most probable of those possible futures.

The people most taken with this idea led fervent discussions on how best to realize the theory in one's own life. Like humans anywhere, they didn't want to waste time. They hoped to reach their destinies as quickly and efficiently as possible—not their ultimate destinies, just their penultimate ones. And so it made sense to try and act as much in accordance with probability as they could.

The executives at the BlackBerry headquarters in Waterloo decided they would capitalize on this desire, and they began producing a machine they tagged *The Mother of All BlackBerrys*. It remained a phone you could email from, but it had an added, special feature: given ongoing inputs, it was calibrated to determine for each user what they were destined to do next.

"It will be a device that determines a person's most likely next action based on previous behaviors. If the input is one's life, then the outcome is one's life," an executive explained to the rest as they sat around a table.

"Brilliant!" said another executive, reaching for a Danish. And they all reached for Danishes, and toasted each other, smiling.

The Mothers—as people began calling them—were at once a huge success. They eclipsed everything in the culture at that moment, like any great fad down through time. People in Waterloo consulted their Mothers at every turn, and it quickly became as impossible to live without a Mothers as it had once been to not check email. People wondered how they had managed their lives before their Mothers. They bought Mothers for their babies.

If life became somewhat more predictable as a result, it was also more comforting, and soon the citizens of Waterloo didn't even notice that they were going in circles; that it was always the same thing over and over again.

The physicists, though nominally to blame for the proliferation of the Mothers, were largely skeptical and had a hundred doubts. It was not unusual to be standing in a supermarket line and hear one of them testily provoke and challenge an amateur physicist who was checking his Mothers, if the physicist was having a particularly bad day. "So do these Mothers calculate quantum or classical probabilities?" the physicist might ask; a question over which the amateur might stumble, only to regain his footing upon consulting his Mothers about whether continuing the conversation would be to his benefit, to which the Mothers would reply that the probability was low.

*   *   *

What will Sunni do without her Mothers? I sometimes ask myself a similar question. What would I do if I didn't know what was to come? If the inputs of my past were to disappear, I'd have no idea how I'd behaved in relationships past, and would not know how to behave in them now. I would play it all differently, not knowing how I was most likely to play it. I might forget how much I once hated to be on a soccer pitch, and how I had avoided soccer ever since. I might, while lounging in a park, say to the soccer players, while rising, *Do you need an extra player?*

If you draw a line across a piece of paper, that is King Street. Now draw a small, perpendicular line crossing King Street near the center. That is Princess Street. That is the part of town where the losers, misfits, and orphans hang out. It's where someone crosses the street drunk, and someone else crosses the street with ripped jeans and a lazy eye.

On either end of King Street, draw a square. These are the two malls. The mall at the right end of town is in the richer neighborhood, near the Perimeter Institute, the University, and the Institute for Quantum Computing—all the institutions representing the heights of Waterloo's excellence. The other mall, the one that the teenagers gathered at, is situated near the Old Town Hospital, City Hall, and the more run-down establishments that deal with the humanities and the human body.

Now watch Sunni speed along the long line of King Street, arriving within minutes at Princess.

"No," said one of the physicists, standing in the park under the gazebo, to the twenty-odd citizens picnicking around her. "We *don't* all believe that time is static."

The picnickers smiled up at the physicist. They continued to eat their bread and sandwiches and throw their strawberries into the grass.

Sunni was like all her friends. And all her friends were like Sunni. Their machines resembled the part of the brain that sees patterns and nothing but patterns. To that part of the brain, everything fits. There is no randomness to life, no chance. If ever their Mothers missed something, or something not predicted occurred, they would correct for the future, learning from what happened and fitting this new thing into a better, more complete image of the whole. In this way, if not everything was already accounted for, Sunni and her friends had faith that in time all would be. Life would proceed as anticipated. One had only to walk the determined path.

Sunni had always avoided Princess Street, since only losers hung out there. But since nearly every teenager whose Mothers broke somehow wound up on Princess, it was where she decided to go. She still had the instincts of someone with a Mothers, and wanted to waste no time before moving on to the likeliest next stage of her destiny. She parked her scooter and walked straight into one of the bars, pushing its red door open.

Two teenagers she had never seen before were sitting on tall stools, smoking and drinking, and upon entering Sunni could hear them whisper: *Doesn't she look like Shelly? No, but she reminds me a lot of my grade-four gym teacher. Actually, today in its entirety reminds me a lot of grade four.*

She went to perch on the stool beside them, and then she said hi. They regarded her blankly. Without waiting for a sign of their interest, she explained that she had lost her Mothers that day.

The boy nodded solemnly. He knew that once your Mothers is dead, it's gone for good. The factory had shut down seven years before due to lack of any demand for the Mothers beyond Waterloo, and not a single repair shop in town knew how to fix the machines.

The boy explained that the very same thing had happened to him four years ago, but told Sunni not to worry; life would not be as different as she feared. Having said this he turned to face his friend, finishing up the anecdote he had been telling about his childhood, concluding, "And I still feel its reverberations today." Then they put down their money and began packing their bags to leave.

"Wait! Wait! Where are you going?" Sunni cried anxiously, and the boy sighed deeply and said, "Relax. Personality is as static as time; it's a fixed law. People don't change. As long as you remember that, you'll be all right. Now we have to go and write in our diaries." Then they left.

Sunni, still sitting there, glanced down at her Elders pin as it began to blink and beep.

* * *

Time is a measurement of change. The change in the position of quantum particles cannot always be known, because they don't seem to exist in any fixed spots. At the level of human bodies, we can see that time has passed because one moment I'm here at this table, the next I'm there at the stove. But at the quantum level, everything is cloudy. This is the mechanism for the disappearance of time. The people of Waterloo liked this theory because, deep down, they felt it. Their lives, in many ways, reflected it. *The End of Time* simply stamped their intuition with the air of authority and truth.

Though Sunni sped down to City Hall as soon as she received the call, she arrived a little later than everyone else, as was typical for her. The other Elders were already there, waiting for the emergency meeting to begin.

The teenagers of Waterloo, whose Mothers had been receiving inputs since the day they were born, were believed by everyone to have a more accurate grasp of what the future would bring. Compared to their Mothers, their parents' Mothers were deeply lacking: twenty, thirty years unaccounted for. So a special place in Waterloo was reserved for the teenagers. They were given much respect. They bore the official title Double Special Elders, since having a particular destiny is the essence of being Special. They were paraded about on ceremonial occasions and called in to advise the city on all the important matters.

Sunni crept quietly through the side door and up to her seat in the fourth row of the dais, which seated thirty across. Already the city's two hundred and fifty-eight native-born teens were in their seats, and they glanced at Sunni and watched her take her place, though she had tried to make her entrance subtle. The mayor, standing at the podium before them, was in the midst of explaining the current crisis, but after two minutes Sunni was still totally lost, so she whispered to the boy beside her, asking him what she had missed.

He replied quickly, "This morning Perimeter received word from Africa that all the problems in physics have been solved."

"*What?*" she whispered back. "Are you *sure?* The measurement problem and—"

"Yes, yes, *everything*," he insisted hotly. Then he rolled his eyes. "Don't ask me."

Sunni sat back in her chair, stunned. The mayor was now on to the mundane, municipal details, explaining how much it cost the city to fund the institute, claiming that it would be humiliating for Waterloo to carry on the project of physics when the field was now kaput. He gestured toward the two physicists who had come to explain the proof, should anyone want to hear it. He said that they represented the physicists who believed the institute should be kept alive—not because the African proof was wrong; it wasn't—but for reasons that he, the mayor, did not completely understand, though if one of the Elders wanted to hear their reasoning, the physicists could give it. As for the rest of the physicists, they were too preoccupied with going over the proof to attend the meeting that day.

"Would any of the Elders like to see the African proof?" the mayor asked.

Sunni looked around tentatively. No one else seemed to want to hear it, but she was interested, so she raised her hand. The mayor nodded at the physicists, and the younger of them stood and went to the whiteboard and began drawing an equation and a little diagram. He turned to the Elders and began to speak. He was only a few sentences into his elucidation when the mayor interrupted him to exclaim:

"Aha—look! It's like an earthworm praying!"

At which point the physicist violently threw his marker onto the ground and left the whiteboard and sat down beside his friend. He was too upset by the events of the day to push forward. It wasn't even so awful that a proof had been found; the pain in his heart was because of how unsatisfying a proof it was. It just wasn't the beautiful, elegant thing that everyone had been hoping for.

Sunni wanted to ask the physicists what the African proof said about the absence of time, but just as she was about to raise her hand again, the boy next to her leaned over and pointed at Sunni's Mothers, which she still reflexively clasped tightly.

"Is your Mothers *dead?*" he gasped.

Sunni, hiding it quickly under her coat, replied with feigned ease, "Nah, it's just a new sleeve. My architect friend made it. He's cool."

"I wouldn't want a sleeve that looked like that."

"Never mind."

"You should take that sleeve off."

"One day I will."

Then the mayor turned to the teenagers and asked, "Should Perimeter be closed?" In this way the voting began.

The first Elder spoke: "Yes."

The second Elder looked up from her Mothers, which knew that once you began talking about ending something, usually that thing ends. "Yes!" she said.

The third Elder spoke. "Yes."

And on and on it went: yes yes yes yes yes yes yes.

Now it was Sunni's turn. She hesitated, glancing down at the blank screen of her Mothers, which she had pulled from under her coat. It was still a twisted, black, charry mess. She took a deep breath and said very quietly, though loud enough for everyone to hear: "I am no longer Special."

Then she stood up from her place on the dais and climbed carefully down the steps. It was a humiliating walk, one others had performed before her while she had watched in pity and fear. Behind her there rose a wall of whispers; it was the world Sunni had been part of, sealing itself closed behind her.

She walked past the mayor and the physicists, toward the doors at the end of the hall. Just before she slipped out, she heard the mayor announce the tally of the vote: it was unanimous. Perimeter was to be shut down within the hour.

"Fucking teenagers," the older physicist muttered.

Sunni stepped out into the warm air of the afternoon, blinking and adjusting to the brightness of the day. She stood on the steps of City Hall, thinking nothing, a blank, faintly bewildered. Her eyes rested on a tree that stood a short distance away in the grass, and she watched it gently sway, moved by the breeze. What would move Sunni, now that her Mothers was dead? With each day, she felt, her destiny would be less and less clear, and less and less would what was probable be the law that ran her life. She tried to imagine what other law might come to replace it, but no other laws came to mind.

Perhaps, she mused, she could learn about living from this tree—let the laws that moved it move her as well. At base, she knew, she was made up of the very same particles as the tree; she must, in some sense, be treelike. She stepped down onto the lawn.

But at that moment her attention was distracted by vague sounds in the distance. She squinted her eyes; there seemed to be a lethargic parade approaching from the far end of King Street. After a moment, she realized what it was: a small tide of dejected physicists was flowing out from the doors of Perimeter. They came closer, heaving down King Street with stooped posture, dazed, carrying boxes of computers, papers and chalk, streaming toward their cars, which would take them back to the university towns from which they had come.

"How pathetic," came a small voice.

Sunni turned and noticed that sitting cross-legged beneath the tree was a scrawny boy around her own age. From the first glance she could tell that he was a loser, but such a loser he wasn't even a Princess Street loser.

"They don't have to leave," he said.

"But it's their destiny," Sunni replied. "I was in the meeting. I saw it happen."

The boy looked at her skeptically, pushing his bangs away. "Destiny? There's no destiny. These physicists don't believe in the future. Most of them don't, anyway. I know. I'm good friends with some of them."

"But—" Sunni shook her head. "If there's no destiny, how can you tell what's going to happen next?"

The boy, whose name was Raffi, frowned. He paused a moment, and then he went on to quietly explain, barely raising his voice above a whisper, so that Sunni had to move closer to hear.

He told her that last year's Bora Bora proof, which contributed to the African proof, revealed that not everything that comes to pass can be known in advance, that everything is in a continuous state of cocreation and coevolution with everything else. The universe is utterly non-computable and non-predictable—possibly not mathematical, at essence, at all. No future can exist until it exists, since we create reality together in a radically flexible present. "Things can go in different ways," he said. "The possibility of creating genuine novelty, while rare and precious, is real."

Sunni sat back hard against the tree. The Bora Bora proof was impossible! She turned her head as the Double Special Elders emerged from the tall doors of City Hall and began spreading across the lawn, moving off, heads bent low over their Mothers as they decided what to do next. She was about to say something when, in the distance, a blue spiral exploded into the sky.

Sunni gasped and turned to Raffi, scared.

"It's the action," Raffi said quietly. "It's coming closer, I see."

"What action?" Sunni asked.

He said slowly, "You're a Double Special Elder through and through. You didn't even know."

Now another spiral burst wildly in the distance, near the mall. A high-pitched radial whistle could be heard emanating from it. Raffi got up like a smooth animal.

He bent over and started rummaging in the large duffel bag that had been lying beside him in the grass.

Sunni pushed herself closer to the tree, astonished. In the distance, a physicist in a red overcoat had turned around and begun to walk back toward them. Raffi looked up to answer the question on Sunni's face and explained, "It's a Turquoise bomb. We might know how to handle this." The physicist came near and Raffi walked off with her, in the direction of the institute and through its front doors.

Now Sunni was alone. She stood up from the ground and watched the Elders, most of whom were gazing up into the distance, where the spiral still hung. She watched as they looked down at their Mothers to make sense of it; to know how to respond. But their Mothers had no valuable insight; could not fit the spiral into the pattern; had never encountered such a thing before.

Get on your scooter and go home, was the instruction on their screens; an instruction applicable to many situations, and the most common one.

The teenagers made their way to their scooters, sure in their movements, for deep in their hearts they felt a cool reassurance: it was not that their Mothers lacked insight, but that the question they had posed about the explosions was not a pertinent one. What happened in the distance had nothing to do with the patterns in their lives. It had nothing to do with all the ways they were special. They got on their wheels and, like the physicists, sped off from the heart of town.

Sunni looked up as an acorn fell from the tree and landed on her head. She thought about what she knew.

Thanks to physicists Sean Gryb, Aaron Berndsen,
Julian Barbour, and Lee Smolin for conversations and advice.

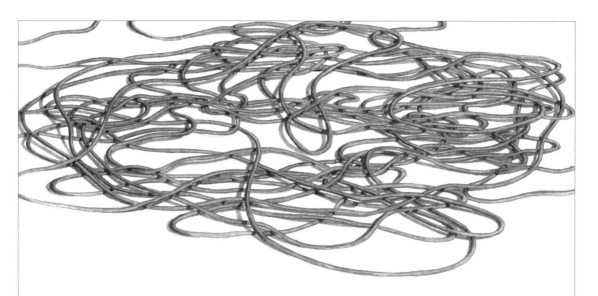

MATERIAL PROOF OF
THE FAILURE OF EVERYTHING

by HEIDI JULAVITS

NOBODY LAUGHED AS GYULA rotated through the revolving glass doors of the Muvész Kávéház, as he caught the belt loop of his overcoat on a protruding nail, as he made another two full turns before managing, gracelessly, to extract himself on the intended side of things.

Nobody greeted him as he ejected at a zigzagging trajectory and attempted to self-correct by grabbing on to the nearest grabbable body, one that unfortunately belonged to Peza Macedone, the woman for whom his penis had failed to erect last night.

Peza, boggling a silver tray on which she carried an *apfelstrudel* and a pot of mildew-stinking tea, cursed him in Hungarian, a phrase Gyula had fielded regularly since arriving in Budapest, one that translated most kindly as *A horse's prick into your ass!*

He put on his sunglasses to ward off the baroque glare of the Bohemian glass chandelier, refracted and somehow amplified by its travels through the sedimentary haze of morning cigarette smoke. The gilt interior of the Muvész, gaudified with pubic-hairy tinsel garlands and blinking Christmas wreaths, worked in legion with his Grüner Veltliner hangover to fortify his misery.

His white paper bag, folded once, awaited him on the counter. The barista peered at him through turquoise horn-rims; he dot-connected his gaze between Gyula and Peza, in case Gyula should be too ruined to catch his meaning.

"It's called impotence," Gyula said. "Understood to be a psychological condition requiring the utmost sensitivity from friends and loved ones."

"Impotence my fanny," the barista said. "It is an insult not to noodle the ladies."

"Lies issued as protection," countered Gyula tonelessly, for he truly hated this barista, "are the only valid expressions of love." Gyula had chosen to spare Peza, her arm threaded through the peek-hole of his boxers, the truth: that he found her unerotically neckless, a flaw unassisted by her penchant for wearing a burglar's hood in winter.

"You need to believe so," the barista said, "loving the Liar like you do."

The barista sponged his milk nozzle, clearly eager for the comeback; he knew Gyula couldn't stand to hear Angy, his work partner, called by a name she absolutely deserved. But today Gyula was too wine-queasy to defend the heartbreak of his life, a woman who was also, indisputably, a mendacious whore.

He opened the paper bag, paranoid that the barista had given him a prune *schnitten* or a much-detested (by Angy) *germspeisen*. Maybe, too, Bela, their so-called boss, had failed to assign him an eavesdropping job, the location of which would be typed on the single industrially perfect square of brown butcher paper that wrapped his and Angy's morning pastries.

This was another reason not to sleep with Peza: she placed the eavesdropping assignments into the pastry bags after Bela delivered the assignments to the Muvész. Sleeping with Peza, thus, would be akin to sleeping with his work superior—a get-ahead strategy that worked, in the long run, for precisely no one. Upward mobility was a dead art. The only beneficial reason to sleep with the neckless Peza would be because Bela—who loved to make Gyula feel like each assignment was potentially his last—professed to admire, "above all other peoples," a handsome man who "fucked below his station."

Gyula's eavesdropping qualifications, after all, were basically nil. A first-generation Hungarian American with a degree in hotel management, he'd worked a five-year stint at the Four Seasons Maui during which he'd manned the beachside cabanas operation and masterminded a down-low call-girl service. One afternoon he'd been summoned to a cabana occupied by a hotelier from Budapest. Bela, in the midst of a blow job tastefully obscured by a beach towel (Bela's preferred manner of conducting business, always there was a girl kneeling beside Bela's desk chair, a suit coat pup-tented over her head), offered him a job. Gyula had, Bela could smell it, the blood of Attila running through his veins; in Hungary, his talents would not be wasted. A decade later this prediction had possibly turned out to be true. But as Gyula followed Bela's breadcrumbing from job to job, he was occasionally prompted to ask himself what, exactly, his talents were, and what use, if not the current use, would constitute a waste.

The barista whistled to a pair of waitresses shift-breaking by the lavatories, their cigarettes drizzling smoke up the walls, and gestured toward an advent calendar taped to a corner of the billboard-size café mirror. He fingered door number 22 open while the waitresses, their cigarettes held jitteringly aloft, awaited the verdict.

Gyula's borderline-bleak mood turned officially bleak. He detested the extreme Hungarian hooplah surrounding the holiday (a half Jew who, as a child, loved Christmas, he self-damningly chose to see something anti-Semitic in the country's enthusiasm), but more than any other Christmas by-product he found advent calendars inexplicably sinister.

"An elf that is also an angel!" the barista announced.

Gyula squinted through his sunglasses; to him, it looked like a maggot with wings.

"Aren't you a little old?" he crabbed.

The barista, a total *nietzfunzen*, started yammering about the history of advent calendars, about how nineteenth-century German Lutherans used to count down the days to Christmas by making chalk marks on doors.

"I don't care about the history," Gyula said. "Though I will note, historically, that Germans do like to make marks on people's doors."

"And so you care about what?" the barista asked.

"You open the door, and then you open the next door, and the next door, and behind every door there's a different drawing of a toy."

"You're saying," clarified the barista, "that you, opening the doors, would rather it be the same toy?"

A waiter walked past with a booze-soaked plate of *rumos golyóks*. Gyula's stomach boomeranged.

He wall-faced the bartender by way of indicating his profound boredom with the man. Then he unfolded the bag. Inside he was relieved to see, tacoed together by the familiar square of butcher paper, two *meggyes rétes*, their sour-cherry viscera bulging suggestively from their pastry casings. Gyula had no illusions about his relationship (if it could be called such a thing) with Angy. The daily joy he took in observing the two nestling, still-warm *meggyes rétes* was proof of this. He compared it to watching a person sweetly asleep, a typically non-sweet person who would never in her caustic waking life express anything resembling fondish feelings for you.

His place of employ, if he could be said to have one, was the entirety of the London Gresham Life Insurance Building, also known as the Gresham Palace Hotel, where he spent his days eavesdropping on guests.

The Gresham Palace had been restored in 2004 to its former Szecesszionist grandeur, and then de-restored in 2018 to its circa-1989 decrepitude by Bela, based on the guidelines supplied to him by the Deszecesszionists. Bela, no moron, savvily opted to become an active participant in the Deszecesszionist bid to attain, for Hungary, a pre-capitalistic, postcommunistic state of *cultural and economic innocence*. He wagered that the initial outlay required to re-ruin his hotel would eventually pay off. It had.

Thus the formerly former Gresham Palace Hotel had an old bronze plaque onto which had been soldered a new bronze plaque designating it as an official *Deszecesszio* building. Thus Bela, though he gave precisely zero shits about anything but courtesy sucks and his bank account, could attend the Deszecesszionist cabinet meetings held in the men's portion of the Gellért Baths and hypocritically pretend to care about the future of Hungary. Thus he could stroll between the thermal pools in his white shame apron, well-blown genitals joggling beneath the thin cotton and appearing twice as obscene for being covered, a so-called "anti-capitalist" who made money as an accidental by-product of his commitment to the Deszecesszionist cause.

Gyula, too, attended these meetings. Himself, he preferred to be naked.

The Gresham's atriumed lobby, a jumble of sad kiosks, stank of cabbage and mentholated shaving cream. Gyula nodded to Martin the Janitor, who was drinking an espresso on an overturned mop bucket beneath a smattering of bullet holes, shot into the glossily new Zsolnay tiles by an interior decorator who'd used photographs from 1989 (and an authentic Mosin-Nagant rifle) to precisely re-create the damage inflicted by the 1944 Soviet siege. The front desk was unmanned; its plastic khaki telephone appeared not to work, though in fact it did.

A sound system played a grainy xylophone loop of "O Tannenbaum."

Gyula freed the butcher-paper square from beneath the *meggyes rétes*.

Room 417.

He pressed the lift button, watching the numbers over the doors ignite sequentially as the lift descended. The bulbs illuminating floors one through four had, for the sake of 1989 authenticity, been removed; below the fifth floor the panel went completely dark, as though the lift had entered a free fall.

If Gyula appeared to understand the Deszecesszio Movement, it was only because such appearances made his life infinitely easier. Three years ago, Dasco, the leader of the Deszecesszionist Party, negotiated a takeover from Hans Lugerschmidt, the German bank CEO who, much to his evident dismay, came to essentially own Hungary when its economy, feebly buttressed by loans from Lugerschmidt's bank, imploded. Subsequently Lugerschmidt ruled from his office in Frankfurt, asserting his domestic presence via low-resolution internet appearances wherein he tonelessly issued financial reports tracking Hungary's still-plummeting economy and how it was dragging his bank, and the entire European Union, into the red. In an attempt to, as Lugerschmidt put it, "isolate the Hungarian problem," he changed the country's currency from the euro to the fleuro (a quaint nod to Hungary's original currency, the florint), but this worthless schizo offspring of two tanking economies quickly worsened the situation. The final insult occurred when Lugerschmidt, at an EU press conference, was overheard referring to the fleuro as "more or less ass paper."

The precise details of Dasco's takeover were never made public, but Gyula suspected, despite the online news headlines comparing Dasco's act to Attila's gory raids, that the takeover was really more of a handover, that Lugerschmidt had been more than happy to dump his parasitic non-asset in exchange for a pathetic fraction of the money he was owed.

Since the takeover/handover, Dasco had moved from his hermit's cottage in the Buda Hills to a more centrally located apartment in Pest. He gave speeches to the nonplussed crowds that gathered on rainy days in the defunct metro stops. He also lectured at the weekly Deszecesszionist meeting at the Gellért Baths.

Regard Cuba, Dasco would say to his naked or mostly naked cabinet members. Dasco—manic, copper-haired, and noodle-thin (the Viszla, the news sources dubbed him)—tended to soapbox with his shame apron tied tightly around his middle like a French garçon's folded tablecloth.

Cuba, railed the Viszla, like Hungary, had rejected communism and embraced capitalism as the panacea to all its ills, and look what it had become. A country full of failed resorts, shoddily built fortresses of Sheetrock softened to oatmeal by the monsoons and condemned. Hangar-size stores that sold expired crackers, glue guns, and hot sauce to an increasingly indigent population. And what about domestic industry? Abandoned for a generation by people lured to the cities and the hastily assembled spa towns for easier work. No farms and no farmers. No weavers and no fishermen. A people infected by the fake promise of ease, and indebted to the point of imprisonment to the Germans.

Hungary, claimed the Viszla, was similarly sick. Many wrong turns had been taken over the course of Hungarian history (such as the aptly named Austro-Hungarian Compromise of 1867 and its crazy-making establishment of the *doppel-monarchie*), but none so fatally wrong as the turn taken in 1989, when the country quivered like a smooth metal ball between those magnetic *doppelmonarchies* of the twentieth century—communism and capitalism.

The only cure, said the Viszla, was to return to that metal-ball-quivering moment, to live again for years in a replicated, highly charged 1989 limbo state, and after existing for a suitable number of years in that state (he refused to make any time projections), choose an original path.

No matter how ridiculous Gyula found the Deszecesszionists and, in particular, Dasco—who wore a dictator's white linen suit in summer and read a book while walking back and forth each day across the Chain Bridge, who vowed (metaphorically, of course; Dasco was a passivist) *Death to Greedy Capitalists* even as Bela made greedy-capitalist money right under his nose—limbo was a fine way to pass one's time on earth. Fuck progress. Fuck ambition. When you live in a country that's never in the history of time won a war, why push toward conclusion? Gyula preferred living each day, as Dasco called it, by *riding the meniscus of the future*, a meniscus that could rupture tomorrow or never. He had a job that could end at any moment but never did. He had a woman he loved who conveniently refused to love him back, which meant he, too, lived in a limbo state that remained pleasingly stagnant and unresolved.

* * *

He took the lift to the fifth floor and knocked on the door to room 417.

"Germspeisen," he greeted Angyalka. Despite his iron smelter of a hangover, Gyula experienced a brief lightening in his soul. He and Angy had been working together for nine months; he knew that one day their partnership would—because of Bela's tendency to whimsically and without warning reconfigure the eavesdropping pairs—be dissolved.

"Schnitten," said Angy.

Her complexion was rashier than usual, as though she'd spent the night rubbing her cheeks against someone's pelty chest, possibly Martin the Janitor's.

She grabbed the bag and flopped onto the cappuccino mohair couch, stuffing a *meggyes rétes* into her mouth. She wore her usual uniform: tight black pants attached to a pair of purely decorative suspenders, a tight black ballet top that made a man, or Gyula at any rate, feel guilty that he'd ever fetishized breasts over the erotically superior clavicle bones, and striped socks, always flopping loosely at the toes and smelling, not unpleasantly, of the abattoirish interior of her cheaply tanned ankle boots.

"You didn't want this, did you?" she asked, holding up the second pastry.

Angy wasn't wearing a bra. She never wore a bra, nor did she need to wear a bra. She had nipples but not breasts—sturdy, screwlike protrusions that, combined with her rigid posture and fuck-all attitude, contributed to her enigmatic vibe of robotic sloth. Add to this the fact that she collected snow globes (preferring those with a commemorative tourist bent—the twenty-fifth anniversary Euro Disney snow globe, for example), and she practically, from a category standpoint, self-negated.

Gyula shrugged his permission. He felt like Grüner Veltliner shit and breakfast wouldn't likely make a difference.

He busied himself reading her handwritten transcripts from the night before. He less cared what had been happening next door in room 419 than what had been happening here in room 417, possibly on the cappuccino mohair couch, which appeared suspiciously deflated to him.

Between 1:30 a.m. and 4:30 a.m., Peter Wallsy and his schipperke, named Crocus, had slept. Wallsy was some kind of political scientist from the University of Vienna and a likely homosexual, given his choice of traveling companion and his decision to visit Budapest, alone, the week of Christmas. *And* a man cursed with a rather bizarre sleep pattern, unless of course he hadn't been sleeping. Angy was known to claim a subject was "sleeping" or "reading quietly" when in fact Angy was watching TV (not for nothing was she called the Liar).

At 4:50 a.m., Wallsy had made a phone call to a colleague in New York City to chat about an upcoming paper he was delivering called "Amnesiacal Trends in the Lugerschmidt Derivative."

At 5:28 a.m., he'd put Crocus in the bathtub and encouraged him to take a shit.

At 6:00 a.m., he'd watched a cable special on wheat hybridization.

At 6:45 a.m., he'd ordered a Continental Breakfast from room service, opting for herbal tea instead of coffee.

At 8:00 a.m., he'd taken some pills.

At 8:30 a.m., he'd gone back to sleep.

Since then, Crocus had been whimpering at the door. Clearly, the shit he'd taken in the bathtub hadn't been enough to tide him over.

"So?" Gyula asked.

"He's a nobody," Angy said. Her ballet top was covered with pastry crumbs. She looked beautiful, as if she'd been gently snowed upon.

Gyula shuffled through Wallsy's file.

"They're all nobodies," Angy said, more bitterly than usual.

"Enlighten me, who is a somebody?" Gyula asked. Meaning, had they ever found out anything of use by eavesdropping, day and night, on the guests of the Gresham? Dasco mandated guest monitoring as a condition for Bela's continuing to operate the Gresham as a hotel, thereby proving to Gyula that, despite Dasco's promises of "cultural innocence," there was no such thing as a post-surveillance state. Once a country has repeatedly violated its citizens' rights to privacy as a means of governance, there was no way a leader could sleep at night unless he knew what people everywhere were secretly thinking and secretly doing.

Not that the people at the Gresham were secretly thinking or secretly doing anything of interest; they certainly weren't planning to assassinate the Viszla. Mostly Gyula, when he wasn't bored out of his moccasins, busted prostitution rings and dealers of prescription selective serotonin reuptake inhibitors (Deszecesszionist-forbidden activities that Bela allowed, but only if he received a sizable kickback).

"What's Wallsy's plan for today?" Gyula asked.

"Baths, according to Martin."

"You talked to Martin," Gyula said casually.

"Wallsy called Martin and asked him what time the Rudas opened."

Martin the Janitor also functioned as the hotel's de facto concierge. The hotel hadn't had a concierge in 1989, thus Martin's concierge activities were strictly "off-book." Still, if a guest pressed the CONCIERGE button on his room phone, he was connected with Martin's cell.

Gyula flipped through the handwritten transcript. There was no record of Wallsy making a phone call to Martin. Nor was there any record of Angy calling Martin, or vice versa. Gyula decided, as he often decided, to doctor the transcript once Angy left. He didn't want to risk her being fired for something that should, in fact, get her fired.

"After the baths he wants to go to the National Gallery to look at heroic portraits of the chicken-hearted dead," Angy said.

Fine enough, your average tourist day. Another form of Hungarian limbo that Gyula found reassuring. No matter what political ideology was stomping through the *utcas*, people visited Budapest as if it were suspended in time unchanging; now, as ever, Budapest was touristically represented by the baths with their inscrutable locker-room protocols, and by the hilariously blinkered artistic vision of Miklós Barabás at the National Gallery, and by the plastic shot glasses of bile-colored Unicum drunk by Hungarians who toasted one another by saying *I fuck the corner of your mouth, dear friend*, and by the bulleted facades in the Jewish quarter, and by the material proof of the failure of everything displayed on gypsy blankets at the Ecseri flea market, the repository of leftover junk from Hungary's succession of doomed regimes.

Angy thrust her things (raisiny leather gloves, Siberian *Vogue*) into her red faux-patent bag. Always after she left he'd find flaking bits of fake cherry-colored skin, backed with a textile grid, in a little pile by the couch.

"What are you doing today?" Gyula asked. Trying to sound casual, but sounding precisely not.

"Movies," she said. "Sleep."

She absently rubbed her mottled cheek with the backside of her knuckles—a wistful gesture, or that's how Gyula chose to read it, so that the rest of his day, sure to be a crippling bore, might hold some interest for him in the form of manufactured anxiety. He'd be listening to Wallsy and imagining Angy at her flat with Martin, two night owls unconscious on Angy's unelevated futon slab, a far worse vision than the two of them awake and fucking beneath her wall of commemorative snow globes. Worse to envision them, post-sleep and pouchy-eyed, sharing a pot of tea in Angy's pitiful alcove kitchen. Worse to envision them on Angy's mangy sectional, eating black-market Mexican and watching movies on the flat-screen he'd helped her disinfect after a Gresham suicide (a guest had aerosolized his brain with a flea-market revolver; his room had been gutted). Gyula was so overtaken by these upsetting visions of sweet domestic squalor that he forgot to entertain his pro forma worry as Angy, without saying goodbye, shut the door: what room he'd be assigned to on tomorrow's square of butcher paper, and who would answer when he rang the bell.

By the following morning, Peza appeared to have forgiven him his failure to erect on her behalf. She smirked at her tray as Gyula rotated into the café, effortlessly this time, no comical spinning about.

He'd spent an abstemious evening reading a dystopian novel set in postrevolution and pre–War of Independence Hungary (he preferred novels to history books; he felt it safer, intellectually speaking, to knowingly acquire factually suspect information). The novel was about a group of boys whose mothers, in the 1950s, during the years of the Ratko Law, had been imprisoned for trying to abort them.

The book, aptly, had been recommended to him by his father, a Hungarian Jew who'd immigrated to Hartford, Connecticut in the 1990s and behaved, throughout his life, like a man whose mother had tried to poke a wire hanger through his heart before and even after he was born. Gyula otherwise knew nothing about his father's past; he'd chalked his reticence up to the diasporic quiet that encased all the Hartford Hungarians he'd met, but this reticence, he'd learned since moving to Budapest, afflicted even those Hungarians who had never left.

Angy's family, for example. She had learned, via her personnel file, the following: her great-grandfather had been trained at the Soviet-style Dzerzhinsky Academy; he'd worn a service cap that bore a red star in a circlet of corn; via his "police work" he'd caused the torture and deaths of many innocent people before being accused of conspiracy himself, and tortured, and presumably killed, since he was taken to the headquarters of the Communist Secret Police and never heard from again.

None of this, Angy said, had ever been spoken about in her family, people she referred to as *spreaders of pig fat on bread*.

To Gyula, however, her family's story sounded less scandalous than typically Hungarian. The root of the Hungarian verb *to inform on* was the verb *to spit*, thus implying that one was as commonplace, and as involuntary, as the other. Hungary, given it had been morally invaded and corrupted by so many foreign tribes and countries, retained only this as its lasting national identity: a tendency to cyclically self-cannibalize.

Or, as Bela had explained it to him, to live in Hungary was to participate in a political pyramid scheme. People, in order to save their asses, cooperated with the regime in power and ratted out their neighbors. But eventually every cooperator became a traitor, ratted out by another person's attempt to appear cooperative, and then the regime was overthrown by a successive regime, which punished the cooperators who'd yet to be ratted out, and then the whole doomed thing started anew.

And what about those who refused to engage? Gyula asked. Were they excused from this cycle of pointlessness?

Oh no, Bela said. They got the immediate rather than the someday ass-fucking.

Thus, given the certain hopelessness of his relatives' situations, Gyula had declined to read his file. He preferred to keep his associations with Hungary heroically mythical—blood of Attila and whatnot. For this reason (not that he needed a reason), despite the fact that he'd lived in Budapest for nearly ten years, he had never visited the village where his ancestors, Jews of a sort, had lived until for whatever reason they no longer did. This was as historically precise as he cared to get—and those muckers-about-in-the-past, those who might scold him with that tired old aphorism about history repeating itself, could welcome the horse's prick right up their asses. Repetition resulted in a form of limbo, a comforting spinning in place.

As if the world were making a mockery of his indifference, a homeless man entered the Muvész's revolving door and took a little ride, going around and around and around, waving at Gyula each time he spun toward him with a fresh look of surprise, as if he hadn't just hand-flapped him five seconds ago.

The Muvész, Gyula noticed, was only a fraction as smoggy as it typically was by this hour. Also, the barista was a different barista. This barista was a younger fellow, with a wispy bread-mold beard spreading along the underside of his chin. He'd taped a sign, in English, to the espresso machine: NO SMOKING UPON PENALTY OF SHOOTING.

Beneath this someone had drawn an inscrutable stick-figure scenario, in which one stick figure smoked a cigarette and a second stick figure held a machine gun to the head of a seemingly innocent third stick figure.

Help me, Gyula thought. *Another* nietzfunzen.

"Gyula," he said, introducing himself.

The barista didn't reply.

"I'm here for my breakfast," Gyula said.

No response.

"Typically this is when you hand me my bag," Gyula said.

"Typically this is when I punch you in the face," the barista said.

Gyula reared back. Not because he feared being punched in the face—really, at his age, with his face, who could muster much concern about that? This was a purely emotional reaction, a true rearing-back of surprise.

"I'm calling Bela…"

"Bela?" the barista said. "I don't know any Bela."

Gyula dialed Bela's cell. A recording informed him that the number was no longer in service.

"See?" the barista said. "Neither do you know any Bela."

The barista lit a cigarette. He pointed the ignited end at Gyula's head.

"Pow," he said.

While Gyula's immediate reaction should have been one of panic—Bela, his official connection to Dasco, was gone, which meant, in practical terms, that Gyula was out of a job—it was not. Instead he experienced an endorphin rush of schadenfreude. Bela, that breadcrumbing middleman whom Angy mockingly called Angel Penis, had been fired, exiled, imprisoned, who knew; Dasco, Gyula could only presume, had finally figured out that the guy was the embodiment of everything he claimed to despise. *Metaphoric Death to Greedy Capitalists!*

Deliciously, he found himself failing to care much about Bela. What he did care about was Angy. Angy was known to skim off the guests who ran prostitution or SSRI operations from the Gresham, following them to the National Gallery and cornering them by the portrait of Count István Széchenyi (a man who lost his mind over the repeated fiascos of Hungarian history and killed himself), with a proposition that involved paying her a comparatively minimal sum to keep their activities a secret.

Worried that she'd been busted alongside their boss, he dialed Angy's cell. The call went straight to her voicemail. That her account still existed he read as a sign that her extortions remained undetected, or had been generously viewed as anti-Bela, thus anti-capitalist, thus, in a sense, loyally pro-Deszecesszionist, and thus above punishment.

Still, there persisted the problem of his sudden unemployment.

Peza approached with an order for the barista, weird smirk intact. She collected two espressos and a plate of *papsapkas*.

"My bag," Gyula appealed to her.

"If you want a bag," Peza said, "you'll have to go to another café."

"Which other café?" Gyula said.

Peza shrugged. "How many others are there?"

The barista sniggered.

Gyula wished he were hungover. He wished he had an excuse to short-out mentally, shove a *meggyes rétes* up the barista's gaping right nostril.

Peza, bless her, saw his struggle. She repeated herself: *How many others are there?* She wasn't being a wiseass, she was actually trying to tell him something. Her tone conveyed to him, even if her words did not: if you're looking for a job, there's only one café in town.

As he was leaving, Peza gave him the sign—two blinks of the left eye.

Before spinning through the glass door, Gyula grabbed the matchbook off the last table on the left. He stood outside the café and theatrically lit a cigarette he didn't want to smoke, then pocketed the matchbook. He waited until he was four blocks away before reading what Peza had written on the interior flap.

The Szimpla—which multipurposed as a café-bar-restaurant as well as the Deszecesszionist headquarters—was located in the former Jewish district, a district Gyula appreciated at this time of year especially, given it was the only part of town not Christmassed to death.

The former Jewish district had also been, more recently, a former luxury shopping district: a Hungarian businessman, in 2009, had transformed the ghetto into a high-end shopping mall, the ghetto's connected courtyards filled with umbrella-ed bistro tables, the tiny, formerly squalid second-story flats dewalled and defloored so that the ground-level shops had, according to the old tram-shelter advertisements that could still be purchased at the Ecseri flea market, "an *en plein air*–like feel." The Hungarian businessman had restuccoed the entire concrete-colored edifice with Mediterranean-pink plaster that glowed garishly in the taupe Hungarian light; the pink had faded over time to a pallid flesh tone, and now that the shops were gone and the broken plateglass had been replaced by sawtoothed, overlapping plywood scraps (on which vandals had jokingly written anti-Semitic slurs), the place had, as Angy liked to say, "a Kristallnacht-like feel."

Gyula turned onto a runty *utca* lined with bullet-ridden apartment buildings and doorway plaques commemorating Jews who'd been killed and forgotten long ago. The Szimpla, a designer relic of Hungary's high-capitalist era, was a classic example of Deszecesszionist inconsistency. No establishment of this sort had existed in 1989, but its film-set decrepitude (the crumbling gravestone exterior, the leaky courtyard, the bombed-out stairwells, the rusted and mismatched furniture, the about-to-collapse gallery lined with small rooms that functioned as offices, the putrefying Turkish toilets) made it, even in the eyes of purists, a nonideologically identified establishment, the perfect environment in which to plan for a blank-slate future.

Gyula knew the day bartender, a relocated American like himself called William the Silent.

This morning William the Silent was working the Japanese tea station. Japanese food was the only foreign food allowed in Hungary, presumably because the ascetic, vegetarian Dasco had a weakness for daikon root.

"How are things?" asked William the Silent.

Gyula shrugged. "Heard from Bela?" he asked.

Wielding a scrap of plaid, William the Silent buffed an ebony pot.

"Not so much these days," said William the Silent.

"Shame," Gyula said, lighting another cigarette he didn't want. "My partner and I are looking for work."

Gyula strategically placed the matchbook on the counter so that William the Silent could read the name written inside.

Sydney Vega.

William the Silent jerked his head skyward, indicating that Sydney Vega was dead in heaven or merely up in the gallery.

"Your timing's good," he said grimly, as if good timing was the ultimate bad thing.

Gyula ordered a pot of green tea and an under-sugared Japanese pastry that was less decadent than a day-old dinner roll. Gyula's craving for a gooey, flaky, sour-sweet *meggyes rétes* hit him in a place that was equal parts stomach and gut; the sudden upset of his morning routine, never taken for granted but, yes, to some degree, taken for granted, gnawed at him abdominally. He looked at his phone to see if Angy had called. She had not. He dialed her cell phone (still off) and didn't leave a message.

He'd just repocketed his phone when he felt it humming against his nipple. A text from Angy. *dont call me schnitten im working undercover*

He wrote: *undercover how do you mean exactly*

Angy wrote: *i mean i went dark*

He wrote: *so long ago you went dark*

To which she did not reply.

Gyula finished his tea and his cake. He bussed the dishes and left a few extra fleuros for William the Silent. Sydney Vega—a Cuban, he assumed—awaited him. It was no secret that Dasco had been in protracted negotiations with the Cubans regarding an economic alliance. He'd heard rumors from the old men at his bathhouse, rumors that claimed Dasco's "takeover" hadn't happened as implied by the news sources; Dasco had, in effect, borrowed back his own country on the condition that he pay to Lugerschmidt, by a certain date, the remainder of the debt. The agreement was time-sensitive and the time, the old men said, was running out.

Upstairs, the gallery buzzed with winter flies trying to escape through the safety-glass skylights. At the north end of the gallery, in front of an office door, sat a desk. At the desk sat a woman. A secretary.

The secretary was beautiful, Gyula thought, but only if you imagined her very much elsewhere, preferably Havana's Malecón, wearing a wasp-waisted halter dress and wedge sandals. Here her tar-colored hair, braided and coiled above her ears, appeared greasily reptilian; here, dessicated by radiator steam heat and lit unattractively by two intertwined strands of green and white Christmas lights, her chestnut face appeared scored by delicate crepe-like wrinkles. She'd encased herself in wool cardigans and a tangle of gypsy scarves. She might have been a multiple amputee for all he could make out of her body.

"The bathroom's on the landing," the secretary said, "next to the blinking Santa head."

Gyula flipped the open matchbook onto her blotter pad. She picked it up.

"How noiry," the secretary said. "Stealth communication via matchbook cover."

She tore a match from the matchbook, lit it, and turned the match back onto its unlit comrades. The sulphur tips exploded blue. She dropped the flaming mess into her paper-filled waste can, ignoring the ensuing blaze that lurched toward the fringe ends of her scarves.

"These silly little fires," she said, staring at Gyula, "tend to burn themselves out. Don't you find?"

The secretary fished a cigarette from the inside of one of her cardigans. She held the tip to the flaming waste can.

Together they watched the fire die down.

"You're one of Bela's people," the secretary stated, inhaling her blackened cigarette.

"Was," Gyula said.

"Bela screwed up," she said. "Wouldn't you say?"

Gyula shrugged.

"I'm just curious," the secretary said. "Do you believe that turning a blind eye is a virtue or a sin? From a workplace standpoint."

"The blinder the eye," said Gyula, "the stronger the ears."

She pushed a manila folder—onto which someone had spilled a copious amount of brown liquid—across the desk.

Gyula opened the folder and examined his photo stapled to the inside cover. According to this photo, Gyula Sigmund Horvath was most likely a middle-aged singer of intensely felt rock ballads for teens—either that or a man whose talents were going to waste. Regard the deadened eyes, propped up by greenish tussocks of skin. Or the Adam's apple–length hair center-parted and frizzing into the frizzy background of leafless trees. Or the sprawling slag-toned cheek mole. Or the features duking it out against symmetry and winning by a landslide.

"You failed to report your partner for offenses of varying severity a total of seventy-six times," the secretary said.

"That's all?" Gyula said.

"Those are the ones we caught," the secretary said. "But you knew you were being watched, didn't you?"

"Of course," he said, struggling to appear unfazed. "That was part of the fun, wasn't it?"

The secretary pressed her lips together, displacing the corners of her mouth to higher ground and creating what might, Gyula thought, among certain ice-hearted women, pass as a smile.

"Not every employer values a man with a blind eye," the secretary said.

"Too true," Gyula said equitably.

She flicked through his documents with a pink nail filed to a switchblade.

"I see you come from a long line of uncooperative Jews," she said.

"Subsequent generations of Horvaths have wised right up," Gyula said. "We play ball, so to speak, no questions asked."

"America will do that to a bloodline," the secretary observed.

She scrutinized the photo stapled to his open file, then his actual face, as if searching for some telling discrepancy.

"We could offer you a tryout," she said.

"Excellent," Gyula said.

"The protocol is the same. Go to the Muvész tomorrow morning. Your paper bag will be waiting for you."

"And my partner, can she get a tryout?" Gyula asked.

The secretary didn't respond.

"We tend to work together," Gyula fumbled. "My partner and I."

The secretary closed his file. She sniffed the brown stain before sliding the folder into a low drawer.

"For all you know, she's already been given one."

"Oh," Gyula said. "Well, good for her."

"For all you know, when offered her tryout, she expressed no concern whatsoever about you and your future prospects of employment."

Gyula watched, as though it were a winged thing busting from a wool-cardigan chrysalis, the secretary's flagrantly bitchy self unfurl.

"And as you probably know from my file," Gyula said, "I wouldn't have it any other way."

"No?" said the secretary. "That's disappointing. If a man has no sense of self-preservation, how can he be manipulated to do things he would never ordinarily do?"

"Nothing starts my day like a good manipulation," Gyula assured her.

The secretary smiled, revealing a single gold incisor riding high on her gum line like a bullet descending from her brain.

"I suppose we'll see tomorrow, won't we?" she said.

She stubbed her cigarette on her desk blotter, branding it with a sooty, heart-shaped mark. Behind one of the closed office doors, a man conducted a heated phone fight in German.

"And can you thank Mr. Vega for the opportunity?" Gyula said, rising. He was done with this woman.

"Miss Vega," the secretary said. "You already have."

That evening, Gyula called Angy three times before falling asleep. He left no messages.

In the morning he had a text from her: *poor me here the meggyes retes suck unicum vomit where's here?* He wrote back, knowing she wouldn't respond. A tiny doubting part of him wanted to add: *and how do i know this is really you?*

of course this isn't really me, schnitten, she'd respond. He'd get precisely nowhere by asking; a peculiar form of the Liar Paradox rendered meaningless all text messages written by sarcastic, unreliable individuals, or people pretending to be them.

The next morning, the bread-mold-beard barista handed him his paper bag as though no enmity existed between them, and maybe none did.

"Where's Peza?" Gyula asked.

Inside he found two *beigli* slices wrapped in the familiar butcher square.

"*Beigli*," Gyula said. He hated *beigli*. The poppy seeds lodged in the horseshoe gaps between his teeth and gums and were impossible to pick free with anything other than the sideways-turned blade of an X-Acto knife.

"New regime," the barista said, referring, or so Gyula assumed, to Bela's replacement, Miss Vega. "Plus it's Christmas."

"How could I forget?" Gyula said. He peered at the old barista's advent calendar, still taped to the mirror—only one paper door remained unopened, the big double-door reward one received on the twenty-fourth.

Thank god, it was almost over.

Gyula walked to work along Andrássy. Spray-on snow covered the fake-fir garlands draped from the lampposts; loose particles drifted down in asbestosy puffs when the wind gusted.

He spun through the Gresham's revolving door and nodded to Martin. The Gresham appeared unchanged; it stank of the same stinks. He roughly disentangled the butcher paper from the *beiglis. Room 726.* He took the lift to the seventh floor. He knocked on the door to room 726.

He almost didn't recognize her out of her Muvész uniform.

"What took you so long?" asked Peza.

She grabbed the paper bag from his hand and returned to her eavesdropping area, a card table with a desk lamp, a black laptop, a swankily blinking digital recorder. She shoved the *beigli* into her mouth; he heard the raining-down sounds of poppy seeds striking the tabletop.

Pushing aside Peza's burglar mask, Gyula sat on the mohair couch.

"You've been demoted," Gyula said.

"We'll see how my tryout goes," Peza said. "You can't just be demoted these days."

Gyula waited to be filled in on the activities in room 724.

"They're asleep," Peza announced. "*Finally.* I don't need to tell you what they've been up to all night. You never told me your job was like watching bad porn without the watching."

"On the whole it's not," Gyula said. "Who are they?"

"I don't know," Peza said. "New rules. Miss Vega prefers anonymity. She's trying to eliminate conflicts of interest."

She showed Gyula her computer screen; in her typed transcript the guests were referred to as *X* and *Y*. And they had, as Peza reported, been having a lot of sex, unless they'd been watching the porn channel and Peza couldn't tell the difference.

"What's their nationality?" Gyula asked.

"They're speaking Hungarian," Peza said.

"Natively?" Gyula asked, though the question was an unnecessary one. Hungarian wasn't a language spoken by many people unless they'd been forced, since childhood, to do so.

Peza nodded.

"Did they say anything of interest?"

"Just some drunken yelling," Peza said. "Nothing of interest."

He watched as Peza pulled on her great-grandfather's old military overcoat, the right lapel shiny where the strap of his machine gun had once rested.

"So who is this Vega lady?" Gyula asked.

"Daughter of a Cuban hotel magnate. Apparently there are plans."

"Plans?"

"For the Gresham. She's heading up the renovation. It's going to be an international spa and business center."

"But what about the meniscus of the future?" Gyula said uneasily.

"Finally we're moving forward," Peza said. "It's an exciting time."

Gyula stared at Peza's laptop. On the cover someone had affixed a Star of David sticker, except that this star had little spider legs, and looked like a cross between a star and a swastika, what might be properly termed a starstika. The starstika was inside a snake eating its own tail; on closer inspection the snake proved to be a pine-bough wreath.

"Have you heard from the Liar?" Peza asked, pausing at the door.

"No," Gyula lied. "You?"

"I don't imagine any of us will be hearing from her," Peza said.

Gyula scrutinized Peza's face—did she know where Angy was?—but she quickly pulled her burglar hood over her head, and all he could see was two eyes and a mouth, disconnected communication nodes separated by a knit expanse of black.

"Merry Christmas," the mouth said.

Gyula put on the headphones and pretended to listen to the sounds of X and Y sleeping, but really all he was hearing, deep in his head, was the radar *boing* of Peza's voice. *I don't imagine any of us will be hearing from her.* He had no need to worry about Angy, he kept telling himself, but the truth was that something about her situation seemed not entirely right to him.

He glanced back at the door. The eyes watched him. The legs moved. The mouth planted a wool-rimmed kiss on his lips as the hands stripped his headphones from his ears, an act more intimate than the unzipping of a fly. "Merry Christmas," the mouth said again, the space between its two front teeth embedded with tiny black seeds.

The people in room 724 had been asleep for over three hours, and Gyula figured, given they'd been strenuously engaged all night, they'd remain asleep for at least three more. It was scarcely a work violation (he imagined explaining to Vega if she busted his balls about it) to take a quick break from eavesdropping on nothing remotely interesting to anyone so that he could attend the Deszecesszionist meeting. He wanted to hear more about this "moving forward" Peza had referred to, and the ideological reasoning behind the fancy renovation of the Gresham.

Icy wind blasted off the Danube. Toxic gusts of fake snow pelted his head, or what he thought was fake snow, until he realized it was actual snow. It was real-snow snowing—or, as Angy liked to say, it was snow-globing, because when it snowed was there any longer a doubt that you lived safely inside a little glass bubble and that doomed giants were watching you?

The wooden ticket kiosk at the Gellért was manned by the usual fusspot individual, who snubbed him for scrimping on his entrance fee, paying for a locker but not a cabana. Gyula ran his card through the turnstile, descended the stairs, and coiled his way through the underground tiled passageways. He presented his Deszecesszionist ID to the attendant and put his things into a locker. Wrapped only in a towel, he passed the curtained massage booths and, wading through the chlorinated foot bath, entered the thermal pool chamber.

Whenever Gyula entered this sanctuary—for despite the Deszecesszionist activities within, it did remain a sanctuary—he was reminded of first arriving in Budapest, and his amazement that every urban center didn't have museum-like spaces filled with water and (more important) the sounds of water, where one could be prolongedly naked with sexually disinterested strangers. It seemed the height of civility to him, a necessary means to combat the loneliness that dehumanizes people in cities.

It being not-yet-noon, the Deszecesszionists had yet to gather in significant numbers; he noticed a few heading for the steam room. Dasco tended to show at a quarter past.

At 12:30, however, he had yet to appear, his snake torso tied with a shame apron, his skin rashy-looking beneath his all-body covering of umber hair, his expression inspiringly inert. Nor had the group grown to more than a few members, most of whom floated in the hottest thermal pool, holding on to the edge and languorously kicking in place.

Gyula slung his towel over the statue head of a nymphet with a fountain spurting from her upturned palm. He crab-walked toward one such man.

"The meeting," Gyula said. "Is it happening?"

The man regarded him drowsily, inserting a carroty index finger into the deep crease of his double-strength jowls.

"No meeting today," he said.

"Tomorrow?"

"No meeting tomorrow," the man said.

The man blew his nose into a small urn on the side of the pool intended for this purpose.

"But with all the changes happening..." Gyula said.

"Changes?" the man said.

"No more limbo," Gyula said.

"Limbo is for men with hazelnuts dangling from their anuses," the man said.

"Oh," Gyula said.

"The blood of Attila," the man said, making a strange salute-like gesture against his hairy chest. "You cannot live your life heeding vegetarian assheads."

He grinned, exposing the predictable mouthful of Unicum-colored teeth.

Gyula took a quick steam. He got dressed. He walked over the Elizabeth Bridge, heading back toward the Gresham. Usually he experienced, after a visit to the Gellért, a pleasant post-soak euphoria; today, however, he felt anxiously confused and adrift. He knew this job was his tryout, he knew he should want to impress Vega with his plodding dependability, he knew this was his chance to maintain his personal status quo in the midst of change, but the thought of returning to room 726 filled him with moody dread.

Already the streets teemed with Christmas Eve revelers, many of them drunk and in charge of small children, who also seemed drunk, and possibly were. Gyula allowed himself to be swept toward Vörösmarty Tér, a square he normally avoided this time of year because of the five-week-long Christmas fair that raged there.

He'd gone to the fair once by mistake during his first winter in Hungary. There he'd eaten caramelized pastry horns washed down with mulled wine until he seethed with sugar, he'd been bullied into the purchase of an official Christmas fair mug that featured a Hungarian phrase that meant, more or less, "Commemorate But Don't Remember," he'd been near-trampled by a stampede of children Pavlovianly cued by the five p.m. clock chimes to rush precisely in his direction. Curious, he'd followed them. What he saw over their bobbling knit-capped heads seemed out of a nightmare, some sickly collaboration between the sugar and his own subconscious—a house-size advent calendar. Soon thereafter, he'd vomited into a mesh trash can. Since then, he'd avoided the Christmas fair.

The crowd pushed him down Dorottya utca and through the gates of twisted elm branches that looked like an arbor of interlocking human bones ivied with white lights. Gyula had to confess that he found the sight an evocative one. Under the bearing-down gray sky, from which sifted, as though pre-measured, the gentlest amount of atmospheric snow, the effect was both cozy and pagan, inspiring in him a nostalgia for childhood holidays he had never experienced— Christmas Eves spent fondling cute girl cousins under wolfskin throws in the backs of sleighs, drinking cow's blood from a bone chalice and singing slaughterous Magyar carols.

Gyula purchased a glass of mulled wine, which was served in a commemorative Christmas mug, and which he was told, when he tried to return the empty vessel to the mulled-wine guy, belonged to him now. The guy also gave him a free refill, and then a second, and translated, with theatrical flourish, the Hungarian saying emblazoned on the mug: "A Window Is Sometimes a Door But Never a Wall." Gyula was already buzzy enough to immediately dyslexify the message: *A door is sometimes a wall but never a window. A wall is sometimes a window but never a door.*

He passed booths of *kürtös kalács*, where ribbons of dough were rolled onto what looked like a giant lint brush and baked over an open fire, and a booth where a pair of metalsmiths smoking cigarettes took turns banging a metal hook over an anvil, and booths strung with peppers, and booths in which puppets, heads cocked at a broken-neck angle, hung in cramped rows. His third glass of wine finished, Gyula paid for a fourth to help him wash down a thick duck sausage and, the clock bell bonging, allowed himself to be borne along on the prevailing current of people.

Again, without intending to, Gyula found himself in front of the house-cum-advent-calendar. He'd learned (since his last ignominious Christmas fair run-in) that this house was the Zserbó House, once a famous Hungarian pastry shop, now more frequented by local drunks than tourists and run by a woman with a double-cataracted Pekingese she carried about in a gym bag. This advent-calendar moment represented the Zserbó's annual return to innocence and prominence, and the Pekingese woman made the most of it—this year she'd covered the front with a trompe l'oeil gingerbread house. Gyula located the twenty-fourth window easily; it stretched double-wide across the facade like the Pekingese woman's unibrow.

The clock continued to bong madly, and the crowd continued to amass around him, also madly, the bonging and the sugar and the wine encouraging everyone to a collectively mad threshold.

All to see what's behind a door, Gyula thought to himself dismissively. *Or a window. Or whatever.*

A peasant trio stepped to the fore and started to play, the horn and the fiddle and the flute building in tempo until, on top of the balcony, two young girls flanking the twenty-fourth door parted the fake-gingerbread panels.

The cheers surged at a wild, animal pitch. Gyula almost vomited from the noise alone, and the inconceivable fact that people were cheering—*cheering*—at the painted scene exposed by the two girls. The scene showed Dasco in his white suit hanging from a noose tied to the branch of a Christmas tree, his neck kinked like the puppets Gyula had seen in the fair booths. Atop the tree blinked one of starstikas he'd seen pasted on Peza's computer.

Gyula pushed past a collection of small children, all of whom were sobbing—*but of course they were sobbing*—except that they were laughing. *Laughing!* Sausage-breathed bacchanalian monsters danced around him in dirndls and leather smocks, impeding his movement. He shoved a man by the shoulders. He punched a woman in the face and she tried to kiss him.

Finally he made it to the front of the crowd, where the Pekingese woman stood, stroking her gym bag.

"Tell me," he said breathlessly. "Who is behind the doors?"

"Doors?" the woman asked.

Gyula gestured toward the gingerbread facade.

"Windows," said the woman.

"Windows are sometimes doors," Gyula said impatiently.

"You missed it when you missed it. Come back next year."

"No, what I meant was…" What he meant was: Who is responsible for the doors? But maybe that was the wrong question to ask.

"If there is a next year," the Pekingese woman added bitterly. "I'm tired of businessmen. My snowshoes are too full of shit."

"Businessmen?" Gyula asked.

"Lugerschmidt and Vega," she said. She made a claw with one hand and uttered a Hungarian curse that meant, roughly, "May God fuck their stinking wrinkled whore mothers."

On his way back to the Gresham—a place he had no interest in returning to ever, ever again (but curiosity, and suspicion, for once beat out his instinct for disengagement)—Gyula anxiously texted Angy about his fair findings. What did she know about Vega and Lugerschmidt? And did she know who was behind the Zserbó's doors?

schnitten, Angy replied, *every window is a door.*

The lobby of the Gresham, since he'd left it four hours ago, had been transformed by an army of men in brown coveralls—the Medusa-hair-pattern tiled floor, the marble statue of Sir Thomas Gresham, all were obscured behind mud-colored tarpaulins. Already the smells of shaving cream and cabbage had been overridden by the sweet stink of solvents. The brown-coverall crew moved with a scissored efficiency Gyula did not associate with Hungarians; from the blankly intent looks on their beer-burned faces he pegged them as Germans. Perched on top of their turnip heads were brown baseball caps emblazoned with the wreath-starstika logo.

Gyula took the lift to the seventh floor and let himself into room 726. His headphones were not where he'd left them—or were they? He slipped them over his head, noting that the pads landed above his ear canals, as though they'd been adjusted to fit someone else's skull.

Still nothing happening in room 724 but sleep. All he could hear, if he listened very intently, was the erratic *rub-whoosh* sound of snoring.

He rewound the digital recorder and then played it back at twenty times the normal speed. No midget voices interrupted the zipped-up block of quiet. They'd been asleep the entire time he'd been gone.

If only he could listen to the sex recording made during Peza's shift, he thought, he might be able to identify X and Y. He moused around the hard drive; Peza's audio file had been emailed to Vega before she'd left, but she'd forgotten to delete it.

He clicked. He listened.

That a man and a woman were having sex was indisputable, though it sounded to him less like a man and a woman having sex and more like a man being attacked by a vindictive, fluffy house cat.

The man, clearly, was Dasco; Gyula could tell from his voice, which he used primarily to moan and to say, repeatedly and drunkenly, *Death to Greedy Capitalists!*

This relieved him (that the value of Y was Dasco, that Dasco was still, at least based on the snoring noises he'd just heard through his earphones, alive) as much as the mysterious value of X frustrated him. X spoke occasionally but mostly she growled. He rewound and listened to the growls again and again and again until he was certain to whom they belonged.

Working undercover, he thought to himself. *Hah.* That was one way of putting it. He was overcome by disgust. This was Vega's idea of a tryout? Assigning Angy to bed the Viszla? Assigning him to listen to it?

He texted Angy.

a pruney germspeisen you are, he wrote, *growling like a whore*

speak for yourself schnitten, she replied, *the walls hear both ways*

personally i've grown a little tired of hearing things, he wrote.

not too tired to kiss that mousse-brained little rigo jancsi, she replied.

Gyula paused. She'd been listening to him?

that's it i'm coming over, he wrote.

dont, she wrote. He could practically hear her toneless insincerity.

here i come, he wrote.

Gyula walked into the hall and stood before door 724, uncertain that he wanted to see what he was bound to see, Angy in bed texting him while the Viszla slept the mercilessly overfucked sleep of the dead. He stood there for, he figured, at least five minutes. He knocked. No answer.

He returned to his room and straddled the headphones over his head to listen to the rest of Peza's audio file. Why, he couldn't say. Because he wanted to hear the sounds of the woman who would never have sex with him have sex with a dethroned vegetarian asshead. That's why.

Peza had been right about the sex: it was endless, and, after a while, phantasmagorically boring. Possibly so boring that Peza had honestly missed (unless she'd been lying to him) their conspiratorial whispering.

Gyula returned to the hallway and stood outside room 726. He withdrew the master hotel-room card Bela had given him.

The bed was made, the black-and-gold jacquard spread pulled tautly over the mattress, the sausage bolster plumped to remove all skull imprints. In the ashtray on the minibar, someone had left a generous five-fleuro tip for the chambermaid. Everything appeared newly straightened and awaiting the next guests except the drapes, which had been loosened from their tasseled tie-backs. They undulated weightily in the breeze gusting through the open window, dragging over the parquet floor and making a sound that was easily mistakable for sleep-breathing.

Gyula parted the drapes. Directly beneath him, two men in brown coveralls mopped up twin dark stains on the cobblestones. The cobblestones, he noticed, were depressed around the stains, as though something very heavy had recently landed on them.

Eavesdropper, he thought. *A person who drops from the eaves.*

The realization possessed a physical momentum; Gyula had to grab the window jamb to keep his body from hurtling into space. He stared at the impressions in the cobblestones and felt himself on the verge of weeping, the sort of weeping that threatens to dissolve one's entire body, starting with the heart.

He fumbled his phone from his shirt pocket.

you're so no longer here germspeisen, he wrote. Letting go meant believing, just for a second longer, that you could communicate with the dead by texting them.

no? the person pretending to be Angy replied.

who will be around to not love me? who? he wrote, the water in his eyes making it impossible to see the tiny keys.

dont be pathetic, came the reply. *i left you a memento in the closet*

Gyula heard a high-pitched whining—the sound of a vacuum nozzling the floor moldings overhead, he thought, before interpreting it correctly as the panicked revving of his own brain. He opened the closet door, expecting to find Angy's cracker-crushed body roped through the luggage rack.

To find her not there was both a relief and not a relief. On the floor, centered inside one of the parquet diamonds, he saw a snow globe. He picked it up carefully, as if it were of forensic importance to leave the snow undisturbed. Inside was a tiny plastic version of the Gresham, Christmassed up with plastic wreaths and red bows. He tried to peer into the windows at the minuscule featureless people who were watching TV, or making love, or about to shoot themselves through the mouth with a revolver, but many of the shades were drawn, and those that weren't blank-eyed onto empty rooms. The only visible figures were the faceless guards in front of the Gresham, wearing brown coveralls and hats with little designs above the brims, which could have been wreath-starstikas but could as easily have been stars in a cir-clet of corn, throwbacks to the past rather than men of an identical future.

In the hallway he heard the tumbling of many footfalls on the carpet, and a woman's voice speaking German.

Behind him, Sydney Vega opened the door of room 724. He saw her fatly reflected in the snow globe's curve.

He shook the globe. The snow wafted upward sluggishly. He pressed the globe against his eye socket, hoping he might spot Angy inside, entombed but safe.

The coverall men escorting Vega paused at the threshold. She stood by the bathroom door, her scarves gusting around her.

"Horvath," she said.

He chose not to reply.

Vega talked to him even though he made it quite clear by the way he peered into the snow globe that he wasn't listening to her. Nevertheless, she kept talking. She complimented him on his sleuthing skills. She announced that certain personnel decisions were being made within minutes—decisions over which he had a clear bodily investment, and about which he might, if he agreed to "play ball" (unlike a few other potential employees), have a say.

But Gyula was too busy watching the fake snow falling on the Gresham to reply. He noticed, with some irritation, that the snow fell too quickly, as if the person who had made this particular snow globe had cut some corners and purchased, for a lesser price, the heavier fake snow, the variety that sank rather than drifted.

He shook the globe hard, practically concussing it in order to fool its equilibrium into keeping the snowflakes airborne. Clearly it was a worthless piece of crap—not a collector's item, the snow made of metal sloughings or some industrial-waste by-product, cleverly repurposed and leaching unknown toxins into this frozen-in-time scene from the past, or the future, not that there was any difference—and so he would be better off hurling it out the window and watching it explode on the cobbles, maybe making a small indent where it landed, inflict some damage to remember it by in this country where all is commemorated and everything forgotten.

But then it seemed shameful to rupture the symbolic meniscus, this material proof of the failure of everything. His bad future was coming for him regardless of what ruptured and what remained intact. Still, he wanted to preserve its destruction as an option. He stood by the window, globe cocked over his head like a baseball or a bomb as Vega's men crept into the room, easing along the walls, their coveralls rubbing audibly against the flocked paper. He one-eyed a man wielding, of all things, a glue gun. *Got you in my crosshairs*, he thought. *Snow globe beats glue gun. I could crush your noggin.*

Gyula fake-threw the globe, theatrically winding up and then freezing at the top of his pitching arc, watching with no small satisfaction as his target flinched. He faked three more throws at three different men; each man jerked like a puppet attached to strings that Gyula was pulling. This made him laugh, and as he laughed his body relaxed, allowing sense to flow back into his head. Of course he wasn't going to peg anyone with a snow globe. This impulse toward self-preservation seemed not only futile but also desperate and cowardly. He was Gyula Sigmund Horvath of the uncooperative Hungarian Horvaths, and he experienced a surge of pride to think that he was joining his long line of contrary Jew ancestors, whoever they were and whatever had happened to them, by refusing to engage in the pointlessness, to immediately, rather than to someday, ass-fuck himself. Better, thus, to save the globe for posterity. When he was gone another hand would shake it, and then another hand after that, and as he looked out the window, contemplating his final act of eavesdropping, he found some solace in knowing that forever it would be Christmas, and forever the metal snow would fall on the Gresham, and forever the people trapped inside would stare out their windows at the proud faces of the doomed.

THE NETHERLANDS
LIVES WITH WATER

by JIM SHEPARD

A LONG TIME AGO a man had a dog that went down to the shoreline every day and howled. When she returned the man would look at her blankly. Eventually the dog got exasperated. "Hey," the dog said. "There's a shit-storm of biblical proportions headed your way." "Please. I'm busy," the man said. "Hey," the dog said the next day, and told him the same thing. This went on for a week. Finally the man said, "If you say that once more I'm going to take you out to sea and dump you overboard." The next morning the dog went down to the shore-line again, and the man followed. "Hey," the dog said, after a minute. "Yeah?" the man said. "Oh, I think you know," the dog said.

"Or here's another one," Cato says to me. "Adam goes to God, 'Why'd you make Eve so beautiful?' And God says, 'So you would love her.' And Adam says, 'Well, why'd you make her so stupid?' And God says, 'So she would love you.'"

Henk laughs. "Well, he thinks it's funny," Cato says.

"He's eleven years old," I tell her.

"And very precocious," she reminds me. Henk makes an overly jovial face and holds two thumbs up. His mother takes her napkin and wipes some egg from his chin.

We met in the same pre-university track. I was a year older but hadn't passed Dutch and so took it again with her.

"You failed Dutch?" she whispered from her seat behind me. She'd seen me gaping at her when I'd come in. The teacher had announced that that's what those of us who were older were doing there.

"It's your own language," she told me later that week. She was holding my penis upright so she could run the edge of her lip along the shaft. I felt like I was about to touch the ceiling.

"You're not very articulate," she remarked later, on the subject of the sounds I'd produced.

She acted as though I were a spot of sun in an otherwise rainy month. We always met at her house, a short bicycle ride away, and her parents seemed to be perpetually asleep or dead. In three months I saw her father from behind once. She explained that she'd been raised by depressives, and that they'd left her one of those girls who'd sit on the playground with the tools of happiness all around her and refuse to play. Her last boyfriend had walked out on her the week before we'd met. His diagnosis had been that she imposed on everyone else the gloom her family had taught her to expect.

"Do I sadden you?" she'd ask me late at night before taking me in her mouth. "Will you have children with me?" I started asking her back.

And she was flattered and seemed pleased without being particularly fooled. "I've been thinking about how hard it is to pull information out of you," she told me one night when we'd pitched our clothes out from under her comforter. I asked what she wanted to know and she said that that was the kind of thing she was talking about. While she was speaking I watched her front teeth, glazed from our kissing. When she had a cold and her nose was blocked up, she looked a little dazed in profile.

"I ask a question and you ask another one," she complained. "If I ask what your old girlfriend was like you ask what anyone's old girlfriend is like."

"So ask what you want to ask," I told her.

"Do you think that someone like you and someone like me should be together?" she said.

"Because we're so different?" I wanted to know.

"Do you think that someone like you and someone like me should be together?" she repeated.

"Yes," I told her.

"That's helpful. Thanks," she responded. And then she wouldn't see me for a week. When I felt I'd waited long enough, I intercepted her on her way home and asked, "Was the right answer no?" And she smiled and kissed me as though hunting up some compensation for diminished expectations. After that it was as if we'd agreed to give ourselves over to what we had. When I put my mouth on her, her hands would bend back at the wrists as if miming helplessness. I disappeared for minutes at a time from my classes, envisioning the trancelike way her lips would part after so much kissing.

The next time she asked me to tell her something about myself I had some candidates lined up. She held my hands away from her and the result tented the comforter to provide some cooling air. I told her I still remembered the way my older sister replaced her indigo hair bow with an orange one on royal birthdays. I remembered the way I followed her, chanting that she was a pig, and the way I was always unjustly punished for that. How I fed her staggeringly complicated lies that went on for weeks and ended in disaster with my parents or teachers. How before she died of the flu epidemic I slept in her bed the last three nights.

Her cousins had died then as well, Cato told me. If somebody even just brought up 2015, her aunt still went to pieces. She didn't let go of my hands so I went on. I told her that, being an outsider as a little boy, I'd noticed that *something* was screwed up with me, but I couldn't put my finger on what. I probably wasn't as baffled by it as I sounded, but it was still more than I'd ever told anyone else.

She'd grown up right off the Boompjes; I'd been way out in Pernis, looking at the Caltex refinery through the haze. The little fishing village was still there then, huddled in the center of the petrochemical sprawl. My sister loved the lights of the complex at night and the fires that went hundreds of feet into the air like solar flares when the waste gases burned off. Kids from other neighborhoods always noticed the smell on our skin. The light was that golden sodium-vapor light, and my father liked to say about it that it was always Christmas in Pernis. At night I'd be able to read with my bedroom lamp off. In the mornings while we got ready for school the dredging platforms with their twin pillars would disappear up into the fog like Gothic cathedrals.

A week after I told her all that, I introduced her to Kees. "I've never seen him like this," he told her. We were both on track for one of the technology universities, maybe Eindhoven, and he hadn't failed Dutch. "Well, I'm a pretty amazing woman," she explained to him.

Kees and I both went on to study physical geography and got into the water sector. Cato became the media liaison for the program director for Rotterdam Climate Proof. We got married after our third International Knowledge for Climate Research conference. Kees asked us recently which anniversary we had coming up and I said eleventh and she said one-hundredth.

It didn't take a crystal ball to realize that we were in a growth industry. Gravity and thermal measurements by GRACE satellites had already flagged the partial shutdown of the Atlantic circulation system. The World Glacier Monitoring Service, saddled with having to release one glum piece of news after another, had just that year reported that the Pyrenees, Africa, and the Rockies were all glacier-free. The Americans had just confirmed the collapse of the West Antarctic ice sheet. Once-in-a-century floods in England were now occurring every two years. Bangladesh was almost entirely a bay and that whole area a war zone because of the displacement issues.

It's the catastrophe for which the Dutch have been planning for fifty years. Or really, for as long as we've existed: we had cooperative water management before we had a state. The one created the other: either we pulled together as a collective or got swept away as individuals. The real old-timers had a saying for when things fucked up: "Well, the Netherlands lives with water." What they meant was that their land flooded twice a day.

Bishop Prudentius of Troyes wrote in his annals that in the ninth century the whole of the country was devoured by the sea: that all the settlements disappeared and that the water was higher than the dunes. In the Saint Felix Flood, North Beveland was completely swept away. In the All Saints' Flood the entire coast was inundated between Flanders and Germany. In 1717 a dike collapse killed fourteen thousand on Christmas night.

"You like going on like this, don't you?" Cato sometimes asks.

"I like the way it focuses your attention," I told her once.

"Do you like the way it scares our son?" she wanted to know.

"It doesn't scare me," Henk told us.

"It *does* scare you," she told him. "And your father doesn't seem to register that."

For the last few years when I've announced that the sky is falling she's answered that our son doesn't need to hear it. And that I always bring it up when there's something else to be discussed. I always concede her point but that doesn't get me off the hook. "For instance, I'm still waiting to hear how your mother's making out," she complains during a dinner when we can't tear Henk's attention away from the Feyenoord celebrations. If a team wins the Cup, the whole town gets drunk. If it loses, the whole town gets drunk.

My mother's now at the point at which no one can deny it's dementia. She's still in the little house on Polluxstraat, even though the rest of the Pernis she knew seems to have evaporated around her. Cato finds it unconscionable that I've allowed her to stay there on her own, without help. "Let me guess: you don't want to talk about it," she says whenever she brings it up.

She doesn't know the half of it. The day after my father's funeral my mother brought me into their bedroom and revealed to me the paperwork on what she called their Rainy Day Account, a staggering amount. Where had they gotten so much? "Your father," she told me unhelpfully. I went home that night and Cato asked what was new and I told her about my mother's regime of short walks.

Each step of the way in the transfer of assets, financial advisers or bank officers have asked if my wife's name would be on the account as well. She still has no idea it exists. It means that I now have a secret net worth more than triple my family's. What am I up to? Your guess is as good as mine.

"Have you talked to anyone about the live-in position?" Cato wants to know. I'd raised the idea with my mother and she'd started shouting that she never should have showed me the money. Since then I've been less bullish about bringing Cato and Henk around to see her.

I tell her that things are progressing the way we would hope.

"Things are progressing the way we would hope?" Cato repeats.

"That's it in a nutshell," I tell her, a little playfully, but her expression makes clear that she's waiting for a fuller explanation.

"Don't you have homework?" I ask Henk, and he and his mother exchange a look. I've always believed that I'm a master at hiding my feelings, but I seem to be alone in that regard.

Cato's been through this before in various iterations. When my mother was first diagnosed, I hashed through the whole thing with Kees, who'd been in my office when the call had come in, and then told Cato later that night that there'd been no change, so as not to have to trudge through the whole story again. The doctor had called the next day when I was out to see how I was taking the news.

Henk looks at me like he's using my face to attempt some long division. Cato eats without saying anything until she finally loses her temper with the cutlery.

"I told you before that if you don't want to do this, I can," she says.

"There's nothing that needs doing," I tell her.

"There's plenty that needs doing," she says. She pulls the remote from Henk and switches off the news. "Look at him," she complains to Henk. "He's always got his eyes somewhere else. Does he even know he shakes his head when he listens?"

Pneumatic hammers pick up where they left off outside our window. There's always construction somewhere. Why not rip up the streets? The Germans did such a good job of it in 1940 that it's as if we've been competing with them ever since. Rotterdam: a deep hole in the pavement with a sign telling you to approach at your own risk. Our whole lives, walking through the city has meant muddy shoes.

As we're undressing that night she asks how I'd rate my recent performance as a husband.

I don't know; maybe not so good, not so bad, I tell her.

She answers that if I were a minister, I'd resign.

What area are we talking about here, in terms of performance? I want to know.

"Go to sleep," she tells me, and turns off the lamp.

If climate change is a hammer to the Dutch, the hammer's coming down more or less where we live. Rotterdam's astride an estuarine area that absorbs the Scheldt, Meuse, and Rhine outflows, and what we're facing is that troika of sea-level rise, peak river discharges, and extreme weather events. We've got the jewel of our water defenses—the massive water barriers at Maeslant and Dordrecht, and the rest of the Delta Works—ready to shut off the North Sea during the next cataclysmic storms, but what are we to do when that coincides with the peak river discharges? Sea levels are leaping up, our ground is subsiding, it's raining harder and more often, and our program of managed flooding—Make Room for the Rivers—was overwhelmed long ago. The dunes and dikes at eleven locations from Ter Heijde to Westkapelle no longer meet what we decided would be the minimum safety standards. Temporary emergency measures are starting to be known to the public as Hans Brinkers.

And this winter's been a festival of bad news. Kees's team has measured increased snowmelt in the Alps to go along with prolonged rainfall across northern Europe and steadily increasing windspeeds during gales, all of which are leading to ominously increased winter flows, especially for the Rhine. He and I—known around the office as The Pessimists—forecasted this winter's discharge at eighteen thousand cubic meters per second. It's now up to twenty-one. What are those of us in charge of dealing with that supposed to do? A megastorm at this point would overwhelm the barriers from both sides and inundate Rotterdam and its surroundings—three million people—in twenty-four hours.

Which is quite the challenge for someone in media relations. "Remember, the Netherlands will always be here," Cato likes to say as her way of signing off with one of the news agencies. "Though probably under three meters of water," she'll add after she's hung up.

Before this most recent emergency, my area of expertise had to do with the strength and loading of the Water Defense structures, especially in terms of the Scheldt estuary. We'd been integrating forecasting and security software for high-risk areas and trying to get Arcadis to understand that it needed to share almost everything with IBM and vice-versa. I'd even been lent out to work on the Venice, London, and St. Petersburg Surge Barriers. But now all of us were back home and thrown into the Weak Links Project, that over-educated fire brigade composed to rush off to address new vulnerabilities as they emerged.

And we all have our faces turned helplessly to the Alps. There's been a series of cloudbursts on the eastern slopes: fourteen inches of rain in the last two weeks. The Germans have long since raised their river dikes to funnel the water right past them and into the Netherlands. Some of that water will be taken up in the soil, some in lakes and ponds and catchment basins, and some in polders and farmland that we've set aside for flooding emergencies. Some in water plazas and water gardens and specially designed underground parking garages and reservoirs. The rest will keep moving downriver to Rotterdam and the closed surge barriers.

"Well, change is the soul of Rotterdam," Kees joked when we first looked at the numbers on the meteorological disaster ahead. We were given private notification that there would be vertical evacuation if the warning time for an untenable situation were under two hours, and horizontal evacuation if it were over two.

"What am I supposed to do—tell the helicopter that we have to pop over to

Henk's school?" Cato wanted to know when I told her. He now has an agreed-upon code: when it appears on his iFuze, he's to leave school immediately and head to her office.

But in the meantime, we operate as though it won't come to that. We think: We'll come up with something. We always have. Where would New Orleans or the Mekong Delta be without Dutch hydraulics and Dutch water management? And where would the U.S. and Europe be if we hadn't led the way out of the financial Panic and Depression, just by being ourselves? E.U. dominoes from Iceland to Ireland to Italy came down around our ears but there we sat, having been protected by our own Dutchness. What was the joke about us, after all? That we didn't go to the banks to take money out; we went to put money in. Who was going to be the first, as economy after economy capsized, to pony up the political courage to nationalize their banks and work cooperatively? Well, who took more seriously the public good than the Dutch? Who was more in love with rules? Who tells anyone who'll listen that we're providing the rest of the world with a glimpse of what the future will be?

After a third straight sleepless night—"Oh, who gets any sleep in the water sector?" Kees answered irritably the morning I complained about it—I leave the office early and ride a water-taxi to Pernis. In Nieuwe Maas the shipping is so thick that it's like kayaking through canyons, and the taxi captain charges extra for what he calls a piloting fee. We tip and tumble on the backswells while four tugs nudge a super-tanker sideways into its berth. The tugs look like puppies snuffling at the base of a cliff. The tanker's hull is so high that we can't see any superstructure above it.

I hike from the dock to Polluxstraat, the traffic on the A4 above rolling like surf. "Look who's here," my mother says, instead of hello. She goes about her tea-making as though I dropped in unannounced every afternoon. We sit in the break-fast nook off the kitchen. Before she settles in, she reverses the pillow embroidered GOOD NIGHT so that it now reads GOOD MORNING.

"How's Henk?" she wants to know. I tell her he's got some kind of chest thing. "As long as they're healthy," she replies. I don't see any reason to quibble.

The bottom shelves of her refrigerator are puddled with liquid from deliquescing vegetables and something spilled. The bristles of her bottle scraper on the counter are coated with dried mayonnaise. The front of her nightgown is an archipelago of stains. "How's Cato?" she asks.

"Cato wants to know if we're going to get you some help," I tell her.

"I just talked with her. She didn't say anything like that," she says irritably.

"You talked with her? What'd you talk about?" I ask. But she waves me off. "Did you talk with her or not?" I ask again.

"That girl from up north you brought here to meet me, I couldn't even understand her," she tells me. She talks about regional differences as though her country's the size of China.

"We thought she seemed very efficient," I tell her. "What else did Cato talk with you about?"

But she's already shifted her interest to the window. Years ago she had a traffic mirror mounted outside on the frame to let her spy on the street unobserved. She uses a finger to widen the gap in the lace curtains.

What else should she do all day long? She never goes out. The street's her revival house, always showing the same movie.

The holes in her winter stockings are patched with a carnival array of colored thread. We always lived by that old maxim that a thing lasted longer mended than new. My whole life, I heard that with thrift and hard work I could build a mansion. My father had in his office at home a typewritten note tacked to the wall: *Let those with abundance remember that they are surrounded by thorns.* "Who said *that*?" Cato asked when we were going through his things. "Calvin," I told her. "Well, you would know," she said.

He hadn't been so much a conservative as a man whose life philosophy had boiled down to the principal of no nonsense. I'd noticed even as a tiny boy that whenever he'd liked a business associate or a woman, that's what he said about them.

My mother's got her nose to the glass at this point. "You think you're the only one with secrets," she remarks.

"What's that supposed to mean?" I ask, but she acts as though she's not going to dignify my response. Follow-up questions don't get anywhere, either. I sit with her awhile longer. We watch a Chinese game show. I soak her bread in milk, and walk her to the toilet. I tell her we have to at least think about moving her bed downstairs somewhere. The steps to her second floor are vertiginous even by Dutch standards, and the risers accommodate less than half your foot. She makes an effort to follow what I seem to be on about, puzzling out that she needs to puzzle out something. But then her expression dissipates. She complains that she spent half the night looking for the coffee grinder.

"Why were you looking for the coffee grinder?" I ask her. I have to repeat the question. Then I have to stop, for fear of frightening her.

Henk's class is viewing a presentation at the Climate Campus—*Water: Precious Resource and Deadly Companion*—so we have the dinner table to ourselves. Cato's day was even longer than mine so I prepared the meal: two cans of pea soup with pigs' knuckles and some Belgian beer. She's too tired to complain. She's dealing with both the Americans, who are always hectoring for clarification on the changing risk factors for our projects in Miami and New Orleans, and the Germans, who've publicly dug in their heels on the issue of accepting any spillover from the Rhine in order to take some of the pressure off the situation downstream.

It's the usual debate, as far as the latter argument's concerned. We take the high road—it's only through cooperation that we can face such monumental challenges, etc.—and another country scoffs at our aspirations toward ever more comprehensive safety measures. The German foreign minister last year accused us on a simulcast of being old women.

"Maybe he's right," Cato says wearily. "Sometimes I wonder what it'd be like to be in a country where you don't need a license to build a fence around your garden."

Exasperated, we indulge in a little Dutch bashing. No one complains about themselves as well as the Dutch. Cato asks if I remember that story about the manufacturers having to certify that each of the chocolate letters handed out by Santa Claus contained an equal amount of chocolate. I remind her about the number-one download of the year turning out to have been *fireworks sound effects*, for those New Year's revelers who found real fireworks too worrisome.

After we stop, she looks at me, her mouth a little slack. "Why does this sort of thing make us horny?" she wants to know.

"Maybe it's the pea soup," I tell her in the shower. She's examining little crescents of fingernail marks where she held me when she came. She turns off the water and we wrap ourselves in the bedsheet-size towel she had made in Surinam. Cocooned on the floor in the tiny steamy bathroom, we discuss Kees's love life. He now shops at a singles' supermarket, the kind where if you're taken, you use a blue basket and if you're available, a yellow. When I asked him how his latest fling was working out, he said, "Well, I'm back to the yellow basket."

Cato thinks it's a funny story. "How'd *we* get to be so lucky?" I ask her. We're spooning and she does a minimal grind against me that allows me to grow inside her.

"The other day someone from BBC 1 asked my boss that same question about how he ended up where he did," she says. She turns her cheek so I can kiss it.

"What'd he say?" I ask when I've moved from her cheek to her neck. She's not a big fan of her boss.

She shrugs comfortably, her shoulder blades against my chest. I wrap my arms tighter so the fit is even more perfect. She tells me that the gist of his answer was: Mostly by not asking too many questions.

My mother always had memory problems, and even before my sister died my father always said that he didn't blame her: she'd seen her own brothers swept away in the 1953 flood and had been a wreck for years afterward. The night after her sixth birthday, January 31, a storm-field that covered the entire North Sea swept down out of the northwest with winds that registered gale force 11 and combined with a spring tide to raise the sea six meters over NAP. The breakers overtopped the dikes in eighty-nine locations over a hundred-and-seventy-kilometer stretch and hollowed them out on their land sides so that the surges that followed broke them. My mother remembered eating her soup alongside her brothers while they listened to the wind increase in volume until her father went out to see to the barn and the draft from the opened door blew their board game off the table. Her mother's Bible pages flapped in her hands like panicked birds. Water was seeping through the window casing and her brother touched it and held his finger for her to taste. She remembered his look when she realized that it was salty: not rain but spray from the sea.

Her father returned to tell them that they all had to leave, now. They held hands in a chain and he went first and she went second and once the door was opened the wind staggered him and blew her off her feet.

He managed to retrieve her, but by then they couldn't find the others in the dark and the rain. She was soaked in ice and the water was already up to their thighs and in the distance she could see breakers where the dike had been. They headed inland and found refuge in the open door of a neighbor's brick home and discovered the back half of the house already torn away by the water. He led her up the stairs to the third floor and through a trap onto the roof. Their neighbors were already there, and her mother, huddling against the force of the wind and the cold. The house west of them imploded but its roof held together and was pushed upright in front of theirs, diverting the main force of the flood around them like a break-water. She remembered holding her father's hand so that their bodies would be found in the same place. Her mother shrieked and pointed and she saw her brothers beside a man with a bundle and a woman with a baby on the roof of the house beyond theirs to the east. Each wave that broke against the front drenched them with spray, and the woman kept turning her torso to shield the baby. And then the front of the house caved in and everyone on it became bobbing heads in the water that were swept around the collapsing walls and away.

She remembered the wind having finally died down by mid-morning, and a mist continuing out of the gray sky, and a fishing smack way off to the north coast-ing between the rooftops, bringing people on board. She remembered a dog lowered on a rope, its paws flailing as it turned.

After their rescue, she remembered a telegraph pole slanted over, its wires tugged by the current. She remembered the water smelling of gasoline and mud. She remembered treetops uncovered by the waves and a clog between two steep roofs filled with floating branches and dead cattle. She remembered a vast plain of wreckage on the water. She remembered that sea-smell of dead fish that traveled along the wind. She remembered two older boys sitting beside her examining the silt driven inside an unopened bottle of soda by the force of the waves. She remem-bered her mother's animal sounds and the length of time it took to get to dry land, and her father's chin on her mother's bent back, his head bumping whenever they crossed the wakes of the other boats.

We always knew this was coming. Years ago the city fathers of Rotterdam thought: This is our big opportunity. We're no longer just the ugly port or Amsterdam with-out the attractions. The bad news was going to impact us first and foremost, so we put out the word: we were looking for people with the nerve to put into practice what was barely possible anywhere else. The result was Waterplan 4 Rotterdam, with all-new approaches to water storage and water safety: water plazas, super cisterns, water balloons, green roofs, and even traffic tunnels that doubled as immense drainage systems, would all siphon off danger. It roped in Kees and Cato and me and by the end of the first week had set Cato against us. Her mandate was to showcase Dutch ingenuity, so the last thing she needed was The Pessimists buzzing about clamoring for more funding because nothing anyone had come up with yet was going to work. As far as she was concerned, our country was the testing ground for all high-profile adaptive measures and practically oriented knowledge and prototype projects that would attract worldwide attention and become a sluice-gate for high-tech exports. She spent her days in the international marketplace hawking the notion that *Here we're safe because we have the knowledge and we're using that knowledge to find creative solutions.* We were all assuming a secure population to be a collective social good for which the government and private sector would remain responsible: a notion not universally embraced by other countries, we realized.

Sea-facing barriers are inspected by hand and laser imaging. Smart dikes schedule their own maintenance based on sensors that detect seepage or changes in pressure and stability. Satellites track ocean currents and water-mass volumes. The areas most at risk have been divided into dike-ring compartments in an attempt to make the country a system of watertight doors. Our road and infrastructure networks now function independently of the ground layer. Nine entire neighborhoods have been made amphibious: built on hollow platforms that will rise with the water but remain anchored to submerged foundations. And besides the giant storm barriers, atop our dikes we've mounted titanium-braced walls that unfold from concrete channels, leviathan-like inflatable rubber dams, and special grasses grown on plastic mat revetments to anchor the inner walls.

Is it all enough? Henk wants to know, whenever there's a day of unremitting rain. Oh, honey, it's more than enough, Cato tells him. And then she quizzes him on our emergency code.

"It's funny how this kind of work has been good for me," Cato says. She's asked to go for a walk, an activity she knows I'll find nostalgically stirring. We tramped all over the city before and after lovemaking when we first got together. "All of this end-of-the-world stuff apparently cheers me up," she remarks. "I guess it's the same thing I used to get at home. All those glum faces, and I had to do the song and dance that explained why they got out of bed in the morning."

"The heavy lifting," I tell her.

"Exactly," she says with a faux mournfulness. "The heavy lifting. We're on for another simulcast tomorrow and it'll be three Germans with long faces and Cato the Optimist."

We negotiate a herd of bicycles on a plaza and she veers toward the harbor. We walk a little ways in single file. When we cross the skylights of the traffic tunnels, giant container haulers shudder by beneath our feet. She has a beautiful back, accentuated by the military cut of her overcoat. "Except that the people you're dealing with now *want* to be fooled," I tell her.

"It's not that they want to be fooled," she corrects. "It's just that they're not convinced that they need to go around glum all the time."

"How'd that philosophy work with your parents?" I ask.

"Not so well," she says sadly.

We turn onto Boompjes, which is sure to add to her melancholy. A seven-story construction crane with legs curving inward perches like a spider over the river.

"Your mother called about the coffee grinder," she remarks. "I couldn't pin down what she was talking about."

Boys in bathing suits are pitching themselves off the high dock by the Strand, though it seems much too cold for that, and the river too dirty. Even in the chill I can smell tar and rope and, somewhere, fresh bread.

"She called you or you called her?" I ask.

"I just told you," Cato says.

"It seems odd that she would call you," I tell her.

"What *was* she talking about?" Cato wants to know.

"I assume she was having trouble working the coffee grinder," I tell her.

"Working it or finding it?" she asks.

"Working it, I think," I suggest. "She called you?"

"Oh my God," Cato says.

"I'm just asking," I tell her after a minute.

All of Maashaven is blocked from view by a giant Suction Dredger that's being barged out to Maasvlakte 2. It's preceded by six tugs in the parade and looks like a small city going by. The thing uses dragheads connected to tubes the size of railway tunnels, and harvests sand down to a depth of twenty meters. It'll be deepening the docking areas out at Yangtzehaven, Europahaven, and Mississippihaven. There's been some worry that all of this dredging has been undermining the water defenses on the other side of the channel, which is the last thing we need. Kees has been dealing with their horseshit for a few weeks now.

We stop on a bench in front of some law offices. Over the front entrance, cameras have been installed to monitor the surveillance cameras, which have been vandalized. Once the Dredger has passed, we can see a family of day campers across the way who've pitched their tent on a berm overlooking the channel.

"Isn't it too cold for camping?" I ask her.

"Wasn't it too cold for swimming?" she responds, about the boys we passed.

She says Henk keeps replaying the same footage on his iFuze of Feyenoord's MVP being lowered into the stadium beneath the team flag by a VSTOL. "So here's what I'm thinking," she continues, as though that led her to her next thought. She mentions a conservatory in Berlin, fantastically expensive, that runs a winter program in chamber music. She'd like to send Henk there during his Winter Break, and maybe longer.

This seems to me to be mostly about his safety, though I don't acknowledge that. He's a gifted cellist, but hardly seems devoted to the instrument.

She repeats the amount it will cost with her pitchman's good cheer, though we don't have it. It's the daily rate for a five-star hotel. But she believes that money can always be found for a good idea, and if it can't, it wasn't a good idea. And her husband is, after all, a hydraulic engineer, the equivalent of an atomic physicist in terms of technological prestige.

Atomic physicists don't make a whole lot of money, either, I remind her. And our argument proceeds from there. I can see her disappointment expanding as we speak, and even as the result contracts my inner organs, I sit on the information of my hidden nest egg and allow all of the unhappiness to unfold. It all takes forever. The word in our country for the decision-making process is the same as the word for what we pour over our pancakes. Our national mindset pivots around the word *but*: as in, *This, yes, but that, too.* Cato puts her fingers to her temples and sheaths her cheeks with her palms. Her arguments run aground on my tolerance, which has been elsewhere described as a refusal to listen. Passion in Dutch meetings is punished by being ignored. The idea is that it's the argument itself that matters, and not the intensity with which it's presented. Outright rejections of a position are rare; what you get instead are suggestions for improvement that if followed would annihilate the original intent. And then everyone checks their agendas to schedule the next meeting.

Just like that, we're walking back. We're single file again, and it's gotten colder.

From our earliest years, we're taught not to burden others with our emotions. A young Amsterdammer in the Climate Campus is known as the Thespian because he sobbed in public at a coworker's funeral. "You don't need to eliminate your emotions," Kees reminded him when he complained about it. "You just need to be a little more economical with them."

Another thing I've never told Cato: my sister and I had been jumping into the river in the winter as well, the week before she caught the flu. That had been my idea. When she'd come out, her feet and lips had been blue. She'd sneezed all the way home. "Do you think I'll catch a cold?" she asked that night. "Go to sleep," I told her in response.

We take a shortcut through the sunken pedestrian mall they call the Shopping Gutter. By the time we reach our street it's dark and it's raining again, and the muddy pavement is shining in the lights of the cafés. Along the new athletic complex in the distance, sapphire blue searchlights are lancing up into the rain at even intervals, like a landscape's harp strings. "I don't know if you *know* what this does to me, or you don't," Cato says at our doorstep, once she's stopped and turned. Her thick brown hair is beaded with moisture where it's not soaked. "But either way, it's just so miserable."

I actually *have* the solution to our problem, I'm reminded as I follow her up the stairs. The thought makes me feel rehabilitated, as though I've told her instead of only myself.

Cato always said about her parents' marriage that they practiced a sort of apocalyptic utilitarianism: on the one hand they were sure everything was going to hell in a handbasket, while on the other they continued to operate as though they could turn things around with a few practical measures.

But there's always that moment in a country's history when it learns that the earth is less manageable than was thought. Ten years ago we needed to conduct comprehensive assessments of the flood defenses every five years. Now safety margins are adjusted every six months to take new revelations into account. For the last year and a half we've been told to build into our designs for whatever we're working on features that restrict the damaging effects *after* an inevitable inundation. There won't be any retreating back to the hinterlands, either, because given the numbers we're facing there won't be any hinterlands. It's gotten to the point that pedestrians are banned from the sea-facing dikes in the far west even on calm days. At the entrance to the Haringvlietdam they've erected an immense yellow CAUTION sign that features two tiny stick figures with their arms raised in alarm at a black wave three times their size that's curling over them.

I watched Kees's face during a recent simulation as one of his new designs for a smart dike was overwhelmed in half the time he would have predicted. It had always been the Dutch assumption that we would resolve what problems faced us from a position of strength. But we passed that station long ago. At this point each of us understands privately that we're operating under the banner of lost control.

The next morning we're crammed into Rotterdam Climate Proof's Smartvan heading west on N211, still not speaking. Cato's driving. At 140 kilometers an hour the rain fans across the windshield energetically, racing the wipers. Gray clouds seem to be rushing in from the sea in the distance. We cross some polders that are already flooded and there's a rocking buoyancy when we traverse that part of the road that's floating. Trucks sweep by backward and recede behind us in the spray.

The only sounds are the sounds of the tires and wipers and rain. Exploring the radio is like visiting the Tower of Babel: Turks, Berbers, Cape Verdeans, Antilleans, Angolans, Portuguese, Croatians, Brazilians, Chinese. Cato managed to relocate her simulcast with her three long-faced Germans to the Hoek van Holland; she told the Germans she wanted the Maeslant Barrier as a backdrop but what she really intends is to surprise them, live, with the state of the water levels already. Out near the Barrier it's pretty dramatic. Cato the Optimist with indisputable visual evidence that the sky is falling: can the German position remain unshaken in the face of that? Will her grandstanding work? It's hard to say. It's pretty clear that nothing else will.

"Want me to talk about Gravenzande?" I ask her. "That's the sort of thing that would certainly jolt the boys from the Reich."

"That's just what I need," she answers. "You starting a panic about something that might not even be true."

Gravenzande's where she's going to drop me, a few kilometers away. Geologists there three days ago turned up crushed shell deposits seven meters higher on the dune lines inland than anyone believed floods had ever reached. The deposits look to be only about ten thousand years old. If that ends up confirmed, it's very bad news, given what it clarifies about how cataclysmic things could get even before the climate's more recent turn for the worse.

It's Saturday, and we'll probably put in twelve hours. Henk's getting more comfortable with his weekend nanny than with us. As Cato likes to tell him when she's trying to induce him to do his chores: Around here, you work. By which she means that old joke that when you buy a shirt in Rotterdam, it comes with the sleeves already rolled up.

We pass poplars in neat rows lining the canals, a canary-yellow smudge of a house submerged up to its second-floor windows. Beyond a roundabout, a pair of decrepit rugby goalposts.

"You're really going to announce that if the Germans pull their weight, everything's going to be fine?" I ask. But she ignores me.

She needs a decision, she tells me a few minutes later, as though tired of asking. Henk's winter break is coming up. I venture that I thought it wasn't until the twelfth, and she reminds me with exasperation that it's the fifth, the schools now staggering the vacation times to avoid overloading the transportation systems.

We pass the curved sod roofs of factories. The secret account's not a problem but a solution, I decide, and as I model to myself ways of implementing it as such, Cato finally asserts as though she's waited long enough that she thinks she's found the answer: she could take that Royal Dutch Shell offer to reconfigure its regional media relations and they could set her up in Wannsee and Henk could commute.

They could stay out there and get a bump in income besides. Henk could enroll in the conservatory.

We exit N211 northwest on an even smaller access road to the coast. Within a kilometer it ends in a turnaround next to the dunes, and she pulls the car about so that it's pointed back toward her simulcast, then turns off the engine and sits there beside me with her hands in her lap.

"How long has this been in the works?" I ask. She wants to know what I mean and I tell her that it doesn't seem like so obscure a question; that she said no to Shell years ago, so where did this new offer come from?

She shrugs, as if I asked if they'd be paying her moving expenses. "They called. I told them I'd listen to what they had to say."

"They called you," I tell her.

"They called me," she repeats.

She's only trying to hedge her bets, I tell myself to combat the panic. Our country's all about spreading risk around.

"Do people just walk into this conservatory?" I ask. "Don't you have to apply?"

She doesn't answer, which I take to mean that she and Henk have already applied, and that he's been accepted.

"How did Henk feel about his good news?" I ask.

"He wanted to tell you," Cato answers.

"And we would see each other every other weekend? Once a month?" I'm attempting a version of steely neutrality but can hear the terror working its way forward.

"This is just one option of many," she reminds me. "We need to talk about all of them." She adds that she has to go. And that I should see the option as being primarily about Henk, and not us. I answer that the Netherlands will always be here, and she smiles and starts the van.

"You sure there's nothing else you want to talk to me about?" she asks.

"Like what?" I say. "I want to talk to you about everything."

She jiggles the gear shift lightly, considering me. "You're going to let me drive away with your having left it at that," she says.

"I don't want you to drive away at all," I tell her.

"Well, there is that," she concedes bitterly. She waits another full minute and then a curtain comes down on her expression and she puts the car in gear. She honks when she's pulling out.

At the top of the dune I watch surfers in wet suits wading into the breakers in the rain, the waves barely enough to keep them on their boards. The rain picks up so that the sea's surface is in constant agitation. Even the surfers keep low, as if to stay out of it. The wet sand's like brown sugar in my shoes.

Five hundred thousand years ago it was possible to walk from where I live to England. At that point the Thames was a tributary of the Rhine. Even during the Romans' occupation, the Zuider Zee was dry. But by the sixth century BC we were building artificial hills out of marsh grass mixed with manure and our own refuse to keep our feet out of the water. And then in the seventeenth century Hulsebos invented the Archimedes screw, and water wheels could raise a flow four meters higher than where it began, and we started to make real progress at keeping what the old people called the Waterwolf from the door.

In the fifteenth century Philip the Good ordered the sand dike that constituted the original Hondsbossche Seawall to be restored, and another built behind it as a backup. He named the latter the Sleeper dike. For extra security, he had another constructed behind that, and called that one the Dreamer dike. Ever since, school-children have learned as one of their first geography sentences *Between Camperduin and Petten lie three dikes: the Watcher, the Sleeper, and the Dreamer.*

We're raised with the double message that we have to address our worst fears, but that they'll also somehow domesticate themselves nonetheless. Fifteen years ago Rotterdam Climate Proof revived "The Netherlands Lives with Water" as a slogan, the poster accompanying it featuring a two-panel cartoon in which a towering wave, in the first panel, is breaking over a terrified little boy before its crest, in the second, separates into immense foamy fingers so that he can relievedly shake its hand.

When Cato told me about that first offer from Shell, I could *see* her flash of feral excitement about what she was turning down. Royal Dutch Shell! She would have been fronting for one of the biggest corporations in the world. We conceived Henk a few nights later. There was a lot of urgent talk about getting deeper and closer and I remember striving once she'd guided me inside her to have my penis reach the back of her throat. Periodically we slowed into the barest sort of movement, just to further take stock of what was happening, and at one point when we paused in our tremoring, I put my lips to her ear and reminded her of what she'd passed up. After winning them over, she could have picked her city: Tokyo, Los Angeles, Rio. The notion caused in her eyes a momentary lack of focus. Then she started moving along a contraction as a response, and Shell and other options and speech evanesced away.

If she were to leave me, where would I be? It's as if she was put here to force my interaction with humans. And still I don't pull it off. It's like that story we were told as children, of Jesus telling the rich young man to go and sell all he has and give it to the poor, and the rich man choosing to keep what he has, and going away sorrowful. Kees said when we talked about it that he always assumed that the guy had settled in Holland.

*   *   *

That Monday, more bad news: warm air and heavy rain have ventured many meters above established snow lines in the western Alps, and Kees holds up before me with both hands GRACE's latest printouts about a storm cell the potential numbers of which we keep rechecking because they seem so extravagant. He spends the rest of the morning on the phone trying to stress that we've hit another type of threshold here; that these are calamity-level numbers. It seems to him that everyone's *saying* that they recognize the urgency of the new situation but that no one's *acting* like it. During lunch a call comes in about the hinge-and-socket joint, itself five stories high, of one of the Maeslant doors. In order to allow the doors to roll with the waves, the joints are designed to operate like a human shoulder, swinging along both horizontal and vertical axes and transferring the unimaginable stresses to the joint's foundation. The maintenance engineers are reporting that the foundation block—all fifty-two thousand tons of it—is moving.

Finally Kees flicks off his phone receptor and squeezes his eyes shut in despair. "Maybe our history's just the history of picking up after disasters like this," he tells me. "Like the way the Italians do pasta sauce, we do body retrieval."

After a few minutes of waiting for updated numbers, I call Cato and fail to get through and then try my mother, who says she's soaking her corns. I can picture the enamel basin with the legend CONTENTED FEET around the rim. The image seems to confirm that we're all just naked in the world, and I tell her to get some things together, that I'm going to be sending someone out for her, that she needs to leave town for a little while.

It's amazing that I'm able to keep trying Cato's numbers, given what's broken loose in all the levels of water management nationwide. Everyone's shouting into headpieces and clattering away at laptops at the same time. At all of the Delta stations the situation has already triggered the automatic emergency procedures with their checklists and hour-by-hour protocols. Outside my office window the canal is lined with barges of cows, of all things, awaiting their river pilot and transportation to safety. In front of them the road is a gypsy caravan of traffic piled high with suitcases and furniture and roped-down plastic bags. The occasional dog hangs from a window. Those roads that can float should allow vehicular evacuation for six or seven hours longer than the other roads will. The civil-defense teams at roundabouts and intersections are doing what they can to dispense biopacs and aquacells. Through the glass everyone seems to be behaving well, though with a maximum of commotion.

I've got the mayor of Ter Heijde on one line saying he's up to his ass in ice water and wanting to know where the fabled Weak Links Project has gone when Cato's voice finally breaks in on the other.

"Where are you?" I shout and the mayor shouts back "Where do you *think*?" and I kill his line and ask again and Cato answers "What?" and in just her inflection of that one-word question, I know that she heard what I said. "Is Henk with you?" I shout, and Kees and some of the others around the office look up even given that everyone's shouting. I ask again and she says that he is. I ask if she's awaiting evacuation and she answers that she's already in Berlin.

I'm shouting other questions when Kees cups a palm over my receptor and says, "Here's an idea. Why don't you sort out all of your personal problems now?"

After Cato's line goes dead, I can't raise her again, or she won't answer. We're all engaged in such a blizzard of calls that it almost doesn't matter. "Whoa," Kees says, his hands dropping to his desk, and a number of our coworkers go silent as well, because the windows facing west are now black with rain and rattling. I look out mine, and bags and other debris are tearing free of the traffic caravan and sailing east. The rain curtain hits the cows in their barges and their ears flatten like mules and their eyes squint shut at the gale's power.

"Our ride is here," Kees calls, shaking my shoulder, and I realize that everyone's in a flurry of collecting laptops and flash drives. There's a tumult heading up the stairs to the roof and the roar of the wind every time the outer door is opened, and the scrabbling sounds of one last person dragging something out before the door slams shut. And then, with surprising abruptness, it's quiet.

My window continues to shake as though it's not double pane but cellophane. Now that our land has subsided as much as it has, when the water does come, it will come like a wall, and each dike that stops it will force it to turn, and in its churning, it will begin to spiral and bore into the earth, eroding away the dike walls, until the pressure builds and that dike collapses and it's on to the next dike, with more pressure piling up behind, and so on and so on until all the barriers start falling together and the water thunders forward like a hand sweeping everything from the table.

The lights go off, and then on and off again, and then the halogen emergency lights in the corridors engage, with their irritated buzzing.

It's easier to see out with the interior lights gone. Along the line of cars a man carrying a framed painting staggers at an angle, like a sailboat tacking. He passes a woman in a van with her head against the headrest and her mouth open in an *Oh* of fatigue.

I'm imagining the helicopter crew's negotiations with my mother, and their fireman's carry once those negotiations have fallen through. She told me once that she often recalled after the flood of 1953 the way they drifted through the darkness for so long without the sky getting lighter. She said that when the sunrise finally came they watched the Navy drop food and blankets and rubber boats and bottles of cooking gas to people on roofs or isolated high spots, and when their boat passed a small body lying across an eave with its arms in the water, her father told her that it was resting. She remembered later that morning saying to her mother, who had grown calmer, that it was a good sign that they saw so few people floating, and her mother had answered before her father could stop her that the drowned didn't float straightaway, but took a few days to come up.

And she talked with fondness about the way her father had tended to her later, when she'd been blinded by some windblown grit, by suggesting she rub one eye to make the other weep, the way farmers did when bothered by chaff. And she remembered, too, a service a week or so later, and the strangeness of one of the prayers her village priest recited once they all were back in their old church, the masonry buttressed with steel beams and planking to keep the walls from sagging outward any further: *I sink into deep mire, where there is no standing; I come into deep waters, where the floods overflow me.*

The window's immense pane shudders and flexes before me from the force of what's pouring out of the North Sea. Water's beginning to run its fingers out from under the seal on the sash. Cato will send me text updates whether she receives answers or not, wry and brisk and newsy, and Henk will author a few, as well. Everyone in Berlin will track the goings-on on the monitors above them while they shop or travel or work. The teaser heading will be something like THE NETHERLANDS UNDER SIEGE. Some of the more sober will think, That could have been us. Some of the more perceptive will consider that it soon may well be.

My finger's on the Cato icon on the screen without exerting the additional

pressure that would initiate another call. What sort of person ends up with someone like me? What sort of person finds that *acceptable*, year to year? We went on
vacations and fielded each other's calls and took turns reading Henk to sleep and
let slip away that miracle that was there between us when we first came together.
We hunkered down before the wind picked up. We modeled for our son risk management when we could have been embracing the free fall of that astonishing *Here.
This is yours to hold*. We said to each other *I think I know* when we should have said
Lead me farther through your amazing, amazing interior.

Cato was moved by all of my mother's flood memories, but was only brought
to tears by one. My mother's only cherished memory from that year: the Queen's
address to the nation afterward, and her celebration of what the crucible of the
disaster had produced: the return, at long last, of that unity the country had displayed during the war. My mother had purchased a copy of the speech on LP, all
those years ago, and had had her neighbor transfer it to a digital format. She played
it for us while Cato and I visited, and Henk knelt at the window spying on whom-
ever was hurrying by. And my mother held Cato's hand and Cato held mine and
Henk gave us fair warning of anything approaching of interest, while the Queen's
smooth and warm voice thanked us all for the way we had worked together in that
one great cause, soldiering on without a thought for care, or grief, or inner divisions, and without even realizing what we were denying ourselves.

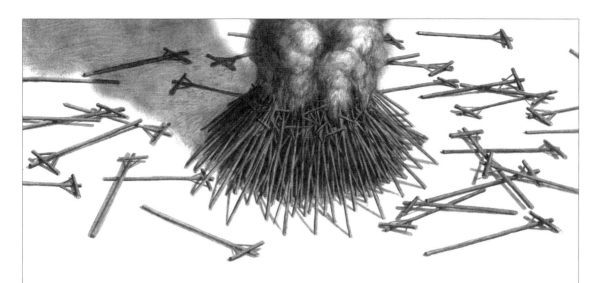

THE ENDURING NATURE
OF THE BROMIDIC

by SALVADOR PLASCENCIA

ENDEARED BY ITS DISREPAIR and moldings, they move into a house with delicate plumbing. Its system colicky, the kitchen sink spits soap suds and swollen rice and the toilet clogs with gently wadded tissues.

In the restroom an old mirror flips the embroidered letters on Cheli's sweater. She reads in reverse, experiments with the toothpaste's lettering and the instructions on shampoo bottles.

"It's like in those Almodóvar movies where *Ambulancia* is always spelled backward," she tells Gonzalo.

The toilet backs up, ruining an afternoon and two area rugs in the hall. They hire plumbers to snake the debris and install compactors into the pipes. After every flush motors grind and faint seismic vibrations reverberate into the furniture and fixtures. The mirror they replace with a smaller slab, but its optics are truer and do not distort the syntax of words.

Pressed against the wall Cheli's vertebrae indent into the soft Sheetrock. Her fossil tracks are spackled over three weeks later, filled with a dense paste. On her belly, the comforter furled beneath them, Gonzalo wipes chalk and flakes of paint from her ridgeline and watches as welts surface and spread their tinge. On the hardwood, cratered by heels and the sudden pivots of the previous tenants, lost strands of Cheli's hair coil into a nest. The bulbs still attached. The exposed patch of scalp she surveys with the tips of her fingers.

Outside the window, its panes pocked and scratched by years of Santa Anas blowing sand against the glass, hazy linemen unlace wire from decommissioned telephone poles. Most posts are removed at the root, but some are left as stumps to be retrofitted one day as cellular antennas. The sign towers—advertisements for carnicerías, a Vietnamese plaza anchored by a phô restaurant, and a Hong Kong diner—are draped in dark hunger cloths, the whole skyline in lent.

Ordinance of El Monte, California, Section 21.50.030 requires that the girth of English words be of the same heft and height as the accompanying language. Forty-five percent of the typographic space must be allotted to English signage. Code Enforcement trucks, using black sheeting, cover violating marquees, free-standing signs, and backlit boards. Strip malls, supermarkets, and bars fall into a mute mourning but soon speak in neon and cursive malaprops and misspellings.

Census data and field surveys find an America fractured into colonies. At root is a linguistic failure to assimilate and label liquor stores in an easily decipherable font and recognizable diction. Cheli and Gonzalo's house sits on an aging sewer system and a census tract of high Cantonese and Spanish saturation. English, the language of emergencies—used to summon police and to instantly reach planes of mutual intelligibility via profanity—ranks a distant fourth. The house's repairs and mortgage are subsidized by an incentive program requiring Cheli and Gonzalo to use English as their primary language and infuse it back into the community.

Chinese meat trucks pass by every other day. Gonzalo waves one down. Early English attempts failed: shoulder butt was confused for marbled chops, ribs for shanks, pork for lamb. Now Gonzalo uses a careful pantomime to order three pounds of ground beef. When he wants a specific and complicated cut he uses the computer to translate and then writes down phonetic spellings. The truck butchers smile as Gonzalo reads his index cards. The vegetable truck does away with language altogether and catalogs its stock pictorially on its side panels, posting custom magnets of carrots and herbs. Seasonal offerings are drawn at distorted angles and taped to the windows.

A stipulation of the English Enculturation Initiative is that all initial encounters be attempted first in English. But when *elote* men and carts of shaved ice, the syrups hanging on the rim, roll by on casters, Zalo automatically defaults to Spanish.

Once, he ordered a cob dusted with parmesan and chili powder using only the promoted and subsidized language. The elote man, his shirt tucked in and pants starch-creased but his eyebrows wild intertwists and snarls knotted and uncombed to counterbalance his neatness, pulled a corn from the pot and stabbed it onto a stick. He buttered it and rolled it in the bed of cheese and sprinkled the ground pepper from a shaker. He inflated the price, handed Zalo the stick, and gave him a look that said, "Your forehead is cactus-stamped. Three prickly paddles sprout from your brow"—a saying his own mother had used against short, dark cashiers who counted her change back to her in strained English.

A quarter of Gonzalo's tuition is provided by the Geographic Society, which has recently reinstituted its cartographic division for sentimental reasons. The rest is paid with loans and Pell Grants. But he often receives letters and electronic correspondences insisting he falls above the qualifying income line. Funding is rescinded and his degree progress stalls in the timeline. He appeals. His pay rate is quarters above the minimum wage and his hours are limited but the auditors respond in terse letters that affirm their previous decision.

Half of his coursework is in geology and land forms. Studio Arts and History of Lines & Contours fill the rest of his schedule. For Lines & Contours 202: Geometry of the First Testament, he writes his notes on index cards: *The first straight line drawn on tan vellum, marking the incision where a rib would be extracted from. The curved line invented to mimic the movements of waves, circles to trace the circumference of unnamed planets, the directional vector to illustrate where to deposit the seeds for Cain and Abel.*

While Cheli is in the library, Gonzalo maps the depressions and fissures of the house. Cartographic exaggerations of nail holes convert into cenotes, and the gaps between the floorboards widen into gorges, plummeting into dark canyons. Overwhelmed by his spatial imagination, Gonzalo free-falls hundreds of feet while sitting in his living-room chair. The fluids of the inner ear swished, he holds his head in his palms until he regains equilibrium.

They attend the same university but their home departments are at opposite ends of the campus. Gonzalo earns credits toward his bachelor's while Cheli is all but dissertation, an ontological condition of tortured pensiveness.

Cheli's dissertation is ten chapters on exhausted literary devices: the dreams of Descartes, kaleidoscopes, old men in brothels, the voices of the dead, Mexicans stuffed into dummy speaker boxes, children with expanded lexicons, God as a slow-moving star, African Americans in Paris.

The first chapter offers a theoretical framework of her study, investigating the comforting nature of reruns and the cliché. How sadness softens by watching familiar television episodes. Suspense slackened and surprises disarmed, the worn shows reassure our sense of safety. Gonzalo summarizes her thesis as a defense of boredom, a justification for passive disinterest.

He questions the epistemological underpinnings: "Why would I want to already know? What's the point of watching and reading if I know what's going to happen?"

Countering theories of fiction as a means of vicarious excitement and trauma, Cheli proposes that the literature of repeating motifs and plots offers a safe home to rest in. The need for excitement and surprises she positions as a bourgeois desire, as an aesthetic of privilege. A mode preferred by aesthetes raised by serene parents, those who know the whereabouts of their mothers and were fathered by men who did not spend nights and paychecks in bars themed after their own deteriorated interiors.

To Zalo she gives a gentler and more restrained explanation. "A story that confirms our predictions satisfies us because through it we perform a small act of prophesy. It simulates the sensation of time travel, of knowledge carried over from a distant spatial-temporal dimension." When Cheli's diction encrypts into academic jargon, Gonzalo concedes.

Her adviser, a modernist Elizabeth Bishop scholar who took family vacations to snow cabins and still has warm memories of her mother, believes in the angular shapes of discomfort and the ninety-year-old refrain of making it new. She approves Cheli's prospectus but only reluctantly.

At night, after eating pasta flavored with olive oil and clustered tomatoes bought from the vegetable van, they suds the dishes using a liquid soap named after spring blooms and then spread their papers and books over the dining table. If there's a surplus of metabolic energy and caloric reserves they copulate against the give of their bed, sometimes against the burn of their wood floors. On hot days, under the rain of their showerhead. They knock down moisturizers, body washes, oatmeal-soap bars, shampoos for color-treated and brittle hair, herbal conditioners, and gentle face scrubs. They dry themselves using towels laundered in Tide and softened by supplemental chemicals.

*   *   *

On paper and student-loan applications Gonzalo is orphaned, left without cosigners. In truth, his father still exists as an operative organism who calls Gonzalo every Tuesday, reminding him to put the trash and recycling bins on the sidewalk.

His father's social—pinged and cross-checked by authorization of the Data Confirmation Act—is returned as the number of a once-removed and now-deceased cousin. HR, holding a dead number in their manicured hands, follow him as he gauges the current of alternators, replaces three burnt fuses, and wanders into the break room. While standing next to a microwave and percolator, he is let go without severance or official pink slip.

"He was your uncle," he tells Gonzalo, misquoting genealogical lines. "When he died I cried and went to the rosary all nine days. I wasn't a pallbearer. I shoveled dirt and patted it down, made it level with the rest. I grieved so they could see me, mournful as a crocodile. Do you know what I mean?"

Gonzalo nods.

"It's an old Juan Sin Miedo saying. It means that your tears are fake, still saline and secreted by your own glands but the sentiment is forged," his father explains. "A month later his mother—still wearing black and a veil—gave me a birth certificate, social security card, and a yellow immunization booklet with two boxes stamped and dated. His name was Andrew González, no middle names or compounded lasts, and I assumed it as my own from that day on."

His father speaks of the name as if it were a streamlined power suit, an invention of NASA and stolen from the wardrobe of Iron Man. A once-state-of-the-art technology with its fuel cell burnt out. Armor reduced to only heft, providing no protective function.

He was born Jose Maria de Jesus Martinez but Gonzalo knows his father only as Andrew, a sequence of letters his own mother couldn't pronounce. Instead, she always called him "*tú*." When addressing him in a crowded room she had to stand next to him. For desperate moments, when centripetal forces separated them or phone operators mediated their connections, she kept "Andrés" in reserve.

Andrew tells Gonzalo, "I worked money into that number for fifty years and now it's all gone." Gonzalo's father is widowed. At home he is surrounded by cupboards he has never opened and kitchen appliances of mysterious specialties. Two years after the funeral, mailings still arrive in his wife's name.

She passed away. Her pulse was delayed, and they waited for it gathered around a hydraulic bed. But Andrew was not a man of idle patience and instead took laps around the hospital's grounds. The atmosphere thin and his despair heavy, the g-forces pulled pigment from his follicles, left gray racing stripes in his hair, and fused his knee caps into a stiff arthritis.

Sitting next to a monitor and IV stand, Gonzalo charted the topography of the floor for future visitors. His mother's room at center, a vending machine to the east, a unisex restroom northwest, a nurses' station too far south, and the lukewarm coffee and lunch trays deep in the mantle of the hospital.

Finally, doctors and nurses offered conclusive evidence: blank printouts of her vitals and the stone of her wedding band softened into a brittle graphite.

Thankfully, she is not here to witness Andrew's dismissal or the follow-ups by the Social Security Administration. The banks block his accounts, confiscate all of his savings and checkings—leaving him only the cash he hid in the wire undercarriages of his couches.

The house, after Andrew opens hatches stuffed with cloth napkins and plugs in kitchen instruments to decipher their gauges and motions, they repossess for fraudulent signing and entering into a contract as a nonexistent entity.

But before the bank's locksmiths arrive, Andrew must undo the corruptions of his nonbeing. Twenty years of invalid upgrades and Home Depot purchases must be reversed, the starter home restored to its dilapidated condition.

The copper pipes and wires, installed by the forged labor of his counterfeit muscles, must also not exist. The new tiles: ghosts in grout. To test their non-essence, Andrew lets the sledgehammer drop at every square. He snips lines of electricity at strategic and obscure points. He pours a sack of cement into the sink and washes it down with a slow trickle of water that will harden into a mysterious plaque that will puzzle even the most veteran plumbers.

Surprised by his feelings of rancor, he does not tell Gonzalo of the shock waves and dust released by ceramic planes, of the darkness of a short-circuited living room, or of the impeded flow of liquid molecules.

"Things ill-got had ever bad success," he says to Gonzalo. "But they were just some old papers of a dead boy. They were no use to him. They were going to go to waste."

He moves into Gonzalo's backyard. He weeps privately but rings of salt ripple down his shirt. From a Swedish dock a house sets sail; a quartered and insulated cargo bin arrives at the Long Beach harbor. Panels fall into windows, a crank slides walls and extends the rear of the container. Outlets and light sockets have been threaded through the beams and a fuse box is readied to receive electricity. Plumbers—dressed in the jeans and thinning T-shirts of their moonlight hours—are hired to run pipes to the main system. An hour into a trench dig, Andrew dismisses them and finishes the installation himself. Sometimes, when Cheli and Gonzalo are in bed, they feel the torque of the motors turning. Gonzalo thinks of his father sitting by himself on Scandinavian porcelain.

"Zalo, it's supposed to be lonely. It's a restroom," Cheli tells him.

In the morning Gonzalo's father drinks tea, a tea that is equal parts heated brandy and manzanilla, and watches twin engines as they seed the sky. They fly in pairs, their tails scratching a thin line into the clear blue. After several passes, the grid thickens into an overcast that slicks the roads and wets the lawns.

Inside the front house, five letters, a *New Yorker*, two postcard utility bills, and a *Penny Saver* fall through the door slot.

The *New Yorker* features a story about a couple inheriting a house and an attic full of documents. Paragraphs Cheli will underline and annotate with several Post-its.

Gas and electricity are due.

Two identical envelopes hold invitations and a badly designed map—off-scale and convoluted—indicating the time and date of Zalo and Cheli's high school reunion.

Two others, heat-sealed and sent by Sallie Mae and the U.S. Department of Education, report that Gonzalo's W-9 earnings are above the qualifying level and his funding for the spring semester will be withdrawn.

Finally, the university follows with a warning that his preregistered courses will be dropped unless payment is submitted for the outstanding balance.

Gonzalo collects the mail and walks over to his father's. On first pass, the cloud seeders send down a warning mist. It pools and channels into discrete drains that empty into the surrounding planters. Zalo opens the letters and translates the gist to his father.

"I have something to tell you," Andrew says, and he explains.

Indebted to the grieving mother who gave him his voucher to America, Andrew repaid her a decade later using replicas of Gonzalo's social security card. Rectangular cuts of blue paper she handed to her grandchildren—the mysterious doppelgängers now scattered in Missouri, Texas, and Puerto Rico, producing taxable income under Gonzalo's nine-digit code, undermining his financial-aid packages.

Andrew tells Zalo he is sorry. Sometimes in the logic of the moment there is a failure toward the future. The qualifying criteria for federal aid is something that is not often considered. He will find a way to help him and repair the damage made by the cloning of his Social.

Gonzalo's father teleported, slowly and belatedly, from a land that malnourished him, a steep valley with its grass fields trampled and chewed to clods of clay. In the mornings, after eating eggs that had been whipped to a froth and fried into a sponge—the proteins broken and divided amongst his brothers—he tracked the steers and led them to a flickering stream. Slobbering snails with splintered hoofs and horns, their dessicated tongues sopped the creek dry.

He does not mention or remember much from these days. His dreams cycle only evidence of domestic appliances: loads of warm laundry and dryer sheets, utensils drying in dish racks, lawn trimmings on sidewalks. But one dream, in the fasts before doctors' appointments, repeats. In it a fleet of cloud seeders flies over a brown and cracked valley, tamping the dust and sprouting grass; sharp bones upholstered in cheap leather graze and fatten into full coats.

Andrew, still Jose Maria de Jesus Martinez at the time, ran away from the ranch to shine shoes in cobblestoned plazas. Once all the wingtips were gleaming, he sold ice cream from an ice chest. When the *tejuino* fad overtook the town and everybody was drinking fermented sherbet, he switched professions and became a sidewalk mechanic, dismantling carburetors and draining oil, promising to have cars ready before morning. Sidewalk ordinances were passed and again he changed his field, directing radio waves and transistor signals back on course. One stray current he followed led him to the house where he met his wife.

In America, despite supplements and fortified foods, he was too late to absorb the proper nutrients. His height remained stunted, his hearing muffled, and his sight blind to muted colors and subtle gradations that clashed when worn together.

After open houses and parent conferences, the Santa Anita Race Track on the hills above, classmates—sometimes lanky girls whom Gonzalo never talked to—asked if his father was a jockey.

"He's a machine technician," Zalo said.

"But he's so little. He should race horses."

In their house they forfeited the obvious tells: government peanut butter, pamphlets of acceptable purchases, EBT credit cards, and Section 8 subsidies. Cautious of testing Andrew's name against the force of governmental databases, they decided to make do. The evidence of their struggle took on more subtle manifestations. Gonzalo's mother reread the fine print of mailers and they shopped in grocery stores where they bagged their own items, using a thin plastic that stretched hesitantly and ripped easily. Security guards stood at the exit cross-checking their receipts against the loads of their carts.

Detergent was bought in bulk, a thirty-pound sack stored under the kitchen sink. After soccer matches Gonzalo showered using the rough soap he scooped from the bag, a dissolving sand of low lather and rough exfoliants. He scooped from it again to wash the dishes and again for loads of grass-stained laundry.

When he reached high school Gonzalo was moved to left defender in a 4-3-3 formation. After two games of rushed touches and guarding a post that would never be in danger, he quit soccer and spent his afternoons walking idle laps, listening to his earphones.

He met Cheli sophomore year. During school—lunches, period breaks, and truant math sessions—they made out in the halls and against the back wall of the cafeteria.

Once, after the final bell, they kissed behind the backstop for twenty minutes, though by Einsteinian measurements and adjusted hormonal levels the duration totaled only sixteen seconds. Cheli's father, returning from his shift, pedaled by wearing a Stetson and ostrich boots. He skidded to a stop and gently set the Huffy in the infield. Zalo looked up as he approached. A puff of dust rose in the background. It was a moment broken from time, the déjà vu of the baseball diamond remembering its days in the Wild West.

By the tether of her hair the cowboy dragged Cheli home. She did not resist or pull. She walked away with her neck and waist bowed to the grip of her father's clench, proficiently stepping as if it was the posture of everyday locomotion.

The next day, using the oxidized blade of a machete, Cheli's father tapped on Gonzalo's door. Through the grate Gonzalo smelled his cologne, a scent milled from cereal boxes. Cheli's dad took off his hat and politely asked for his bike back, but kept the machete in plain view.

It's not the ranch, you don't walk around with a machete, Zalo wanted to tell him. Instead he bent his finger and pointed to the wall behind the garage.

From a propped portal more cowboys emerged. They stood in front yards, using the kinetic energy of the old country to belt their sons for bleaching their hair, for the effeminate cut and fit of their jeans, for baggies with residues of suspicious origins. Their horses, unable to travel across time, stayed behind, so the men walked on sidewalks and gathered in parking lots. Their gait melancholy, longing for a distant time and terrain.

One Wednesday in mid-October lasted for three days. Cheli's father, caught standing at a conveyer belt packing sugared corn puffs into boxes, sat with his wrists zip-tied inside a van with reinforced roll bars and lined with cage mesh. He and his coworkers were unloaded at an INS detention center. For two weeks the paddy wagon and sleeping bunks all smelled of cereal and sweat.

The scent, brought home on her father's clothes and in trash bags stuffed with overtoasted flakes, had already seeped into Cheli's things, but she burned a heavy incense to counter the cinnamon and breakfast starch. Her room was furnished with Margaret Thatcher's England. Posters of the Smiths and skinheads in Fred Perry shirts dancing on checkered dance floors insulated her walls. Her sink was stained red with hair dye, and matching smears stained her towels. She wore stockings, which Gonzalo did not pull off at first, but eventually he wanted to see all of her. Dandruff glistened in her hair; beneath her panties razor rash and nicks reddened her skin, and her elbows ashed and flaked against the friction of coarse sheets. When he gripped her hair, a streak of red in his wadded fingers, the hinges of her limbs slackened. Like a pet grabbed by the nape, she deactivated into a sad limp. Her frame regained its structure only after Gonzalo apologized and released the snakes of her hair from his hand. In a silent reconciliation they ate cereal flavored with the undertaste of burnt steel.

When Zalo finally returned home his mother was on the stoop waiting for him. She should have been at work feeding fabric into an overlock machine and joining jeans at the seams. He had never been hit by his mother before and she was a respect-ful woman who did not use slurs. A switch furrowed his back into purple rows of skin and she beat him for being a nigger. For two days she'd waited for him to come home. Eighteen work hours lost, hours he had to break into his savings account to reimburse her for.

Cheli's father returned after months of being stopped by checkpoints and thermal-imaging technologies, which sensed body heat emanating from car trunks and mal-formed upholstery. The humiliation of contorting into tire compartments and posing as the stuffing of bench seats invigorated him. He intercepted phone calls, patrolled the school on his Huffy, and at night he called Zalo's phone while drunk and tapped the machete into the receiver.

"I'm not with her," Zalo told him.

Two weeks before the winter formal Cheli and Zalo broke up.

Gonzalo spent the next three terms with Kristi Johnston. She was six inches taller than him, her hair pulled back into a ponytail exposing her domed forehead and peach-fuzzed ears. Her pores nearly microscopic, the flop of her hair a cascade free of split ends and breakage, her armpits and legs smoothed by creams safeguard-ing against burns and irritations.

With her parents always stuck in overtime, deportations were unnecessary. Gonzalo went over after school and on weekends, but made sure to be back home before his mother arrived.

He kissed Kristi until their mouths cottoned and she undid her bra into a Rubik's tangle. Her motions he remembers as guided by instructional arrows. The wedge-capped lines found in chapter eight, reengineered with sticks and sharp stones by Indians and reappropriated back to paper by geometry and sport tacticians. Her moans cribbed from videos, positions rehearsed and scripted from magazines. All of her movements and utterances plagiarized from the same pages he secretly bookmarked and hid. When Cheli now pontificates on the virtues of the rerun as an aesthetic, he wants to cite Kristi as a counterexample of the dulling effect of a bro-ken imagination.

Still, Kristi's neatly contained areolas, her trimmed tuft and trail of moles he cataloged and drew as a sloping landmass, a geologically perplexing alluvial fan materialized miles removed from any ranges or foothills. Her veins, almost at the surface, he inked as rivers in a bruised hue.

Culled from locker-room legends, from jokes about the struggles of miscegenation, and from the wisdom of older brothers, a concordance of knowledge emerges. Verified data, true at varying elevations and grade levels: white girls are the most permissive. They may be folded at sharper angles, salts deposited onto any of their surface areas, their follicles easily pulled and uprooted like onions.

But for Gonzalo there was a crass ungratefulness in these experiments. He never tested Kristi's pliability beyond her natural range, her hair he held not like a rope but as fibers he separated with the pick of his hand, and his starches he directed away from her or kept sealed in baggies he tied and carried away.

Kristi moved away at the end of senior year. Gonzalo now wonders if her presence was incentivized. An emissary sent to give contact with the America that was promised. A white girl who walked barefoot down carpeted stairs. Her ceilings punctured by skylights, her restrooms sharp with extra ledges designed to hold lotions, sun blockers, and other ointments formulated to protect her low melanin count. An exemplar inserted to demonstrate to a population what it is to wash with proper soaps, how to exfoliate tender faces, condition follicles and scalp, and lubricate the skin against triple-mounted blades and an increasingly brutal sun.

Cheli explains to Zalo's father what it is that she is working on.

"It's about the enduring nature of the bromidic."

She tries to translate into Spanish but she can only summarize it as a study of English.

He says he studied short and long waves but they no longer exist. He fries an egg on the Teflon, just lightly touching the white with the spatula. His Swedish design house comes equipped with an integrated electric range, coils of heat which brand a labyrinth into the tortillas.

"The Swedes have a good eye and know how to fold and collapse everything into a box, but they've never warmed a tortilla in their lives," he tells Cheli.

It's a year of sequels: *Street Fighter VI*, the return of Anton Chigurh, Vatican III. Cheli takes notes: Latin doubles back, pneumatic weapons endure, Ken and Ryu are readmitted into the tournament. Nostalgia becomes reliant on the cliché, on the worn and overused. She extrapolates: love as a longing for the tired.

As she writes, revising chapters and footnoting allusions, Andrew mixes water and a box of dry compound into a bucket. He stirs with a spatula until he achieves the viscosity of dough. In the living room he patches nail holes and hairline faults. He lifts the bucket and takes it into their bedroom. The bed is unmade and their clothes are stacked in to-be-washed and to-be-folded piles. Andrew fills the dents made by Cheli's spine.

While the compound dries, he mallet-taps the floorboards into alignment and nails a warped board flush. Once the compound has crusted and hardened, he sands the excess into a fog of floating particles, which settle on the peaks of the laundry.

Conceptually, she understands what a father is. A progenitor, a reservoir of cells that transfers biological data into her musculature, fating her to diabetes and providing her with the modest inheritance of green eyes and a defined nose.

But beyond the vain replication, she is perplexed by their internal mechanics and circuitry. How after years of an overbearing jealousy—after welding rebar on her windows and dictating the route she would walk home from school—one night he leaves the front door open, the screen mesh torn and never to be mended. When she calls him, his voice is bloodshot. He is at a bar but its name is cloaked in a tattered black plastic; the owners in protest refuse to update their signage, fines accumulate but the engendered solidarity and increased patronship offset the penalties.

And meanwhile Andrew, a man of the same title, perhaps aided by the dignity of not having to bunch his being into confined and converted spaces, industriously hammers and sands. When he drinks it is in the company of his own son, not with strangers who talk about the size and gallons of their hats and exchange tips on the oils used to buff their footwear.

Andrew tells Cheli what he did, how he vandalized his own house. "But you shouldn't let Zalo know," he says. "He grew up in that house, helped me do most of the work."

He knows he has botched Gonzalo's grant-and-loan eligibility. "I'm sorry, but I think I can fix it."

The seeders are parked in the hangars. Clouds arrive by the haplessness of air currents. A low-yielding awning, a sprinkle at best. But the day turns cold and the radiator takes all day to warm. They stay under sheets. Zalo touches Cheli, feeling for a cluster of hair but finding only stubble. She shaved for him two days before but he spent the evening in the little house talking to his father. Now he presses up against her and places his flaccid penis between her buttocks, but she reaches back and cups him in her hand.

"Not right now, Zalo," she says, and falls asleep watching a television she has looped on replay.

Meanwhile, from the living quarters of his phone booth, Andrew calls Gonzalo's clones. In Missouri the Spanish is slow but proficient. In Texas heavily cut with English and similes drawn from a life of cattle raising. Puerto Rican Spanish operates at hyperspeed; words are windburned and must be digitally recorded and slowed to rescue them from the blur.

He wants his son to finish school. He tells them this. Maybe, just for two years or so, they can rest the social. But they have families, responsibilities, car payments, he hears. Their grandmother gave him exclusive use of a whole set and he is asking them to give up theirs?

Not give up, just rest.

They say they wish they could but no. Besides, they're paying into his son's retirement and unemployment insurance and they can't even file to recoup.

The next morning Andrew and Gonzalo share a pot of coffee and the pages of *La Opinion*. The paper, save the soccer coverage, runs syndicated and computer-translated articles, the conjugations touched up and slangs regionally adapted. The original English columns run in parallel spaces to increase the paper's federally subsidized revenue.

Its headlines tell of a broken, fragmented, unintelligible babble nation. A polyphony of nonsense with no common language. Restaurant menus coded, bars with hidden services, grocery-store items labeled in illegible lettering. The legislature moving on strategies to bring the country toward a bridge, ways that we could speak to our fellow citizens.

Zalo and Andrew talk about the upcoming Súper Clásico. Chivas—the team of bricklayers and farmers beloved for signing only Mexican players—versus Mexico City's C.F. América, a club led by two mercenary Brazilian strikers.

From soccer, the exorbitant price paid per goal, Andrew segues into tax questions. He asks Zalo if he has filed.

"No. I've been below the income threshold for years."

"I think there might be some money in there." Zalo's distant cousins have been pumping credits into the number, he explains. Maybe some penalties for failing to file, but also years of accumulated returns and interest waiting to be claimed.

Later that day, Gonzalo types in his number and downloads the W-2s, consolidates the sum of various boxes. Everything is on-screen. He files for the block of 2019–2023. Fifty-six thousand dollars, minus some punitive but small charges, is to be returned. He can go back to school, concentrate, and finish off his degree.

Zalo tells his father and they walk to the Super Saver for a celebratory half-case.

When Cheli gets home Andrew and Gonzalo are drunk and sitting on the Swedes' planters. The refrigerator can fit six beers, which are systematically pulled and replaced.

As they drink they reach once-elusive conclusions. The Mexican Selection, El Tri, is forever cursed on European soil; they will need a real goalie for 2026 when the Cup returns to the Americas, not just a failed basketball player tending the net. The gateway into English is movies and rock music; all the funding should go there. Gonzalo misses his mother, Andrew misses his wife. GPS makes navigation easier but at the loss of one's spatial IQ; we are never lost anymore—if we are, we don't know it. Unpracticed, map-reading will gain the density and strain of Pynchon. Half of what they say is lost to Cheli in the esoterics of soccer but she interjects to explain Pynchon: a man famous for his dense, punning sentences and a visage of anonymous meaning. Entangled in the intricacies of offsides traps and the demise of cartography, Zalo had neglected to tell Cheli about the tax return.

"Cheli, we're rich," he says.

At the high school reunion, while Cheli is in the restroom, Kristi and Gonzalo sit at the bar overlooking a freeway and its clot of brake lights. She tells him what she didn't say eleven years ago: "Your cock always tasted like Ajax." After, she would spit into the sink trying to purge the flavor of cleanser.

He explains, "It was the house soap. I didn't think it was weird until I saw your shelves."

The homecoming prince and princess are crowned. Jokes about the enduring beauty of Loren Siguenza's face, now attached to a snowman's body, circulate.

At the Department of Internal Revenue Services the operations are automated; forms are processed, fines assessed, and refunds calculated. A check is printed in thermal ink on hologrammed and watermarked paper and its serial number transferred into a spreadsheet.

The digital geography software raises a red flag. Gonzalo (Social Security Code: 409-52-2002; profession: "student") is designated as one point in Southern California. But other dots blot the continent: in Texas 409-52-2002 is a cattle rancher. In Kansas City 409-52-2002 drives a forklift and has just made a down payment on a two-bedroom. A lighthouse, on an island hesitantly anchored to the U.S. sea floor, also flashes. 409-52-2002 of San Juan, Puerto Rico is employed by a multinational and spends his nights in lounges bantering in double entendres and undressing in back rooms.

The controller, on the last hour of his double shift, packs his briefcase and Tupperware. He overrides the alert as a glitch and logs a rushed line. Nonessential vowels omitted, he explains the occurrence of a single body occupying four distinct and distant points on the same plane as improbable but theoretically possible. A breakthrough in quantum mechanics but outside the jurisdiction of tax code.

Depending on who is home, Gonzalo, Cheli, and Andrew greet the postman in person and receive the magazines and letters with their own hands. The envelope passes through two routing centers, a mechanical sorter jams, and delivery stalls as new motors are installed and the system recalibrated. Eventually it is a junior postman on the first day of his novitiate who delivers the refund check accompanied by a newsprint mailer. He is cheerfully received by Andrew and offered a beer he must decline.

SKY CITY

by SESSHU FOSTER

To ADVANCE THE PROLETARIAN *interests of the community and counteract the military-industrial propaganda of the oppressor government, which goes so far as to categorically deny the existence of the High Low Radiance Corridor, disregarding even the cars that disappeared many years ago and that abruptly reappear nowadays falling precipitously out of the sky to wreak havoc on community members, community gardens, and street traffic, pirate radio Ehekatl 99.9 on your dial broadcasts this report—during our irregular broadcast hours of 2 a.m. to 6 a.m. from various hilltops in northeast Los Angeles—to examine the Mysteries of East L.A., and to confirm the existence of one of the biggest: the long-rumored but never-before-sighted* Sky City. *Through eyewitness investigation by one of our undercover reporters during her night job as pilot trainee at the allegedly phony and/or "underground" company East L.A. Dirigible Air Transport, pirate radio Ehekatl 99.9 is ready to provide firsthand evidence that* Sky City *is real. As our reporter, with her unsuspecting master zeppelin pilot watching over her shoulder, has already assumed the flight controls of a seven-hundred-foot-long state-of-the-art postmodern dirigible and ascended to eleven thousand feet in altitude (the signal's fading in and out because of air-pressure fluctuations, not to mention the engine noise, but we can't help that), we go live directly to our Report in Progress:*

Which is it gonna be, Captain?

Which is it gonna be what?

Which is it gonna be?

What? The heading's off the compass bearing, altimeter right there in front of you, pitch and yaw, wind direction (remember there's two gauges fore and aft—that's important in a ship this long), *both* hands on the wheel—

Which? Is it gonna be a story or what?

You want a story? The USS *Agnes Smedley* drifts across the misty night above the devastated West, too boring for you?

You know, your usual whatever it is, surrealism bullshit. People get tired. That's not really considered a story, is it?

It's not—

Is it?

It's not—

Come on!

It's not surrealism!

What? That's not what they call it?

No.

It's kind of psychedelic or something, isn't it? Doesn't that qualify—

Surrealism goes back to World War I. It was French. It's supposed to be a reaction to the First World War.

Thank you, doctor. Doctor Barnswallow.

No—thank *you!* I always like a little European history and iced tea on night flights over the greater L.A. basin.

I'd like a little iced tea with my iced tea.

Now you can get virtual iced tea with—or in place of—your actual iced tea.

Doctor Barnswallow!

Mister Doctor Barnswallow to you.

So what's the best love story you know? I mean one that you actually know *about*. Not—

You mean not like *Romeo and Juliet* or *Wuthering Heights* or—

Exactly. Something that happened to you—

Brokeback Mountain, eh? What about, like, *The Fly*? That's kind of a love story. There's a love story in there. The scientist's wife has to kill him by crushing his fly head to put her husband out of his suffering. I feel like something like that happened to me. Or it could!

You know what I'm sayin'. Best thing you can come up with.

Something I heard about?

All right. Something you heard about. Someone you actually know, though.

Personally, eh? Somebody we know personal. *Personal-like*.

Who you know. Yeah.

The love of a middle-aged Arizona couple for their Chihuahua? The love of a whole people for their land? The love of an old retired dude for a patch of lawn and his lawn chair?

For a woman!

I thought—

Make me spell it out!

Thought so. Woman always wants a story about a woman. How about someone you know, someone you and I both know?

Let's see if you know any. You ever know any? Let's see if you were paying attention.

I see. It's a test. Everything these days is like a test.

Let's go back to the facts, then. You're a flagrant anarchist, an individualist subject to no party discipline, who can't even get his partners to show up for work—Jose Lopez-Feliu, Swirling Wheelnuts, clandestine backers to whom you cannot even allude—so you have to yank me, an innocent paper girl and communist, off the streets, teach me to drive this thing toward the dawning of a New Something Era—

Complaints and whining, that's the thanks I get for teaching you a salable skill? You'd rather still be selling that useless cult-propaganda sheet?

Cult! You anarchists can't even—

All right, all right! The whole yawning proletariat shall one day bust a move in a Bollywood dance number, waving a sea of red flags—

You think they won't? Just like everything else in America, media for the people is winking out in the darkness. My organization happens to be developing real alternative community-news outlets! For all you realize, my captain, I could be broadcasting this across the greater northeast Los Angeles heights and San Gabriel Valley on a pirate radio station, to arm our communities with the knowledge you won't—

Pirate radio!

You laugh, my captain! But the workers are the ones who deserve collective ownership of the skies. If your fleet of solar dirigibles proves to be—

If! If? You mean when!

That is exactly what these flights may prove, Captain—sir! But—come on, tell us—say—for the sake of our listenership (even if you don't believe our listenership exists, like the authorities don't believe this zeppelin exists, like they deny the existence of Sky City)—tell me the story behind it all, as if this big wild airship was wired for sound as it swung through the vast purplish night—a floating boom mike for the sounds of an empty universe—a personal story, give 'em a sense of your personal motivation, heisting abandoned materials, welding titanium-frame airships in collapsible folding sections, portable solar technology capable of eluding the downpressor forces (I know, you said you can't afford the *insurance*, but you can afford our listeners the true story—)

Comandante Che said the real revolutionary was guided by feelings of love. At the risk of appearing ridiculous.

Let us not go gently down the slippery slope of sarcasm, Captain. How's that square with the one about that girl you used and abused, she was so young and sweet, what was she? Just a baby—eighteen, nineteen, baby sister of your best friend, she looked up to you both, threw herself at you like only a kid could, but there was something sinister going on between you and your *compa* so you took it out on her, kept her on the line, strung her along until you were in such a state you couldn't recognize her as something fully human—in the end, what? Left her all in a mess? Gave her a dread disease? Wrecked her car? What were you planning next, kill yourself? Double-suicide, Japanese style? Must've used all the towels to clean up after that one, yeah? Is that where love gets you?

Sounds like you heard that one before. The whole story in a nutshell, eh? I'm not sure that has anything to do with me.

So they say. In the twentieth century, you know, they thought the world was going to end with an apocalypse—death and destruction raining down on all nations through nuclear war, viral agents, genetic engineering, ecological disaster. There wasn't going to be enough left of us to make fossils out of—that's what they were having nightmares about during my great-great-grandparents' golden years. They had *no idea*, not the vaguest, about global warming, the obliteration of the auto industry, the complete collapse of aerospace, the death of the world's oceans, the airline bankruptcies that led to the economic depression we've been in for more than a generation now, the landscape of the nation completely erased and, Katrina-like, replaced by a scene of utter devastation, the past not even the vaguest dimness, not even nostalgic, not even a memory evoked by *I Love Lucy* reruns—

But so what?

What?

So what about it?

I was just going to say that I agreed to train for this position because besides needing a real job (I'm tired of selling revolutionary newspapers up and down Figueroa) and liking you personally, as a person I mean, and respecting your loco plan to build clandestine (because uninsured) dirigibles in abandoned warehouses and all kinds of foreclosed office parks atop the hills of El Sereno, Highland Park, and northeastern Los Angeles, to be launched at the perfect moment—

There is no perfect moment.

You said it, Captain. But this is my idea, Captain. Hear me out. They have denied the existence of Sky City, the downpressor government, till their political credibility (such as it is, strained even among their most vocal supporters, probably about ready to combust like the so-called evangelical vote) depends on this lame and weak fabric of lies. We prove the existence of Sky City, Captain, it will bring the downpressor government to its knees.

Then the people will rise up, eh? I think that's a fantasy. Legend from the mists of time.

I don't make these things up. That's too much of a whole lot of extra work.

John Brown said the slaves would rise up across the South when he took Harpers Ferry. Che went down saying he only needed fifty more men in Yuro Ravine.

Sure. But what they didn't have was the radio audience of potential millions; you got the perfect broadcasting platform up here floating over the entire city. They'd be on the edge of their seats, I bet. Even if all they could hear was the droning of propellers—three on each side driven by electric engines powered via auto-charging titanium frame—and the occasional weird structural noises that John Cage–like the great long airship nose makes nosing through the wild empty darkness of winds. It's kind of spooky up here, just me and you. You marked our location?

Just northeast of Burbank airport, abandoned acres and acres of lots, old hangars and warehouses and service facilities that used to—

Boys' hangout. Playground for youth—

Reminds you that when they planned for the expansion of the airport they didn't plan on the airlines going out of business. All these empires coming to an end, leaving junk landscapes in their wake—socialism imploded, Sea of Azov dried up, capitalism collapsed, exploded, toxic wastes strewn across burning dead forests, public entitlement programs gutted, billboards for shit that people can't recognize let alone hanker after, malt liquor and "gentlemen's clubs," cell phones and house-hold cleaners, peeling off to reveal the coruscating undersurface, faces somebody might've seen on TV decades earlier, dimly recognizable except that now nobody cares. What's left that's worth risking your life for?

Isn't that Mount Washington, or Glassell Park? San Fernando Road doglegging away from the river?

We'll get there. Our hometown.

Scene of the crime.

It's all conspiracy and no crime, Cadet—just trying to survive, fanning insignificant dreams and desires like a tiny campfire on the stormy side of some immense mountain—maybe squatting in some empty building, making unpermitted renovations... Calling it the headquarters of East Los Angeles Dirigible Air Transport Lines! Taking calls at all hours. Attempting to broker deals allowing for the production of great new fleets of revolutionary airships. Where other people looked at the vast huge old empty hangar and saw a derelict building with torn orange fiberglass insulation hanging out of smashed-out windows furling in the breeze, we saw *opportunity*. Vast opportunity, I might add.

Wow, can I work in telemarketing? Hello, Mister Investor, this is the East L.A. Dirigible Company. We are headquartered in Burbank. Yes. That's right, for a soft loose ten thousand pesetas you got hanging in that sack there—

Scoff and mock! Scoff and mock at will. Professionals have made careers of it. But where are those professional mockers and scoffers when you truly need 'em? Where are the Marx brothers now? In Hollywood Resurrection Cemetery, where all the smart-asses end up, watching the movies from the solid side of the wall, listening to punk bands on Dia de los Muertos.

Sorry, sir. Sarcasm isn't maybe my best side. I apologize. But why the big secret? Why operate underground?

Why do you broadcast on pirate radio? Why don't you publish your own newspaper, buy up the long-lost and defunct L.A. *Times* and call it the *Post-Everything Herald*? Next you'll be asking me why do we bother to resist in the first place, commie girl. What, do you expect the same government that was behind Wounded Knee and AIG and every war that bankrupted the whole world system to drive up in our driveway with a suitcase of cash and signing papers? You think they'd overlook our lack of friends who are state and federal representatives, no credit, no permits, paperwork, investors, insurance, licensing? Don't you even read your own newspaper?

Okay, okay—

No, no, follow me on this now. Western civ brought the equivalent of the Black Death to the original Tongva. But from this angle, we're watching the whole show in decline. Industry came to L.A. like George Harrison at the end, like Steve McQueen heading to the Tijuana peach-pits cancer clinic, like Janice Joplin in room 105, fixing in the Landmark Hotel, like Sam Cooke shot with his pants down at the Hacienda Motel, like JFK in the Ambassador Hotel—

RFK. Ambassador Hotel Wilshire Boulevard was Robert Kennedy—

You know what I'm getting at. Look down two o'clock, south by southeast.

At the cops? That looks like one of those, what do they call it? Pursuits where they go slow?

But look at the streets—what I'm saying is that they got streets and buildings named after those "people," but it's all just like black-and-white shadows flickering—without sound—in the collective memory of some windy abandoned hangar—

Did your ears pop right now, too? Mine just did.

Tupac and Biggie Smalls, heroes of the crack wars, where are they now? Che T-shirts, brown berets, and the grape boycott, where are they now? Purple Hearts, field jackets, the Doors at the Troubadour on Sunset, all those rock stars living in Laurel Canyon, Topanga, and Malibu, where are they now? Sam Yorty calling Tom Bradley a communist? Freeway Ricky Ross's conduit for CIA crack cocaine, the prison postindustrial system! San Fernando Valley porn industry boom? All those unemployed porn stars trying to find work as strippers? The desert-acres real-estate bubble? L.A. riots of '65 and '92 and 2021? "Crystal meth," "Earth Day," "public education," "rap music," "U.S. steel," "the United States Merchant Marine"? What happened to all of it? It didn't just blow away on a Santa Ana…

That was then.

This is now! Hey, you can see water in the arroyo! It's gone now, but I swear I saw it shining.

So what if there's no aerospace industry? Fifty thousand gangbangers and a hundred thousand cops, they're still there. Maybe if you sift out End-Time suicidal Christian cults, the movie business, the real estate shuck-and-jive, $1.37-per-gallon gasoline, "physical culture" and food fads—that was what was real, finally…

Cops?

Or gangbangers. Did you see? The cops had 'em lined up on the sidewalk way back there. In the spotlight.

Well, we aim to love it anyhow, as is. So what if the twentieth century was a wash? We aim to love it by floating our boat. We aim to change the whole look of this landscape. This solar dirigible will rise from the El Sereno hills, ferried across the San Andreas fault at night, in the early hours before dawn, to some secret mooring location. We consulted the example of Uruguayan urban Tupamaros, organizing an underground movement to develop alternate forms of pollution-free air transport, to revolutionize and revitalize the Southern California grid. Job creation for the masses, turn around the bankrupt culture of despair, Cults of Eating Shit and Liking It. We will use the current state of total neglect, disrepair, and entropy of urban centers to launch an inversion. Electro-titanium dirigible "of the new day" on the scale of the *Graf Zeppelin* will appear like the rising sun over the San Gabriel Valley, and when the people will see what can be done, *they will rise up*, across the nation, in every dead city and wasteland suburb—the will to live—desire to prevail, the prevailing of desire—

What do I get if I invest my life savings in this imaginary scheme? A pound of queso fresco, a clay-statue Colima dog?

Such a deal! Where else can you find an offer like that?

So why wait? What better time for them to rise up than right now?

What, why—if it weren't for the lack of a handful of investors—

What, you're gonna pretend cash is all that's holding you back?

We can't operate forever out of abandoned buildings, moving storage and assembly sites one step ahead of the bulldozers. We don't have outlay for lithium batteries, critical materiel, utilities, everything is borrowed against to our eyeballs, every time I want a new part, I find Vice President of Sales Swirling Wheelnuts out back sitting on a woodpile in the weeds, drinking up the profits, clinking beers with passersby—

I think you're holding back the real reason.

I assure you it's all a house of cards improvised on the point of a pin, balancing on tiptoe, walking through fire—

You got the look of motion sickness on you. But I don't think it's from vertigo, from fear of actual heights.

You think it's not daunting, piloting improvised pirate dirigibles across the night skies of Southern California, conversing in code on the radio so as to fool air traffic and controllers into thinking that you're either one or the other? Aircraft heading away from them on standard corridors at lawful altitudes or emergency craft making unscheduled rescues? To give at least the radio appearance of being strictly legit at the same time as we avoid all visual recognition, collisions, charted air corridors?

I know you can spin it for the customers—huge, hovering airships droning across the south-facing slopes of the San Gabriels in the dark, hiding behind black clouds, pretending to be the slowest helicopter that never was, maneuvering through air pockets, isotherms, and cold fronts, carrying forth into the new era alternative technologies lost to history and salvaged through derring-do. But a while ago you had something like this same green look on your face when you told me you were waiting in your car in the alley outside the Smell to pick someone up—

No, Isaura had to drop off something for the band—

Whatever—you saw her come out of the club, smashed. The guy she was with had to carry her out. They fall against the side of your car (I see you sitting stone cold in the dark and not even twitching at this point) and slide off the hood (very slowly off the wheel well, as you described it) and stumble down the alley…

Yeah, I told you about that. That was the guy she married.

Her enabler, I know.

You said that.

Not true?

I wouldn't begin to know.

No?

I don't pretend—

No? Come on—she was calling you. I know you were taking her calls.

Once or twice a year. Yeah, I might get a call.

Maybe more than that. She's drunk or wasted and always starts crying. She's gone from L.A. to El Paso, Austin to San Jose, San Jose to Chicago, Albuquerque to San Diego, burning her bridges everywhere. The constellation of mutual friends is winking out one by one. Even you stopped lending her money when she told you it was for her mom and then you found out it wasn't. Her mom has one in jail, one out on parole at home, and this one—

I knew her when she was better than that. Everybody else just sees the latest mess. She used to be somebody else. Some other person entirely.

You got that color in your face again.

I heard she broke up with that guy, anyway.

Of course! Within six months of the wedding (to which you didn't go) she and the guy are fighting all the time. Eventually she calls the cops, apparently there's visible bruising and redness so they arrest the dude. She changes the locks and gets a court order barring the guy from getting back inside his own house for three months! When he does, he finds she backed up a moving van to the place and cleaned him out. She was already off to Texas or Chicago or wherever when the guy walks in and finds it clean as a whistle—

Sniggling and giggling. Here, let me assume the controls. Go use the restroom, even if only to check it out—upstairs, down the hall to the left. Check out the workmanship—wall-to-wall tile, full-length mirrors, all brass fittings—better than anything Boeing or McDonnell Douglas ever produced. No second-class Mexico

City train with a hole in the floor where you can see the ground going by. Go. I'll play music for you on the PA.

{"Little Train of the Caipira," by Heitor Villa-Lobos, Toccata, Bachianas Brazileiras No. 2 for Orchestra}

You were right! This thing does have great bathrooms! Did you design all that tile yourself? What a blast of gleaming brass—no wonder you don't have money to pay your bookkeeper. Give me those controls back, would you? I'm feeling much better now, more relaxed. You know, this ship is mighty spacious. It's like we're in the belly of the whale, but once you get the hang of it, with your hands on the wheel…

It's not a hummingbird. It's not a helicopter.

It's not an eighteen-wheeler. It's not an oil tanker or ship of state.

You do seem to be getting a feel for it.

I think I am! Does this mean I have a job?

Looks like it.

Outstanding! Congratulations, new girl pilot! No cop choppers or—

No surveillance or hostile interference visible at this time. All screens are clear. Steady as she goes.

Good! Look at all those people sleeping down there. America's sleeping dreamless. Tired out, tossing and turning—I can see them all in their beds. Dreaming of a blank future! Unimaginable! I wonder what they'd think if they could see this ship in the clouds?

You got a real imagination on you.

I can see them. I can see everyone.

I can't see anything down there but streetlights, houses, big shadows of trees on the avenues. It's a dark landscape, dark fields of the republic rolling on under the night. I can't see any people at all.

I can see everything from up here—their individual lives flickering like candles. What a feeling.

It's all just a blobby blackness sprinkled with a few random lights to me.

Wow, what happened to you?

I don't know. I think I got burned out working on all these secret plans, underground utopias, machines to transport our future. I think they were killing too many people while I was working hard on something else. Time went by, stuff happens.

Really? You look down there across the whole city at night, you don't see those souls burning and scattered like stars against the dark?

I don't even see the stars anymore. I think you might be talking about the streetlamps.

No, I am definitely not talking about the streetlamps. I am talking about the people.

Yeah.

You're embarrassed about that, I see.

It is a little embarrassing.

Is it?

Sometimes I feel like my feelings for people went out with the last century. I'm looking down on the eviscerated cities of America's urban landscapes day and night from my floating technological vantage like a squinty-eyed Captain Nemo and I feel like I lost most of my soul somewhere along the way. Or maybe it just dried out completely and stuck on me like a scabbed-over herpes sore on the corner of my mouth.

Yeah, that could be kind of embarrassing. What're you gonna do about that?

Thanks for the sympathy. I appreciate that.

Welcome.

Really.

Hee hee.

I have bared my scars and here you are snickering.

Sorry. Habit.

See those gauges in the yellow off to your left? That means that bank of batteries is reduced; switch over to Bank Three. Bank Two off, Bank Three on.

Roger that.

That's the professional air-transport lingo I like to hear.

I feel like I'm really flying this thing.

We're flying!

We're flying?

We're zooming.

So gimme the rest of the story. And not just some cheap allegory, either, like we're the all-seeing Eye of Surmise, of the Flying Id above the dreaming mind of sleeping America. In a bed of ideological rubble, its subconsciousness submerged in the ruins of everything it has consumed and discarded like the Indian nations and the Civil War dead and the slaves and the Chinese who built the railroads and the Mexicans in the fields. Dead-dreaming America except for cops and gangsters running around shooting each other. That's not a story.

I didn't say it was.

So just say it. You're taking me to Sky City, aren't you? If not now, then… But wait a minute. This all has something to do with her, doesn't it?

I didn't tell you I saw Isaura last month.

Really?

We had lunch. She wanted to talk.

Uh oh!

She looked good. Looked great, as a matter of fact.

I've seen pictures.

Better than the pictures.

Pictures may lie. What did she want to talk about?

She's turned her life around. She's taking care of herself now.

That's what she told you? Did you laugh? Did she ask you to lend her a down payment?

She looked like she's got a handle on it. She might have been coloring her hair, but she looked like she'd put down some demons. Maybe they went down hard, but they went down.

Her? After what everyone's told you, in the face of your own experience, you're going for that? After everything she's done? No wonder she keeps calling.

She didn't mention money once, except to say she could pay me back.

Really. I don't know whether to believe you. Is there any actual verifiable fact associated with her at all?

I'm relating it exactly as I have been told. I heard she's been working in South

Central, gang intervention for at-risk kids, getting them off the street, into school, changing some lives. I did some checking up.

News to me! Secondhand, too. I can't say I'm believing it as yet.

I relate it just as I was told. She said she got into it after the riots of 2021. She had to drive through the intersection the TV choppers were circling, where the cars were being attacked and the trucker was pulled out of his cab and beaten unconscious. That intersection. She drove through it for years to get to work and she was on her way to work that morning and she saw cars mobbed, people dragged from their vehicles and beaten. One car on fire. They smashed out the windows and—

Yeah, I saw it on TV.

For Isaura it wasn't on TV. She'd almost made it through—people were on the ground—when a guy smashed out her window and hit her in the head with a piece of concrete. She said she hit the gas and dragged him along till he fell off. Blood pouring down her head, glass all over.

She didn't, like, pause at that point, light a cigarette and look at you from the corner of her eyes and ask for a favor?

She wasn't sure how badly she was hurt. She felt wet, she knew she was hurt but not how bad, and *she wanted to live*. The guy was trying to grab the wheel from her and push his way into her car and she was thinking, *I am not going to die like this! I am not going to die today!* She decided, then and there, when she hit the gas pedal and got herself through the intersection, dodging groups of people and other cars, the whole neighborhood in chaos, that she was determined to live. So she leaned over and drove as far as she could—her windshield was smashed and she couldn't really see through it—without looking where she was going, peeking around every once in a while. Then she got dizzy and had to pull over to the side of the street and stop. But a woman had seen her. The woman got in and told her to move over and stay down, and drove her out of there. She looked ten years younger when I saw her. She'd lost weight. She was taking care of herself. She looked like the sister of the Isaura I knew. That promise she'd made the day it looked like—

You believed her?

Whatever she said to herself when she got through that intersection, it carried down through the years. She changed her life.

Hard to believe.

Some of this shit is real. Exact words. Verbatim.

Was she happy?

She seemed very happy, yeah.

There's hope for us all?

There is, yes.

If she can do it, we can do it?

We can do it.

Maybe I can do it. Not sure. What about you?

Maybe, eh?

Is that a dead reservoir there, by those white buildings?

Hahamongna. Most of the big shore places are closed now, there's hardly any lights… And as the moon rises, that's JPL, Jet Propulsion Laboratory. You may not believe this, but one time they had hundreds or thousands of people working on a Mars mission. There's plywood on the windows now. Check your altimeter, we're catching a rising draft off the San Gabriels. Time we start the climb.

Where is she now? Why aren't you and her hooked up? Is that all over? She burned even you one too many times? End of story?

You know, I looked for her.

She disappeared again? Where to now? Maybe she's over in Ethiopia somewhere.

I always knew where she was, before. I could always call somebody who knew.

What now? Now what?

I checked my people. New York, no, eastern seaboard, nada, I even checked Miami. Texas was out, Chicago was a blank. St. Louis, somebody there pointed back to L.A. San Diego pointed back to L.A. The same thing with the Bay Area.

Montana?

Overseas! London, Lisbon, Brazil, nothing. Cape Town, nothing, Melbourne, the same. Ho Chi Minh City, Shanghai, some of it by internet, but still. Not even a whisper, no trace at all, and anyhow, it all pointed back to L.A. as last residence. L.A. like the black hole you can't escape from.

Except apparently she escaped. Maybe you missed something.

Could have, but we found her last apartment, talked to the manager. Her family boxed up her stuff and cleaned out the place after she'd been gone for a couple months. I talked to her sister. Her sister was worried about her for the first time ever. I promised I'd keep looking. But she was the one who realized where Isaura must be.

Where?

That's where we're going.

El Monte?

We're under way already.

Coachella Valley? Victorville? I thought we were on a run to rescue illegals from dehydration or transport sneaky drugs expressed from cochineal beetles or something. Or conduct mysterious scientific light-wave research over a crater in the desert.

I admit I mentioned some of those possibilities.

That was a cover story.

I had to say something halfway plausible. It's not like we don't find ourselves engaged in practical pursuits to pay the bills. We can't all be like you—spend all our days selling revolutionary newspapers on street corners along Figueroa Boulevard and spending all night in the Echo or the Airliner or dives like that.

Oh, low blow!

Deny it.

I stopped going to the Echo last year. But, wait—where to now, then?

Exactly about the time Isaura disappeared, the National Oceanic and Atmospherics Administration published its data on atmospheric anomalies caused by global warming. Hurricanes along the gulf coast and eastern seaboard chronically engorged, scouring the lower-right-hand corner of the U.S., Florida swept under the sea surge like Bangladesh. Tornados hopping from Oklahoma to Colorado, touching down in Pittsburgh. Africa turning into a hellish baking continent of Saharas to the north and Namib deserts to the south. Australia and southern Europe burning off, killing thousands, desertifying. Vast areas of earth depopulating, turning into heat-blasted wastes.

Didn't Al Gore win the Academy Award for that?

The earth is turning into Venus. We're churning out thick stratospheres of smoke, debris, waste gases that have a measurable cooling effect. Making a dark planet of blasted ideologies, bloated sick passions, corrupted by viral pandemic apathies—

Tell me something I don't know. That's why the working class has to subscribe to the *Daily Red Revolutionist*. Then the revolution—

We're rising to check out that ring of litter, particulates, and trash that now rains down on the globe. That's why you brought the radio transmitter aboard in your cute Guatemalan bag, right?

You knew about that? I didn't mean—

My police scanner picks up all frequencies. For this airship to remain invisible, I've got to monitor all currents. These multicolored gauges and flashing lights aren't Christmas decorations.

Where to, then? What's the course adjustment?

You're the one driving.

We're on a heading 130 degrees, 80 knots, sixty-mile-an-hour wind speed from the northwest, resulting in a heading correction of about five degrees.

Perfecto!

But where?

You just said—

You know what I mean. On this heading, we won't see much out this way except vast freeway interchanges, concretized floodplains and flood-control channels, gravel pits, nurseries under the power lines, the Miller brewery and the Rose Hills Cemetery, Fry's electronics, massive warehouse districts and truck-distribution facilities. Chino Hills.

See, even you—

When the moon comes out, they'll be able to see the shadow of the dirigible sliding across all that cement. It's all parking lots and gravel down there.

We'll be climbing.

We're already at thirteen thousand feet. How much higher can we ascend?

We're going to Sky City, rookie. That's why you're flying this ship. You aced the interviews and I collated a whole file on your skills.

But then you must've, I mean—you knew? You knew about my membership in the Punk Faction of the Red Underground Party, affiliated with I.T.S.C. point one?

I knew about all of that except for the I.T.S.C.-point-one part—I don't give a damn about that! I seen you around the neighborhood since you were carried around in diapers by your mom when she was looking for your MIA dad. Basically, I see that you got heart; who else would sell those damned newspapers on the street corner and even get me to subscribe to that fishwrap?

It's true, then? It's really there?

Sky City? I want you to adjust the ailerons for maximum climb (maximum torque) and drop the last of our water ballast, because we're entering the isotherm. My studies on Sky City's origins and existence have provided me with reasonable information that Isaura and her yellow Volkswagen bug were likely swept up in the recent series of tornadoes and atmospheric disturbances which created and maintain the conglomeration of debris in the stratospheric rings—agglutinated by force—that continues careening through the upper atmosphere, circling the planet. If my information is correct (and I've every reason to believe it is, since we've gotten *this far* based on my calculations), Isaura's only one of hundreds—perhaps thousands—of people trapped in their vehicles and other bubbles of shelter in the swarm of packing sheds and pipelines, condo-construction materials, cars and planes, entire trains and a couple small towns torn out of east Texas and Oklahoma. All of it ripped off the face of the earth by windspouts and tornado-like phenomena, crunched together in the rusty blood-brown rings that permanently swirl above our planet. I expect the diversity and variety of the debris to include enough plant and animal life and atmospheric water to have sustained even a totally marginalized invisible population, in spite of the occasional 1979 Pontiac El Caminos, delivery vans, old tires, and broken water heaters that fall out of the sky at approximately 145 miles an hour terminal velocity, landing in schoolyards and shopping-mall parking lots, which the government blames on Muslims and maintains is yet another thing soon to be fixed by tax cuts—

Fourteen thousand feet. Fourteen thousand four hundred.

Steady on this course.

Fifteen thousand feet. Fifteen four hundred.

We'll be there in just a few damned minutes. Just as an entire distorted aquatic ecosystem and weird society have developed around floating villages on stilts in the midst of the Great Pacific Trash Vortex, I expect we'll find the poor marginalized inhabitants forgotten and stranded in Sky City fending for themselves. They've reconstructed a semblance of lives and livelihoods in the wind, dust, and trash storms of the sky—

If we get there—

When we get there. You're going to come about, so the gale-force currents don't crush the lateral bulkheads against the swirling edges and jagged parts of the debris rings—in fact, it's almost time you turn about and reverse course, transferring the remaining ballast into the nose—

But—

If you don't do it quick the winds will crush the power-generating titanium frame against the trash. Before we get to the edge, the rift in the stratospheric isotherms, I'll leave the ship strapped into a paraglider and expect I'll instantly get sucked up into the vortex, straight into Sky City. The hard part won't be getting in—the hard part will be avoiding ending up ripped to pieces on a tangled mess of radio antennae and radar dishes knotted in high-tension power lines, flatcars and water tanks, oil tankers and remnants of Amazonian rain forests. But if I can drop anchor on a stable structure of some kind, I should be able to pull myself in on the ropes or rappel into shelter.

What about getting back on the ground? What about getting home?

I'll be in radio contact if I make it. First I want you to drop down a thousand feet and circle clockwise at fifty knots against the south-by-southwest wind. If I find survivors, I'll bring them out via paraglider. One at a time, as many as I can.

The first eye-witnesses! Unbelievable! Everything's gonna change when they start telling what they've been through—ambassadors of the new era! You, sir, will be a hero! Our party's always maintained the existence of this phenomenon and some others, recognition of which by the masses would provide the credibility that would be the first step to power—I'd almost believe I was shaking and trembling if I didn't know it's the wheel vibrating like crazy. How can the ailerons take it? Won't there be structural damage?

Titanium. Steady as she goes. You realize, don't you, that these people might not tell a story that serves the interests of your party? From the Plan de Ayala to the Plan de Aztlán, from the Soviet Five-Year Plans to Let a Hundred Flowers Bloom, none of these ideas ever look the same in the daylight. On the ground. Oh, now— are you crying? Don't cry, kid!

Sorry!

Come on, I'm relying on you. I'm gonna release my paraglider into the slipstream and it's gonna be hell getting back against those gale-force winds. Meanwhile it's all on you whether any of us lives or not.

I know. Sorry! It's just a little... I struggle my whole life in the streets with the blown-out industries of civilization collapsing on all sides about our ears, to survive to be here, to be able to see this day...

I'll take the wheel a second. Dry your eyes; you've gotta see clear to make the maneuver, turn about, and descend into a calmer air column.

I'm all right. Just... I know everything might not go the way they say. I don't really think it will. Nothing ever goes like anyone plans. I'm grateful we even get the ghost of a chance. Even if I find out later it was all some fairy-tale, sci-fi-fantasy daydream, I won't even care. Because we took the chance. That's all I've wanted. I'm so grateful, at this moment, that's all. Whatever happens.

I am, too! I thank you for your heedless skills and reckless youth, pilot! Let me shake your hand. A comradely embrace. Take the wheel. You've given me a chance at the happiness of a lifetime and given the masses a glimpse of a glimmer of a new day. Here on, it's up to you.

Thank you, sir. I'll turn about and make the descent; I'll get the berths ready for our first survivors while I stand by. Karl Marx and Friedrich Engels! Would you look at that? That looks like some terrible thunderhead—you can see the debris sticking out of it like torn-out tree roots, stuff swirling inside of it like flocks of birds—

That's just the leading edge of the tumorous fulminating debris cloud. According to my charts, the densest interrelated conglomeration is a few miles south of us—

Augusto César Sandino, what *is* that? What just hit us?

That's the wind I was telling you about—I estimate that thousands or millions of plastic bags, whipped by a hurricane-force gale, are layering in dangerous greasy encrudescences like warm slush on the fins, rudder, and engines—

Already? Sounds like the ocean smashing against us.

Just the beginning!

Very hairy and scary, señor!

Just beginning!

Oh!

Yeah, it's going to test the tensile strength of the titanium frame for all it's worth! To think I disguised the frame for years as the outer housing of the Zep Diner on Main Street, where people stepped inside as if it were an ordinary restaurant. I'd hate to lose the income from that business. I built my whole life on *carnitas* and *posole.* Are we almost about?

One ten degrees. One thirty five.

I'd better go suit up.

Good luck, sir! One sixty. Two more minutes!

How do the engines feel? How's the ballast?

Ballast set, hundred twenty-five degrees, nose tending to drop five to ten. I can barely hold it up.

But it's holding?

Holding. Holding for now. Feels like four to five minutes at the most. The position is already degrading.

I'm going, then. Remember you drop a thousand on my signal.

Terrible wind shear—

Yeah. Good luck, kid! Radio headset channel on—I'll be talking to you.

Roger that. Let me know if…

What?

Good luck!

You won't be able to see the paraglider released from the cargo bay doors. I'll communicate over the headset.

It's on and I'll be listening.

I'm away! {continuous hiss of static, sometimes rising to a sound like tropical rain on a sheet-metal roof—electrostatic slapping and snarling}… paraglider wings whipping like a banana peel… I will buy a subscription {percussive torque reverberating with resounding clanging through titanium struts, weird twanging like Nels Cline guitar}… It's really blasting, no control of glider… Visibility lim… {hissing of static slashed by sudden silence}… in range… outskirts of Sky City above me, looming towers like wrecked cranes festooned with jagged sheet metal, trailing cables, plastic sheeting... Just a few—to hook the ropes. {loud popping, percussive clanging} Yes! Now if I can secure the glider! {grating metallic shrieks} Cables... swirling like octopus tentacles in the cloud—

East L.A. Dirigible *Agnes Smedley* descending to three miles. Waiting for your call.

{electric crackling, popping} {insistent hiss of static, silence}

{"El Pueblo Unido Jamas Sera Vencido," by Quilapayun...}

Ehekatl 99.9 on your dial.

CONTRIBUTORS

CHRIS ADRIAN is a Fellow in Pediatric Hematology-Oncology at the University of San Francisco. Farrar, Straus, and Giroux will publish his third novel, *The Great Night*, next summer.

CHRIS BACHELDER is the author of the novels *Bear v. Shark* and *U.S.!* He lives in Amherst, Massachusetts with his wife and two daughters.

ANTHONY DOERR is the author of three books—*The Shell Collector*, *About Grace*, and *Four Seasons in Rome*. His short fiction has won three O. Henry Prizes, and has been anthologized in *The Best American Short Stories*, *The Anchor Book of New American Short Stories*, and *The Scribner Anthology of Contemporary Fiction*. He also writes the "On Science" column for the *Boston Globe*. He is at work on a novel and a story collection.

SESSHU FOSTER is the author of the novel *Atomik Aztex* and the hybrid text *World Ball Notebook*. He has taught composition and literature in East Los Angeles for twenty-five years.

SHEILA HETI is the author of *Ticknor* and *The Middle Stories*. She lives in Toronto, where she regularly collaborates with other artists; recently, she appeared in Margaux Williamson's film *Teenager Hamlet*. She is presently finishing a book titled *How Should a Person Be?*

HEIDI JULAVITS is the author of three novels, most recently *The Uses of Enchantment*. Her fiction and nonfiction have appeared in *Harper's, Esquire*, and the *New York Times*, among other places. She is a founding editor of the *Believer* and the recipient of a Guggenheim Fellowship. She lives in Manhattan and Maine.

SALVADOR PLASCENCIA is the author of *The People of Paper*. He lives in Los Angeles.

JIM SHEPARD is the author of six novels and three story collections, including *Like You'd Understand, Anyway*, which was nominated for the National Book Award and won the Story Prize. His short fiction has appeared in *Harper's*, the *Paris Review*, the *Atlantic Monthly, Esquire, Granta, Tin House*, the *New Yorker*, and *Playboy*. He teaches at Williams College.

J. ERIN SWEENEY lives and works in Philadelphia. Her stories have appeared in *American Short Fiction, Spork*, the *Licking River Review*, and elsewhere.

WELLS TOWER is the author of *Everything Ravaged, Everything Burned*, a collection of short fiction.

MARGAUX WILLIAMSON is a painter. Her latest project, *Dance Dance Revolutions Co.*, is on YouTube.